The Circle of Na'mow

Inspired by Real Life Events

Anna McDermott
Gretchen Wiegand

The Circle of Na'mow
by Anna McDermott and Gretchen Wiegand

Published in the United States by Anna McDermott and Gretchen Wiegand

Cover and book design by Nick Zelinger, NZGraphics.com
Editing by Mark Graham, MarkGrahamCommunications.com
Author photographs by Stephen Collecter
Wildfire Photo (on cover) by USFS Region 5

ISBN 978-0-9904712-0-2 (soft cover)
ISBN 978-0-9904712-1-9 (hard cover)
ISBN 978-0-9904712-2-6 (e-book)

Library of Congress Control Number: 2014914304

10 9 8 7 6 5 4 3 2

McDermott, Anna and Wiegand, Gretchen
Anna McDermott and Gretchen Wiegand
1. Colorado—Fiction 2. Friends—Fiction 3. Women—Fiction

Authors' Note:
The events in this book are based on the song of our soul and the rhythms of our life dance that encompass our past, present and future truths. Our fictional characters are written to awaken the passion in each and every one of us. This is a work of fiction. Names, characters, places and incidents either are the product of the authors' imagination or are used fictitiously. Any resemblance to actual persons, living or dead, events, or locales is entirely coincidental.

First Edition

Manufactured in the United States of America

Thanks to our beautiful Rocky Mountain environment
and mountain community that we call home…the inspiration
of our hopes and dreams.
~ AMc and GW

Foreword

July 20, 2011

Anna and Gretchen:

"I was deeply moved to share, if only so briefly your mountaintop. It was immediately clear to me that it is a rejuvenating, spiritual, cosmic center. The group who have endured there have made magic in love, support, survival, humor, relationship, and character building.

I have always felt I should have been on my own mountaintop ever since I did my first hitchhike through Colorado in 1971 and fell in love forever with the mountain air. To be there in your organic, warm spaces tells me much of what I might have evolved out of a life in the thin fresh air of the high country. And it surely reflects a good life, deep in meaning, rich contemplation and connection to all that is worthwhile. Thank you so much for your generosity, strength of spirit, and friendship. It means much to me."

John Hueber, a visitor of Na'mow

*"We come spinning out of nothingness, scattering stars ...
the stars form a circle, and in the center we dance."*

~ Rumi

FIRE

Day 1

"Your journey of discovery starts with me."
~ Na'mow

September 14, 1996, Saturday afternoon

The warm gentle breeze turned violent, tearing and scratching at the earth and blinding the eyes of creatures and men alike. The long dry grasses nurtured by the heavy spring rains bent downward unrelentingly in the face of this ferocious wind. The rumbling of turbulent air roared across the landscape. The sun's rays were obliterated by the accumulation of charcoal gray cloud formations colliding like mindless gladiators.

Rabbits, foxes, coyotes and all those of dens, burrows, and lairs sought whatever shelter this parched ground offered. Eagles, hawks, turkey vultures, and songbirds hunkered deeply into the sturdiest of nests. Deer, elk, cattle, and horses hunched like battle-tested warriors against the onslaught of flying debris. Angry crashing whitecaps swept the lake's steely surface, inspiring those inhabiting its waters to seek calmer depths.

The final torment was the rainless thunder and lightning. In a deep ravine, a fiery bolt struck one of the tallest ponderosas, traveled down the tree's broad trunk, and ignited the tall arid grasses beneath it. The tree exploded in flames, sending a fountain of sparks outward and providing fuel for the burning edge of the blaze.

Once the destructive electrical charge had done its job, the storm moved westward, lifting its cloudy veil and revealing the fire for all to behold.

LOLA

Lola retreated into her mountain house when the squall hit. She'd been reading a steamy paperback on her back deck and had forgotten to bring the book inside. When she went back out to retrieve it, she was struck by a distinct lack of natural sounds, struck, in fact, by a moment of complete silence. In that moment, the sky cleared to the hot rays of the sun. The dogs in the yard next door were suddenly quiet. Not a single bird stirred. The air was dead and stagnant.

"Ohhhh, I don't like this," Lola said to no one in particular. The hair on the back of her neck stood at attention. She sniffed the air and sniffed again as she walked the perimeter of her deck, trying to identify the smell.

"Nick!" She craned her neck and called to her teenage son. Seconds later, he glanced down from the upstairs bathroom window, a razor still in his hand.

"What is it?"

"I don't know, but something is definitely off. I can feel it in my being. My heart's pounding and my nerves are on high alert. I've got goosebumps all over my arms. Do you smell that?"

"Yeah. But it's too hot for someone to have their wood stove burning," he called down to her.

"And no one would burn slash today, would they? Not with the fire ban." Her mind searched for plausible explanations but the only one that echoed in her head was the one she dreaded the most: forest fire.

2

She heard Nick's footsteps pounding down the stairs and the screen door opening and closing. He came up next to her. They scanned the horizon and saw nothing. But it was the smell that confirmed it. "Call dispatch," he said.

"I can't. I've embarrassed myself too many times with false alarms. I'll call Ella and see what she thinks." Lola was halfway to the phone when it began ringing. It was John, her ex. The last person she expected to hear from. "John?"

"There's a fire," he said. "I was talking to a client over in Coal Creek Canyon, and they can see flames."

"Damn! I thought so." Lola fought off a wave of panic. Coal Creek Canyon lay to the south on the backside of the mountain, not ten miles away. "I can smell it."

"It's heading up the north ridge," John said. "If you don't see it now, you will soon."

Lola marched over to her south window. Sure enough, a steady stream of gray smoke funneled up from behind the ridge. "God-damnit. I see it! Gotta go, John."

"I'm coming up."

"No, you're not," she practically shouted, but her ex-husband had already hung up.

Nick was looking at her as she dropped the receiver back in the cradle. He said, "Why does something like this always have to ruin my weekend. It just sucks!"

Lola gave him the evil eye. With a determinedly calm demeanor, she walked into her bedroom to gather the most sentimental of her items and then prayed to every powerful force she could imagine that they wouldn't have to evacuate. "Hope that was fervent enough," she said in a low whisper.

The photo on the top of her stack was more than sentimental; it was priceless. It showed Lola as a wide-eyed four-year-old standing small against her stunningly beautiful parents. The black and white photo had faded to gray and sat lopsided in the frame. A cat's head and tail spilled out the crook of the little girl's arms; the cat's name was Tiger, and she had been Lola's best friend back then.

A smeared lip imprint blurred the images after she kissed the photo's glass coffin. Wow, she thought. *Look at us...so damn young... fourteen years later...poof...they'd all be gone except me. Orphaned. Lost...disappearing...searching...always looking...it's taken me this long to finally feel whole...loved...a part of something bigger. Thank God I'm not alone now. But my heart still misses them. Guess I always will.*

Lola opened the door to her closet, stood on her tippy toes, and reached behind some sweaters on the high shelf. She pulled down two metal urns. "Hey Nick, help me here. We're going to have to figure out what to pack up in case we have to leave."

Nick poked his head into her room and spied the urns. "Mom, what're you going to do with those? I mean, I can't believe you haven't figured out where to spread their ashes yet."

Nick had never met his grandma and grandpa on his mom's side. They'd died when Lola was 18 and still living in Las Vegas. "Well, I hate to say this, but I kind of forgot about them until just now," she confessed.

Summer 1974

Lola knew about death.

She was five when the car her dad was driving accidentally struck and killed her beloved cat, the one she called Tiger. Tiger's mangled and bloodied body was sprawled out over the centerline of the street running out front of their house, and Lola remembered standing over her. Lifeless. Dead.

She also remembered how unsympathetic her dad had been. She could hear him saying, "Tiger's time was up and unfortunately it had to happen today. I told you that cat should have stayed indoors, because now she's paid the price of being free and gallivanting all over the neighborhood. There's nothing we can do about it now. It was an accident. We're sorry. She's gone."

All Lola had wanted to do was hold Tiger. To kiss her glistening fur. But she had fainted at the sight of the cat and never got the chance. By the time her parents got to her, she was unconscious in the middle of the road, her head and hair wet from her own vomit.

Thirteen years later, death struck again. This time it was her parents. A car accident: dead.

Lola Ferraro found it such a constrained word, unlike most of the words she used in her buoyant way of speaking. No melody came from it. "Dead" started and ended in the mouth directly behind the teeth. No intake of breath and definitely no lingering exhale when the word was spoken. Even when people used substitutes like defunct, gone, extinct, inert, offed: these words too were restricted inside the mouth's cavern. No wonder phrases like "passed over" or "gone to meet his maker" or "joined the angels" were so often spoken instead. At least these phrases actually had some life to them.

That day, however, at her parents' memorial, you could bet that the mourners would never think to utter the word "dead" in her immediate vicinity. The truth was, it didn't matter. Death was alive and well in Lola's memory and wreaking both emotional and physical havoc on this bereft eighteen-year-old.

The funeral director held Lola's hand as she mustered enough strength to take her place in the front pew. Photos of her parents were displayed on easels at the foot of the altar and reminded Lola, not for the first time, that she was the perfect physical blend of the two. Her mother's high cheekbones, heart-shaped face, and straight nose dominated Lola's face and were perfectly accentuated by her father's dark black eyes rimmed with long eyelashes. Her full, pouty lips were hers alone. Lola guessed that her long wavy brunette locks were another gift from her mother, but she had only known her as a bleached blonde reminiscent of Marilyn Monroe.

She looked from the photos to the center table where the two urns holding their ashes were dwarfed by bouquets of flowers. Her parents were cremated "because of the unusual circumstances surrounding their deaths," as the funeral director had so ingraciously told her. Lola wasn't sure what to do about the urns and couldn't imagine finding them in a closet nearly twenty-five years later in the face of a roaring forest fire.

After the service, the reception room was filled to capacity. *Amazing how many complete strangers are bold enough to call themselves family*, Lola thought with an extra dose of cynicism. She swallowed hard. She was scared. Scared now and scared for what the future would bring. She stole a deep breath, shaking her hands to calm herself. She pasted on one of her bug-catching, toothy, ear-to-ear smiles, hoping someone would be blinded by it. Then she flipped her long walnut-colored hair back away from her puffy, bloodshot eyes. Her posture heightened to its full 5'3" stature, and she walked right into the sea of relatives and friends, swaying her hips and leaving a path of stares.

That was about the last thing she remembered before ushering the last mourner out the door and paying off both the funeral director and the caterers with a handful of cash. After her parents died, Lola had found the stash of bills along with a handwritten will in a box on the top shelf of their bedroom closet. It was just a big unassuming cardboard shoebox that her father told her was off limits unless there was an emergency. He also had a small life insurance policy, all of $35,000 worth. And then there was the very modest house that her parents had scrimped and saved to buy years back. It was Lola's now. Everything was hers.

"Have a sandwich." Her best friend Sandy emerged from the kitchen with a paper plate stacked with miniature roast beef sandwiches and a mound of potato salad.

She found Lola staring skeptically at the brown metallic urns containing her parents' ashes. "What am I supposed to do with these? God, I hope they don't haunt me for the rest of my life?"

She didn't wait for Sandy's reply. "I'm fine, okay? Really. No, I'm not fine, but I think I will be fine when I figure this all out. I might cry a lot, and I might not. I don't know. I've never had to deal with so much pain." The words spewed out of her mouth. "I'm on my own. It doesn't matter what I do. Wrong or right. I'm on my own."

"Not completely." Sandy set the plate on the coffee table. "You've got me."

"Yeah, I know. Thank God. But I just want everything to be like it was before…you know, before the accident. There are too many damn decisions to make and I need some time here to sort things out. I'm just not sure what to do. I'm scared…really really scared and really really sad."

Sandy embraced Lola. "I'll be here for you. You'll make it through just like you always have."

"If you say so," Lola sighed.

Sandy stayed until Lola was safely tucked away in bed; she never did eat the roast beef sandwiches or potato salad.

For weeks thereafter, Lola woke up every morning believing her parents were still alive. Her reality and dream state switched places. She felt more alive and happy when she was sleeping than when she was awake.

"You're grieving, that's all," Sandy said to her over dinner nearly a week later. Sandy refilled their wine glasses and leaned across the table. "So, don't you think it's about time you explain what happened to your parents?"

Lola covered her forehead with her hands. "I guess I can't keep my head buried in the sand forever. You better light up the pipe."

The story began after the second glass of wine and a couple of hits of some very good weed. "Okay, let me just say that Dad adored my mother and me."

"Yeah? And?" Sandy said this after Lola seemed to run out of words.

"Well, I can't say the same for Mom. She could be…" Lola shook her head fiercely. "Oh jeez…I feel so guilty saying this because she's gone. Aren't I supposed to be glorifying them or something?"

"I don't think there's a hard and fast rule about that," Sandy said calmly.

Lola fortified herself with a gulp of wine.

"Okay, my mother pretty much was an emotionally vacant, promiscuous bitch. Okay, now it's out there and I can't take it back! Dad knew it too and still just adored her."

Lola waited for Sandy to fall out of her chair in horror, but she just took a sip of wine and waited. So Lola forged ahead. "Actually, we both adored her. She knew it and used it. She knew he'd never leave her so she took full advantage, staying out until the wee hours of the morning. You know…she was a dancer in The Follies. Then she'd waltz in reeking of alcohol and cigarettes. She'd sleep all day – or not, if you know what I mean – while he worked, and I learned at a very young age to entertain myself. It's why I have such an incredible, hyperactive, off-the-charts imagination."

Lola bowed dramatically, and they roared with laughter. The laughter felt good. Eventually, Sandy reeled her back in, saying, "Lola, you've kind of gotten off on a tangent here, don't you think?"

"Oh, yeah, it's this weed…totally spacey."

"Lola, the story of your parents' car accident. Tell it!"

Lola composed herself with more wine. Then she said, "It was Mom's birthday and Dad decided to take her to Lake Tahoe for a long weekend. He saved enough money to stay in a fancy hotel and also bought her a beautiful new dress. My mother seemed genuinely touched and very excited. I even saw her pack a flimsy negligee.

"Well, they called me once from the hotel to tell me they were leaving and that they'd be home at around eleven, so not to wait up.

So I didn't. But I still had a restless sleep. The moon was full and so bright that night, and it lit up my room like a spotlight. It always makes me have such weird-ass dreams. I didn't wake up until I heard the knock on the door and I realized it was the next morning. It was a state patrol guy. He asked me if this was the Ferraro residence. I just lost it. I knew something bad had happened, because I peeked around him and my parents' car wasn't in the driveway. I fell on my knees sobbing hysterically. Poor guy. He just asked one question and I totally freaked out."

"Can't blame you for that, girl." Sandy filled the pipe. She lit it, took a toke, and passed it. "This is some killer weed. No doubt about it. Then what?"

"Good thing you're a great listener because it only gets longer and weirder." Lola blew smoke toward the ceiling. "The officer told me there had been a bad accident and it took them a while to identify the bodies. 'The bodies.' I will never forget him saying those words. 'The bodies.' I must have blacked out for a very long time because the next thing I knew, I woke up with neighbors standing around the couch and staring down at me like I was some sort of alien. When they got there, I have no idea. Then suddenly, I heard myself screaming, 'An owl killed my parents! An owl killed my parents!'"

"An owl?" Sandy raised an eyebrow dubiously.

"That's right. An owl. I saw it. I dreamt it. I felt it. Sandy, I'm telling you. I saw what happened. It's totally crazy!" Lola slammed her hand down on the table.

"Okay, so it's totally crazy. Tell me anyway."

"My parents were happy. They were smiling and laughing as they drove down the highway toward home. Beaming. The sky was clear, and the moon was so bright that even the sagebrush was casting shadows. There were a million stars twinkling above them. Mom was about to ask my dad a question when a huge black shadow came out of nowhere and crashed into the windshield."

"What the hell? You mean, the owl?"

"Yeah, the owl. Dad freaked. He veered sideways and lost control. The car rolled. A rock punctured the gas tank and POOF, a spark ignited the whole thing. Fire. Flames. I just saw it all. I heard the crackling and groaning. It seemed so lonely for them out there in the middle of nowhere, and…" Lola took a deep breath and shook her head.

"Hold on. I need some water." Sandy got up, went to the kitchen, and brought back two big glasses of water. "So let me get this straight. This state trooper comes to your door and tells you there's been an accident. He mentions bodies. You black out and have a dream. You then wake up to a room full of people and you're yelling about an owl killing your parents."

"That's exactly right."

Sandy stared at her. "Hmmm. Okay, but who told you what actually happened? I mean, that an owl hit the car?"

"Well, that's the funny part. Nobody said anything about an owl. Not one person," Lola said.

"Okay, then what?"

"So after everyone left, I talked Tim into driving me out to the scene."

"You talked Tim into driving out to the scene? What? Are you crazy? Weren't you scared?" Sandy sounded incredulous.

"Of course," Lola said calmly. "But I had to see it with my own eyes, or I'd be wondering about it the rest of my life. I just had to know."

"Yeah, okay. I get that. So?"

"It was about an hour drive from here. In the middle of nowhere really, but you couldn't miss the scene. The fire had blackened a huge area along the road, and there were still pieces of scrap metal everywhere. By the time we got there, Mom and Dad's car had been hauled away, so we just started walking around. We followed the skid marks back down the highway. It seemed like we walked forever, but sure enough, we found a huge, dead owl lying on the ground. But it wasn't like it was all mangled or anything. It was like…like it was asleep. Perfect. No animals had even touched it. I mean, the hair on the back of my neck stood straight up. That's how weird it was. And then all of a sudden, this old man just appeared out of nowhere. One minute he wasn't there, and the next he was standing next to Tim and me, staring at us."

Sandy's eyes nearly popped out of their sockets. "What old man? Where did he come from?"

"I don't know. But he had this raspy, parched-like voice…like he hadn't had a drink of water in years. He said, 'Watcha going to do with that owl?'"

"And I said, 'We don't know.'" Lola looked at Sandy and grinned. "You would have been proud of me, I said this as nonchalantly as if all of this friggin' weird shit was as normal as could be. Then Tim nudged the owl with his foot.

"The old man squatted down for a better look and said, 'It's a federal offense to have an owl or any part of it, including feathers, in your possession. Only a shaman with permits is allowed, and he has to follow strict guidelines. You two shamans?'

"I was thinking, oh my God! We aren't shamans, but we were two friggin' morons. Did we look like shamans? Are you kidding me?" Lola had worked herself into a tizzy. "But, Sandy, here's the best part. Tim, the biggest moron of all says, 'Come on, you're just trying to scare us. How do we know you don't want to take this thing for yourself? Sell the feathers or whatever? And who the hell would know even if we did take it anyway?'

"Then the man stood up and very calmly said, 'The owl would know. Just let it be. Let nature do with it what it wants.'

"'You mean, leave it out here? Why should we do that? If we don't take it, some animal will just get to it,' Tim said to the guy, and not very respectfully, I might add.

11

"The old man said, 'Exactly my point. Whatever nature intends. You've heard of the cycle of life, haven't you?' the man smiled, and then added, 'Looks like it did its job here anyway.'

"'What job is that?' Tim asked.

"'To forebode death. Transformation.'"

Lola looked at Sandy and shook her head. "Can you believe he said that? 'To forebode death.' That's something someone says in a creepy horror film."

"So what happened next?" Sandy asked.

"So I did the only thing I could think of under the circumstances. I puked. We never even saw the guy leave. No car, no nothing. Tim didn't even come to the memorial, he's still so freaked out."

Sandy and Lola stared at each other. Finally, Sandy stood up, leaned in Lola's direction, and announced, "Shit, Lola, you really need a change of scenery. How can you even think of staying here with all...all these sad memories? You're coming to Colorado with me and that's that."

———

Lola didn't have time to argue. In less than two weeks she was calling Boulder home. She was rooming with Sandy and two roommates who introduced themselves as students at a local Buddhist college.

Lola jumped into the scene headfirst. She got a job at a funky coffee shop where musicians jammed whenever the urge moved them. Poets read their latest musings. If she had to work – a reality she could hardly comprehend – she was going to work at a place where lots of people congregated and the operative word was fun.

Lola was not a good waitress. In fact, she very often forgot what people ordered, was slow to pick up finished orders, and was clumsy any time she was faced with carrying more than a single plate or a coffee cup. What counted was that the customers loved her. She was genuinely interested in them. She'd sit down beside a customer and gab until the manager dragged her away. No topic was off limits. She could carry on simultaneous conversations about everything from UFOs, aliens, cattle mutilations, and the latest movie releases to books, philosophy, religion, and the politics of the day.

Lola had a knack. Laughter seemed to fill the coffee shop whenever she was on the job. She exuded an energy that enveloped people with its enchanting simplicity. Men and woman alike were drawn to her. She embodied all that was feminine in one exquisitely divine package.

She would walk into the room wearing a mismatch of the brightest and most unusual colors and pull it off like a fashion model. Her perky breasts never needed a bra. Flowing, see-through peasant blouses paired with multi-tiered long skirts swirled with every step. Her musk perfume lingered like a mist within the room. A big turquoise and silver pendant adorned her chest. Bulky cuff bracelets lined her wrists. An ankle bracelet made of tiny bells tinkled when she glided by.

People routinely asked her what kind of drugs she was on because they wanted some. Her standard reply was, "Drugs? I'm high on Life."

And that she was: high on her new life far, far from the memories of her broken home, a mysterious dead owl, and an even more mysterious old man she couldn't completely purge from her mind.

FIRE

Day 1

*"Nature's circles and spirals contain the rhythms
of the universe."*
~ The Circle of Na'mow Handbook – Chimalis, First Generation

September 14, 1996, Saturday afternoon

A grateful respite from the wind lasted less than an hour.

When it returned, it returned with increasing ferocity. The flames were relentless in their pursuit, destroying anything and everything in their path. Mother Nature had conspired to create the perfect conditions for a fast moving wildfire: a rainless summer, low humidity, a forest floor thick with natural kindling. Parched grasses, pine needles, twigs, and decaying branches ignited like a tinderbox. Densely populated acres of pine, juniper, and aspen trees awaited their fate.

The hot afternoon sun super-heated the air, adding to the landscape's dehydration. As the fire sucked oxygen from the atmosphere, it generated its own terrifying weather pattern. Bursts of tornado-force wind shook the air. Embers shot out like missiles into the air, igniting the crowns of distant trees and starting fast-burning fires acres away.

The flames used the steep slope of the gulch to slingshot up the ridge, leaching every ounce of moisture from the fire's perimeter and immediately engulfing it. Erratic and unpredictable, random areas were totally untouched by the flames, and it was this unpredictability as much as anything that wreaked havoc in the minds of residents and firefighters alike.

ELLA

"So you're going to take the money your grandparents gave you for graduation and jump ship for a year, is that it?" Ella was practically shouting at her eighteen-year-old son Brice.

"I'm not jumping ship, for Christ sake," he replied aggressively. "I want to take a year off before I head to college, that's all. I want to pursue my music. You know that. And L.A. is the best place to do that."

"You made a commitment to college. Not just to me. To yourself." Ella's husband Gary and fourteen-year-old daughter Alena sat ringside of this ongoing battle and were smart enough to keep quiet.

"I need to find myself, Mom. I want to play my music and have a little adventure before life gets 'too real.'" Brice glanced at his father. "You get it. I know you do, Dad. Tell her."

Gary was a musician himself and all for the move. In fact, he was a bit jealous. One of Brice's music buddies was driving out to the coast in a couple of days and had asked Brice to join him. What musician wouldn't want that? "Yeah, I get it, Brice, but it's not quite as cut and dried as you're trying to make it."

"Damn right it's not," Ella was saying when the phone rang. Gary answered it. His expression and tone of voice changed from casual to great concern in less than five seconds. The shouting match between mother and son came to an abrupt halt. He said the word "fire" to the person on the other end of the phone, and everyone in the room froze.

Gary slammed the phone down. He looked at his family. "It started in Coal Creek Canyon and is heading this way. It's kind of far off right now but..."

"But we have to prepare for the worst," Ella said, calmly.

After Bridget's house fire five years ago, Ella had typed up a list of everything they would need in case of evacuation. "I have most of our old photos and stuff in a couple of suitcases upstairs, and I kept three or four empty ones in the attic for a situation like this. We can use those for all the other stuff we want to take. Alena, maybe you could help your dad grab those, okay?"

They had always been amazed by Ella's organizational mind; sometimes it drove them nuts, but today they were grateful for it. Ella looked at her son. "Brice, start calling all the neighbors and tell them where the fire is even though we don't have much information to go on."

"No way, Mom," he protested. "I'm sorry about the fire, but I'm not missing this opportunity. I already have my backpack loaded and my guitar ready to go. I'm outta here before the police or fire guys decide to shut down this road. My future is calling me, and it's in California. I don't have time for this!"

Brice headed for the door, but he didn't get far. His dad stood in the entrance with Brice's guitar dangling from his hand, effectively blocking his departure. He said, "Not happening, Brice. You heard what your mother said! You aren't going anywhere until you call the neighbors and warn them. You **will** help us pack, and you **will** load up the cars if need be. I'm telling you right now, you will never see this guitar again unless you do what you know needs to be done right now. Then, and only then, will we talk about when and if we release the money for you to go to California or anyplace else for that matter. I don't mind you following your dream, but when your family's lives and property are at stake, that's a whole other deal. I thought we raised you better. You're acting like a self-centered spoiled brat!"

Ella was about to second this assessment of their son when they heard Alena yelling from her bedroom. "I can see flames. On top of the ridge."

Not ten seconds later, they heard the wail of sirens and hurried out the front door to the porch. The lights of the fire trucks flashed as they raced down the lake road, twenty or thirty volunteer fire-fighters on a collision course with danger.

"We gotta move," Gary said. They hurried back inside and started hauling the suitcases Ella had packed with their heirlooms down from upstairs. Whether it was because he was still pissed off or whether he tripped coming down the stairs, Brice lost his grip on one of the suitcases and it broke open when it hit the floor, family photos and scrapbooks strewn in every direction.

"Goddamn it, Brice!" his mother yelled.

"Shit. Sorry." Brice knew he had crossed the line and quickly started cleaning up the carnage. He picked up his parents' wedding album and couldn't help thumbing through the pages. He whistled, saying, "God, everyone looks so damn young and so damn happy. Look at those cheesy smiles."

As angry as Ella was, she knelt down next to her son and reached for a box with "1970s" scribbled in magic marker across the top. Inside were stacks of photos rubber-banded together and organized under headings like, "Before Colorado," "College at CU," "Mountain Thanksgivings," "Parties," "Before Kids," "Alena in NY," "Friends on the Mountain," "Life after Intervention," and "Family."

Gary and Alena joined them. Yes, there was panic in the air, but something caused them to slow down for a few minutes. Gary put his arm around his wife's shoulder as she flipped through a random stack from their wedding twenty-one years earlier. "Look at Mom and Dad. Underneath that smile, he's all worried about the cost. And Mom. She went around with that fake smile pasted on her face for our entire wedding day. She was so angry at me for leaving home and heading out here."

"I remember," Gary said.

"Every opportunity she got that day she told me, 'At least you had the good sense to have this wedding at home and let me plan it. And I did do a fabulous job, didn't I sweetheart.'"

"And what did you say?" Alena asked her.

"And I probably said, 'Yes, you certainly did. But at least I had the good sense to move far, far away from your obsessive need to control everything and everyone you ever came in contact with.'"

Alena's eyes widened. "You said that?"

Ella looked at her daughter. "She and I didn't really like each other very much. God, thank God, all the years in between have mellowed us. I was just a girl back then wanting to make *my* life, just for me. And that's what I did."

Summer 1974

"Darling, it's time to go," Ella's mother called to her.

Ella descended the staircase and did so the way she seemed to do everything of late: reluctantly.

When her mother saw the dress she had chosen, she squished her nose up like something in the room smelled awful. It was her infamous look of disapproval; Ella had seen it a thousand times. "Is that what you're wearing?"

"I like what I'm wearing," Ella replied. This was their life. If Ella said black, her mother said white.

"Oh, honey, you don't have time to change. Your father's waiting outside in the car. You'll just have to go like that, I'm afraid."

"I wasn't planning on changing." Ella was used to her mother's constant condescension and breezed past her, out the door, and into the back seat of the air-conditioned Lincoln Continental.

"Why the long face, Ella?" her father asked from the front seat.

Ella held out her hands, palms up, and swiped the front of her clothes.

"Oh," he muttered, unconcerned as her mother, reeking of Chanel No. 5, carefully sat down in the front seat. She immediately pulled down the visor and looked in the mirror. "Ella, darling, you will tell me if I have lipstick on my teeth, won't you? And stop twirling that silky blonde hair of yours. You'll get split ends. I've told you a million times. Stop it!"

Three long miles of deadened silence followed. Her father parked the car in front of the country club because they were early. They were always early. Ella's mother looked back at her and said, "Honey, don't forget to stand up straight. I've...I mean your father and I have noticed how you've been slouching lately. That kind of posture always reminds me of someone too lazy to care."

Ella got out and slammed the door behind her. Shirley, a name Ella was glad not to have inherited, waited for her husband to open her door. By the time she had taken Robert's arm, their daughter was already inside and ready to partake of the never-changing Friday night fish fry.

Doctors, lawyers, and financial analysts lived in this affluent neighborhood. Shirley and Robert Hoffman did not come from money. They had both put themselves through college, being the first ones in their families to do so, and were damn proud of the fact.

Failure had no place in their view of the world. They accepted no excuses. Ella had grown up privileged and understood the opportunities that money could buy. The country club provided swimming, tennis, golf, and dancing lessons. Her piano teacher was a member. Ella was an excellent classically trained pianist. It wasn't that she had an innate aptitude for it, but it was a cultural requirement for a girl of her social stature. She hated recitals. She hated the attention. She was terribly shy and perpetual stage fright almost always prevented her from finishing the music she had supposedly memorized during endless hours of practice. It was in these moments that she could feel her parents' disappointment, sitting in the audience watching their daughter struggling to finish a piece of music she'd come to hate. Actually, there were lots of moments when she felt their disappointment. Well, such was life.

Ella had returned home from her sophomore year at Cornell harboring two secrets. One she would never reveal. The other she hoped to share soon. The first was her abortion, an experience tucked away forever into the farthest recesses of her mind and heart. That final decision not to have her baby was the most difficult she had ever faced, quite the opposite of the irresponsible spontaneity that caused her to lose her virginity with unprotected sex. Stupidity, she discovered, had big consequences, ones you had to live with forever. Now all she wanted was to be as far away from upstate New York as possible.

The University of Colorado at Boulder had accepted her application for her junior and senior years; no, her parents didn't know this yet. Ella had rehearsed her speech a hundred times – her biggest concern was whether or not they would agree to pay out-of-state tuition, not whether they would approve or not – but it turned out to be much simpler than she had expected. Her parents, it turned out, felt confident that a couple of years away from home would remind Ella in no uncertain terms of all the benefits they had provided her. They also felt confident that she would come running back to them, repentant and contrite. Oh, how her mother would hold that against her.

So, instead of a fight, her bon voyage gift was the family's five-year-old station wagon. Ella couldn't believe her good fortune.

She didn't wait a day to pack and organized the process with the precision of an orchestra conductor…fluid, precise, and efficient. On the outside of every box, she and her mother listed every single item; no use wasting time unpacking. Her parents stated that under no circumstances would Ella drive alone out to Colorado, so her older brother John rode along. It was a three-day journey that set Ella's life on a new trajectory.

Her first discovery was the stark realization that there was more to the west than snow-topped mountains and frigid temperatures; in fact, it was hot as hell in Boulder in August. The air was dry enough to make her nose bleed. Her first purchases were lip balm for her chapped lips and moisturizer for her skin. An advertisement on a bulletin board in the university's registration office led to an apartment and a roommate: Joan. When she called her father to tell him the news, he couldn't believe how pricey living in a university town was compared to their small town in upstate New York.

The apartment complex that was to be her new home was occupied entirely by students. Lawn chairs filled every balcony and every available square inch of lawn. Beautifully tanned bodies soaked up the sun. The students here were fit, and Ella took this to heart. Fit was good. Joan, on the other hand, was neither fit nor neat, dubbing them the latest version of the odd couple. But Joan had met the guys next door, and the guys next door were having a party on Ella's third night in town. Joan talked Ella into going even though she hadn't unpacked all of her boxes yet; maybe a new Ella was already emerging.

The party was seriously jumping the minute they walked in. The music was loud and so was the laughter. Someone handed Ella a perfectly made Sloe Gin Fizz, which she carried out to the balcony. The first thing she noticed in studying her fellow classmates was the fashion, or lack thereof. It was a casual, rugged, outdoor look. The girls wore revealing halter tops and short jean cutoffs. And from what she could tell, long straight hair parted down the middle was the norm for both sexes and she was glad her long blonde hair was no different. Bandanas served as headbands or scarves. Wool socks and hiking boots covered their feet. If people weren't wearing hiking boots, they wore Birkenstocks, and Ella determined to get a pair of both. Why not? After all, this was the new Ella she was talking about.

The sky's inky blackness accentuated the brightness of the full moon, mesmerizing Ella as she downed her second drink. Joan reappeared and introduced her to a couple of guys whose names she didn't remember. She didn't remember their names because Joan was handing her a joint at the same time. Ella didn't know a thing about pot. But she sure as hell didn't want to demonstrate her lack of worldly acumen in front of two guys she'd only just met, so she stared at the lighter's flame at the end of the joint and inhaled her newfound freedom.

FIRE

Day 1

"Knowing that sunrise and sunset begin and end my day is a comforting constant in a life full of surprises."
~ The Circle of Na'mow Handbook – Martha, First Generation

September 14, 1996, Saturday afternoon

The mountain's volunteer firefighters may have been the first on scene and the first to test their skills against the growing blaze, but they wasted no time calling in reinforcements from fire departments all along the Front Range. That's how dire things were and how quickly the fire spread.

The terrain was treacherous. Steep slopes covered in rocks and boulders, slippery pine needles, and soil made from a thousand years of decomposed granite made for dangerous hiking under the best of circumstances. Laden with firefighting gear? Nearly impossible.

Water, or a lack thereof, was the other problem. This was the heart of the Rockies, and water was a precious commodity up this high.

The firefighters' best bet was the lake, a huge body of water west of the growing danger. Accessing it, however, proved difficult. Trucks could fill up without much problem, but then, heavy with water, found it almost impossible to navigate such steep terrain. Even at that, the huge wall of flame and smoke dwarfed the small mountain tankers, and the helicopters and slurry bombers that authorities had summoned wouldn't be available until the next day.

In any case, you didn't put out a fire of this magnitude; containment was the best anyone could ask for.

While the fire raged, the power company worked on shutting off power to the neighboring subdivisions. Sheriff's deputies went house to house telling people to make sure they shut off their main gas lines. They were strongly urging people to gather their livestock and their pets and get out. Some did. Some didn't.

On the perimeter, it was a circus. Looky loos, bicyclists, joggers, hikers, and tourists clogged the main road, even as the police set up their roadblocks and fire personnel made a mad dash up the mountain.

BRIDGET

Bridget was exhausted.

A week in London. Fifteen-hour days. Ten hours in a plane. Now she faced an hour and a half car trip from the airport back home. Thank God it was Saturday. At least the traffic would be manageable. After the streets of London! Hell, this would be a piece of cake.

Bridget worked for a thriving technology company, and she had been spending one week a month in their London office for the last six months. It was like her second home. She liked the energy; she hated the travel. Oh, yeah, and she also liked the money. *Never forget the money*, Bridget reminded herself, using the locker in United's Premier Travelers suite to change out of her skirt, blouse, blazer, and pumps – her "corporate uniform," as she called it – and into a pair of jeans, a tee shirt and hoodie, and sneakers. All she could think about now was sitting on the back deck with her husband and kids, sipping an ice-cold margarita, and watching the sun set behind the mountain.

On her way to the car, she called home and got the answering machine. She left a message. "Hey, everybody. I'm home. Where is everyone? See you in a bit."

Bridget noticed the gray cloud hanging over the foothills as she merged from I-70 onto I-270; the cloud started changing to a disturbing black color and obstructing more of the sky as she turned onto the Boulder Turnpike.

She tried the home phone again, and this time her husband Dan picked up. The first words out of his mouth were, "We've got a fire."

"Oh, shit!"

They'd lost everything in a house fire in '91. Everything. The house burnt down to the foundation. They planned to rebuild, but for now they were renting a house next door, determined to stay the course of longtime residents of the mountain. It sounded so romantic. The problem was not rebuilding, not the brick and mortar, not months and years. The problem was in their hearts and heads; fire never let you forget. So now every time there was even a hint of smoke or a rumor of fire somewhere, panic set in.

"We got a call from Ella's kid about two hours ago. I got out the binoculars, and there it was. Right on the ridge line." Dan was trying his best to stay calm. "Charred trees. Thick black plumes. We could even see flashes of orange as it took to the top of the trees."

"Shit, Dan, a crown fire. We're fucked."

"Don't say that."

Bridget ignored this. "How are the kids?" Michael was sixteen and Shauna was two years younger. They'd lived most of their lives on the mountain.

"Freaked," he said. "Shauna saw a herd of deer crashing through the currant bushes, hightailing it for who knows where, and she literally screamed. Poor kid."

Bridget could picture the fear in her kids' eyes, and she wanted to cry. Of course, she didn't. She never cried in front of her family. She could cry with the girls. "Dan, you get them moving?"

She meant doing the jobs each of them had on their list in case of fire. "Yeah, they're on it. Michael's digging out our backpacks. He's filling up as many empty containers with water as we can find."

"Don't forget to fill the sinks and bathtubs too," Bridget reminded him.

"Shauna's putting flashlights in every room in case the power goes," he said. Bridget could tell he was pacing. Dan always paced when he was anxious. "I'll get the computers and all that paraphernalia together."

"You better start packing," Bridget said.

"Yeah, and I'll move the cars so they are pointing toward the road in case we have to evacuate."

There was a moment of silence. "I'm on the turnpike just outside of Broomfield. I'll get there as soon as I can," Bridget said.

"Good. We need you."

"Let me talk to Shauna. And don't forget the kids' school stuff, Dan."

Shauna was crying when she got on the phone, and Bridget felt guilty about the time she was spending in London. "I'm sorry I'm not there yet, baby. We're going to be fine."

"You promise?"

"I give you my word," she said quickly. "Help your dad, okay? I'll be there soon. I love you, baby. We're all going to be fine. You stay strong for me, okay?"

"I will, mom."

Bridget hated to end the call, but they had work to do and she was still an hour away. Bridget strained her neck to look up through her driver side window when she heard the engine noise of a small spotter plane on its way toward the foothills to survey the fire. It didn't look good.

The protective mother bear in her took over as she raced west on Highway 36 toward the smoke-shrouded mountains. It was amazing how thick it was even from this distance. Bridget was a hands-on person. She was a hands-on wife and mother, and she hated this feeling of helplessness. She was left with her imagination, and her imagination conjured up a dozen different scenarios that might await her at the bottom of the mountain; she plotted a course of action in every case.

And then came the questions. Would they even let her up the mountain? Would it be better just to go the back way? And now that she thought of it, would the four-wheel-drive road even be passable?

The shock waves of a police siren brought her back to the moment and caused her to jump in her seat. She peeked at the speedometer. Eighty miles an hour. Damn. She glanced in her rearview mirror and saw the squad car tailgating her.

"Goddamn it!" She pulled over.

Bridget dropped her license and insurance information as she handed them out the window to the patrolman. She looked down at her hands and realized they were trembling. And then she understood why. It wasn't the damn speeding ticket and it wasn't the damn cop chasing her paperwork down the highway. It was something far more important than that. She scrabbled for her cell phone and speed-dialed her home number again. Dan answered after one ring. "Bridge? Hey, you okay?"

"Don't forget my scrapbooks, Dan."

"Got 'em," he said reassuringly. "They were buried under all our winter stuff in the front hall bench. Shit, Bridge, our whole lives are in those albums. We're not leaving those behind."

Summer 1974

The cigarette smoke in the dive bar drove Bridget outside for a breath of fresh air, and the rotting garbage in the alley was seconds away from forcing her back inside when she caught sight of the glorious full moon overhead. Its beguiling brilliance surprised her sober, and she was suddenly comforted by its roundness in a world full of sharp angles. Here she was standing in an alley in the heart of downtown Detroit, and there was no way to escape the irony. On the one hand, the putrid smell of garbage reminded her that she too was rotting away and going nowhere in a godforsaken town she despised. On the other, the moon reinforced her private vow to "get the hell out of Dodge," and the one-way bus ticket to Colorado hidden in the messy recesses of her big leather purse spoke for itself. She was going. No one could stop her.

This wasn't a spur of the moment decision. The wild frontier of the Rocky Mountains had called to her ever since she was a child playing cowboys and Indians, and her heart yearned for the endless vistas and the impressive elevations. A place she could call home, a place where she felt connected to the land just like her ancestors had been connected to the misty moors of Ireland.

The thought of her escape caused a huge smile to crease Bridget's lips, and she felt an inexplicable urge to lift her head toward the moon and let out a spine-chilling howl, just for the hell of it.

The plan was to celebrate with her friends tonight and tell her parents about her decision over Sunday dinner tomorrow. She hoped she'd survive the next twenty-four hours.

The next morning Bridget rolled over in her bed and groaned, unconsciously wiping the small trickle of drool from her cheek. She had to fight her way through her mane of crazy red hair to see the light of day. Her eyes tried to squint to see. Only one emerald green eye cracked open but it hurt to focus. She pulled her quilt over her head and snuggled in deeper, trying to ignore daylight's reality, but as usual unrest began boiling to the surface of her consciousness, making her head pound even more viciously.

Her mother climbed the stairs to her daughter's room in a huff. A loud crash and yelp made the sleeping redhead bolt upright.

"What the fuck?!?" Bridget yelled, instantaneously massaging her temples.

Mary held onto the wall trying to regain her balance and pride. "Bridget!!! You'll not be using words like that in my house! You have a mouth like a drunken sailor headed for the gates of hell. I swear I'm gonna burn those darn cowboy boots always sittin' in the middle of the room and just look at your clothes thrown all over the floor. You weren't raised in a barn! GET UP NOW! GET READY FOR MASS!"

"Fuck!" Bridget yelled out loud, not caring if her mother heard her or not. She yanked her unruly mane of hair up into a ponytail, fixing it with a rubber band. It was Sunday and Bridget was pissed off that she had to go to Mass and then help fix a huge Sunday supper, then help clean up while her two brothers and father retired into the living room to watch TV. Her life consisted of helping her mom clean up everyone else's crap, and she was sick of it.

Bridget's parents raised her with a great respect for their Irish heritage, their religion, and hard work. Her father, Joseph Jameson, worked in an auto plant as a laborer as did his father and grandfather before him. Mary, her mother, cleaned houses for the executives in the auto plant, as had three generations of women before her. Making an honest living through hard work and sacrifice was a badge of honor that they wore well and instilled with pride in their three children. "It's a good life" they could be heard quoting frequently to their children. Bridget was going to break the family tradition! She wanted something different and better for her life.

This Sunday dinner was definitely going to be different. The reality of leaving everyone and everything she had ever known behind gripped her heart, but fear was not going to stop her, not now, not ever. She tried to keep that in mind when she announced after the pink frozen gelatin dessert that she would be leaving for Colorado the next morning. The looks on her parents' faces were impossible to bear. Their love for her was palpable. She regretted hurting them because she knew they had given her their best.

Her father exploded. He slammed the tabletop with a meaty fist and nearly came out of his chair. "By God, you'll be going nowhere. We're a family and families stay together. That's all there is to it! Period."

Her mother hid her face in her linen napkin, a vain attempt to stifle tears that eventually erupted into wracking sobs. Bridget was used to her father's outbursts, but witnessing her mother's deep sadness was almost too much for her to bear.

Neither accompanied her to the bus station the next morning. She promised to call when she reached Colorado, even though her father said, "Don't bother."

The bus wasn't very comfortable, and Bridget had a splitting headache from one too many Irish whiskeys with her friends last night. She was too nervous to sleep, and her head rocked back and forth against the window as the bus bounced along a boring stretch of highway in eastern Indiana. She missed her pillow but was glad her mother had insisted she bring along one of her grandmother's Irish quilts. A tear rolled down her cheek and a lump formed in her throat as she relived her departure from the only place she had ever called home. There were things she would miss, of course. Her friends, her family, and what was left of their Irish community. But there were more things she wouldn't. The dirty, filthy city, the poverty, the lack of opportunity, the caged feeling that never seemed to go away.

She had a thousand dollars in the money belt strapped around her waist – money from waitressing and house cleaning jobs – and she hoped it was enough to get her new life started.

She must have dozed off for a couple of hours, because the changing Iowa landscape and its vast fields of corn were suddenly upon her. Corn gave way to soybeans and finally to endless fields of golden hay baled into tight bundles. Bridget saw a tractor working the fields and sending up a trail of dust in its wake. She couldn't make out the farmer driving the vehicle, but she imagined a hardened man who would know every detail of his farm's landscape, much like he would every curve of his wife's ample body. Bridget imagined a man tending to both farm and wife, knowing that any rewards worth reaping in this world would come from them.

Bridget knew she needed to sow her own seeds now and hope for the best, and this new sense of freedom appealed to her immensely.

In Omaha, a guy wearing a University of Colorado tee shirt boarded the bus and took the seat next to her. His name was Larry, and he was quick to explain that he was returning to Boulder after spending a grueling, hot summer back home. And though Bridget found his company a bit grating, he did invite her to share the six-pack he had stowed in his backpack. Bridget's face lit up. "You're kidding me!"

"Want one? They should still be cold."

"Imagine asking a redheaded Irish girl if she wants a beer," was her response. And indeed Bridget had the most magnificent head of red hair Larry had ever seen.

Two beers made Larry a bit less grating and the trip a little less boring. Bridget prodded her companion for as much information about Boulder as she could process, and he eventually asked her if she had a place to stay.

"Well, no, actually. I was planning on finding a youth hostel. I know there's one in the middle of town somewhere. Not sure how to get there, but I'll find it."

"Sounds like a major headache, if you ask me," Larry said. "Why not crash on our couch for a couple of nights until you get settled. I'm sure my roomie will be cool with that. We're in a huge apartment complex close to campus, and who knows? You might find someone looking for a roommate."

"Thanks. I'll take you up on that," Bridget replied. "I mean, if it's not too much trouble."

"No trouble."

As Highway 36 crested a last hill before dropping into the broad, lush Boulder valley, Bridget got her first view of her new home. She had read about the Flatirons, but seeing these huge slabs of stone that formed such a magnificent backdrop to the town of Boulder, and a gateway to the forested mountains beyond, was jaw-dropping. Her father had a saying: "Jesus, Mary and Joseph, I have arrived in heaven." And that was exactly what Bridget was thinking. If only her mom and dad could see the majesty of these mountains now. The sight filled her with so much excitement and anticipation that she could barely stay in her seat.

"Sure as hell beats Detroit!" she said to no one in particular.

The day after her arrival in Boulder, three girls who lived in the same complex as Larry posted a note on the office bulletin board looking for a fourth roommate. The rent was only $55.00 a month, and this included utilities and furniture.

Bridget didn't need convincing. She moved in the next day.

FIRE

Day 2

"Mother Nature manifests duality best, forever spiralling around us."
~ The Circle of Na'mow Handbook – Phoebe, First Generation

September 15, 1996, Sunday morning

Once the electricity shut down, so also did the usual sense of optimism normally so prevalent on the mountain.

People resorted to battery-powered radios and "mountain mouth" – what flatlanders referred to as word of mouth – to gather bits and pieces of information from neighbors and friends and to hear updates from fire officials and police.

The wells most of the mountain homes used for their water supply needed pumps to propel the water into their storage tanks, and with no electricity there was little to no water for showers or inside toilets. If you'd lived in the mountains for long, you knew to fill as many containers as possible for drinking water, so that was rarely a problem.

There were also no lights, no heat – at least for some – no stoves, no microwaves, no televisions, no radios. With all the modern conveniences gone, creative survival came into play. It was either that or leave. Most would leave. But then the question arose: where does one go? The Red Cross had set up an evacuation center at the local church, but most evacuees would stay with friends or family in Boulder or Denver or some other town close by. Most people hadn't even checked with their insurance companies to see if their policies might pay for a hotel, but then, chaos didn't leave much room for clear thinking.

Fire was one of the most unpredictable forces in nature. You could prepare and plan for the moment it struck, but you couldn't plan for the sheer power and destructive force of the blaze, and you really couldn't predict how you would react until it was breathing down your neck and threatening your future.

LOLA

The sooty smoke of a billowing campfire consumed her; it was like inhaling the purifying aroma of a sage smudge stick. Her ears vibrated to the steady beat of drums. Indian women in a trance-like state danced in steady rhythm with the drums. Dancing as one, the movement of the women picked up speed, and Lola heard a baby crying in the distance. She caught the droning hoot of an owl. She heard herself cry out in pain and didn't know why. Her eyes popped open. She felt a sheen of sweat on her brow. She spent a confused moment trying to recall the details of the dream and found herself coughing uncontrollably.

An instant later, the smell of charred wood teased her nose, and she shouted, "Fire." Half panicked, she bolted out of her bed, only to faint into a heap before getting to the bedroom door.

When she came to, John was cradling her in his arms and Nick was holding a cool washcloth to her forehead. She sat up and pushed them both away. She looked at her ex-husband. "What are you still doing here?"

"Yeah, yeah, I know. Long story. Didn't mean to freak you out," he said as if trying to quell her suspicion. "I was planning on driving back down to my condo after we got the cars loaded up, but you and Nick both fell asleep. I didn't want to wake you up, and I didn't feel right leaving you alone. I don't remember closing my eyes, but I obviously did. Next thing I knew it was morning. I got up in time to make coffee before the power went out and was bringing you a cup when I heard you take a header onto the floor."

"Maybe you need to eat something, Mom," Nick suggested. "There are some power bars on the kitchen counter..."

Lola held her hand up at the mention of power bars and dry-heaved into the washcloth.

"Mom sure doesn't handle stress very well, does she?" Nick shrugged at his father.

"I handle stress just fine. I gave birth to you, and that was pretty damn stressful," Lola said. "Help me up. You're right, I need something to eat."

Lola settled for saltines and some kind of electrolyte drink as the havoc raged outside her house. The smoke was getting intense and so were John's blow-by-blow descriptions of the blaze as he watched the ridge through binoculars. She could even smell it on him when he reappeared from outside.

As soon as her stomach felt a little less like someone had sucker-punched her, Lola went out on the deck. She saw Nick standing down by the road trying to gather information from their neighbors. One thing was obvious: people were very hesitant to leave the mountain. Evacuation was a last resort. Maybe that was silly, and maybe it was stubborn, but it was still a fact.

Lola looked skyward as the roar of planes and helicopters rushing toward the scene corrupted the atmosphere, and billowing smoke and indiscriminate wind added to the chaos.

The blaze crept steadily toward the mountain's longtime community; its arrival seemed inevitable. Visibility was terrible.

Breathing conditions continued to deteriorate. The rush to safety included deer, birds, bears, and anything else on four legs.

An hour later, Nick returned from his neighborhood reconnaissance mission reeking of sweat and smoke. His eyes were lit with excitement and worry. "Brice is missing," he said to his parents.

"What do you mean, 'missing'?" Lola wanted to know. She couldn't imagine how worried Ella had to be.

"I ran into Gary. They had a fight over Brice leaving for L.A., and he split on foot to meet a buddy in town. Just left."

"He left with all this going on?" John threw his hands in the direction of the fire, but they knew what he meant. "That sucks."

"Maybe so, but if I know him, there's no going back," Nick said. "The L.A. music scene is all he ever talks about."

They went back inside. Not an hour later, John said what they were all thinking. "I hate to say it, but we've got to get out of here. I know how much you guys hate to bail on the house, but it's getting too damn close."

"You're right," Lola admitted. "It's out of control."

"You okay with that, Nick?" John said to his son. "Because once we're down in town, we're stuck there until this thing's contained."

"You're right about one thing," Nick said. "It feels like we're bailing. But I guess it's time to go."

"You can both stay at my condo. Besides, half of Nick's stuff is already down there and you, my dear, have a few things there too." He winked at his ex-wife.

Nick noticed the wink. "Gross."

"Nice of you to offer. Thanks." Lola blushed.

"John, why don't you head down now, and Nick and I will be right behind you. I've got a few more things to throw in the car."

"Okay, but don't wait. We should have probably left already."

"We're right behind you. Promise."

Watching John leave brought up so many emotions for Lola, so many memories, and so many questions. Her eyes filled with tears when she realized how grateful she was for him in her life despite living apart. He waved as the car rolled down the drive, and the tenderness she still felt for him swelled in her heart. She touched her hand to her chest as if to contain the feeling for a little bit longer and brushed a tear from her cheek.

She felt Nick's eyes on her and heard him say, "A crazy question, I suppose, but why the hell did you two ever get divorced in the first place? It's obvious you both still care."

That was the last thing Lola needed to hear, and a swell of tears obliterated her vision. She turned on her heel and walked right into the doorjamb, stubbing her toe and wincing with pain. Then she hit her head when she bent over to grab the injured foot.

"Goddamn, Mom. You okay?" Nick tried not to laugh as he helped her through the door, but he wasn't very successful. "I don't mean to laugh."

"My goodness, I'm just so emotional today, Nick. Probably these damn photos." She and Nick maneuvered the box toward the door, but she stopped him before he carried them out. She plucked an album at random from the box and threw it open to an even more random page.

The photos carried her back in time nearly thirty years ago, and her son chuckled. "I mean, shit! Look at you. Look how young you are."

"Good Lord. And look here." She held up a picture of a much younger Lola at a campsite she couldn't put a name to. "I was just a clueless girl hiding in hippie clothes."

"And not much of a camper either, by the looks of it," her son teased.

"Yeah, but I loved the outdoors even then. You couldn't keep me inside even when the weather went to hell."

Nick nodded toward the photo. "So is this before you met Dad?"

"Oh, yeah. Before…before a lot of things. Before I moved up here. Before I met Ella and Bridget. Before I met your father and found love."

June 1975 – Summer Solstice Weekend – Rock 'n Blues Festival

The car bumped and swayed its way up the winding mountain roads of southwestern Colorado. This was Lola's first trip to this part of the state, and Mother Nature's beauty was majestic and even a little hypnotizing as the thinner air caused a pleasant drowsiness in everyone in the car. Well, except the driver hopefully, and since Sandy was their driver, Lola felt pretty confident.

The drive was breathtaking. Steep canyons rose to elevations so high that everything seemed slow to respond: your breathing, your muscles, your need for anything but the expanse opening up before you. The rock walls were splattered with every shade of brown and red imaginable, and they towered like skyscrapers over everything else. Below, meandering valleys cradled creeks and rivers that ran past groves of aspens, junipers, and pines. The leaves of the aspens were drenched by intense sunlight, and fluttered and shimmered a fluorescent green. The sun's rays pierced through the cloudless blue sky, making the temperature hot and the air dry and perfect for the festival.

Lola and her roommates had one thing in mind: Get as far away from the city as possible for a long weekend, and the Rock 'n Blues Festival in the San Juan Mountains was the perfect excuse. Music, camping, and adventure were the perfect combination, even though Lola was a virtual novice at the camping and adventure parts.

Sandy, her best friend, knew about a campsite not ten minutes from town, and she pulled the Jetstar 88 off the road and into the trees like she'd been here a hundred times. "We're here! Yippee!" She jumped out and slammed the door.

Sandy was already opening the trunk as her three passengers sleepily climbed out. "Let's get unpacked and set up camp. This place will be flooded with people in the next couple of hours, and we want the best place we can find." Sandy was an experienced camper, and she knew how to pick a campsite. A sweeping aspen forest surrounded it on four sides. The ground was flat, rock free, and perfect for their tent. It took the four of them twice as long as it would have if Sandy had done it herself – with a lot less complaining to boot – but they finally got it done and started unpacking.

"Look at this," Caroline said when they spied the huge suitcase Lola had spread open next to the tent.

"Holy crap!" Sandy knelt down and held up two pairs of rhinestone-studded sandals. "What are you going to do with these?"

They all joined in. The blonde named Cindy peered into Lola's treasure chest and said, "You've got to be kidding me. You know how to travel, that's for sure."

"Travel, yeah. Camp, no." Sandy surveyed the contents in disbelief: a cotton eye mask, a spray bottle of Jovan musk perfume, little containers of colored lip gloss, a small jewelry bag, a big travel alarm clock, a couple of frilly peasant blouses, two scarves, a shawl, two long skirts, a blow dryer and straightening iron, deodorant, a jar of face cream, packets of lubricated rubbers, KY jelly, rolling papers, a small jar of purple buds – "Very primo," Lola assured them – matches, four bottles of wine, a tambourine, maracas, a huge handheld mirror, comb, brush, toothpaste and toothbrush, red nail polish, a big puffy pillow, and the book "The Joy of Sex, A Gourmet Guide to Love Making - The Complete, Unabridged, and Illustrated Edition."

"Lola, where's your mind?" Sandy held up the book. "As if we have to ask."

Caroline laughed. "Girl is ready for anything. Good for you."

Then Sandy held up the blow dryer. "This is not a resort, you know. Do you think these trees have electrical outlets? A blow dryer and hair iron? And all this makeup and smelly crap? Every bear and mosquito within a hundred miles will know exactly what tent to hit."

"Bigger question," Cindy said. "Where's your sleeping bag?"

"My what?" Lola looked from one girl to the next, right index finger tapping her lips. They all laughed, and Sandy rescued her.

She said, "Good thing I always bring an extra bag for emergencies. And, yep, I'd say you are that emergency, Lola. Where's your coat, rain gear, socks, hiking boots, hat, sun tan lotion, and water bottle? Lola, did you bring anything essential?" Sandy stood with her hands on her hips.

"Hell, yeah, I did," Lola answered. "Wine, pot, and four hits of acid for later tonight."

"Now I know why we brought her," Caroline said.

Sandy shook her head and walked back to the car. "Well, it's nice to know someone is providing the entertainment in camp the next couple of days. Let's grab these coolers."

The camping area filled up quickly that day, just like Sandy predicted: trucks, cars, tents, and loads of people. Lola's Kodak Instamatic 104 was getting a serious workout. She had never seen so many musicians, hippies, and scantily clothed free spirits in one place. Singing, laughter, and endless conversation filled the air with a never-ending gaiety of spirit. Lola fit in perfectly and realized she was the happiest she'd been in months.

And then, typical of the fickle weather in Colorado, the storm hit and hit with a fury. Dark clouds exploded with deafening thunder and frightening bolts of lightning. The temperature dropped forty degrees in a heartbeat. Unrelenting rain forced everyone inside to their cars or tents.

For the first few minutes the coolness gave relief to a day of stifling heat. But then sleet, and then snow quickly transformed the rain. It got very quiet. Mother Nature had silenced these drugged, boisterous animals and made them retreat back into their dens. Falling snow suddenly transformed acres of blackened, trampled mud, littered disrespectfully with bottles, cans and food wrappers, into a perfectly tranquil paradise.

When the frenzy of the storm passed, Lola and her friends peeked out of their tent door and saw an assemblage of brave souls building a huge pyramid of wet wood at the campground's far end.

"What the hell! Look at that," Sandy said. She clapped her hands. "Let's get out there. It looks like a party in the making."

The girls put on their warmest clothes and ventured out. They did their part by snapping off small dead tree branches to add to the future bonfire.

When the pyramid reached a respectable six feet, some brave soul poured gasoline on the pyre and someone else struck a match to it. The wood burst into flames. The fire burned fiercely and glowed intensely, and the girls gathered around. True, Lola looked ridiculous with the socks and gloves and wool blanket she'd borrowed from Sandy, but she didn't care. No one was trying to make a fashion statement here in this circus-like atmosphere. Style was in the eyes of the beholder, and it seemed that everything went.

The warmth of the bonfire and the heat of the blanket quelled Lola's shivering. She took a hit of acid, and Cindy and Caroline joined her.

A dozen musicians took up their instruments – drums, guitars, a dulcimer, a saxophone, a flute – and Lola felt her body begin to move. Mesmerized by the music, she raised her blanket, waving it like wings above her head, side to side: dancing, twirling, humming, traveling to places unknown in her mind. She heard an unfamiliar language swimming in her head, speaking to her, softly nudging her on.

Suddenly, boundaries faded. First one woman joined her dance, and then another. Then many. Each dancing to her own drummer. Each free. Each connected.

Summer 1977

Lola's love of the mountains and the freedom she felt when she was dancing only grew stronger as the years passed, but not all days were perfect. Take today. A musician friend from the coffee shop had invited her to a softball game up in the mountains. The mountains

41

she was drawn to like a magnet, but softball was something she knew nothing about. Maybe that's why she had to go.

First, she couldn't find an outfit to wear. Major headache.

Then her ride decided she didn't want to go, so Lola had to bribe her with extra gas money. The nine-mile drive rose 2,500 feet along a narrow road with no guardrails. Dodging bicyclists and joggers made the drive even slower and more frightening.

They had no sooner arrived when the accident happened. A petite girl with a long brunette ponytail caught a softball right in the eye. She went down hard, right in the middle of centerfield.

"Ohhhhh…that looks bad, really bad." Lola cringed. "Sort of like my whole damn day."

Because the rest of the players on the field were too stoned and too drunk to help, and because they were laughing way too hard, Lola and her friend Darby grabbed some ice from a nearby cooler and raced to the girl's aid. Darby wrapped the ice in her bandana and placed it over the girl's eye. "This should help," she said, though Lola wasn't sure anything was really going to help except maybe a trip to the emergency room.

The injured girl sat up, shaking her head and laughing. "Damn mescaline. Threw off my whole depth perception. I thought for sure I'd catch that ball."

"You caught it all right," Lola said, gasping when she saw the dark purple circle forming around the eye socket and spreading over her cheek. "Sorry to say, but you look like Spot the Dog, and I'm not sure that's a compliment."

They helped the girl to her feet and escorted her off the field.

They found a shady spot under a tree and left her with the ice pack. Lola made a beeline back to the coolers and discovered a pitcher of frozen daiquiris. She poured herself a healthy one and wondered if softball might not be a sport worth avoiding.

Then she heard someone saying, "Hey, we need a centerfielder." Lola looked up. The voice belonged to the stocky kid playing first base, and he was looking straight at her. "How about taking Candi's place?"

Now he pointed toward the meadow and the spot where Candi had met her misfortune.

"Me? But…this baseball field is all sloped and uneven," Lola said. "And I don't see any bases."

"Cow pies," the guy said. He nodded toward three strategically placed piles of cow pies. "It's open range up here." Then he smiled.

"Cow pies? Are you crazy?" Lola said.

"We don't plan on sliding." The pitcher was a hippie with thin stringy blond hair and a businesslike voice. "Grab a mitt."

When the game ended, no one could remember what the score was or who had won. Nobody cared. And nobody cared that Lola more or less sucked and would probably never wear a baseball mitt again.

"You did good," the hippie said as they walked off the field. "We're moving the party up the road. Why don't you and your friend join us?"

"Thanks. We will," Lola answered.

The "Party House," as they called it, was a huge log cabin on the edge of the meadow, and twenty cars were parked out in front when Lola and Darby arrived. Inside, the horizontal logs ran the length of the walls and huge wood beams crossed the ceiling. A double-sided moss rock fireplace dominated the living and dining rooms. Gigantic picture windows framed stunning views of the lake and the Continental Divide.

"Damn! What a place for a party," Lola said.

Guitars, a standup piano, and a set of bongos were set out in the living room. A smorgasbord of food overflowed from the dining room table. Coolers heavy with everything from rum and Coke to St. Pauli Girl beer were strewn along the outside deck. Everyone from the softball game refueled on food, booze, and drugs of every make and model. A motley crew of musicians strapped on their guitars, took up their places at the piano and the bongos, and filled the house with their soulful voices. The music motivated the partiers to get up and move; some danced either spastically or in a slow sway depending on the drugs they had ingested. The green shag carpeted living room floor wasn't the ideal dance floor.

Learning from her camping experience, Lola had brought extra clothes in a backpack, "just in case." She changed into a silky halter top and low-cut jeans, and her body looked toned and beautiful. When a hit of acid started coursing through her veins, she hopped up on the huge tree trunk coffee table that dominated one end of the room and untied the long scarf she'd been wearing as a headband. She started dancing, gyrating her ample hips in a slow sensual circle as her upper torso undulated in the opposite direction. Using her scarf as a prop, she playfully "captured" first one person and then another, enticing them onto the table top with her, bumping and grinding and laughing as if time had stood still.

Suddenly, she was Lola the Enchantress, bewitching guys and girls alike with her lilting, graceful movements. From that night forward, the casually choreographed moves would forever be known as "Lola's scarf dance," and many years later, the girls of the Circle would make it a lighthearted part of their ritual.

The night rolled on.

Above the scent of incense, pot, and hash wafting among the revelers, Lola caught the scent of the pine forest outside filtering through an open window. It made her smile. Above the flickering candles and the otherworldly shadows they created against the walls and ceiling, she saw a moonbeam illuminating the black forest, and it gave her a sense of place she'd never experienced before. Above the strumming, drumming, and singing, she heard coyotes howling and a pair of owls hooting, adding magic to an already magical night and signaling a change Lola subconsciously knew was in the offing.

Living on her own in the college town of Boulder brought out Lola's resourceful side, what with rent and food and things like that hanging over her head. However, there was always a more impetuous, spirited side waiting to pounce, and it happened later that summer when she was riding her bike back from an early shift at the coffee shop, and the dark clouds forming overhead unleashed a serious downpour. And as much as she loved getting to and fro on her bike, inclement weather like this was a pain.

She was a half block from her apartment when she passed an orange "Thing" parked on the street with a For Sale sign hanging inside the windshield. The sign also said: "Make an offer." The "Thing" was a boxy Volkswagen 181 that looked like a military vehicle with four doors and a removable top; in this case, a complete wreck that Lola fell in love with instantly. An hour later, she was calling the car her own.

Racing into her apartment, she called Sandy's name. "Hey? You home?"

Her roommate appeared at the kitchen door a moment later holding a dishtowel and saw the keys dangling from Lola's hand. "Uh-oh. This looks like trouble."

"Yeah. I just got a car."

"What do you mean by 'got'? Not bought or inherited or some other verb. Just 'got'? Lola, what does 'got' exactly mean?" Sandy dried off her wet hands.

"It means I just bought the Davises' car next door."

"That ugly orange thing?"

"Exactly. And I love the orange color. It's the sex chakra color, you know. Sex, money, and power. I definitely need my sex chakra activated. Maybe this is a start. Oh, yeah, and it's four-wheel drive," Lola proudly announced.

"Sex chakra. Yeah, right." Sandy stared back. "I thought you weren't going to touch your inheritance. How much did you pay for the damn thing?"

"That's the beauty of the deal I made. You know the shady characters we see hanging out over there. Well, I think they're in over their head with all the drugs they're dealing and need cash. They're moving out as soon as they can, and…"

"Lola! Lola! Your imagination just takes off…what shady characters?" Sandy didn't wait for an answer. "Tell me about the deal you made."

Lola held up the title. "Two hundred in cash and my bicycle."

"Wow! What did you do, mesmerize the hell out of them?"

"I didn't have to. That's how desperate they are. They even offered me their furniture for $50. They're bringing it over later."

Sandy was staring again, clearly in awe. Then she looked around their apartment and shrugged. "Yeah, pretty sparse in here, now that you mention it. What's that?" She pointed to the newspaper sticking out of the top of Lola's purse.

"My horoscope. You ready for this?" Lola opened the paper with a flurry.

"'Aquarius. Because yours is the air sign, people often perceive you as being spacey, indecisive, and wishy-washy." Sandy couldn't help but laugh. Lola ignore her. "'But over the coming days, the element of air will blow good fortune your way. Yours will be a magic carpet ride. Opportunities will pass before you. Don't let them get away. Be decisive. Your future looks bright. Your lucky star is illuminating your path. Follow it.'"

"Crap, Lola, some people get all the great horoscopes," Sandy teased.

"Oh, shut up, Sandy. You're just jealous." Lola folded the paper and stuck it back in her purse. "Let's go try out my new wheels."

So that's what they did, driving around town with the top down so the new owner could "get the feel" of the car. Eventually. Sandy pointed toward the mountains on the west side of town and said, "Let's see what kind of power this baby has. Find us a nice wind-y mountain road and take us out of the city for a while." Sandy pointed, and the driver obeyed.

They took the only road Lola knew out of the city and the soaring pines quickly swallowed them up. The mountains came alive. There were tourists and joggers that made the going slow, but there were also wildflowers of every imaginable color blooming along the hillsides that made it all worthwhile. Abert's squirrels with their tufted ears scurried from one pine tree to another. Deer grazed unconcerned. Ravens caught thermals and circled overhead. A big fat marmot dodged in between the huge boulders, and Lola and Sandy both laughed.

They stopped for a moment to get their bearings. The view of the city from this high up was surreal, like a panoramic postcard. It was the perfect place for a picnic, and a dozen people had already staked out tables.

Forty-five minutes later, Lola and Sandy drove through a small mountain subdivision of modest summer cabins now converted to yearlong residences. Lola slowed down. A huge steer was blocking the narrow dirt road. He stared at the "Thing." His nostrils flared as he lifted his tail and emptied his bowels. The pile steamed as he slowly lumbered off toward a shady grove of pines.

"Oh, I forgot…it's open range up here," Lola remembered.

"Ah yes, smell that mountain air," Sandy said, closing her eyes. "It smells just like…a huge pile of steamy shit!"

Lola held her breath as she navigated around the odorous heap.

As they continued on, they saw kids playing soccer in a small clearing surrounded by aspens. They passed a couple walking their black Lab, and Lola waved. They rounded a tree-lined bend, and Lola saw the For Sale sign staked in the yard of a cute and very modest wood cabin. "Look! How cute is that," Lola practically screamed. She eased the car to a halt out front. "Get a pen and paper out of my tote. Write down the number."

"What's up with you? Lola, we're just out for a drive, not a shopping spree."

"Write down the number. I have to see what my numerology book says about the address," Lola insisted. "We have to see if it's auspicious."

"Auspicious? Lola, you're beyond impulsive today." Sandy scribbled the number down. "First a car. Now a house?"

"Impulsive, ha! I'm just seizing an opportunity. Remember my horoscope? I need to be decisive. That's what I'm doing. And I love the people up here…at least what I've seen so far. It's just one big melting pot, and they seem to know how to balance fun with… with…I don't know."

"The reality of day to day living?"

"Exactly. Damn, I wish it wasn't so late. It's going to be sheer torture waiting until tomorrow to call," Lola said. "But at least we can go home and celebrate with some wine."

"Aren't we celebrating a bit prematurely?"

"Look at that cute little house, Sandy. It has my name written all over it."

And so it did. Five days later, Lola paid $35,000 cash for the house. She explained to anyone who would listen that her horoscope had predicted her good fortune. A car, furniture, and a house, all bought within a week's time. Luck seemed to be on her side.

Lola moved a month later.

She used beer and pizza to bribe anyone willing to help her move, and she had nearly a dozen takers. It took three hours and three pick-up trucks. When they were done, Lola politely asked everyone to leave. She wanted to smudge the house and commune one on one with it. Walking into every room and visiting every nook and cranny, she revitalized the house with her sage smudge stick. Her last stop was the closet in the guest bedroom where she found a kitty litter box, two empty bowls, and a bag of kibble.

"Oh my, that's odd. I know that wasn't here earlier in the day or…was it?" She stared at the box and the bowls, and tears spilled down her cheeks as thoughts of her beloved Tiger overwhelmed her; it had been nearly seventeen years since the cat's untimely death, and yet this was all it took to bring the memories rushing back to her.

Lola held the smoking sage in front of her and twirled around, trying to purify the memory into the ethers. Satisfied with the result, she continued through the rest of the house, coughing as the house filled with the pungent aroma.

Finally, she turned off all the lights and lit two candles, wanting to experience the mountain and the house under the silvery light of a waning moon.

She was clearing a box off her one and only chair when she saw a ghostly silhouette with shining eyes staring at her through the sliding glass door off the deck. Lola jumped and screamed at the same time. Then she saw it. A cat pawing at the window and meowing loudly, as if Lola were the intruder and not the other way around.

"Hey! Are you lost, little guy? Where's home?" she asked, pretty certain that the cat was already home. She opened the door, and the Tiger-look-alike raced into the back bedroom, eyed the empty bowls and protested loudly. Lola switched on the bedroom light. She clapped her hands and knelt down next to her new friend. She stroked her with a gentle touch, and the cat arched her back in response.

"Thank you, Universe," Lola heard herself whispering, a single tear rolling down her face. "Thank you, angels and divine masters. Thank you for guiding me here to this mountain, to these people, and to this house. Thank you, thank you, thank you."

After her new roommate was well fed, Lola carried her out onto her deck and the two of them nestled in the chaise lounge Lola had arranged there. The song of the crickets and the frogs and the distant sound of a train set her at ease. She gazed skyward, fixed on the moon and the one star shining brighter than all the others: Venus, the evening star. "Hi there. Shine your love down on me. Protect me. Guide me."

They sat like that for the better part of an hour before coyotes began yipping and howling. Lola took this as a sign. She grabbed the kitty and ran into the house, glad she wasn't alone.

The click of the deadbolt echoed into the sounds of the night, and Lola knew she was, without question, home.

FIRE

Day 2

"The will towards expression builds your future.
Magic happens in the present moments of happiness
celebrated within the Circle."
~ The Circle of Na'mow Handbook – Olive, Second Generation

September 15, 1996, Sunday morning

All wildfires have personalities.

This one could be called angry, but it was almost too calculating. Listening to it howl, you could almost hear its many voices, voices from so long ago that they were beyond the memory of all except the mountain. Every tree that exploded in flames was part tribute, part sacrifice.

Everyone who made their home in the mountains – even those who lived in the cities within view of the mountains – understood that Mother Nature would sooner or later raise her hand and demand that the course of things play out. You couldn't control that. Hundreds of years ago, the Indian child who first called the mountain Na'mow also gave a name of tribute to this unstoppable force most know as Mother Nature. She called her Eru'tan. Giving praise to Eru'tan did not cause her will to soften, not when her forests grew overly crowded and humans became too possessive.

This fire seemed to have intent. You could say it was a servant to the winds, but it seemed just the opposite. It appeared to use the wind to drive itself up and over the ridge and to set its sights on the human dwellings that had invaded Eru'tan's paradise.

Yes, you could call the fire angry, but it wasn't wise to deny its purpose.

It was coming.

ELLA

Five hundred acres burned overnight.

Ella had been up for hours. If the fire had intent, so did she. And hers was to make sure nothing would be forgotten if they had to make their escape. Which seemed more likely by the hour.

However, the slurry bombers dropping their red liquid were an encouraging sight. When Gary, Brice, and Alena roused from their fitful sleep, they stood as a family on the deck and watched as several helicopters refilled their huge buckets from the lake, drenching hot spots whenever and wherever they flared up.

As the heat of the morning increased, so did the blaze's intensity. Yellow-jacketed firefighters dotting the hillsides seemed so small against the backdrop of the Rocky Mountains. Fear was palpable. Stress flaunted itself.

They went back inside to the items on the lists Ella had prepared for them. One of Gary's was purposely large: the word HERB written in big black block letters. "I know you checked on him yesterday," Ella said of their elderly neighbor up the road, "but you'd better do it again."

"Yeah, probably should." Gary carried a box of electronics out to their SUV.

Ella went upstairs. She was digging through her closet when she found the vodka bottle. Her heart skipped a beat. She stared at it, and then cradled it to her chest.

The shelf with all of her purses had once been among her favorite hiding places when the drinking was out of control. It was a terrible time. She now had four years of sobriety under her belt, and the bottle had long been forgotten. But now, with the fire and their impending evacuation, anxiety coursed through her veins. Old and dangerous feelings took hold.

Her chest tightened as the talons of alcoholism gripped her. The urge was strong...just to unscrew the top and smell it. *What the hell...just one small sip won't hurt?* she thought. She closed her eyes, and her mouth moistened with the thought of the cool liquid flowing over her tongue.

The cap, she found, wasn't sealed and came off easily in her fingers. She held it to her nose, but there was no hint of the potent alcohol aroma she was hoping for and expecting. Her brow furrowed in confusion; the answer popped into her head an instant later and then she was laughing. Laughing so hard and for so long that when she finally stopped, Gary and the kids were standing in the room staring at her, their faces shot through with concern. Gary grabbed the bottle.

"You think this is funny!" He emphasized the word "this."

Ella finally managed to catch her breath. She shook her head and said, "It's water. Just water. I poured the vodka out years ago. Those first few months after I quit were hard as hell, and I knew there was always the possibility I might relapse. And the water...that water..." She pointed to the vodka bottle. "...I knew it would stop me. It was a symbolic gesture, you know, to remind me that the real elixir of life is water."

She laughed again, shaking her head. "Can you believe it? I had to trick myself...how lame is that?"

Gary breathed a sigh of complete and total relief. "It worked. That's all that matters," he replied and wrapped an arm around her. The kids joined in.

"You scared the shit out of us," Brice said.

"So sorry," Ella said, her arms tight around them. "Wow! You know what's funny? Back when I was eight or nine…something like that…someone asked me what I wanted when I got older. You know what I said? 'I just want a roof over my head. I want a family. I want to be happy.' That was it! Simple, right? I never expected it to get so complicated. Happy…isn't that all anyone wants?"

June 1975 – Summer Solstice Weekend – Rock 'n Blues Festival

"Wow!" Ella clasped her hands together in delight, her deepset blue eyes widening as she and Gary walked toward the entrance of their enchanting wedding gift, a beautiful Victorian home tucked away at the base of a new ski area near Telluride. "This is going to be so awesome, Gary!"

They were on their honeymoon. The two had met in a psychology class and had partnered on a project to gather data about party games students engaged in while drinking. Yes indeed, serious academia.

After dating for less than a year, they decided to get married. Ella's mother was ecstatic about planning the wedding, especially the lavish reception at the country club in their hometown. She wasn't at all excited, however, about how the happy couple planned on spending their honeymoon. Camping in the mountains of Colorado? "Crude" was how she described it.

So they compromised. The first week they spent camping near Durango and fishing in the Animas River. And now they were here. Five days in the old Victorian was Ella's parents' wedding gift to them.

They pulled into the drive. "Look at this place. It's magnificent," Ella said. A lush grove of aspens framed the house from the rear, and a river ran out front. They went inside. "Running water and electricity. What a treat after a week in the woods. I'm first in the shower."

When Gary heard the shower running, he stripped off his clothes and joined her. "Let me wash your hair," he said.

This was part of their sex ritual. Actually, at this point in their relationship, everything was part of the sex ritual. Reading a book led to sex. Taking a hike led to sex. Laughing led to sex. Sharing the shower most certainly led to sex.

This was how they spent the first half of the week. Hiking, eating, listening to music, and as much sex as they could fit into an eighteen-hour day. Everywhere they went those first few days they heard the buzz about the Rock 'n Blues Festival, and decided they needed one last adventure before heading home.

The campground, at least from afar, was a picturesque mix of ponderosa pine and aspen trees framing a meadow filled with tall grass. The day was hot as the sun glared down from a cloudless blue sky, perfect for camping and a concert. They parked, found a campsite under tall swaying aspens, and then went exploring.

The first thing they saw was a guy selling firewood from the back of his pickup. This wasn't so unusual. That he was stark naked and selling firewood from the back of his truck was. Gary bought a bundle of wood from "Buck" while Ella put on her sunglasses to hide her wide-eyed gaze. Buck was deeply tanned…everywhere.

Ella gripped her jacket under her chin when she realized how uncomfortable she was with the guy's nakedness, and it only got worse as she saw one woman after another going topless with the same ease as she would wear a bathing suit. "I hope I'm not the only one here who doesn't intend to take her clothes off," she said to Gary.

"I'll save my nakedness for you and the bedroom, if that's okay with you," he said, taking her hand.

By late afternoon, the camping area had transformed into a ramshackle shantytown made up of tents of all sizes and fabrics, makeshift lean-tos, and plastic sheeting hung from tree branches flapping in the breeze. The portable johns stood downwind of the major campground, but the event organizers had so underestimated the crowd that toilet paper was soon a commodity in extremely high demand.

"I've never seen so many people so unprepared for a weekend in the mountains," Ella said in amazement. "No camping stoves, no sleeping bags, no warm clothes, no food, no nothing."

"Yeah, but on the other hand, I see plenty of booze and drugs, and what else do you need for a music festival."

"You see that girl over there with the high-heeled sandals and the red lipstick? I mean, what the hell?"

"Ella, relax, honey. Forget about it. It isn't your concern. Your only concern should be having fun with me, your new husband." He put his arm around her waist, pulled her close, and kissed her hard on her mouth. He caressed her butt and the back of her thighs until she interrupted his groping by pushing him forward. "Come on, let's get closer to the stage before the band starts."

Gary grabbed her hand, and they made their way through the growing turmoil. Ella was disgusted, especially when she stepped in a peanut butter and jelly sandwich that someone had left to rot in the middle of the path. "Look at this place. People are just such pigs. I mean, one minute a beautiful meadow, the next minute a trash dump."

The music kicked in well before dark and played until the storm hit. The rain and hail compelled people to seek shelter. The fear of electrocution forced the band to pack up their precious instruments. Tents and tarps blew over. Bodies huddled together for warmth, and the stark naked guy with the firewood started passing it out for free.

Everyone gathered around a growing bonfire. Ella and Gary huddled together on a big log, sipping whiskey out of a flask. Joints and pipes made the rounds. The storm had blown over, and the weather no longer was a concern. The music started up again.

Ella indulged in a hash pipe that someone put in her hand and not five minutes later was leaning heavily against Gary, floating pleasantly upward into a white void. She couldn't make out where the treetops ended, but out of the corner of her eye she witnessed small twinkling lights darting in and out of the tall grass and illuminating the flowers as bright as rainbows. Sparkling winged creatures danced above a small waterfall. Birds chirped. The scene transformed.

It was dark. Trees stood vigilant over a group of women gathered around a fire – all of them holding hands and chanting and moving rhythmically to the music – and then the chanting stopped. Ella was falling.

She didn't remember hitting the ground, but suddenly Gary was shaking her and shouting, "Ella! Ella!"

Ella heard the crackling of the fire. She heard a distant echo that sounded like singing. Then she heard Gary calling to her. She was too paralyzed to respond; her tongue seemed to be soldered to her jaw.

She tasted bile rising in her throat, and her one thought was that she sure as hell wasn't going to let herself throw up on her new Jansen ski jacket. An energy circulated in her very core swirling in her solar plexus, intensifying and building, willing a power in her so great that it stretched her jaws open, and her tongue and lips moved to scream, "SICK."

Suddenly Gary and some other guy were yanking her to her feet, and she projectile-vomited into the fire. The wetness sizzled. Her legs could not support her weight, and she started to wobble. But her eyes opened just long enough to see a woman dancing near the fire with a blanket for wings, and another with a cowboy hat and long wild red hair, their movements sensual and inviting.

The last thing Ella heard was the howl of a coyote. Or was it one of the women? She would never know.

The next morning, Ella was lethargic, dehydrated, and nauseated. Her muscles were incapable of understanding her brain's directives. She was embarrassed about having lost control: her worst fear. The newlywed sobbed uncontrollably as she tried to explain to her husband how the experience had scared the bejesus out of her, but Gary was not buying it. He was unable to console her and was plenty pissed at Ella for ruining "his" night. That was, until he found out that the hash she had smoked had been treated with some kind of chemical.

"Damn, Ella! Listen to this. I just talked to a guy who said a whole shitload of people had the same experience you did. It was the hash. It was laced with something called Special K."

"What the hell is Special K?" Ella sounded scared.

"It's a fucking horse tranquilizer, that's what." Now Gary was pissed at whoever had been passing around hash contaminated with a horse tranquilizer. "No wonder you couldn't move a muscle. You have enough of the shit and you disassociate from reality and start hallucinating. It's called being in the K-Hole. One of the girls in this guy's group told him that she actually saw God. I guess she wouldn't shut up about it. How crazy is that? Talk about a trip."

Not so crazy, Ella thought. *Not so crazy at all.* She put on her sunglasses and got into the car. It was time to go home.

Summer 1977

Two years later and Ella was even more captivated with the Rocky Mountains than when she first came west. Her search for tidbits of new information and unusual facts about the area was insatiable, and led her and Gary this warm summer night to a library lecture on the history of Boulder, the Flatirons and the surrounding mountain communities.

She and Gary had arrived very early because Ella wanted a front row seat. Less than a month earlier, she had found the perfect little arrowhead while hiking with friends on a trail near Twin Sisters rock formation west of Boulder, and now wanted to know more about its origins.

"You're fidgeting. Stop twirling your hair," Gary whispered. He grabbed her thigh. Ella uncrossed her legs and planted her feet firmly on the floor.

"I'm always fidgeting and I'm trying to stop playing with my hair but I don't even realize I'm doing it," Ella reminded him. Actually, the fidgeting was a relatively new thing, a state of affairs tied directly to the stress of marriage, school, and work. In May, she had graduated from CU with her MSW, a far more grueling task than she had ever imagined. Juggling a husband, her entry-level job at the Mental Health Center, and an apartment they had long since outgrown was taking its toll on her. Now Gary was talking about getting a dog, and a friend wanted him to adopt his one-year-old black Lab because a new job had him on the road most of the time. One more thing to think about.

The lecturers entered the room. Olive and Hazel were retired high school teachers from Michigan and acquaintances of Gary's. He introduced the pair to Ella and wondered if they might have time for a brief conversation after the lecture.

"Ella has something she'd like you to look at," Gary explained.

"Glad to," Hazel said as she and Olive headed for the stage and the warm applause of their small, but appreciative audience.

Hazel began the lecture. "If I can start with a little history. Olive, my partner in crime, was born and raised here in Colorado, but moved to Michigan soon after she got married. That's where we met. Olive's frontier mother instilled in her the importance of education and was a stickler for women's rights. Both of our husbands died young, I'm afraid, so she and I continued to support our families teaching English and history at the local community college.

"One summer nearly thirty years ago Olive invited me out to Colorado to visit her mother, who lived at that time with her brother 'on the Hill.' Olive wanted me to see firsthand the picturesque community of Chautauqua, which you all know sits at the base of the Flatirons. Back then, it was a place that focused on adult enrichment courses.

"To be honest, we both wanted to surround ourselves with the many women, strong both mentally and physically, who first settled the area and those who continue to make their homes here even today. I wanted to be a part of that and Olive wanted to be a part of that again."

She looked out at her audience. "Did any of you know that Colorado was the first state in the Union to give women the right to vote? A constitutional amendment to that effect passed in a popular vote on November 7, 1893. 1893! Imagine that! Let me just read you a quote from a Colorado newspaper written back then. It says: 'There are women here so shrewd as to manage to make a husband support them. And there are others smart enough to take care of themselves and their husbands too.' Isn't that just grand?

"For instance. A neighbor's grandmother used to walk twelve miles at night to sell butter in one of the silver mining towns. She walked in the darkness, cross-country, alone at elevations from 6,500 feet to 8,500 feet."

Olive interrupted, "We call any kind of difficult walk or hike, 'The Butter Walk.' They'd just about do anything to make money for the family. Talk about hardy and resourceful!"

Hazel clapped her hands in delight, and the audience joined her. "That's the kind of people we wanted to associate with. So, two decades ago, Olive and I rented a cabin up near the Lake, and we've been coming out here every summer since. Now we're two old bats with all the heart we've ever had but only half the energy."

Their lecture was captivating. Ella hung on every word. Olive and Hazel covered everything from the area's geography and its geology to the history behind the Cheyennes, Utes, and Southern Arapahos who roamed the area for centuries.

They talked about the first ranchers who arrived there and the first towns that sprang up with the arrival of brave and adventurous settlers. They talked about the floods that consumed the rivers and the fires that thinned the forests. They chronicled families who lost relatives and friends along the way, but somehow found strength through their connection with a burgeoning community. They explained about the mining booms that came and went and the fortunes that were made and lost. They talked about the growth of the cities and the influx of people to a land no one ever wanted to leave once they experienced it.

When they were done and their audience made their way slowly to the exit, Ella and Gary got their private audience with the two women. Ella showed them the arrowhead she had found.

"Ute or Southern Arapaho," Olive said, studying it closely. "We've found similar ones not far from our cabin."

"A cabin we're desperately trying to get rid of," Hazel said suddenly. "We're finally admitting to getting older. Traveling is harder on us and this altitude is making breathing difficult for Olive. That and the cigarettes."

"Any chance you two might know someone decent who would want to rent it?" Hazel asked out of the blue.

"Now Hazel, don't be hasty. I told you that you could come out next summer by yourself and leave me back in Michigan next year," Olive scolded.

"Oh, don't be silly, what fun would that be. You've been my best friend for half a century and I don't have the energy to find another one," Hazel chuckled. Olive lowered her teary eyes.

Ella nudged Gary with a very pointy elbow, and this got him talking. "To be honest, Ella and I are looking for a new place ourselves, so we might actually be interested. The problem is we can't get out of our current lease until August."

"Perfect. That's about the time we'd be making our way back to Michigan anyway," Hazel said, and Olive nodded in agreement.

"Why don't you two lovebirds come up this Saturday and see if the place is something that will fit your needs? We'll discuss rent and all that other good stuff that landlords like to discuss."

⁓

"Can you believe this? We're starting a new life in the mountains," Ella said, as Gary steered their car over a curving dirt road filled with switchbacks, potholes, and fearless squirrels.

"Yeah, I particularly like the lack of guardrails and the steep cliff. Should make driving at night a blast," he replied sarcastically, two hands wrestling with the wheel. Then he glanced over at Ella, a look of concern on his face. "Seriously, are you sure you can handle this road? I mean, especially in the winter?"

"Really? If the first settlers could handle it, so can we," Ella said pointedly. "For God's sake, don't be such a wuss."

After nine miles and a 2,000-foot climb in elevation, they saw the battered wooden address sign Olive had described to them and pulled into the dirt driveway.

"Oh, my gosh. Look at this place," Ella squealed with delight. It was everything she had imagined it would be, but so much larger. It was a log cabin, but it also had a covered porch, a garage, and a large side deck. There was even a charming freestanding stone and wood building off the back that made her think of a Hansel and Gretel cottage, and a dilapidated-looking shed tucked away in the trees between the house and cottage.

"What's with the shed?" she asked the women first thing.

"Something you don't want to live without up here." Hazel grinned, and Olive chuckled. "It's an outhouse."

"Oh! Got it."

Hazel and Olive took them on a tour. The lot was a little over an acre and populated on three sides with ponderosa pine, blue spruce, and a huge aspen grove. On the south side was a beautiful view of a lake that Olive called, well, The Lake. Then Olive led them to the small cottage Ella had been admiring.

"We had this cute little refuge built some years back. We use it for...oh, how do I say this? For special meetings just for...for us women."

Olive took a breath and Hazel finished her friend's thought. "Women of like mind."

"Like a book club," Ella suggested.

"Broadly speaking, yes. We definitely talk about books. But we also talk about a good many other, shall we say, topics," Hazel answered.

"It's got all the basics," Olive added, "but I'm afraid we can't find the key. We've been meaning to get a locksmith up here but just haven't found the time."

Olive noticed Ella giving the cabin's exterior the once-over and tried to guide her off the porch. But Ella was already pointing toward the entrance and the round windows on either side of the door.

"I love those," she said, then turned her gaze to the odd symbol carved into the bottom half of the door. It looked like a spiral with a circle of stars surrounding it. Ella took a step closer. There was a word spelled out with small twigs on a weathered wooden board above the door, though some of the twigs were dangling from loose nails and others had completely fallen off. "Oh darn, I can't quite make it out...I think there's an N...and an OW at the end. What's missing?"

"We'll have to fix that before we leave," Olive said, more or less ignoring Ella's question. She coughed, and Hazel tenderly rubbed her shoulders. "Some of the happiest and saddest times of my life."

"All I hope for you is that you two find as much joy living up here as we did," Hazel said. "Let's take a look at the main cabin."

Inside, the cabin took on all the qualities of a fully functional house with plenty of amenities. There was a living room, a dining room, three bedrooms, a bathroom with tub and shower, and a kitchen with a gas stove and a dishwasher.

When the tour was over, Ella jumped up and down like a small child on Christmas morning, and Gary was more impressed than he could articulate. It was perfect.

"There's a phone," Hazel said, "but you have to get used to using a party line."

"And you never want to leave the birdfeeders out at night because of the raccoons and the bears," Olive warned.

"I think we can handle that," Gary said.

"Once a bear knows he can get a free meal," Olive explained further, "your house will be on his circuit. He'll keep coming back over and over again. And believe me you don't want that. Hazel, remember the time we tried to shoo that black bear away with our pots and pans."

"We nicknamed him Trouble," Hazel told them. "Old Trouble just stared at us like we were loony and started lumbering toward us. It had rained that day, and the grass was slippery as all get out. Both of us turned to beeline it back to the front door and made it about two steps."

"We fell over each other like a bad vaudeville act, and pots and pans went sky high and rained down on us like hail the size of basketballs," Olive continued. "So we ended crawling on our hands and knees back to the porch."

"Scared out of our wits, mind you," Hazel added.

"When we looked back, all we could see was Trouble's behind."

"Figured we weren't worth the aggravation."

"He got halfway down the hill and stopped long enough to give us a good roar and to relieve his bowels."

"Just to mock us," Hazel said, and Ella and Gary split a gut.

"And that's what we did. We laughed. Probably because we were so darn glad that bear didn't eat us alive."

"We never did explain to anyone why we had big bumps on our heads and shoulders," Hazel continued. "Anyways, I digress. Just remember that you have to keep your trash locked up too or every critter in the forest, from bears and coyotes to raccoons and ravens, might get to it."

Olive said, "The ravens are the worst. They make a huge mess pecking through the bags and spreading trash everywhere. They are smart birds, those ravens."

"Speaking of smart," Hazel said, "you have to be smarter than the wildlife because they have learned how to survive up here. Don't forget to look up." Ella raised her eyebrows, not understanding. "Those mountain lions and bobcats, and even bear for that matter, climb trees. One time, I remember I had the hair standing up on the back of my neck. Now that's a sign you don't want to ignore, especially here. I happened to look up in a big old fir tree and sure enough, a mountain lion had a hindquarter of a deer tucked up into a tree branch. I remember seeing blood dripping right in front of where I was standing and that big old mountain lion looking down at me just licking his chops."

"Hazel, you're scaring the dickens out of these two, just when I was starting to get used to the idea of being a landlord." Olive laughed until she coughed.

Hazel continued to ramble. "You kids are going to love it up here. Here's the most important fact of living in the mountains. Don't be afraid to ask for help if you need it. Only the hardy survive here. The year-rounders check in on us and are the nicest people you could imagine. Everyone's in the same boat up here, so even if it's for a cup of sugar, some wine, or just conversation...ask. Pantries in people's houses up here are fully stocked because it's a thirty-minute ride to town if you forget something. Remember, this isn't like living in the flatlands; we're a community up here. We depend on each other, especially when the going gets tough. The tough stay, the weak leave.

"Your alarm clock will be the birds chirping as they awake in the morning. Oh, and there's a flock of turkeys that are so tame they'll eat cracked corn right out of your hand. The deer sleep under the trees and the hummers – the hummingbirds – make that shrilling noise as they approach the feeders. It's like music to the ears."

"That reminds me," Olive said. "We're leaving all the feeders for you. And, as an extra bonus, most of the furniture."

"We just don't feel like dealing with all this stuff until we absolutely have to. So, enjoy it. And if you decide this is home, well, we could work out a deal for you to own this place. But…all in good time." Hazel got up to make some tea.

"We don't know what to say," Ella said. She and Gary were both a bit stunned. This was more than they had ever expected. "Thank you. Thank you, thank you, thank you."

"Oh, stop." Olive waved her off. She said, "Ella, I never finished telling you about your artifact. You were very lucky to have found such a stunning arrowhead and…I don't want to know anything about where you found it. Take it from me. Keep that a secret. The Southern Arapaho loved this area, and we've found so many artifacts over the years that we donated them all to the Anthropology Department at CU, so I have nothing to show you. I will say that the Arapaho were wonderful human beings who believed in peace with the settlers. The head of their tribe was a man named Chief Niwot, and he was apparently quite the male physical specimen, tall and handsome. Unfortunately, the white men weren't so gracious and wiped out most of his tribe and a Cheyenne tribe at a site somewhere in southeast Colorado. It was a massacre of monumental proportions. It makes me sad just to think about it, but Chief Niwot's name lives on even now. There's a canyon named after him; you may have heard of it. Also a little town just outside of Boulder and who knows how many businesses.

"It is said that the beauty of this area would cause people to not want to leave and that overloading this area with whites would be its undoing. It's called 'Niwot's Curse.' Just look at Hazel and me. We keep coming back year after year because we cherish this place so much. Ordinary is somehow 'amplified' up here. It's simple things, like that first snowflake in the fall that's wrapped in the damp smell of autumn. It's a smell that you can actually taste. Or feeling sheer delight being awakened at dawn by the pure melody of a singing house wren. Or it's the surprise you feel when an errant ray of sun escapes though a prison of clouds and catches on a gray granite outcropping, and suddenly it becomes a field of diamonds." Olive paused in her dreamy repertoire, catching a sidelong gaze from Hazel, a gaze filled with loving sentiment and knowing. "Well, anyway...you'll see. Trust me, if you make it through the first year up here, it's safe to say that you won't be leaving...for a very long time."

FIRE

Day 2

"Eru'tan always has the last laugh."
~ The Circle of Na'mow Handbook – Chimalis, First Generation

September 15, 1996, Sunday morning

They heard it all the time up here. Why the mountains? How many fires do you have to see before you pack your fantasy up and head back to civilization?

The owl, the coyote, and the bear called the mountains their home, but under the auspices of The Ruler of the Wild, they were wise enough to flee when Eru'tan decided to thin her forests. Sometimes it was lightning. Sometimes it was manmade. Mother Nature didn't step in when lightning struck, and she stood back and watched when her creatures were to blame.

Sometimes humans fled along with the Wild Ones. Humans called it evacuation; the animals relied on instinct. The fire didn't care. It would burn until its force was spent. If men stepped in and stopped its progress, it would just return another season. It always did.

It wasn't personal. It was just Eru'tan's way.

Fire was nature's way of dealing with overcrowding and over-population. Sometimes nature just needs to start over. When the little Indian girl took to calling Mother Nature Eru'tan a century ago, it wasn't out of disrespect. She believed that every force that influenced her life deserved a name special only to it: Ra'los, the Sun; Ra'nul, the Moon. These names were not only special to her, but they would eventually become a permanent part of the Circle's special language. In the Indian girl's world, the Circle included every living thing, not just the women who grew to celebrate it.

When Phoebe Winston and Martha Addison, members of the first Circle and the mountain's first settlers, took a cue from the stories they had heard about the Indian girl and her daughter, they decided to describe their natural world with their own names as well: Sla'mina, the Ruler of the Wild; Toh'ria, Enchantress of the Warm Wind. The names became part of the Na'mow handbook and passed down to Hattie, Betty, Olive, and Hazel, the second generation of the Circle.

BRIDGET

The smoke, the acrid smell, and the metallic taste that sat heavy on the tongue all held Bridget captive. Her logical mind believed she could ward off its grip by willing it away. But that wasn't working now. Its heavy, choking presence surrounded her entire being.

Bridget shoved her exhaustion away. She fought desperately against the anxiety welling up with every breath. The cellular memory of their house fire six years ago overwhelmed her. It punished her physically, emotionally, and mentally, and there was no escape. Knowing she had no control over the fire or the memories pissed her off. Ironically, anger helped.

She stood at the railing of her porch, and the anger spilled out. "Damn you fire. I will not let you control me," she shouted. "This is the place I love. This community is full of people I love and I will not let you terrorize me." Her kids were staring at her in awe, but she wasn't quite done. "You may try to kill us, but I have made the choice to fight and to get my family to safety. We will be back…back to this wild, beautiful place. A place that brings me immeasurable joy…so FUCK YOU very much! I have a family to take care of!"

"Mom!" Michael tried to turn her off, but Shauna pumped her fist and said, "You tell it, Mom."

"Damn right," Dan called from the doorway. "Now could we get back to work?"

There wasn't that much more to be done, but Michael and Shauna were becoming increasingly anxious, and their dad was trying his best to distract them with the requisite duties of evacuation.

Shauna wasn't cooperating. She followed her mother around like a lost puppy, refusing to let her out of her sight. Bridget didn't mind. She was too strong to succumb to fear, especially at a time like this. She knew that everyone was counting on her to be the courageous and strong one, and she wasn't about to let anyone down. She knew she had to get her children away from the fire, and the sooner the better.

At least now they had a landing place. Dan's brother Will had invited them to stay at his home in town. He had also issued the same invitation to Ella and her clan, a wonderful gesture. Lola would be staying in town with her ex, John, and that made Bridget feel so much better.

There were some other pieces of good news too. Their household was the only one in the neighborhood that still had power, because they were on a separate power line that ran westward. They were also the farthest away from the fire's perimeter. Even though the house was a rental, Dan and Bridget treated it as if it were their own, and thanks to him and the kids, the garden hoses were put to good use watering down the house and surrounding land. The old shake shingle roof was cause for particular concern, so they soaked that down as well as possible. And until they evacuated, they had a gas-powered generator that sat outside the garage as backup.

The one thing that was always in short supply at times like this was water, so they'd taken to going to the bathroom outside, girls included. After Bridget was done cursing the fire, she snagged her cowboy hat from the hat tree by the front door – she always felt more like an outdoorsman when she wore her hat, and it looked particularly sexy, Dan told her, over her fabulous mane of red hair – and headed into the small grove of ponderosa pines out back. She unzipped her pants and squatted down to pee.

Surprisingly, it was that sequence of events that sent her mind colliding into the past.

June 1975 – Summer Solstice Weekend – Rock 'n Blues Festival

The overloaded yellow VW bug carried four weekend vagabonds in its cramped interior: Bridget, her friend Connie, and her roommates Janis and Beth. The bug's trunk was filled to capacity. Extra camping equipment and backpacks were tied precariously to the roof.

The Beetle crawled forward, now part of a long parade creeping into the small town. After a few short blocks, the caravan turned into a wooded camping area. The "Festivarians," as Bridget and her companions called the growing masses, were already assembling.

"Doesn't look like any weekend party I ever saw in Michigan. This is gonna rock!" Bridget passed the first of many joints they would share that night and started to unload a cooler from the trunk.

"Bridget! Let me give you a hand, for God's sake," Janis exclaimed, hurrying over.

"What for?" Bridget yelled back. "I could haul a cooler full of beer up that mountain if that's where the party was." Bridget walked over and dropped the cooler down beside the tent. "I'll get the last load out of the car and you guys get me a cold beer. I'm workin' up a fierce thirst."

No sooner were the words out of her mouth than a gust of frigid wind tore through the canyon and the campground, carrying with it anything and everything that wasn't nailed down. "I think we're going to need those extra coats we brought," Bridget said, hugging herself and shivering. "Is this normal for June? I swear, it feels like it's twenty degrees colder than when we pulled up thirty minutes ago."

"Yeah, girl. You're in the mountains now and anything could happen." Her companions were all Colorado natives and were plenty used to this type of erratic weather shift. "Mother Nature can be a bitch this high up."

"No shit," Connie said, pulling a down parka over her halter top. "Have a hit of whiskey. That should warm you up."

The weather, however, didn't dampen anyone's appetite for fun, and just like everyone else, Bridget, Connie, Beth, and Janis made their way to the huge bonfire that attracted everyone's attention later that night.

Bridget was left with three indelible images. The first was the chick with the blanket and the magical dance that everyone seemed compelled to join in on, including Bridget, her flowing red hair, and her cowboy hat. "Mushrooms must be involved," was her explanation.

The second was the girl passed out like a light right next to the fire. "God, let's hope someone drags her into a tent before they go to bed."

And the third was the puddle of water that Bridget inadvertently stepped in, soaking her cowboy boots and putting her feet in a deep freeze. "Okay, I've hit my limit. I've gotta pee and get some sleep," she said to Connie and Janis, who were pretty much at the end of their ropes by this time too. "But I'm not going into the woods in the dark by myself. You two come with me, okay? God only knows what could be hiding out there."

Bridget had a right to be leery. As she squatted in the cold and dark, her broad shoulders tapering down to form a magnificent "V" at her small waist and her muscular, rounded glutes complementing the masterpiece of her womanly physique, the woods let out an awestruck moan. "Nice butt," a voice called.

Bridget scrabbled to her feet, wriggled back into her jeans, and spun around in a fury.

"You son of a bitch!" she yelled at the guy who was staring at her. "If I had a gun in my hand right now, I would have shot your ass!"

"Well then, I guess this is my lucky day." He laughed an easy, relaxed laugh. "I got to see a great piece of ass and didn't get shot."

"A gentleman would have fuckin' turned away and not scared the shit out of a lady like that!" Bridget fumed.

"And here I thought you were only peeing. Guess I'd better watch where I step," he teased. "And pardon me, but with a mouth like that I am not sure the term lady applies."

Furious, Bridget stormed back to camp, Connie and Janis trying to keep up and laughing. "Stop laughing! You're not helping here," Bridget snapped. "I'm really pissed!"

Connie's only response to this was to say, "Damn, he was cute!"

"Hell, yes," Janis said as they slipped into their tent. "And for all you know, Red, that guy could be your soul mate."

"Yeah, well, even if I believed in that crap, it sure as hell wouldn't be him," Bridget replied.

Bridget stepped out of their tent the next morning and recognized that flirty voice Connie used whenever she wanted a guy to do something for her, in this case help them take down their tents and pack everything up.

"Hey, Red, come join us," Connie called. She was grinning from ear to ear, which made Bridget immediately suspicious. "Come over here and meet Dan...and...maybe you could show him your face this time."

Bridget shoved her cowboy hat further down over her brow and marched over. Connie said, "Dan, let me introduce you properly. This is my roommate, Bridget Jameson. Bridget, this is Dan Mullins. Now shake hands and be nice to each other."

Dan put out his hand. *Yep, same guy, same shit-eating grin,* Bridget thought. "How are you?" he said when she just stared.

Bridget didn't say a word, so Connie filled the silence. "I just found out that Dan lives in Boulder too, so I invited him to come over for beer and burgers tomorrow night."

"You're fuckin' kidding me, right?" Bridget was irritated in the way a girl was when she knew how pissed she should be, but really wasn't. The problem was she was also noticing how attractive Dan really was, with his easy grin and weathered cowboy hat riding low on his forehead.

Dan smiled, his teeth white and straight, and said, "Hey Bridget, how about a peace offering?" He held up a beautiful feather, took a step forward, and deliberately stuck the feather in the band of her cowboy hat. "After you ran out of the woods last night and me being real careful not to step in anything steaming, you know, I found this feather lying at my feet. I think it's meant for you."

Try as she might, Bridget couldn't hold back her smile, and a blush as bright as a rose washed over her white Irish skin.

Summer 1977

"Damn!" Bridget screamed as water sloshed up and over the rim of the filthy toilet bowl she was scrubbing.

How in the hell had it come to this, scrubbing someone else's john? She swore to herself when she left Michigan three years ago that she was not going to follow in the footsteps of so many of the other women in her family. Cleaning houses hardly fit her dream of living in Colorado, but that's exactly what she was doing.

"Shit! It's all shit and my hands are a fucking mess!" Her hands were chapped and red and looked like old lady hands. Her feet look like hooves. Even her lips needed heavy-duty balm on them every fifteen minutes. "Never thought I'd miss Michigan's dampness."

But she had no intention of going back. After the Rock 'n Blues Festival, she and Dan became a couple. They shared a love of the mountains and nature, shooting guns, riding motorcycles, dogs, and pretty much everything else. They had fallen into a comfortable routine, and she had begun spending more and more nights up at his place in the mountains.

Dan had inherited some money when his grandpa died and used most of it to buy a piece of land for his dream house. Bridget loved the property. It felt like the Wild West to her, untamed and untrampled. Huge boulders, aspens, pine, and spruce trees dominated the landscape. Herds of deer and elk moved along century-old game trails. Even wild turkeys could be heard gobbling in the early mornings. Bald eagles nested nearby and could be seen riding the thermals every morning. The organic smells of the land, and the chirping of nuthatches and chickadees along with the call of hunting redtail hawks, filled Bridget with a longing to be surrounded by all the mountain had to offer. Her senses awakened on the mountain. She knew this was the place she was supposed to be.

The views were breathtaking. On a clear day, it felt like you could see halfway to Kansas. At night, the city lights of Denver twinkled forty miles to the east. While Dan built his dream home, he lived in a god-awful 1950s trailer that had about 300 square feet of living space. The 52-foot monstrosity, rusted and pink, sat off to the side of his long driveway. Its louvered Floridian style windows looked ridiculous and provided no shelter from the wind or snow. The plumbing was a whole other nightmare that Bridget couldn't begin to figure out. Dan, on the other hand, was so impassioned with building his own house that he didn't seem to notice. When he wasn't working on the house, Dan worked part time at his brother's automotive business fixing cars.

Coming home from a night at Dan's was always a shock to Bridget's system, almost like landing on another planet. Her apartment didn't feel like home. Her roommates were great, but they had very different lives and interests from her.

One of her roommates was engaged to a guy from Kuwait, who hung out with twenty other Kuwaiti engineering students who didn't drink alcohol or swear. Some were related. All of them were incredibly smart.

Bridget was hard pressed to find someone to party with in her own apartment, and she refused to drink alone.

New experiences were great, but Bridget started to feel like a fish out of water with her apartment filled with strange people and customs.

It was one in the morning when Dan dropped off Bridget at her apartment that night. He shut off the clackety engine of his 1963 Ford pickup – everyone called it Moby because it looked like the huge white whale – and put his arm around her.

"God, Dan, I hate coming back to this place. My life sucks right now. My job is shit. I have to watch every penny I spend so I can have a nest egg. I have zero privacy here. And if I can't drink and swear in my own home, then it's not a home. I'm fucking Irish after all!"

"God, you turn me on when you talk like that," he said. It was more than just her bawdy language. It was the fire in her green eyes, her outrageous red hair bouncing wildly, her athletic body, and her pure, natural beauty. Throw in the laugh and her substantial partying skills and she was everything he wanted in a woman.

"Bridge, I know we've had this talk before, and I understand your concerns, but I need to bring it up again. Listen, you've been on your own for a while now and proved you can be independent. I also know you like having your own space and you can't move in with a guy until you're married because your parents will freak. The whole living in sin thing and all that. But hell, girl, you're pretty damn miserable," he said. "Maybe not as miserable as you were in Michigan, but it's getting pretty damn close. You love the mountains and maybe you even love me a little too. Why not just move in with me? We'll make it work. We can save some money and have some fun at the same time. Besides, I could really use your help building the house."

Silence.

"Shit, Dan, that's about the most unromantic proposal any man could ever come up with! No wonder I haven't jumped all over it!" Bridget hopped out of the truck, slammed the door, and stomped up the stairs to her apartment.

Sleep eluded her as she tried to figure out what to do about her life. "I didn't move this far to be this fucking unhappy, I know that much," she whispered to the walls. "I wanted passion and adventure and I can have both. A win-win for everybody. I could move in with the man I love and live exactly where I've always dreamed of living." She sat up. "Hell, girl, just do it."

Late Summer 1977

Neighbors. It's funny how people come together. In this case, the connection was guns and dogs. For the mountains, this actually made sense.

Dan had a shooting range off the ridge behind his trailer. He and Bridget also had a dog named Laska, a ninety-pound husky mix, who hated guns and hated gunfire even more.

The firing range in question was along the ridge behind Dan's property. Dan's father used his range to teach a national rifle team competition shooting, and Dan had very strict rules.

Those rules included no alcohol or drugs consumed before or during shooting. One person shot at a time and all others had to place their guns on a table, which meant no one walked around with a loaded gun in his hand. Everyone stood behind the shooter until he or she was done. Loading a gun took place at the table and nowhere else. In exchange for using Dan's guns and ammo, he requested one or all of the following: six-packs of great beer, pot, cash, and replacement ammo.

This day, Dan's brother Will and several of his buddies had come up from town to shoot with Dan, and Dan interrupted the proceedings to give Bridget and her friend Candi a chance to take a few shots.

"It's the girls' turn," Dan announced.

There probably would have been more groans from the men had the two girls not been dressed the way they were. In other words, showing way more skin than clothes and looking fantastic. Candi, weighing all of ninety pounds and dressed in a bright red Indian print halter top over her perky chest, was first to shoot. Once Dan convinced her to take the big mood ring off the index finger of her shooting hand, he started her off with a Smith & Wesson Model 17 revolver, a 22 LR with a 6" barrel. It was loaded with a standard 22-rimfire cartridge. Her hands were small for the gun, but she managed it just fine. Even though the recoil was minimal, she still flinched and shut her eyes when she pulled the trigger. Thank God for the earth berm behind the targets.

"Let's try that again," Dan said, patiently talking her through his instructions. "Keep your finger off the trigger until you are ready to shoot. Get square to the target. Arms straight out in front. Cup your left hand upward under your right hand so that your fingers are wrapped around your right hand and wrist. Line up the sights with the target. Gently put your finger in front of the trigger and squeeze slowly while keeping your eye on the sights and the target."

Candi fired off the rest of the cartridges, and yes, her last shot actually hit one of the paper targets pinned twenty yards away to a hay bale, a little low and to the right, but still a hit. She beamed with excitement.

"Nicely done," Bridget said, giving her a high-five and stepping up to the table. Bridget had some gun experience with a shotgun, putting away big varmints back home, and a BB gun to shoot squirrels on her friend's Midwestern farm, so firing a gun wasn't new to her. She was much more comfortable handling the gun than Candi. In fact, she was a natural. She wasn't even flinching after the first couple of shots with the Smith & Wesson revolver, nailed the bull's eye with her third shot, and moved quickly over to the beer cans Dan had lined up. After nailing three cans in a row, the men started calling her Annie Friggin' Oakley, much to her delight.

Dirty Harry was Dan's hero and just about every woman's fantasy, so of course Dan's brother brought along his Smith & Wesson Model 29, 8 3/8" barrel, 44 Magnum. This modern day double-action revolver was a real piece of eye candy. It had been around since the late fifties and was made extremely popular when Clint Eastwood played Harry Callahan in the movie "Dirty Harry." His portrayal of an unconventional cop caused this firearm to be coveted by all handgun enthusiasts.

Dan had also broken out his Ruger Blackhawk with a 6 1/2" barrel chambered in 41 Magnum. This was a single-action revolver loaded one cartridge at a time through a gate on the right side of the frame, reminiscent of the nineteenth-century cowboy era six-guns. His was of modern manufacture.

The sound of those guns thundered around the mountain. The recoil was significant, the muzzle flash was bright orange and about two feet in length. When the sky darkened with clouds, the sight of either of those guns going off was more than impressive. It was also downright scary.

Candi, with newfound confidence, held the rather heavy 41 Magnum in her hand. She was shaking and Dan talked her back down to calm. She fired and was knocked right on her butt with the gun pointed skyward. Everyone held his or her collective breath.

She was laughing. She looked up at the rather startled group and asked, "So which one of you fine gentlemen is going to help a lady off her ass?" That got them moving. Dan and his brother both offered their hands, and Candi was soon upright and grinning. She handed the gun back. "I think one shot is good enough for me."

It was Bridget's turn, and she held the 41 Magnum like a pro. She braced herself for the recoil, shot and almost got a bull's eye. She yelped like a wild woman and shot the rest of the cartridges, taking a deep breath and centering herself in between each shot.

"Let's try that sucker, Will." She pointed to the 44 Magnum, and Will passed it over. Bridget took aim and fired. Every time she hit the target, she yelled, "Shit, yeah. Take that you mother-fuckin' beer cans. Boys, don't mess with me, Bridget 'Sure Shot' Jameson! I love this!"

When she was finished, she said her hand was getting sore and that she'd had enough. For the first time in her life Bridget was glad for the hardened calluses on her hands from cleaning houses. The beer cans were barely identifiable after her turn. All the guys thought she was just about the sexiest woman they had ever seen. Her long lean legs in short cutoffs stood slightly apart. A cowboy hat sat atop fiery hair, dark big sunglasses, and a big-ass grin lit up her face. Bridget's incredible body rivaled Raquel Welch's and to top it off she was holding one powerful handgun. She was breathtaking in a primal animalistic sort of way. It was a sight no one would soon forget. The men had to remember to close their gaping mouths in order to catch their drools of saliva.

That's when it happened. She was extending the gun in two hands when something ran by them at lightning speed.

"What the hell was that?" Greg jumped.

"Laska!" Dan yelled. "Damn it. Escaped his damn pen again. He hates this shooting. We're going to have to call it quits until I find him. I don't want to leave any of the guns and ammo out while we look for him, so holster up your guns and help me find him."

Dan gave Bridget and Candi each a leather belt that held a holstered 22. "The guns are loaded so be careful." The oversized belts were made up of 24 cartridge loops filled with 22 ammo and were too large to fit around the girls' waists, so they slung the belts over their heads and diagonally across their chests. It was a comical sight that gave new meaning to the word "bandito."

When everyone was ready, Dan said, "Let's go down the road to the cable. Laska usually takes the easiest escape route right down the road."

Dan was in a legal dispute with the county on whether the road that cut through his land was private or public, so he temporarily had put up a steel cable at his property's entrances. They all headed toward the south side of his property.

That's when the forces of the universe brought them together.

At the very moment when the shooting stopped, Ella and Gary were stepping out on their porch with their newly adopted black Lab, Bear. Unlike Laska, Bear wasn't the least bit scared of the gunfire. He loved mountain living. Unfortunately, he had taken a fancy to the neighbor's chickens a mile down the road, and Ella had caught him red-handed not a week before, a dead chicken flopping up and down in his mouth. Not five minutes later, an out-of-breath man with a 22 rifle cocked and ready marched right up onto the porch and picked up the dead chicken.

He glared first at the dog and then next at Ella. "The next time your dog kills one of my chickens or even sets foot on my property, I'll shoot him dead," he snarled.

He had stomped away without another word of conversation. Stunned hardly described Ella's reaction. By then, Bear had hidden himself under a porch chair, his ego badly deflated. "Great job," Ella said to him with as much sarcasm as she could muster.

From then on, Ella and Gary agreed that Bear would have to be leashed. No more free roaming.

With a certain peace restored to the mountain, the trio set out on a walk, Bear tugging at his leash every step of the way. They entered a beautiful aspen grove that lined either side of the dirt road and came face-to-face with the Western Wild Bunch: Ella, Gary, and Bear on one side of the cable, and Dan, Bridget, and their well-armed friends on the other.

"Where do you think you're headed? I assume you can read. You just chose to ignore that big-ass orange and black Private Property, No Trespassing sign then?" The man who said the words was young and menacing, menacing mostly because of the huge holster hanging from his belt, which in Gary's eyes meant one enormous gun occupied it.

"Or our reading skills are pretty well honed actually," Gary replied calmly. He noticed that the entire group had guns. And while they didn't look much like bandits or thieves, it was still an unsettling sight.

The hand holding Bear's leash loosened for an instant, and the dog took full advantage of the situation, hauling ass straight for two of the most attractive gunslingers Gary had ever seen. All eyes turned from the intruders to the dog, who stopped in front of the girls and allowed himself to be petted. Then, in one swift swoop, he snatched Candi's flowing headband and ran down the road shaking it from side to side. Bridget and Candi started after Bear, and the sight of them running with their bandoliers bouncing up and down broke the tension and everyone started laughing.

"Looks like your dog doesn't obey much better than mine," Dan said lightheartedly. "You didn't happen to see him, did you? He's a husky malamute mix named Laska?"

"No, but he probably didn't go far," Gary said, extending his hand. Introductions were made all around, and Gary said, "We've rented the house just down the road. From the Michigan school-teachers."

"Ah, Olive and Hazel. Great folks. And any friends of theirs are friends of ours." Dan smacked Gary on the shoulder. He shook Ella's hand. Ella smiled politely in return, but her mind was working overtime and taking in every nuance. *Gun-bearing crazies. That's all we've met so far. Gun-bearing crazies with bad tempers. Oh God.*

Fortunately, the next person she saw was neither bearing a gun nor ill tempered. It was, in fact, an exotic brunette looking like a Grecian goddess wearing sandals laced halfway up her calf. She was calling, "Yoo hoo, yoo hoo," two hands gripping Laska's leash, and allowing herself to be pulled more or less down the road by the huge dog.

"Guess who came to my house looking for a doggie treat again?" she said, her smile moving from Dan to Gary and settling on Ella. "Laska's kind of like my boyfriend here. He only comes around for food. Just like a man."

"I know the type," Ella replied.

"Lola! Thank you," Dan said. "You're my hero."

"Hero, my ass. Don't you ever feed this dog?" The woman named Lola didn't wait for an answer. "And you obviously need to build a stronger fence, because his urge to see me is stronger than that flimsy thing you call a pen. He scared the crap out of me. Came right up to me while I was busy doing a little nude sunbathing and planted a very wet tongue on my cheek."

Dan didn't have a chance to reply because Bear came barreling out of the woods with the scarf still in his mouth and headed straight for Laska. Candi and Bridget weren't far behind. The redhead was shooting profanities out her mouth just as fast as her earlier bullets. Laska's brute strength pulled the leash out of Lola's hand. The two dogs reared up, butting chests and falling over into the tall grass, wrestling and chomping and growling. It was more play than fight, thank goodness, but both Gary and Dan felt compelled to call their dogs off. Finally, Laska heard his name and popped up. Bear did the same. They paid their owners less than two seconds of attention, and then started their play all over again.

"Holy shit, that could have been bad." Bridget tried to catch her breath. She looked at Bear's owners. "Laska looks scary, but he's really just a big pain in the ass teddy bear."

"Same with Bear," Gary said, laughing. "Now it looks like they both found someone their own size to play with."

"Hey, no fair partying without me," Lola said, sauntering over to the group. She said her hellos to Dan and his crew and then shook hands with Gary and Ella. "Now, how do the two of you know this crazy group?"

"We just met. Sort of," Ella said. "When the guns stopped, we decided to take a walk and ran into the posse not two minutes before you arrived."

"Well. I'd watch out for those two if I were you," Lola said, glancing over at Candi and Bridget. She shook her head and smiled. "Oh, Candi, I had no idea you were into such macho stuff. I thought all you hippies were into was peace and love."

"Fuck that shit! We're just learning how to protect ourselves from the wackos that wander up here from the flatlands." Bridget extended her hand to Lola. "Hi, I'm Bridget, Dan's roommate, house building helper, and after today, his own personal Annie Friggin' Oakley."

"Wow, and I thought you were only his girlfriend." Lola teased. "I thought he was just using you for sex. Come to find out there's a lot more to you than meets the eye."

"Damn straight." Bridget patted the gun belt hanging over her chest. "Dan, what d'you say we put these guns away and treat these new neighbors to some mountain hospitality?"

"You game?" Dan said, looking over at Ella and Gary. "Our place is just up the hill."

"Sure," Gary said, answering for them both. "Be good to get to know our neighbors."

They walked up the hill, and Ella's baby blues nearly popped out of her sockets when she saw "Big Pink." She poked Gary in the ribs and said under her breath, "Get a load of this. They live in that rundown thing?"

"Looks like," Gary said, shrugging.

"Well, that house better get done soon. I'm glad I'm not in Bridget's shoes. I better start counting my blessings," Ella said. "They MUST be in love."

Tree stumps, old lawn chairs, and cinder blocks served as chairs out in the driveway. Everyone gathered around. The guys told bawdy jokes and bullshit stories. The girls never ran out of conversation.

Bridget served up plates piled high with cubed cheese, saltines, potato chips, and a dip comprised of canned shrimp, sour cream and cream of shrimp soup. Everyone drank beer except Bridget, who drank whiskey straight up. Greg passed around a couple of joints of something he called "creeper."

The party carried on into the evening. A beautiful orange and pink sunset lit up the turquoise sky and was as dramatic as the varied personalities. After a couple of hours of loud and enthusiastic laughter echoing off the ridge behind Dan's trailer, friendships that would prove to be as lasting as the coming decades were sealed with an undeniable melding of guns, dogs, pot, food, booze, and tall tales.

FIRE

Day 2

*"Step into the center of the circle and perfect order
will revolve around you."*
~ White Sun, Mother of Chimalis

September 15, 1996, Sunday afternoon

Fire was a constant threat. From mid-June to mid-September when
the heat rose and the rains grew scarce, the mountain became a
tinderbox awaiting a stray bolt of lightning, a tossed cigarette, or
an unextinguished campfire.

The western slope's winter runoff, which had raged down
streams and rivers earlier in the summer, had ceased. Streams were
dry and cracked soil replaced the moist earth.

The lake's water level dropped as man and beast consumed its
priceless commodity.

Slopes of tall parched grasses that were green and supple in
spring offered little support in keeping topsoil in place. Relentless,
gusting wind created suffocating dust bowls in the open meadows.

Fishermen, kayakers, bikers, and hikers flocked to the area,
anxious to have a last outing before the snow started flying. Often,
these lovers of nature brought with them the worst of their city habits:

loud music, litter, nonchalance with fire. It was the carelessness with fire that was the biggest cause of concern for the mountain's residents, and yet, it also united them together as a neighborhood to be forever vigilant in protecting their precious landscape...just as past generations who had called Na'mow home had done.

⁓

The Indian Girl was born in 1851. She was the first daughter of the peace-seeking chief of a Plains tribe known for their shrewd trading abilities. Her father and mother named her in honor of the White Sun. Her parents were multilingual. They were fluent in the Arapaho, Sioux, and Cheyenne tongues and spoke English nearly as well as they did their own language. White Sun was equally as fluent in the tongue of the white man by the time she was five.

The symbol that identified her tribe was the circle. The men had three circles tattooed horizontally across their chests and would tap their tattoos to indicate their place as members of the Plains tribe. The women tattooed one circle in the middle of their foreheads by scraping their skin with yucca needles. They achieved the bluish color by smearing wood ashes into the wound. The entire tribe connected through this one powerful unifying symbol. It was not ornamental; it spoke of their connectedness at the deepest level.

White Sun spent her winters camped in the tribe's village at the foot of the mountain she first christened Na'mow. Her whole life centered around Na'mow, for the mountain provided her with food, shelter, and the magic of the natural world. Since nature was an intimate part of the tribe's connectedness and the circle that bound them, so was Na'mow.

It was on the slopes of Na'mow that White Sun married and gave birth to a daughter she named Chimalis after the bluebirds that called the mountain home. Blue also was the color of the cherished circle tattoo of her people.

It was on Na'mow that Chimalis chronicled her mother's stories, knowing the mountain had spoken to her mother as it now spoke to her.

White Sun recalled Na'mow's first conversation with her, and it became the very essence and very foundation of what later would be known as the Circle of Na'mow Handbook. Powerful words to be given to such a small child perhaps, but Na'mow knew that White Sun's soul was one with the Ancient Ones.

These were the words White Sun heard: "I am the mountain you call Na'mow. You have intuited my presence, therefore, you are aligned to the magic of the natural world – the Circle of Life. As it has been and always will be, I will provide the lessons and challenges required for you to recognize your full feminine expression. It is time to awaken the sacred fire within you. You will not be alone. Others will find their way to me, and I will provide the backdrop on which their destinies lie."

It was also on Na'mow where the first generation of the Circle took shape in 1911, when Chimalis befriended Phoebe Winston and Martha Addison, two of the mountain's first settlers, and shared with them the wisdom and humor of her ancestors. She shared the importance of being connected and joining together in the beauty and power of the universe. The women became fast friends, confidantes, and hardened survivors.

Phoebe lost a home, a child, and six cows in the fire of 1914. Martha and her family fled the great fire of 1921 and stayed away for nearly a year. But the mountain and the Circle called to her, and she, her husband, three sons and a daughter returned. Her husband suffered a heart attack eleven years later when lightning struck not a hundred paces from their front porch. That was life on the mountain.

The Circle back then was more about keeping alive the traditions that the women had left behind, Phoebe from her home in Virginia,

Martha from her farm in Missouri, and Chimalis from a life that hardly resembled that of her mother and grandmother.

The one thing it shared with the generations to come was community. And when fire struck, the community always looked out for one another.

LOLA

Brice spent the entire morning calculating his escape down the mountain.

With his family distracted and packing for their own evacuation, he grabbed his coveted guitar, backpack, and the $2,000 in cash that his mother had stashed in her purse. Earlier, he had watched her go to the small safe in the bedroom and remove the money, saying, "You always want to have some cash on hand for an emergency, and it looks like this fire constitutes an emergency."

Well, Mom, so is getting the hell off this godforsaken mountain! Brice thought, as he ran off the porch loaded down with his few earthly possessions, down the drive, and onto the road. Freedom was his at last.

He lit up a joint and started walking. The smoke was worse the farther he went. It invaded his nose and throat and made him realize how close the blaze was. He stuck out his thumb as a couple of cars lumbered by, but they were both too overflowing with people, pets, and belongings to make room for Brice and his stuff.

He kept walking. Just about the time he thought the weight of his backpack and guilty feelings were too heavy to carry another step, a horn beeped. He turned and saw Lola's ex-husband John pulling up next to him. "Hey, kid. Where you headed?"

"Town." Brice opened up the door and a load of sweaters, coats and boots started tumbling out.

"You look pretty full in there," Brice said, scrambling for the clothes.

"Always room for one more," John said. He got out and started rearranging things. He opened the back door and pulled out a huge box containing all of Lola's computer equipment. He set it down on the ground and let out a low, painful groan. When he looked back at Brice, beads of perspiration rose on his forehead and he shook his arm. "Damn box is heavy."

"You all right?" Brice asked.

"Fine. What about you? Aren't you headed in the wrong direction? I thought your family was still up on the mountain."

"I'm headed down," was all Brice said.

"Nick saw your dad. He's out searching for you. Don't you think they have enough to worry about without you running off…especially during a wildfire?"

"I gotta go." Brice stuffed the clothes back in the car.

"This could be fixed right now. Why don't I take you back home? What do you say? Really, Brice, they need your help. You're their only son, for Christ's sake. Did you hear me…in the middle of all this chaos…your father…was out…looking for you." John was struggling to catch his breath, stuggling with every word. "And…by the way…is that pot I smell? Not…a good idea…with police…police roadblocks all over the place."

John was gulping for air, but Brice didn't seem to notice. He turned and stormed away, shouting, "I'd rather hike all the way to town than get in a car with a scum of the earth lawyer interrogating me all the way down."

The crash startled him. His feet froze mid-step, and he looked back. The box with all the computer equipment had obviously broken open when John tried picking it up again, and now John was flat on his back groaning, hands to chest. Brice stripped off his gear and sprinted back. He fell to his knees and bent over John. His moaning had stopped and his eyelids started to flutter.

"Oh, my God. Oh, my God. John, I'm so sorry." He slapped

John's face hoping for some sort of reaction. Nothing. He shook his shoulders and yelled, "Come on! John! John! Wake up!"

Time stood still. No pulse. No breathing. Nothing. Brice tilted John's head back, pinched off his nose, and began mouth-to-mouth resuscitation. He breathed into John's mouth twice and watched John's chest rise. Brice couldn't remember how many chest compressions to do, but finally decided on twenty-eight. As if in a trance, Brice repeated the pattern over and over again, praying that John would wake up.

He didn't even hear the car pull up behind him or Sam calling his name. It was only when Sam's hand touched his shoulder that he finally looked up, half in shock himself. Brice's eyes were swollen and bloodshot and his cheeks were wet with tears. He tried to say something, but Sam was already talking into his cell phone and requesting medical assistance. "Make it fast. We've got a man down. Looks like a heart attack."

Sam put aside his phone and jumped in beside Brice.

"Let me jump in here a minute, son," he said, taking over CPR duties from Brice. The young man collapsed, hands covering his face as he wrestled with his own internal demons. Within minutes a fire emergency team showed up, and an ambulance was right behind them.

"You all right, kid?" one of the paramedics said to Brice.

"I just want to go home."

"I'll take him," Sam said.

Brice's posture sagged as he gathered his backpack and guitar and climbed into Sam's car. They headed back up the mountain. They drove in silence until Sam pulled up in front of Brice's house. He didn't see Ella or Gary, but their car was out front.

"Do you want me to come in with you?" Sam asked.

"No…I have to do this on my own." Brice paused. "Do you think John will be okay?"

"I sure hope so. I'm going to head to Lola's right now."

"Tell her I'm sorry."

"Just remember this, son: you did everything you could possibly do for him. Always remember that." Sam touched Brice's arm. "And just one more thing. A piece of advice my Daddy gave to me, and I'm going to give to you right now. 'Be as careful as a naked man climbin' a barbed wire fence' when you start explaining things to your family. Your words have power, if you catch my drift."

"I do." Brice smiled, inhaled deeply, opened the door and waved to Sam as he straightened to his full height and headed toward his home. Sam waited until he saw him disappear inside before he drove toward Lola's place.

Lola's car was parked in front of her house, and her son Nick had the radio blaring when Sam pulled up. "Where's your mom, Nick?"

"You know Mom," he answered, turning down the volume. "She's somewhere doing God knows what while everyone is waiting for her. We were supposed to be at my Dad's an hour ago. I thought I saw her go around the back of the house."

Sam scanned the perimeter of the house. Lola had just zipped up her jeans and was staring down at a white Popsicle-like stick in her hand when he peeked around the corner. "Lola. Hey."

"Jeez, Sam, you scared the bejesus out of me." She hid the stick behind her back and glared at him. "Not having water sucks when a woman has to pee. Easy for you guys though. You just whip it out and that's that. Me? I'd like a penis just for that reason…hmmm…I guess I could think of a few other reasons too."

She stopped short when she saw that Sam wasn't laughing. Lola had lost none of her beauty, and she still possessed such innocence about her that men just wanted to take care of her. Sam couldn't find the words to tell her about John, so he uncharacteristically wrapped her in a comforting embrace. Lola squealed a bit as she hugged him back. That's when the stick fell out of her hand, and Sam reached down to retrieve it.

"Damn!" Lola said as he stared down at it.

"Is this what I think it is?"

She shrugged her shoulders.

"This is my third test in two days because I just didn't want to believe it. Nick's almost seventeen, for Pete's sake. I'm too old for this, Sam." She took the pregnancy test stick and threw it into the trees. "I don't know what I'm going to do, so as far as you're concerned this never happened."

Sam's eyes asked the question he didn't have to utter.

"It's John's," she said. "The baby is John's."

Sam couldn't bring himself to tell her about John's apparent heart attack, so he said he had come to escort her to town. She would ride down with him and Nick would follow them in her car.

Lola flirted with Sam all the way to town.

"Sam, this isn't the way to John's condo. What do you have up your cowboy sleeve?" she teased.

She was still flirting when he turned into the hospital parking lot. "The hospital? Oh, no you don't. I'm not having another pregnancy test. Those home tests are almost 100% accurate. And besides, Nick will be wondering why we're here. You tricked me..."

Sam put his index finger on her lips to stop her from talking. He stared into her beguiling black eyes and said, "Lola, this isn't about you. This is about John." He explained about the incident on the mountain.

When he was done, Lola crumpled in her seat, whimpering as Nick walked up beside the car. "What the hell are we doing at the hospital?" she heard him say. Sam jumped out. Lola saw him take her son aside.

Her reeling hormones and surging adrenalin battled up against an overwhelming guilt that crystallized into "could've, should've, would've" as she watched Sam take Nick by the shoulders and talk to him eye to eye.

She mumbled, "And me flirting at a time like this…my God, my God…John, John…you've always been the love of my life…me playing games…people always saving me from myself… I just played stupid games all the time with life and love…I guess I didn't know any better."

November 1977

Lola lifted her legs high in the snow, grunting from the effort. "Oooo! This is work." She managed to grunt, pant, and look up in the general direction of her destination all at the same time.

Her destination and the house belonging to her neighbors Judy and Joe were one and the same, and the blizzard they were experiencing was starting to adversely affect all parties concerned. Twelve inches of snow had accumulated overnight and another twelve had fallen before noon. Judy and Joe had invited Lola to spend the Wednesday night before Thanksgiving with them so they could all celebrate the next day together. The JJs, as Lola called them, were vegetarians, and Judy had already prepared the tofu loaf and vegetables for tomorrow's dinner. Lola couldn't wait.

The power and phones had been flickering intermittently all afternoon and Joe was worried about keeping the house warm, so he brought in firewood for the woodstove. Judy had already filled eight pitchers and the bathtub with water, knowing it was just a matter of time until the power and therefore the pump went out. Candles, hurricane oil lamps, matches, and flashlights were strategically placed throughout the house. Joe shoveled a path for a couple of yards and then dug out a four-foot diameter flat area that would serve as the makeshift latrine out back of the house, just in case. The JJs had lived through many a blizzard here in the high country. They knew the fine art of preparing. No power meant no water, no electrical heat, no stove, no lights, and usually no phones.

Lola was an hour late, and they were worried about her. Joe put on his hiking boots and went outside, scanning the road and the path.

Lola would be glad that he did, because she was getting a little worried herself. At this point, she just hoped she was headed in the right direction. The path was nicely obscured by this time, and the light was fading. Her backpack was full; Joe had put her in charge of wine and pot, and Lola wasn't going anywhere without her tambourine and maracas. She realized the wine bottles were really starting to weigh her down as she lifted her right foot over a snow-covered rock, lost her balance and fell with the rock in between her legs. The weight of her backpack forced her deeper into the snow. Her face was exposed to the falling snow, and she tried to blink away the flakes. Lying there, she opened her mouth and stuck out her tongue to catch the snow. She heard a noise behind her but couldn't turn her body or head to look. The sound of heavy breathing got closer. Suddenly Joe was standing next to her with his hands on his hips.

"Lola? What the hell are you doing?"

"Catching snow and making snow angels, Joe. What else?" she said with a wide grin. "Help me up."

"We were expecting you over an hour ago. Judy is worried sick. She tried to call, but the power and phones are all screwed up."

"So, here you are, my knight in snowy armor."

"Exactly." Joe reached down and pulled her out of the drift. He relieved her of the backpack, but not without a grunt. "What the hell do you have in here? An entire liquor store?"

"That and my instruments. And some of the best pot you'll ever smoke." Lola smiled one of her typically mischievous smiles.

"Good thinking. Definitely things essential for surviving a blizzard."

As Lola and Joe entered the house, Judy crinkled her nose and said, "What's that dead rat smell?"

"Oh, my! I think it's my bunny coat," Lola said, pressing her nose to the fur. "It's never been wet before, and it does kind of smell primal and wildly animalish, doesn't it?"

Joe's eyes opened wide. "You're wearing a coat made of rabbit fur. Well, guess that explains it."

"I just love this coat. It's so soft and cuddly, but I guess it isn't a very good winter coat, now that I think about it." Lola looked around the kitchen. "Are you expecting more people? Why all the water pitchers? And the flashlights and candles? And there's…"

She was interrupted by the bleep of the phone and the flicker of the lights. Suddenly, they were plunged into darkness.

"There goes the power," Judy said casually. She picked up the phone, listened a moment, and set it down again. "It's dead."

"Well, how cozy. I guess Mother Nature has other plans for us, like reminding us to slow down and enjoy this…" Lola pointed outside. "It is beautiful if you don't have to go anywhere. The good news is that we have all we need right here: friends, pot, booze, and music."

"On that we agree," Joe said.

"And now that we've settled that, you open a bottle of wine, Joe, while I go pee. And then we'll get this party started."

Lola headed for the bathroom, but Joe cut her off. "Oh, no, you don't." He pointed past the sliding glass doors toward the shoveled-out path. "When the power went, so did the toilet. Sorry, but you're gonna have to go right out there."

Lola dramatically crossed her legs. She smiled and said, "Oh, maybe I can hold it for a while longer."

FIRE

Day 2

*"The heart of a woman is the most powerful force on the
planet for it connects to the essence of life itself."*
~ The Circle of Na'mow Handbook – Hazel, Second Generation

September 15, 1996, Sunday early evening

By day two of any fire, you know what you're in for. If things aren't
somewhat contained by day two, then you're probably in for the long
haul. When a fire thirty-six hours old has taken hold, it has almost
certainly spread in at least two different directions by then; that's
how fickle the winds are up this high. It has gained enough heat to
burn hundred-year-old trees from the top down. By then, it's clear
that sentimentality has no place in the circle of events.

Every generation of the Circle had dealt with fire. You don't live
in forests as thick with ponderosa pines and lodgepoles as those
blanketing the mountain and not feel the turn of Mother Nature's
wheel.

There was always a running debate between the members of
the Circle's First Generation and those of generation number two –
Hattie, Betty, Olive, and Hazel – as to the impartial nature of the
force they called Eru'tan.

"Heaven and earth are not sentimental," Phoebe White liked to say.

"The only thing you can count on is things changing," Martha Addison added to this thought. "Transition. The ephemeral nature of things."

"Eru'tan is in tune to all things," Hattie argued. "Every blade of grass that burns in a fire is part of what she aspires."

"Because it's necessary," Olive put in on this discussion.

"On that we agree," Phoebe replied.

"But destruction is not the point." Chimalis usually had the last word in these discussions, not because she was the most forceful or the most outspoken, but she had a knack for bringing most of their conversations, no matter how lively, full circle. "It's all a cycle of life. Sometimes we just get in the way."

BRIDGET

Dusk dimmed the light over the neighborhood. The "mountain mouth" spread the news that Bridget and Dan's was the place to be, and a mini neighborhood command center took shape there. Dan's garage rooftop was the perfect lookout for anyone sporting binoculars.

Despite the danger, a festive atmosphere took hold. The men brought coolers of food and drinks, and Dan fired up his grills. Every "man toy" on the mountain made an appearance: walkie-talkies, camcorders, ATVs, dirt bikes, binoculars, cameras, scanners, and radios.

"It's looking more and more like a tailgate party," Bridget said with a trace of dismay in her voice. "I don't think that's what we intended when we opened our doors to everyone."

"We have to get you and the kids off the mountain," Dan said.

"I don't want to have to worry about you and the rest of these guys if we go," Bridget replied. "Remember our house fire? You were hunting and there was no way to contact you. You came home to ashes, not knowing if we were alive or dead! That's what it'll be like for me...for all the women if we go down without you. It's just a damned added stress that we don't need. All these people staying become your responsibility. Don't you see that? There are consequences! You'd never be able to live with yourself if someone got hurt or worst case scenario, died. Sure, our phone works now but if this fire continues, who knows if I'll be able to get a hold of you. I don't like it one bit!"

Dan held his ground. The men would stay. "At least for another day."

Bridget wasn't happy. She didn't believe in the order of things "according to men." *We strong, you passive.* Total bullshit, and Dan knew she felt that way.

She and the other women started evacuating anyway, knowing that the children had school the next day, and the thought of them in town, in a safe place, was comforting.

Michael didn't like it one bit. At sixteen he thought of himself as one of the men, certainly not one of the "kids" to be evacuated. He was going to stay with his dad. Period! His protests were met with unyielding directives. Bridget was relieved that Dan supported her 100% in this decision.

She and the kids headed up the ridge to the four-wheel-drive road that curled behind the house. Bridget had parked her car on the shoulder of the road earlier, and it was chockfull with her family's belongings.

Bridget's body shivered. She sensed something. She paused for a moment. Her kids ran ahead of her, up the hill toward the ridge. She could hear them, but she lost sight of them for a moment among the forest shadows. "Hey, don't go too far, you guys."

Darkness descended over the landscape like a swipe of the hand and only made the orange glowing lines of the fire to the east that much more startling. Bridget gasped when the blaze took to the treetops and sudden bursts of flame lit up the sky.

The devastation was growing, but at least for now the wind was blowing away from the neighborhood. Every so often the smell of burnt timber encircled her, a stark reminder of the danger. She started up again and then stopped, wishing she had the flashlight from the glove compartment of her car.

Once again her sixth sense went on high alert, and she sensed something off her right flank. She squinted, an unconscious effort to increase her night vision. Movement. Slow, but steady. She held her breath. Listened. Pine needles and twigs crunched under its weight. The creature moved out of the shadows and stopped, looking directly at her. Standing perfectly still, Bridget stared into the eyes of a mother bear, tall, proud, and protective. Two cubs quietly and obediently stood on either side of her huge frame.

The essence of the bear, a thing Bridget sensed instinctively, enveloped her, summoning a deep, mutual empathy. Her body firmly rooted itself to the land as the earth's vibration awakened her to the sacredness of this mountain. She intuited the presence of the ancient ones that had occupied this very same space.

As the veil between two worlds lifted, their ancient chanting swirled around both bear and human, Mother Nature rousing both to move their offspring to safety. And just like that the bears were gone.

Blinking back tears, Bridget stared back into an empty dark shadow. She heard herself say, "You just never know what's going to happen up here. Help us, God. Please protect us all, protect this mountain." Then she crossed herself.

November 1977

Bridget rolled over to Dan's side of the bed. She reached out, fully intending to snuggle up against his warmth when she realized the bed was empty. *What the hell?*

Bam! She heard the trailer's front door slam shut followed by the sound of Dan stomping off his boots. Then his voice calling, "Hey Bridge, there's already over a foot of snow on the ground. You should see this."

He turned on the TV to a local news channel, listened for a moment and then switched channels.

Every channel was broadcasting winter storm warnings for most of the state. "Holy cow, this is going to be a dump! It looks like we might not make it to my brother's house for Thanksgiving."

Bridget stumbled out of the bedroom headed for the coffee maker. "We're really low on supplies. If we get snowed in we won't be having much of a Thanksgiving dinner. All we'll be eating are the pies I made last night. We'd better run into town this morning and get some groceries. Oh yeah...and beer. We are completely out of beer."

At that moment, the lights and the TV started to flicker. "No friggin' way! Don't tell me we're losing power! Dan, could you fill the tub just in case? I'll fill up the water jugs."

The words were barely out of her mouth when a CLICK, CLICK, CLICK, CLICK. POOF filled the trailer. Then dead silence.

"CRAP!" Bridget yelled and stamped her foot in protest. "This is a pain in the ass!"

"Come on, Bridge, settle down," Dan said calmly. "It could be back up in a few minutes. Relax."

"Yeah, right, just like the last time. Power was out for twenty-four friggin' hours. Remember?" Bridget wasn't very good at relaxing at moments like this. "I haven't even taken a crap yet and now I'll have to go outside. My ass will freeze!"

Dan cracked a few windows and spent the next hour getting the propane heater set up and working. After that, he and Bridget shoveled out his truck. As he inched the truck down the driveway, it kept sliding into the drainage ditch, so he decided to get chained up. By the time his truck was ready to go, it was midafternoon and over 24 inches of snow had fallen. The snow was blowing horizontally, and the trees were starting to bend from the force of the wind and the weight of the snow.

Thirty minutes later and Dan had made it less than two miles down the road, and now he could see that two county snowplows were stuck up ahead, blocking the entire road. *Just great!* He spent another ten minutes getting his truck turned. By then, the tracks he'd left no longer existed.

He was within a hundred yards of his driveway when the truck tires started spinning. "Okay baby, let's rock," Dan crooned to his truck. First gear, reverse, first gear, reverse: Dan kept trying to rock the truck forward. No such luck. The truck finally gave out and seized up.

"Unbefuckinglievable!" he groaned. "I burned up the clutch!"

FIRE

Day 2

"The circle is a wheel of eternity depicted in symbols by all ancient cultures. A timeless continuum. It is that potent."
~ White Sun

September 15, 1996, Sunday early evening

This natural disaster created a fascination for those who weren't intimately involved in its chaos. People from all over the county and state were glued to their TVs, waiting for media updates on the uncontrolled fire. Many viewers would want to volunteer in some capacity in an attempt to alleviate their feelings of helplessness. Broadcasts announced phone numbers for hotlines providing information on shelters, food, and clothing donations for would-be volunteers and survivors alike. Animal rescue resources were set up at local fairgrounds.

For the people on the mountain, these reports never reached them since there was no power. Cell phone and laptop batteries were long dead. Besides, these residents were too busy fighting for their own lives and those of their loved ones. It was only when they had finally decided to evacuate and found themselves gathered together at strategic checkpoints that this critical information began to circulate. It was at times like this, a crisis, that even complete strangers armed with food, water, blankets, and other aid suddenly became a part of their ever-growing family.

The Circle was no exception. Fire always brought them closer. You cared as much about the safety of the other members as you did your own, because now you were so closely tied to them; they were family.

⁓

One of the saddest days in the life of the Circle of Na'mow was the passing of Chimalis, daughter of the Indian girl who first christened the mountain Na'mow and introduced the idea of Eru'tan, the essence of Mother Nature.

June 11, 1957 was a most auspicious day for her funeral, because the brilliant full moon ignited robust creativity and potent imagination in the hearts and souls of her most beloved friends. After the burial, Hazel and Olive invited the Circle to their cottage to celebrate the life of their dearly departed friend. Phoebe and Martha, original members of the Circle's first generation and both in their seventies by that point, huddled for two powerful and emotional hours with Hattie, Betty, Hazel, and Olive, of the Circle's second generation.

It was a way of preserving the memory of Chimalis and her mother. It was also a way of giving a firm foundation to the whole purpose of the Circle: community, longevity, and sharing.

"Goodness," Chimalis liked to say, "has a place inside your heart, and that place never stops growing as long as you have a community where goodness is valued. That's what we have."

"Chimalis knew how important community was to her own survival, and she chose us," Phoebe said. She was a large, boisterous woman some would have called nosy except for the size of her heart. "How did we ever get so lucky?"

"Having a place you know you can be completely yourself. No judgments. No falsehoods. Just a life full of possibility. Hell, I didn't even get that from my own husband," Martha said. Smart and insightful, it was only when Martha met Phoebe and Chimalis that she had a place where no one criticized and no one counted your flaws. "I remember her saying, 'All we care about is who you are. That's the person we love.' I never cried so hard or felt so cherished."

Chimalis was the keystone of this shared sisterhood and everything she did flowed from that. Her mother instilled in her that burden of responsibility and sometimes it weighed heavily on her. During her last week on this planet Chimalis seemed to quietly loosen her moorings one by one, with the silence and lightness of a falling feather, but even as she drifted towards her true center she was compelled to provoke the women's conscious minds by leaving a legacy of thought written in a letter to her sisters of the Circle.

They read Chimalis's words out loud.

"The Circle is neverending for it embodies the clock of All time. It is eternally moving and at some point in our lives when we find the center, we too spin, spiraling upwards and outwards to begin yet another cycle of possibility. It is at this very moment, you know without any doubt, that you...each one of you...will never be alone...for you are forever in full circle...connected."

And thus, the Circle of Na'mow Handbook was born.

ELLA

Ella took one look at Brice as he opened the door, and she knew something was wrong, wrong beyond the fact that her son had taken money from her purse, bolted at the worst possible time, and caused them to be sick with worry.

No one spoke as he collapsed into the couch, head in hands, and sobbed. His clothes and face were dusty and grimy. Gary knelt down in front of him and placed his hand on his knee. "What made you change your mind?"

Brice searched for the right words. Once he found them, the story surrounding John's heart attack came quickly.

"I had to do CPR on him. He was dying right there on the side of the road. I was such an ass to him. I apologized, but he was dying. I tried my hardest to keep him going. Then Sam showed up out of nowhere. Thank God. He called for help. The fire guys and an ambulance finally showed up, but it seemed like it took for hours. I think John was still alive when they took him away, but…" He took a breath. "Sam was the one who brought me home. He was on his way over to tell Lola and Nick. All I wanted to do was get back here to you guys… I just kept thinking it could be you Dad, or you Mom, or even Alena. God, what was I thinking… I'm sorry for running off." He took a deep breath. "Poor Nick. He must feel like shit."

Ella could see that the news about John had Gary on the verge of jumping out of his skin. She could see that what he really wanted to do was scream or rant or cry – maybe all three – something to escape the fear that was percolating inside of him. She was proud of him when he squashed those behaviors and started talking to their traumatized son in a quiet, calm voice. Ella put an arm around Brice's shoulder and gave her thoughts to Lola, as good and close a friend as she could ask for; what she must be going through right now, Ella could only imagine. *Thank God Sam is with her.*

Ella may have wanted to be with Lola in her time of need, but that wasn't possible right now. The phones were out, and the task at hand was trying to get off the mountain as quickly as possible.

Ella's strength had always been her resourcefulness. It had always proved helpful in the past, and it would serve her now too.

November 1977

"Oh, shoot! Yuck! Just twenty pounds of slippery flesh!" Ella was never shy about talking to an empty room; putting her thoughts into words always gave them more gravity, even if the task at hand was trying to get a damn Thanksgiving turkey in the oven. She made a face and used the back of her hand to brush the hair from her eyes. The turkey slipped from her grasp, tumbled to the floor, and slid across the kitchen. It ended up in an awkward position up against the refrigerator, looking more like a lost orphan than an uncooked piece of poultry. As she drew near she noticed that something indescribable had tumbled out of the turkey and was now stuck in the grate at the bottom of the fridge. "What on earth is that? Oh gross! It's the gosh darn gizzards. Completely forgot. I would have cooked the damn turkey with that bag of gizzards still in it. A blessing in disguise, I guess."

Ella wrestled the turkey back to the sink. She was washing it off when a knock echoed off the front door.

"Gary? Hey Gary, can you get the door?" No response. Ella drew an exasperate sigh, "Never around when I need the guy." She wiped her wet hands on a dishtowel and stomped across the kitchen floor.

She yanked the door open without thinking, and a two-foot snowdrift literally fell onto her mudroom floor. Ella's eyes went from the mess at her feet to the big, burly man standing in her doorway. "Yes?"

"Hi there. Name's William Stanley. I drive one of the county snowplow trucks."

"Please, please, come in out of the snow." Ella stepped aside and the snowplow driver crossed the threshold with his hat in his hand, his nose and face a scarlet red from the cold.

"Just wanted to let you know that my plow is stuck in the road just a few hundred yards up from your driveway. Hell of a mess. I came up to dig out another plow, and now we're both dead in the water. Unfortunately, the road to town is completely closed off and our two trucks are stuck in the middle of it all. I radioed our dispatch for someone to come and get me, but apparently they can't get within five miles of this place tonight. My bad luck. The other driver got a ride back to town just in time. I never should have stayed and kept working on the road. I always think I have super powers when I'm in my super truck." He laughed easily.

Gary walked around the corner and into the mudroom at that very moment. "Ella? Who you talking to?"

"Gary, meet William Stanley."

"Stanley to my friends," William Stanley said. He took off his glove and stuck out his hand.

"He's stranded up here. Looks like you'll be spending the night with us. Stanley, I'm sure you want to get out of those wet clothes but before anyone gets too comfortable, could you men bring in a couple of loads of firewood? It's getting really wet out there and that wood will be useless tomorrow if we don't start drying it out. Looks like we may be snowed in for a while." Ella put her hands on her hips and shook her head as if Mother Nature had once again made her presence felt in the most undeniable way. "Gary, I'm calling Todd and Sue and asking them to let everyone know they won't be able to come up tomorrow. So much for Thanksgiving dinner with the troops."

Then she raised her eyes in the direction of the stranded snowplow driver. "William…I mean Stanley. I'm sure you have some people you need to call and let them know you won't be home anytime soon."

"Not really. My roommates don't worry too much when I don't come home. They just assume I got lucky." A boyish grin crept across his face.

While Gary and Stanley were hauling in firewood, Ella got on the phone. She rang through to Todd and Sue, but the phone was crackling so loudly that hearing them was nearly impossible. She ended up yelling something about the road being closed, but before she could finish, the phone went dead.

Ella stared at the receiver. "Well, if you're watching the news, hope you figure it out and call everyone else."

She hung up, placed herself in front of the sink once again, and patted the bird. "You look like a lot of leftovers to me," she said to the turkey.

The kitchen went dark just then and the hum of the refrigerator silenced. "Power's out!" yelled Gary from the living room.

"No kidding. Long night ahead," Ella whispered calmly.

Come morning, the devastation of the blizzard hit the mountain's inhabitants square in the face. These were people used to the unflinching power of Mother Nature at this altitude, and yet the effect of three feet of snowfall in less than twenty-four hours was startling to all. Tree branches by the thousands lay twisted and broken. Drifts caused by the wind's fury buried cars and left hundreds of miles of roads impassable. All was frozen in time until the animals shook snow from their coats and feathers and began their hunt for food. Then their human counterparts appeared, all with their winter tools, all straining with the weight of each shovelful of the white wetness. Lungs breathed heavily and then coughed out the frigid air in frosty streams.

Some of the mountain's creatures had been caught unprepared for such a furious storm and faced death: a deer and her fawn, pastured horses, stray cows. For the prepared, however, winter's blast brought renewal and enjoyment.

Typical of Colorado, the passing of the storm also brought a cloudless blue sky. The sun's brilliance lit up every snow crystal like a diamond, glittering and shimmering. The warmth from the intense light warmed and moisturized the earth. Birds big and small filled the air with their morning songs. Herds of deer and elk wandered in search of food. Coyotes hunted in packs like well-coordinated machines. Men, women, and kids were forced to slow down, which led to enjoying each other's company. Neighbors helped those who couldn't help themselves.

"Gary," Ella nudged the lifeless form next to her. "The power just came back on. I can cook that turkey after all. God, we better get up." But Ella didn't get up just yet. She lingered in bed listening to the whooshing sound of the appliances, the furnace kicking on, and the beeping of smoke detectors. Beside her, Gary mumbled something indiscernible and inched deeper under the covers.

Ella's head felt, well, like she probably drank a little too much last night. And, as usual, the alcohol didn't do a thing for a good night's sleep. Now she was paying the price. With no lights and nothing but a deck of cards to entertain themselves, drinking seemed like the only thing to do. Ella finally decided to call it a night when she realized she had consumed a whole bottle of wine by herself.

She pushed the covers aside as the rising sun's rays lit up the bedroom. The ambient temperature made her shiver, and she threw on a pair of sweats before heading downstairs. By the time Gary got up, the kitchen was humming with activity. Ella had just popped the turkey, stuffed and trussed, into the oven and was preparing for phase two of her culinary extravaganza: peeling the potatoes.

"Good morning. Where's our house guest?" Gary said. He was already dressed in jeans and a sweater.

"He's already up and outside digging out his plow."

Gary rubbed his hands through his hair and leaned down to give Ella a kiss.

"Yuck!" Ella grimaced. "Morning breath. Go brush your teeth if you want a kiss from me. Otherwise go kiss Bear. He won't care."

Bear, their big lovable black Lab, responded to the sound of his name by lifting his head and grinning. He jumped to his feet.

Gary looked his way. "Hey, boy, how about a kiss and a walk?" Bear happily obliged, planting his big tongue across Gary's face and wagging his tail hard enough to stir up a breeze.

The pair headed for the front door. It open and closed, and Ella was alone again. Everything about Thanksgiving Dinner is big work, so you might as well get going, she thought and started peeling. The phone rang right as she was putting the pot of potatoes on the stove.

She picked up the receiver and heard a chorus of "Happy Thanksgiving, dear!" It was her mom and dad and she could picture them holding the phone between both their ears.

"Happy Thanksgiving to you too," she said.

They exchanged all the normal pleasantries, including how much they wished they could have been together for the holiday.

"Good thing you didn't try to fly into Denver yesterday," Ella said, recapping the storm for them. "You would still be sitting in an airport somewhere. That would have been a nightmare for you."

Gary and Bear walked in the door at that very moment, and Ella shoved the phone at him. "It's Mom and Dad. Say 'hi' and wish them a Happy Thanksgiving."

Gary put out his hand and shook his head. "No, thanks. You tell them," he whispered. Gary liked his in-laws just fine, but they were a little too overbearing for his taste, especially when it came to the everyday details of their life. It drove Ella and him crazy.

She said, "Just tell them someone keeps picking up the party line and you can cut the call short."

Gary grabbed the phone and gave Ella a little tickle in the side. She giggled, and he put his mouth to the phone, booming, "Happy Thanksgiving, Shirley and Bob! How are you two?"

They talked for two minutes, and then Gary played his ace in the hole. "I'm sorry we have to cut this short, but someone else wants to use the party line. They probably want to talk to their family too. We love you guys. We'll call you on Sunday." Gary hung up the phone, relieved but feeling guilty about the little white lie he had just told. Not that the party line excuse was a complete fabrication. The truth was, they never got more than five or so minutes on a call without being interrupted, so it was probably only a matter of minutes before someone else on the mountain picked up the phone anyway.

Ella paced around the kitchen. "Gary, I was just thinking about Dan and Bridget stuck in that ugly pink trailer of theirs. I'm sure they spent a miserable night. They were planning to have dinner at Dan's brother's house in Boulder, and we know that won't be happening. We should ask them over. We have enough food to feed an army."

"Honey, that's a great idea! I would really like to get to know them and what better way than Thanksgiving Dinner." Gary grabbed his wife's hand and gave her a little twirl.

"So you want to dance this early in the day, do you, Mister? Well, I'm game." She swirled into his arms and rested her head on his shoulder. He caressed her back, and they danced a half-dozen steps to whatever song might have been going through their heads at that moment. Where this might have gone, no one could say because Stanley opened the front door and shuffled into the kitchen at that very moment.

"Oh. Sorry to interrupt." He stopped dead at the threshold.

"Morning, Stanley. Coffee?" Gary said. He kissed Ella on the cheek, and the couple disengaged. *Too bad.* Gary stepped up to the coffee pot, and Ella picked up the phone to invite Dan and Bridget to dinner.

⁓

Bridget groaned. She struggled to a sitting position, which wasn't easy given the constraints of the sleeping bag she was zipped into. The effects of last night's whiskey wrapped tightly around her head. *You did it again, girl. Damn, aren't you ever going to learn?*

Humor, she decided, was the only thing that had any chance of keeping this snowstorm in perspective. Up to now, Bridget believed that her love of the wild, wild West would get her through pretty much anything, but she hadn't foreseen freezing to death. It was, after all, the twentieth century. Despite sleeping in a hat, gloves, and parka, she was still shivering.

When she saw the little drifts of snow covering their sleeping bags, she gave Dan a rough shove. Nothing. He appeared to be quite comfortable snoring away his worries, so Bridget shoved him again and his snoring halted.

The clock ticking made her realize they now had power. She could make coffee, pee in the toilet, take a shower, and have some heat in the trailer, four things that made her oh so very happy. Her momentary joy was stopped short as she turned the faucet on and heard nothing more than a gurgle.

"Dan, get up now! The power is on, but there's no water!"

"Good morning to you too, Sunshine. You sound like a damsel in distress. How may I be of assistance to you today?" He clearly wasn't in the mood to react to his lover's bad temper.

Bridget counted to ten. The storm wasn't his fault, true enough, but she still resented his lack of motivation when it came to their basic needs, simple things meant to keep them safe and at least somewhat comfortable. After all, he was the one who had pleaded with her to move in with him, not the other way around. In Bridget's mind, she'd given up a lot in order to help him build his dream house. The least he could do was follow through on his promise to take care of her. It was not like she needed all that much: water, heat, and the occasional TLC.

"Dan," she said, trying to control the tone of her voice, "by some miracle the power came back on but there isn't any water."

"Bridge, I have a bad feeling that the pipes might be frozen. There isn't much insulation protecting them. I've been so busy working on the house that I never got around to taking care of that."

Bridget, whose bladder was ready to explode, pushed past him and yanked open the front door, ready to storm down the steps. She hit the top step and suddenly realized that the rest of the stairs were buried under forty inches of fresh snow. With no time to recover, the redhead lost her balance and fell headlong into the white icy cold mattress. Dan raced toward the door to help, but her pride and anger warded him away.

Bridget rarely cried. She couldn't recall the last time she'd been brought to tears. She hated crying. So as an abundance of tears intensified and tinseled her cheeks, so did her anger. She was pissed off.

Seeing his girlfriend in tears motivated Dan. He grabbed a shovel, dead set on digging out the side of the trailer that was presently buried under a five-foot snowdrift. Bridget decided to help him because she wanted the water and septic fixed yesterday, and it took a good hour to work through her rage.

By that time, Dan had retrieved some heat tape from the construction site and was wrapping it around the water lines. The ice blockage in the water line would melt in a few hours. He just hoped none of the pipes had cracked.

Then he showed Bridget the sewer lines running out from the trailer, down into the ground, and under the driveway. The line reemerged in a partially covered ditch on its way to the buried septic tank.

"So there's the septic line," he said, panting and sweating from his efforts. "The problem is, it's also frozen and needs to be thawed out. I haven't figured out how to do that yet, but at least we've got it uncovered.

"Hold this shovel for me, will you?" Bridget took the shovel as he got down on his knees for a closer inspection.

"Yep, we're almost there." Dan was feeling pretty good about himself until he heard the untimely *snap* of the sewer pipe, not inches from his face. "AAAGGGHHH!"

"Holy crap! Shit!" Bridget jumped out of the way. But at least she had chosen her words well because that's exactly what Dan was covered in: crap and shit.

He scrambled out of the hole and reached for Bridget's hand.

Bridget shook her head and backed away. "No way am I touching you as long as you're covered in sewage. You're on your own, buddy." She felt vindicated. Pinching her nose, she trudged her way to the trailer. She opened the door and the phone rang once and stopped. Within seconds it rang again; this was the code their friends used. Bridget's parents had no idea she had moved in with her boyfriend and were known to call at unheard-of early hours. So if the phone rang normally, Bridget answered. If a caller used the "code," it was okay for Dan to answer too. So far, the plan had worked perfectly.

When the phone rang a second time, Bridget answered. "Happy Thanksgiving," she said. "That's if you don't mind camping in four feet of snow."

Ella laughed. "Bridget, it's Ella. You sound cold."

"That's my middle name. Cold and bitchy."

"Why don't you and Dan come to our house for dinner? We have plenty of food."

"Are you kidding? That's awesome! But just to warn you, we might have to feed Dan outside since I doubt you'll let him into the house smelling the way he does."

Ella started to question this last proclamation when someone else on the mountain picked up the party line. "Sorry to interrupt. It's Joe."

"Hey Joe. It's Ella. No problem. Bridget and I are just finishing up trying to put together an impromptu Thanksgiving dinner."

"Really? Well I have plenty of tofu loaf and sweet potatoes if anyone is interested," Joe interjected.

"What the hell is tofu loaf?" Bridget asked, eliciting a wave of laughter.

When Ella was finally able to contain herself, she said, "Joe, why don't you just come over to our place and we'll celebrate together? Bring all your goodies."

"Great idea. But I've also got Lola here, and we were talking about calling our stranded neighbors to try to pool our resources. You game for that? I'm sure everyone has food and alcohol to contribute."

"The more the merrier," Ella said, gleeful at the prospect of having a holiday rescue party. After all, rescuing people at work every day was the story of her life. This would just be way more fun. "Good way to finally meet all the neighbors."

"Anything else we can bring?" Joe asked.

"Now that you asked, what I'm really short of is firewood. Gary hasn't gotten around to bucking up and splitting much wood yet and we burned a lot of it last night trying to keep the house warm."

"Lucky you, at least you had a fire. We decided to rough it "cause we love it so much,'" Bridget groused. Then she said, "What about Sam Winston? He has a ton of wood split. I'll have Dan call him and entice him to haul a load over to your house in exchange for a home-cooked meal. He's a bachelor and I doubt he gets much old-fashioned hospitality."

"Great. So we have a plan. I'm so excited!" Ella squealed. "Tell Lola and Judy to plan on 2:00, Joe, and we'll launch the Snowstorm of 1977 Turkey Day Celebration with a grand toast. On second thought, maybe you should put Lola on the phone."

Lola woke up with a start. She'd had a restless sleep, dreaming about her parents, so full of life and welcoming her home for the holiday. She wanted to believe it so badly, but now that reality was setting in she only felt a deep sadness. "I miss you guys so much," she said out loud.

She swung her legs off the bed and noticed she was still completely clothed. "I must've been really tired. Well, at least I'll look presentable for breakfast."

That's when she heard Judy calling her name. "Lola, Lola. Pick up the phone. It's Ella. She wants to talk to you."

Judy handed her friend a cup of coffee and then the phone. After listening for a few minutes, Lola said, "Sounds great, Ella. I'll make some calls and let you know what our head count is."

"Thank you, Universe," Lola said after her last phone call was made. This was Lola. She didn't care if Joe or Judy or anyone else heard her. When she wanted to talk to the Universe, she just did. "You conjured up a beautifully sunny day to lift our moods after whipping up one helluva storm. Oh, yeah, digging my house and car out is going to be quite the ordeal, and I guess I won't think you're so wonderful when I'm slaving away with that! But you know what would make this whole weekend perfect? If you could find me a man. I need a man, Universe. A man who could dig me out."

⟋⟍

Bridget watched dubiously as Dan hooked up Laska to his home-made dog sled, a compilation of scrap wood and pieces salvaged from the house project. She shook her head and said, "I have my doubts about this contraption. I don't know if it will make it all the way to Ella's."

"Of course it will. I know what I'm doing. Oh, ye of little faith." Dan covered a laundry basket full of banana bread, pies, and cookies in a plastic trash bag and strapped it on the seat of the sled.

"Okay, MUSH!" This exclamation was meant for both Laska and Bridget, because the task of trailblazing had fallen to her.

The snow was deep and the going was slow. Bridget stopped to brush away a layer of chest-high snow.

"Tell me again why I'm the one breaking the trail for you and the dog sled?"

"MUSH!" Dan pretended to crack a whip over their heads. They trudged another hundred yards before Bridget gasped, "BREAK!"

She doubled over, feeling like her lungs were about to explode. When she was able to right herself again, she looked westward and saw a herd of a dozen elk. "Oh Dan, look in the trees over there. It's a whole herd of..."

Laska spied the elk at the same moment and bolted. Dan screamed, "LASKA! WHOA! Dammit! WHOA!"

The dog would have none of it. He bounded through the snow, the sled bouncing behind him, catapulting the laundry basket skyward. Two seconds later gravity took over, and the basket disappeared into the snow.

"Son of a bitch! My pies!" Bridget started laughing so hard she fell backward into the forty inches of snow. Eventually, she fought her way out of the snow, sputtering and laughing, and proclaimed, "I peed my pants!"

"But is the whiskey okay?" her boyfriend teased. Dan made his way over to Bridget and gave her a hand. "Whew! You smell like piss and I still smell like shit. We're like a regular walking outhouse."

Dan grabbed his sides, trying to catch his breath from both the exertion and the humor. Bridget checked her backpack to make sure the bottles of booze hadn't broken. That was the good news.

Laska, who was no match for the speed and agility of the elk, eventually gave up the chase. He made his way back to his owners with the remnants of the sled still attached to him.

"You mangy mutt!" Bridget held on to Laska while Dan went in search of the laundry basket and their dessert bag. It took another fifteen minutes of heavy-duty walking before they spotted Gary and Ella's house, and by then they hesitated even knocking on their door. Dan heaved the black trash bag over his shoulder à la St. Nick. Bridget gave him a sheepish grin and shrugged her shoulders.

"We're really going to be a test of their holiday spirit." Bridget yelped as the door opened and the leash was ripped out of her hand. Laska charged forward, racing into the house and nearly bowling Ella over in the process.

"Oh, jeez! That damn dog! I'm sorry about that. We've had our share of problems this morning, starting with this bag of mush that used to be desserts. And boy, I hope you don't have a sensitive nose because, as Dan put it, 'We're like a walking outhouse!'" Bridget was rambling. "Dan here is now called 'shit head' because of his encounter earlier with a sewer pipe and I, well, I peed my pants."

Ella burst out laughing, tears streaming down her face as she waved them inside. "Get in here," she said to the pair. "Let's get you two cleaned up. Can't wait to hear the story."

A white snowflake pattern adorned a horizontal border across Lola's chest. She checked herself out in the guest bedroom's full-length mirror. The sweater was gray wool in an Austrian winter-styled design. Reds and greens made up the border around white stylized snowflakes. Lola had bought the sweater during a winter sale a year ago and had never worn it before. It would go perfectly with her rabbit skin coat.

"Lola, we have snowshoes for you. What are you doing?" Judy asked as she walked into the guest bedroom.

"Don't you just love it?" She struck a pose. "I bought it to wear skiing. Anyway, it's a holiday and this is so definitely a holiday sweater. Look at these snowflakes."

Judy rolled her eyes. "Yeah, yeah, I'm looking at a flake all right. Let's go."

Lola, Judy, and Joe sat on the front porch and struggled into their snowshoes. Beyond the porch lay an endless sea of white.

"I'll break the path for the two of you," Joe announced as he muscled through the yardstick-high wetness. The girls followed.

"It's beautiful." Judy threw a snowball at Lola, missing her by a mile.

"But so much work," Lola complained. She ate some snow. "Are you sure these things are better than just walking in boots?"

"Way better," Judy said. "The thing is, you can't really fall because the snow's too deep. It holds you upright."

"I'll take your word for it."

They all squinted at something disturbing the snow up ahead. "Look at that, will you? It's a coyote," Joe said. The coyote sprang high into the air and then dove back down into the whiteness, again and again. The pouncing antics were hysterical, and they all stopped to watch him.

"Think he's hunting something? A mouse maybe?" Judy said.

"Could be." Whatever its prey, the coyote seem completely focused on it; that is, until it saw Lola.

Sizing her up, the furry critter headed straight for her. Judy and Joe threw snowballs and yelled, trying to divert his attention. Too bad they were such bad shots.

"Oh, my! Why is this coyote so close...to me?" Lola ate more snow.

"Shoo! Shoo! Bad, bad coyote. You just shoo now," she half-heartedly commanded.

Joe yelled, "Make jabbing motions with your poles."

Lola tried and looked like a pathetic fencer.

"He's behind me! And I can't turn around. The snow's like concrete around my legs. And...I'm not even the one carrying any food." Lola gave a fitful glance toward the heavy backpacks on Judy and Joe's backs, both evenly distributed with the likes of tofu loaf, deviled eggs, green bean casserole, sweet potatoes, wine, and pot. "I have nothing."

Lola tried twisting away from the coyote, but this only caused her to sink further into the snow. She became frantic. The JJs tried to walk toward her but it was like moving through quicksand.

"Shoo, shoo," Lola said and then finally yelled, "You damn coyote, stay away from me. I have friends in high places. My angels and invisible protectors will get you and I have special powers." She hesitated for a moment and then screamed, "Help me!" as the coyote sniffed her from a foot away.

"Take off your coat," Joe told her.

"My coat?" Lola screamed. "Take off my coat so then he has less in his way to devour me? You'll have to live with the memory of watching him tear me apart as blood and pieces of my flesh are strewn all over your front yard!"

"Lola, now focus. Listen to me. It's your damn bunny coat he wants," Judy stated. The couple finally reached her.

"Unzip your coat," Judy instructed Lola as she and Joe practically ripped it from her body.

"Now, throw it toward the coyote." Joe pointed toward the animal.

"I'm not throwing my coat to this coyote. I love this coat. It's my favorite."

"The coyote loves it too, Lola. He thinks it's his next bunny meal. Throw him the coat!"

Joe grabbed the coat and tossed it toward the hungry predator. The coyote snatched it and ran off into a stand of trees. They watched as the animal whipped it from side to side in its mouth. Lola was stunned by the coyote's focused ferocity and glad that Tig, the cat she had befriended her first day on the mountain, was safely locked up in her house.

"I loved that coat." Lola sadly lowered her eyes. "May the coyote love it as much as I did. I sacrificed my coat for the greater good of nature."

Judy shook her head. "For God's sake, Lola, get a grip. Give it up and get moving. Sometimes you're the biggest pain in the ass! You're going to get hypothermic if you dilly-dally now. We've got to get to Ella's."

Adrenaline kicked in and made short work of the rest of their trek. Ten minutes later, they were knocking at Ella's front door.

A hunky, muscular man opened the door and greeted them. "Hi, there. I'm Stanley. I'm Ella and Gary's stranded visitor and dinner guest."

Lola smiled. "I don't know where you came from but you're just the man I need. How perfectly coincidental. Could you help me get these things off?" She pointed to her snowshoes.

"Sure." Stanley knelt down at crotch level to untie her snowshoe laces, and Lola couldn't help but notice his thick, dark hair. Being totally and completely Lola, she gave in to the urge to run her ungloved fingers through his hair and then bent next to his ear and whispered, "I really appreciate your help. If you could just hug me and keep me warm. I happened to lose my coat along the way and think I might be hypothermic."

Before he could answer, she embraced him and walked him back into the house. He rubbed her shoulders to warm her up. Lola cooed.

"I see you've met Stanley. Where's your coat?" Ella looked around for it.

Judy piped in, "It's quite the story. Lola seems to attract all sorts of male animals. Her pheromones are on overdrive and her musk perfume doesn't help matters."

Everyone laughed except for Stanley, who looked baffled. "It's okay," Lola assured him. She patted him sensually on the ass and smiled her sweetest smile.

<hr>

Sam opened his back door and brought in the case of beer he had cooling down for Thanksgiving dinner. He took a cold one from the case, opened it, and downed half of it. Then he went into the tiny bathroom of his log cabin and stared at his reflection in the mirror. "Christ, you need a haircut. Guess the least I can do is trim my mustache and sideburns. Shit, I guess I'll have to shave too."

Sam was grateful for the invite from Bridget's friend, Ella; he had to wonder, however, if it was worth all this trouble just to get a decent meal. Watching Sam from the bathroom doorway was an Aussie-blue heeler mix named Bullet, who was never far from Sam's side. Sam glanced his way. "Bullet, a few hours ago it was just me and you, football, and a frozen TV dinner. Now, I got to bring firewood and beer..." (both of which were plentiful around Sam's place) "...and set myself down to socialize and eat."

Bullet whined as if he understood every word. "Sorry, bud, but that means you'll be spending the day looking after the house. Oh, but don't you worry that cute little dog face of yours. You know my motto. 'The more I get to know people, the more I love my dog,'" He reached down and patted Bullet on the head. "Oh, yeah, and my horse."

Sam looked like Sam Elliot. His curly brown hair and thick mustache contrasted with steely blue eyes that crinkled in the corners. His ruddy complexion had just enough wrinkles to look distinguished.

After a bit of sprucing up, Sam went into the bedroom to dress for the occasion. His good cowboy boots were a bit muddy, but he didn't own any Sorel-type winter boots. Besides, those kinds of upscale boots didn't fit in his stirrups, and the plan was to ride his horse – Sam's favorite form of transportation – over to Ella and Gary's.

He was glad he had already pressed the center crease in his dress jeans, the ones without the dye fading out to white in the knees. He snapped the pearl snaps on his yoked shirt and buttoned up the black leather vest adorned with Indian head nickel buttons. The turquoise and silver bolo was his only accessory except for his gun, which he kept purposely concealed. He grabbed his drover overcoat, black cowboy hat and beer, and headed for the barn.

Bullet may have been Sam's best friend, but Lady was the love of his life. She was a chestnut brown thoroughbred with a fickle disposition that Sam more or less expected from all females, horse or otherwise.

"Lady, you're putting on some weight," he said as he saddled the horse up, talking to her like he would any good friend. "Now, I'm not blaming you, but I need to get you out more and today is one of those days."

Lady whinnied and nuzzled his shoulder. "I love ya too." He rubbed her nose and whistled a tune.

He tied a makeshift travois, fashioned from an old toboggan, behind the horse, loaded the beer and firewood in a tarp, and secured the load with rope.

They set out, walking lazily through the snow. "This turned out to be one fine day, Lady, and I'm building up a fierce hunger just knowing there will be home cooking."

The words were hardly out of Sam's mouth when Lady unexpectedly reared up. "WHOA, Lady, WHOA," Sam shouted, almost swallowing his chew in the process. He spit out a brown stream of tobacco juice into the virgin snow and ran his hand along the horse's neck, soothing her. "Just settle down, girl. Just settle down. What's got you spooked?"

Sam wasn't prepared to go much further until he found out what exactly had caught Lady's attention, and then he saw the coyote running out of the woods carrying something strange in its mouth. "Now what do we have here?"

When the coyote saw Sam and Lady, he seemed to lose interest in whatever it was he was carrying and sprang like a nervous jackrabbit into the woods. Sam, ever curious, rode closer. He looked down at the strange, furry thing the coyote had just abandoned and noticed neither blood nor bones. Then he grinned. "I'll be damned. It's somebody's fur coat. I can't even begin to imagine where it came from, can you, Lady?"

Sam shook his head in bewilderment, and Lady seemed to do the same. Then they rode on.

Ella stood in the doorway between the kitchen and the living room, delighted to hear her guests talking and laughing as if her impromptu gathering was the most natural thing in the world. That was both good and bad, because it was time for dinner, and Ella wasn't very good at inserting herself into such energy-filled situations. So instead of ringing a bell or shouting over the noise, she walked into the room and cleared her throat, hoping to get everyone's attention. "Excuse me! Excuse me! I hate to interrupt, but dinner is ready."

She felt invisible. Funny how often she felt that way in a crowd. So instead of calling out again, she walked in her unobtrusive way among her guests, tapping them on their shoulders, and politely letting them know that dinner was ready to be served if they wouldn't mind sitting down. Again without much luck.

When her redheaded neighbor saw this, she did what she did best. She yelled. "Hey, everyone! Ella wants us all to sit down. Time to eat!"

Not surprisingly, given the force of Bridget's personality, this worked like a charm. Everyone headed eagerly for the table. They said grace and dug in. While the food was going around, Lola, ever sexy and captivating, started clinking her fork against her glass.

"Since we all don't know each other as well as we might, I would like to propose that we all tell a little bit about ourselves while we eat. Any takers?"

"Lola! Are you asking us to talk about our sex lives?" Joe forked a sweet potato onto his plate and chuckled at the same time. After all, he knew how capricious Lola could be.

"Well, Joe," Lola replied, taking the bait, "I know that's what you would like to share, but why don't we let everyone else decide for themselves."

At that very moment, the slamming of the front door and the stomping of boots heralded the late arrival of Sam Winston. "Sorry I'm late," he called, shaking off his long duster and slapping his cowboy hat against his legs.

Lola took it in stride. She said, "Sam Winston, you've arrived just in time to tell us the most intimate secrets of your life. I'm so anxious to hear about them."

She wriggled out of her chair, sauntered enticingly over to the latecomer and planted a welcoming kiss on his cheek, leaving a red lipstick imprint.

Sam reacted to this by saying, "Golly, girl," and headed for the table. His eyes traveled around the table. "I have to say, I'm mighty hungry. And I sure do appreciate the invitation Ella and Gary, wherever you are."

Gary stood up and shook the newcomer's hand. "Hey, I'm Gary. The host." He nodded in Ella's direction. "That's my wife Ella."

"Ma'am. Thanks for having me," Sam tipped his head in Ella's direction.

"Sit down here next to me where you'll be safe," Gary said, winking at Lola. "We're all sharing a little bit about ourselves."

"Okay." Sam pulled out his chair and smiled with a lopsided grin. "Sam Winston's the name. Private Detective's the game." He straightened his bolo with a flourish. "I like my beer cold and my bourbon neat."

Gary did his best western drawl imitation: "Where d'ya'll hail from, Sam?"

"Right here, born and raised. I inherited my parent's homestead – just down the road from here. I tried my hand at ranching but it didn't pay the bills so I attended the police academy. Thought I wanted to be a cop. Worked some years for the sheriff's department. Still have quite a few friends there. Then I figured out I'm just not cut out to work for the establishment. That's when I decided to start my own gig and became a P.I. It lets me spend a lot more time with my buddy Bullet and my Lady. They miss me when I'm not around. Only ones that do."

"Your Lady!" exclaimed Lola. This was news to her. "Where is she now?"

"Out in the front yard tied to a tree," Sam said matter-of-factly.

"What?" Lola swallowed a mouthful of mashed potatoes. She jumped to her feet, ran to the front door, opened it dramatically. When she saw the horse, Lola closed the door gently and returned to the table with a slight blush on her face.

"Yeah, Lady's my horse. Sorry, I guess I should have said so." Sam winked at her.

"Roasted turkey!" Dan exclaimed. "My favorite smell in the world. It's enough to make a starving man cry! Delicious, Ella."

"Glad you like it." She smiled. *Okay, so far so good,* she thought.

Joe chimed in. "Judy and I brought the tofu loaf in the blue dish, so don't let any of it go to waste. You're going to love it!"

Ella could see the look on Bridget's face when she heard this and was pretty sure there was no way in hell the white tofu slime would find a place on her plate. And when she sensed everyone else's hesitation as well, she said, "Here, let me get that passed around. I'm sure it's wonderful." Then she looked at Joe and said, "So Joe, how did you and Judy meet?"

Joe didn't hesitate. He and Judy had met at Antioch College in Ohio, he told the group. Both came from wealthy families back east and their parents didn't particularly care for their life choices. In fact, their families were not impressed with much of anything about them, from their choice of college to the VW bus that carried them out west to the fledgling business they'd launched, distributing natural snack foods to convenience and grocery stores. "To be honest, our families consider us more or less failures."

"More," Judy clarified.

Everyone laughed, and Lola turned her attention to the couple that looked to her like Mr. and Mrs. America. "What about you all? I'm sorry, but we weren't formally introduced." Lola was being a bit sarcastic, since the pair looked as if they could grace the cover of any outdoor magazine. Perfect Anglo features with the lean, tan, and muscular bodies of Olympians and the perfect amount of smug. "You two look like you might have some interesting secrets to share. Indulge us."

"Bill and Sue," the man said, and launched into a flowing discourse about their high-powered technology jobs, their incredibly fine-tuned gym workouts, the triathlon and marathons they ran with ease, and the really, really busy schedules that made the idea of kids unrealistic.

Lola stifled a yawn when Sue told them, "And what we really pride ourselves on is the fact that we're best friends."

"As it should be," Lola said, doing her best not to roll her eyes. Having heard far more than she needed to from Mr. and Mrs. America, Lola looked at the one elderly couple at the table and said, "I'd love to hear from you both."

"Well, thank you. And thanks to our hosts," the man said. "We're the Baumgartners. I'm Herb and the lovely lady next to me is Betty, and I would like to propose a toast."

"Oh, how nice," Ella said. "Please do."

Herb beamed. He held up his wine glass and said, "First to my beautiful bride, who is the one true ray of sunshine in my life. And then to all of you. May your lives be filled with as many riches and pleasures as Betty and I have found...especially living up here on this mountain."

"Hear, hear," chimed in Betty, and everyone raised their glasses.

Ella watched as Betty smiled and patted the back of her head, making sure the three-foot braided coil was still firmly in place. Betty thought that one of these days she was going to let her hair down at a party and shock everyone, including her husband. After all, Herb hadn't seen her hair down since the night he retired from the university five years ago. Back then, he would take her hairbrush and tenderly smooth the long locks before taking her to bed, and it had been too long since they'd shared such intimacies. Betty smiled to herself and pointed to the dish she had brought. "Now did everyone get some of my salad? I couldn't decide whether to make the red, green or orange salad but the orange Jell-O with grapes and marshmallows looked more like Thanksgiving to me. Doesn't it look festive? I hope you like it."

In fact, the Jello went fast. In fact, everything did except the tofu dish, which Ella hoped she could dispose of before Joe and Judy noticed how little of it had been eaten. In the meantime, she gave her attention to Stanley's plate and said, "Stanley, have you gotten enough to eat?"

"More than enough," he said, patting his belly.

"Everyone, just so you know," Ella said, taking in the entire table, "Stanley's the fine young man who maintains our road. His truck got stuck yesterday, so today he's having his Thanksgiving with strangers instead of his friends. I hope you're enjoying yourself."

"Heck, yeah, I'm having a good time," Stanley assured her.

"Good." Ella gave her attention to Candi and Greg, the last couple at the table, and said, "I think most of us know Candi and Greg, but I'm not sure everyone knows your story."

"Drugs and music," Bridget said helpfully.

"Yeah, I guess that about sums it up," Greg said.

"And we really don't care who knows it," Candi added with a laugh.

Candi was as petite as Greg was stocky. Partying like rock stars was high on their list, and since Greg worked as a stage lighting expert and Candi worked as a bartender, they had plenty of opportunity to indulge themselves. "But we also like being with good friends, and we're really glad to be here."

When dinner was over, the guys moved into the family room to watch football, while the girls, as always, cleared the dishes from the table and put food away. When that was done it was time to party, and Candi took charge. With all the presence of a drill sergeant, she marched into the family room, snapped off the TV, and made her announcement. "The TV is officially off limits. It's time for this party to rock."

Yes, there was some grumbling from the guys, but it didn't take long for everyone to get in the swing of things. Music, alcohol of every type and description, and some very high-test weed did the trick. It also didn't take long for the younger revelers to nickname the Baumgartners the Bombers, a name the elderly couple gladly embraced. Getting into the spirit of things, Gary broke out his impressive array of musical instruments, and soon there were bongos, maracas, rattles, guitars, and harmonicas scattered about the living room. When Gary began strumming his guitar, Ella realized that she hadn't seen him so excited since the Rock 'n Blues festival. His enthusiasm was infectious, and Ella pulled up a stool in front of the upright piano that stood against the west wall. Even though she was classically trained and paralyzed at the thought of playing in front of a crowd, for some reason she found herself playing the blues effortlessly today. It probably helped that she wasn't stuck in front of page after page of sheet music. And maybe it helped that she was a little bit tipsy as her fingers flew over the ivories. She smiled, then laughed, and realized this was the greatest Thanksgiving she had ever been a part of. Naturally, there was always a bit of guilt weaseling into her happiness, especially when she thought of how appalled her parents would have been at the scene taking place in her living room. *I'm just glad they're in New York and I'm here*, she thought.

The only thing that brought the music to a halt was Bridget's overpowering desire for dessert, and no one argued when she "suggested" it. But before everyone crowded into the kitchen, Lola sauntered out carrying a turkey leg bone topped with whipped cream.

"Lola, what in the hell do you have there?" Sam stopped her as she walked past.

"Well…it's my idea of dessert," she replied and sensually began to lick the whipped cream off the bone.

Sam stared at her, his mouth open with drool accumulating at the corners. He quickly closed his mouth and swallowed hard.

"Want a lick? I can spray more whipped cream on it." Lola wiggled the bone in front of his face and then slowly used her tongue to lick off the white goo left on her lips.

Sam held his beer bottle up between them and took a long draw. "No thanks, I prefer my beer," he lied.

"Oh my God, if only my roommates could witness this," Stanley murmured out loud. "Is she always like this?" he asked Bridget.

"Stanley, she's only getting started." Bridget laughed heartily, slapped him on the shoulder and continued, "Looks like you're next, she's headed this way."

"Sweet Jesus," Stanley whispered as he quickly followed the rest of the neighbors into the kitchen, where plates were filled with pie and cookies and every sort of confection. Drinks were poured, and Stanley raised his glass: "A toast to our hosts Gary and Ella for putting on the best Thanksgiving I have ever had the pleasure of attending. I don't know if you realize it, but you guys have one helluva great neighborhood. Lucky you! Make the most of it! Cheers!"

The JJs followed, giving thanks for the good fortune of being in Colorado. Dan thanked his grandfather for dying and leaving him money to buy land and build his house. He even thanked the storm for all the "shit" he had to go through to get to the party. Even Sam got in on the action when he quoted his favorite cowboy creed:

"A cowboy never fails
When there's call for a good deed,
So gladly lend a helpin' hand
To someone who's in need.

Kindness warms the coldest heart
So treat folks with respect,
And you just might come to find a friend
In one you least expect."

"I'll drink to that," Lola said and latched onto Sam's arm. Then she did her best imitation of an old Marilyn Monroe song, singing in a rather saucy voice: "Happy Thanksgiving to you, Happy Thanksgiving to you, Happy Thanksgiving Mr. Winston, Happy Thanksgiving to you…" She puckered her mouth and held the note far longer than required, then blew Sam a kiss.

No one uttered a word – probably because they didn't know quite how to react to the performance – and suddenly Lola could no longer control the emotions that had been building up in her all day. She sat down, closed her eyes, and cried. Between sobs, she told them about the loss of her parents and how much she had missed them when she woke up this morning.

"It's the holidays. And they just make me so sad." Then she recovered, and a smile creased her lovely face. "I'm thankful for all of you, my newfound friends and family. And…the great and ancient goddess that brought all of us to this place and time and for the wonder and beauty she delivered to us on this special day. Oh, and thank you nymphs of the woods, fairies, angels, white light and, um, the divine presence. I think that's about all." She hiccupped.

"Just when I thought you might actually be normal, you end with a stream of New Age weirdness." Bridget gave Lola a smile that told her a little New Age weirdness wasn't about to get in the way of a new friendship, and proceeded to adopt her best Irish brogue for her own personal toast. "This is a simple wisdom that my grandmother imparted to me, wisdom that was learned by so many generations before her, generations that fought for their survival in the devastation of Ireland's rich land. Today I understand better than I ever have before what the words mean:

"With food there is warmth,
With warmth there is hope,
With hope all things are possible."

She held up her glass and looked around the room. "Thank you for all the hope we feel today and for a feast I never thought was possible."

And finally it was Ella's turn. Fighting hard to hold back her tears, she gathered up as much inner strength as she could muster and forced herself to address the group. "Gary and I want to thank all of you for blessing us this Thanksgiving Day with your presence, your passion, your energy, your laughter, and your love."

"And all your stories, booze, and kick-ass food!" Gary piped in.

"Gary!" Ella said.

"Sorry," he said, when he saw how his crudeness had distressed her.

Betty reached over then and wrapped Ella in the kind of hug only a grandmother knew how to give. The embrace was filled with a lifetime of love and security, and created a special bond that would eventually link one generation of the Circle to the next.

"By the way, I have a key to your precious cottage out back. Olive gave me one for safekeeping. I'd like to clean the place up for you as kind of a welcoming gift. That is, if you don't mind. Olive, Hazel and I used to spend a lot of time in there. It'll be nice to…" Betty paused, thinking about her words. "Did Olive and Hazel tell you that the cottage is a kind of refuge just for us women? I mean, the women of the mountain. Our escape, so to speak."

"Well, to tell you the truth, those two were pretty secretive about it. Maybe you could fill me in?" Ella put out her bait, but Betty didn't take it.

"All in good time. All in good time. Timing is everything," Betty said and kissed her on the forehead. "Patience, my dear."

Herb patted them both on their backs, sensing the connection they had made. Then he said, "I think Betty and I need to start heading home while we can still walk. My bride and I are not as nimble as we used to be. But the night is still young for the rest of you. Party on."

And party on they did, cementing new friendships, and forging a tighter bond with the mountain and all its offerings.

FIRE

Day 2

*"The sacred essence of woman is to create, nourish
and evolve. She is the full circle."*
~ The Circle of Na'mow Handbook – Betty, Second Generation

September 15, 1996, Sunday Early Evening

Ella carried a box outside to her car. The fire was pressing down on them. They had waited as long as possible, hoping for a shift in the wind, but that time had passed. They needed to head for town, and they needed to do it now.

Ella jammed the box into the back seat. She closed the door and stopped long enough to look through the haze at the small stone cottage that she so often retreated to when the need for some peace and solitude reared its head.

The cottage represented a respite against the physical and emotional rigors of daily living. It also brought up fond memories of her friend, Gaia, who rented the place whenever she visited Colorado.

Ella blinked. Floating soot and smoke blurred her view. Anxiety trumped the fond memories and she turned away.

Standing amidst the last boxes yet to be crammed into her car, Ella looked at her family, each scurrying about collecting his or her most precious items. Then without pause, she yelled, "I just want you all to know how much I love you. I love you."

Brice set down a box and walked toward his mother. He was crying. He reached out with his arms and hugged her. "Me too, Mom. I love you too."

Gary held Alena's hand as they scurried down the steps and joined in, the four of them embracing amidst a symphony of crackling wood and roaring flames. No one wanted to break the spell, because in that moment they knew how lucky they were to have each other.

August 18, 1956

BETTY

Betty never thought of herself as a mentor. She was never in the business of giving advice. She wasn't that confident, and she wasn't that self-absorbed. When Hattie and the girls invited her into the Circle, it was a blessing. Betty liked people, but she wasn't a people person. She needed people, but she wasn't great at reaching out; that was Herb's job.

But that all changed the day the synchronized powers of Na'mow and Eru'tan came together in one precise moment and inspired the Circle to expand, to embrace Betty into their fold. The timing was perfect.

It was an unseasonably cold and snowy day in August, nearly forty years ago.

Betty was scared, and she tasted the bile of fear rising in her throat. She was a 37-year-old mother with a two-year-old son. She and Herb had moved to the mountain less than two months ago, and the unexpected snowstorm that blew in from the Continental Divide had dropped the temperature fifty degrees in less than two hours.

Betty's hands shook uncontrollably as the frigid winds battered the windowpanes of a house she was still trying to get used to, and she chided herself for this obvious show of weakness.

"Get a hold of yourself," she whispered. Henry, her two-year-old, had no idea what was going on. At the moment, he was sleeping soundly on the sofa, his face as chubby and angelic as if it had been plucked from a Renaissance painting. Betty questioned herself almost every day over her ability to handle motherhood at such an old age – was 37 really that old? – and she wasn't deaf to the whisperings of the younger mothers in the community. But it didn't matter; Henry was a blessing after years of childlessness.

She and Herb had been married for just five years. He taught year round at the University of Colorado. They'd moved into their dream home on the mountain in June, and two months later Betty was asking herself if she was really cut out for the life. She hoped that Herb would be able to navigate the ten miles of ice-hardened road from Boulder to their house. Betty didn't want to face her first night alone with her baby.

A ferocious whirling of snow, dirt, and ice continued to swallow the house, and the roof creaked and moaned with such despair that Betty found it hard to believe that it would hold through the night. A flash of lightning and clap of thunder materialized from the whiteness, and Betty stood protectively over her boy. A brutally loud pop followed the thunder and with it went the electricity. Everything – lights, water, toilets, stove, baseboard heat – gone.

When Betty looked at the empty woodbin next to the fireplace, her defeat was complete.

"Oh, Henry. What are we going to do?" She cradled her baby in her arms and held him close to her chest.

She picked up the phone, praying for a dial tone, and the hissing and crackling mocked her. She slammed the phone down and raced to the window. She pressed her face to the glass and stared across fields of white to the house owned by the two Michigan schoolteachers. There were four cars parked in their driveway, and light filtered from the windows of the little cottage hidden out back. The women were veterans of mountain living. They would know what to do.

"We're going outside, Henry. I'm sorry."

It took nearly twenty minutes for Betty to navigate less than a hundred yards in whiteout conditions, Henry cocooned in a woolen blanket and too overwhelmed to utter a sound. Every muscle in her body ached by the time she got there, and she could barely muster the strength to climb the one step to Olive and Hazel's porch.

In her exhaustion, her eyes came to rest on a cluster of twigs above the door that spelled out an unrecognizable word: Na'mow. A spiral surrounded by stars had been crudely dug into the wood on the lower half of the door. The round windows flanking the entrance were fogged over with condensation.

She pounded on the door. Then pounded again and again. When there was no answer, she wrapped fingers numb and half frozen around a frigid metal doorknob. She could hardly grip it. She tried again and lost her hold on the bundle that was her son. A bloodcurdling howl came from the precious cargo, and Betty managed to catch him with the last of her strength.

"Help!" She could barely hear herself, coughing from the strain. Then she filled her lungs and managed a plaintive scream. "HELP!"

She leaned her head against the door, defeated.

Not a moment later, the door opened, and she and Henry virtually fell through it and straight into Olive's arms.

"Oh, dear me!" Now it was Olive's turn to scream.

"Help us," Betty managed to say. Henry was more emphatic. He wailed, and the wail caused the other five women gathered in the house to come running. They relieved Betty of her bundle and helped her out of her coat.

"Well, where in the world did you come from?" one of them said to her.

"And who do we have here?" the one cuddling Henry said with a wide smile. "My, don't you have a pair of lungs."

The light Betty had seen was an otherworldly orange glow emanating from several oil-filled hurricane lamps and candles standing upright in sand-filled mason jars. They helped her into a seat in front of the stone fireplace, and the numbness in her hands and feet gave way to a painful prickling.

"Get our guest some hot tea, Olive," she heard one of them say.

"I would recommend a shot of brandy." This said by the woman sitting with Henry in her lap and rocking him in a squeaky old rocking chair. "Though our little friend here might do better with some warm milk."

"Coming up," the one named Olive said. "Oh, how exciting."

Betty was a battered island in a sea of smiles, loving glances, and reassuring pats on the back. The raw scent of freshly picked wildflowers made her inhale deeply, and she was finally able to take in the cozy interior: lace curtains, whitewashed log walls; a shadow-box filled with Indian arrowheads hanging near the front door.

"Such a wonderful room," she managed to say. And then a meager: "Thank you."

Vases filled with assorted mountain flora lined a rustic table along with piles of neatly stacked pencils and paper. Uncorked wine bottles stood among half-filled goblets.

"I'm Hazel. Remember me? Co-owner of this fair cottage." Hazel gently wiped Betty's face with a beautiful linen handkerchief that smelled of lavender, while Olive handed her a snifter of brandy. "And I think you know Olive."

"Yes. Hello." As the warmth of the brandy coursed through Betty's veins, she noticed the dainty circlets of green foliage with tiny yellow flowers that crowned the heads of each woman. And then she saw that each also wore a necklace adorned with the very same symbol etched on the door.

A woman with twinkling eyes and a deep voice said, "And I'm Hattie, former mountain resident, now a farm wife and part-time teacher, up from the flatlands visiting my two most favorite summer friends and hosts for our women's circle. My, my. Na'mow gave you a place to call home and Eru'tan blew you our way! How magical."

"What?" Betty's mouth gaped open.

"Don't scare her back out into the blizzard," Olive said. "My darlings, this is Betty and her son, Henry. New arrivals on the mountain."

"Um, ah, hello." Betty didn't normally stammer, but the last hour, she thought, would have made anyone stammer. "I'm not thinking so clearly…this is real, right?"

"As real as it gets. Oh honey, in our everyday lives, we're just a harmless group of seemingly ordinary women, but when we gather together, the mundane is left behind and the spectacular is revealed." The woman who held out her hand had beautiful copper-colored skin, and the blackest hair Betty had ever seen. "I'm Chimalis."

"And I'm Phoebe," the one cradling Henry said. "We're the members of The Circle of Na'mow and today's lesson is about identifying the bounty of the glorious mountain that goes by the same name."

"She has no idea what you're talking about, honey." This last woman had a smile that shouted warmth and humor. "Call me Martha."

"What is that?" Betty pointed at Martha's necklace. Then glanced at Chimalis. "Did you say Na'mow?"

"A name given by my mother to this wonderful mountain we call home," the Indian woman said. "And she called the Great Mother of the Earth and Sky Eru'tan. She who orchestrates earth's seasons and the cycles of the moon and watches over all things Wild."

Chimalis emphasized the word "wild" and shared a mischievous smile with their new guest.

"Eru'tan. It has such a lyrical sound." Betty sipped her brandy.

"We have special names for everything we hold dear," Hattie said. She was Betty's age by the look of her and spoke with a touch of irony in her voice. Betty liked her immediately.

"Have you ever fallen in love with the piece of ground you called home? The land you live and breathe on?" Chimalis asked. It came out like a question, but she didn't look to Betty for an answer. "Have you ever felt like a protective mother over it? I'm talking about the very soil upon which you live."

"I'm not sure," Betty said. "I'd like to feel that."

Martha said, "Have you ever stared at the moon and let its magic carry your thoughts away?"

"Do you dream?" Phoebe asked, her smile contagious.

"Well, yes."

"And do you believe in your dreams? Because we do. That and the magic of the moon and so many other things."

"We love this place we call Na'mow. And we have a special relationship with her," Chimalis said in a soft voice. She seemed old and ageless at the same time, and her strange beauty transfixed Betty. "But Na'mow and Eru'tan don't always make mountain living easy for us, like today, but we believe it strengthens our resolve to enjoy her beauty even more."

Olive took a seat next to Hazel and said, "Could you in your wildest dreams believe that two 'semi-normal' schoolteachers could have this kind of secret? Honey, the majesty of Na'mow called you. She invited you. And now you are bonded together with us in the magic of this place. Now are you worthy to stay? Well, we have all been tested. Some just didn't get it, and obviously they're not sitting here tonight. Believe me, Na'mow and Eru'tan can scare the bejesus out of anyone, man and beast alike!"

Betty surprised everyone by laughing, "Sure beats a class on knitting."

"Glad to hear you laugh," Hattie said. "Because humor plays an important role up here and, believe me, you're going to need it!"

Phoebe held up her wine glass and said, "Ladies, grab yourself a glass of dandelion wine, a precious gift from Na'mow and Eru'tan, and toast to our newest member! Na'mow, this wondrously massive granite rock who bestows us with the feminine essence of ALL, is now your home. May you treat her and all things that call her home with respect and protect her integrity."

"But most importantly, revel in her majestic glory," Martha added quickly, helping to fill everyone's glass.

"Yes, indeed. And like those who came before us, we are bonded together by our love for this mountain," Phoebe said. They all drank, except for the Indian beauty who reverently held her wine goblet to her chest. "So come on, Chimalis, let's continue with your talk about the power and wonder of being a woman of the mountain."

It made sense to Betty. Nurturing, supporting, creating. All from a place deep in the soul.

It would be many years before Betty would find exactly the right person to share this astounding message with, but that's what would happen when she met Ella. It just felt right. Nothing preachy. Just conversation over coffee, kind of the way it started with Hattie and the girls. They wouldn't anoint the Third Generation of the Circle for a long while, but it was a start.

August 1978

A PIECE OF WORK

Tears began welling in Ella's eyes. She swore at her post-pregnancy mood swings and wiped the tears away.

Brice's conception wasn't planned, but she and Gary were in love with the idea of being parents. Had she known she was pregnant, Ella wouldn't have drunk so much over the Thanksgiving holiday;

at least, that's what she told herself. When the news was confirmed in December, she expressed her concern to their family physician.

"Well, you can't change the past, Ella, so you're better off dwelling on all the positives now," the doctor had told her. And he was right. Everything went fine. Brice was a perfect, beautiful baby boy.

He was six weeks old and growing like a weed. She hoped that sooner rather than later he would get over his colic, because that and an absence of sleep were beginning to take a toll on her.

The lack of air conditioning in the old office building was unbearable, especially when the bright afternoon sun baked the west side like it did right now. She fanned herself with a sheaf of papers and turned the electric fan up to medium. The heat made her sluggish and sleepy. She wished her maternity leave had been longer so that she didn't feel so guilty about dropping Brice off at a daycare every morning, and just the thought of it made her cry again.

It was a year ago that Ella received her Masters of Social Work. She found a job within three months of graduation with County Social Services, and her life changed. Her salary doubled. Ella was so proud of getting her dream job while so many of her classmates continued waiting tables that she couldn't wait to call her parents to tell them. How could she have been so stupid? Her mom, in her typically disparaging fashion, responded by saying, "Welfare! You're working with clients on welfare? How could you?"

Ella, always quick to defend herself, snapped back, "Mom, what do you think an MSW does? Who do you think needs the most help out there? Nobody from your country club needs a social worker. They all have their private therapists at $100 an hour."

Her dad was just as condescending. "We're happy if you're happy, honey."

Ella hung up the phone that day knowing without a doubt that she had made the right choice leaving New York when she did.

There was a knock at the door, and Ella threw off the memory. These days, she counseled pregnant, unmarried women who qualified for government assistance. Her job was to help them explore their options and make informed decisions for their future. Many had never finished high school and lived in poverty. Most days, Ella felt good about providing support and compassion for these young women, knowing that nearly all of them had no one else to confide in. Then there were the others, like Celia, her next client and a real piece of work. No matter how much she tried, some people refused to be helped. They didn't want to take control of their lives. They wanted to cry and complain and make someone else responsible for their problems.

"Celia, you're late again." The clock on the wall said 4:25. "That means your time is going to be cut short."

"What? Come on, I really need a full hour today, I'm freakin' out and you gotta help me." Celia leaned over Ella's desk, revealing way too much cleavage.

"If it was really that important to you, you would have been here on time. I have to leave here at five to pick up my baby or it costs me $10 for every fifteen minutes I'm late. Sorry, but I can't afford that," Ella said. "Now you have exactly twenty-five minutes left, so let's not waste any more time."

Celia launched into her usual script, complaining about her plight as if the world owed her a favor, and Ella realized she was barely listening. She was thinking about her friends and how much she missed hanging out with them since Brice's birth. They rarely called these days, and Ella felt increasingly alone and isolated. They were all still single and carefree, and they couldn't possibly understand what she was going through. At least that was Ella's view. More than anything, she craved friendship; that and the occasional glass of wine to take off the edge.

When the clock struck five, Ella snapped to attention and said with a very practiced countenance, "Yes, Celia, it's five o'clock, and we're done for today. Let me know how I can help you with your next steps, and I'll do what I can."

Ella was out the door and in the car five minutes later. As soon as she saw Brice's smiling face and heard his loud cooing, her heart filled up with love and reminded her not to forget how much joy he brought into her life. She picked him up, kissed his cute, chubby cheeks, and the workday was instantly a thing of the past.

August 1978

LOVE AT FIRST SIGHT

The crunching sound of metal on metal hurt Lola's ears. She was jolted forward, then jerked sideways, hard enough to hit her head on the side window of the car. The sudden jolt snapped her back into reality. She spun the wheel, skidding over the loose gravel, and stopped abruptly on the narrow, almost nonexistent shoulder of the road. She glimpsed the car she had hit and heard its brakes lock up.

"Shit, Lola, that was stupid," she said out loud. She craned her neck and glanced at the other car again. "God, I hope no one's hurt."

She'd been driving in a trance – not particularly unusual for her – and fuming over the fact that Ella had begged her to pick up Brice's prescription in town. Brice had some kind of sinus congestion. He had a perpetual case of colic and who knew what else. *A nightmare child if ever there was one*, Lola thought. Too bad Ella hadn't listened to her birth control advice when they talked about it a year ago. Diaphragms didn't work, she told her. They're messy, she told her. They didn't allow for sexual spontaneity, and Lola was all about sexual spontaneity. Ella, on the other hand, planned everything down to a tee. Funny how she was the one who ended up getting pregnant.

"Well, Universe, you certainly have my attention now!" Lola threw open the car door, and two bicyclists nearly hit her as she stepped out. "Fuck you! You don't own the road!" she yelled as they zoomed past.

"You tell 'em," Lola heard someone say. She looked in the direction of the voice and saw the most gorgeous man walking towards her, obviously the driver of the other car. She first noticed his sky-blue eyes and beautifully thick brown hair. He was dressed for hiking in Vasque boots, khaki shorts, and a yellow Izod golf shirt. There was a beautiful turquoise ring on his right hand and no wedding band on his left; naturally, this caught Lola's attention right off.

"Are you okay?" he said. "You're holding your face. Did you hurt your head? I think you better sit down. You look pale."

The man took her by the elbow and led her away from the busy road. She was half expecting him to yell at her for being a terrible woman driver and say, "What were you thinking, swerving across the road like that?" Instead, this total stranger's concern was clearly genuine, and it brought tears to her eyes as he comforted her with a hug.

"Aramis," she said, stepping completely into his embrace.

"What?" He stepped back. The woman was sexy in a disheveled, innocent sort of way, and he felt himself getting hard. What the hell?

"Aramis. You've wearing Aramis. It's my absolute favorite."

This clearly caught the man off guard, but he managed to say, "Yes, it's Aramis."

He took a deep breath, inhaling her musky perfume. But it wasn't just her perfume; it was her exotic face, her flimsy flowing clothes, and the infinite blackness of her eyes; everything about her was intoxicating.

Lola being Lola was staring at his crotch, and the bulge in his pants pleased her. John's eyes followed hers; he blushed with embarrassment and a sheen of sweat rose on his forehead. Lola giggled and said, "Wow, it's amazing what adrenalin does to the body. I'm feeling a little faint and, from the look of it, you might be feeling a little lightheaded too."

He couldn't believe his ears. Flirting with him so intimately and not two minutes after a car accident. What the hell?

"I'm John Harte," he managed to say. The sun was at a perfect angle, profiling her round breasts and erect nipples, and he knew he was in trouble. "And your name?"

Lola didn't reply. Perspiration beaded above her upper lip. He was hard as a rock. Time stopped. It was just the two of them feeling the fire of passion, lust, and desire ignite right there on the side of the mountain road.

Lola was wet with desire, and her heart was pounding a million miles an hour. Lola didn't believe in coincidence. She didn't believe that they had just "run into each other." It was meant to be.

John felt it too, something so forceful and magnetic pushing him toward her. He also felt his heart opening and this show of vulnerability scared him. He didn't believe in love at first sight. Didn't believe in it until now, anyway. All he knew was how protective he felt of this stranger, how much he needed to be with her...to know her.

"I'm sure it was my fault," he managed to say. "Listen, we need... I don't know...talk or... My car is fine parked where it is. I'll take care of it later. Let's go into town. I want to make sure you're okay. We can take your car."

He grabbed her hand, guiding her back toward her car. "You never did tell me your name."

"Lola."

"Of course it is."

Lola squeezed his hand even tighter, wanting never to let go.

July 1979

ROGUE – THE LIONESS

Eru'tan felt the cacophony in her soul alerting her to the danger. She lamented over the severely tainted feminine essence and desperately attempted to infuse the creature with the harmony of feminine instinct and wisdom. It was futile. Eru'tan had lost control of the lioness to the darkness of lunacy. Now she was rogue.

Rogue, dangerous, and alone.

The felis concolor's mother had taught her excellent hunting skills for bringing down deer and elk but now she was on her own; her mother had met an untimely death with a truck's bumper, and the lioness's world was turned upside down.

During the winter past, when huge snows blanketed the mountains, her mother had acquired a taste for the forbidden delicacies of domestic pets and expensive livestock, a taste she had passed down to her daughter.

The young lioness had honed her skills on neighborhood pets and the occasional livestock, knowing the risk of failure and injury was very low. She patiently observed the habits of the humans and their domesticated creatures, strategizing and planning.

Timing was always crucial, and so she waited…

The sun was at its zenith, an opportunity presenting itself that the lioness couldn't overlook.

She recognized this particular feline by its small size and distinctive tawny color. She had often observed it roaming around the construction site and craving the attention of the workers there. But not today. Today was different. Today the kitty was alone and distracted by a mouse she had cornered under a log. The little tabby's defenses were on low alert, and the stealth attack happened so swiftly that she had no chance to react. The cat's huge jaws broke its vertebrae in less than a second and caused a mercifully quick death.

Felis concolor, as the mountain lion was called, ran half a mile to one of her favorite trees to eat the tasty snack. Two ravens watched from the branches of a nearby tree, waiting to scavenge. A day later all traces of the pet were erased from the landscape, which was a blessing for the kitty's owner.

July 1979

VENUS AND THE CIRCLE

This was life in the mountains. You gave up certain things and you gained a measure of freedom far from the tumult of city living. Lola understood this. She accepted it. Embraced it.

That's what she was thinking as she put the final touches on the newly finished deck on the west side of her house. Love had found her that day on the road when a freak accident brought her and John together.

A whirlwind courtship was finalized by a quickie marriage and a luxurious honeymoon in Hawaii. The remodel was John's idea. He was used to living close to the creature comforts of Boulder, where restaurants and shops populated every other block and where he also kept his office, but he was willing to live in the mountains if the cabin was enlarged. Now, with an expanded living area, kitchen, and master bedroom and bath, it was.

Yesterday Lola had bought new deck furniture, and today she wanted to show it off to the girls.

So while Gary watched their one-year-old son and Dan dirt biked with his motorcycle buddies, Ella and Bridget sipped cocktails on Lola's new deck.

"Lola, this is a killer-ass drink and you know how I usually feel about these girlie concoctions. It tastes like a strawberry smoothie with a hint of coconut," Bridget said as she stirred her drink and rolled her eyes at the paper umbrella adorning the cup.

"Yummy." Ella licked the frothy mustache from her upper lip and held up a plastic thermal glass adorned with flamingoes. "These glasses are a hoot. Did you buy them just for us?"

"Of course I did. You don't think I'm letting some man drink out of my flamingo glasses, do you?" Lola took a long sip on her drink and changed the subject. "Hey guys, have you seen Tig anywhere around? She's been MIA for three days. I thought all the construction might have spooked her, but she's not spooked by anything. I'm starting to get worried."

"She'll be back," Bridget said, even though Dan had mentioned to her that several other family pets had gone missing over the last several weeks. Lola might not want to hear that.

"God, I hope so. But I don't want to think about that." Lola held up her glass. "I got the recipe from a bartender at our hotel in Maui. I named it 'The Potion.'"

"The Potion. Perfect name," Bridget said.

"Potion? What kind of potion?" Ella asked. "You mean like a love potion? Or a magic potion?"

"Any kind of potion you want it to be. For me, it was my get-lucky-potion, because John not only gave me his credit card while we were there, he also made mad passionate love to me in every room in every conceivable position. Did I mention what he can do with his tongue…?"

"Enough!" Bridget held up her hand. "I don't want to hear about it."

"That makes two of us." Ella blushed. Then she turned the conversation back to "The Potion." "So what's in it? The drink, I mean."

"Well, there's a story to that," Lola assured them. "Kai…"

"Who's Kai?" Bridget asked.

"Our bartender."

"You're in Hawaii and your bartender's name is Kai. How perfect is that."

"Shush," Lola said. "In the beginning, Kai was making them with canned cream of coconut. Delicious, right? But the coconut alone was over 700 calories a cup."

"Yikes. That'll put on the pounds," Ella said.

"So true. So then he switched to coconut milk, which was a mere 500 calories. Still too much," Lola continued. "I said, no way. Just water it down. Because I knew if I kept drinking them his way, I would have weighed a ton before the honeymoon was even over. So I developed my own version. Don't eat your calories, just drink them, all 280 of them."

"Ingredients, girl. I need the ingredients," Ella demanded with a smile.

"Start with eight ounces of orange juice, add one to two teaspoons of powdered concentrated cream of coconut, as many frozen straw-berries as you want, two to three ounces of vodka, and lots and lots of ice. Voilà. The Potion." Lola held up her glass again. "A toast. To the sun, us, and my new deck!"

The girls drank and drank some more. It was an hour after sunset when Lola jumped to her feet and pointed toward a strange light in the sky. "Look at that! See how bright that is? It's got to be a UFO. Oh, yeah, definitely an alien space ship about to land in our backyard. I wonder if it's the mother ship or just a small one doing reconnaissance?"

"Holy mother of God, oh alien temptress, you're about a five on the woo-woo scale." Bridget shook her head, even though her eyes were still glued to the object overhead.

"What's the woo-woo scale?" Lola wanted to know. "Is it like scientific, you know, like that chemistry scale we had to learn in high school...you know, the period something...the period scale?"

Bridget looked at Lola like she was stark raving mad, but Ella got it. She said, "I think you mean the periodic table of elements."

"That's exactly what I mean." Lola straightened her posture. Her eyes narrowed, and she looked at the side of Bridget's face. "I'm serious. Is there really some scientific basis for woo-woo?"

"Not that I know of. Of course YOU would think that, given the fact that your basis of reality is so fucking out there." Bridget pointed to the sky. "I made the woo-woo scale up in order to gauge just how out there you are."

"Oh, and how far out there is that?"

"On a scale from one to ten with ten being really fucked up… over the top…out there, like actually participating in things like voodoo, magical spells, card readings, and that number symbol thingy, that to me is ten on the scale of woo-woo."

"Oh…I would think a ten would be believing that a spiritually evolved person could levitate while deeply meditating, or that human beings have been abducted by aliens that come in ships just like the one hovering over us."

"Holy shit! My woo-woo scale doesn't even go up that high; that's more like infinity!" Bridget said, holding back a laugh. "You're a five on the scale tonight. Unidentified flying objects, ghosts, invisible beings…That's a five. Maybe a six."

Lola looked disappointed. "So I have a question for you. Why didn't you name the scale after me?"

"You mean, like the Lola Scale?" Ella said, teasing.

"Exactly." She looked at Bridget. "So?"

Before Bridget could say a word, the object in the sky seemed to flare brightly.

"Shit! Did you see that? It does look like it's moving." Eyes pinned to the sky, Bridget jumped up, took two blind steps forward, and tripped over a planter, scattering dirt and flowers everywhere. Bridget's drink flew out of her hand. It spilled all over Lola's legs, and she ended up facedown on the new deck.

"Yikes! That's cold. And sticky," Lola screamed. And then a devilish grin spread across her face. "Maybe I'll just have to wait until John gets home and have him lick it off!"

"Hello! Hello, earth to Lola," Bridget yelled. "Get your alien ass over here and help me up."

Ella cracked up. She was laughing so hard that her sides hurt.

"Oh my God, I'm going to wet my pants. I'm not kidding. Gotta get to the bathroom!" She bolted for the door and disappeared inside.

"What's this?" Lola was staring at a small knife. It was encased in a leather sheath and lying on the deck not two feet from where Bridget was so unceremoniously sprawled. Lola bent down and picked it up. Then she looked directly at Bridget. "What is this?"

"For Christ's sake, Lola, don't look so surprised. I hide it in my cowboy boot. You never know what's lurking around up here," Bridget said. "It fell out when I tripped over your God damn fucking garden in a bucket!"

"Planter," Lola corrected calmly. "It's a garden planter."

Ella came back with some paper towel in hand and wiped up the spill while Lola helped Bridget to her feet.

"Well, we did a proper job of initiating your deck, I think, Lola," Ella announced. "We've got Bridget's blood, some good earth, some broken flowers, and a healthy dose of the Potion."

"And on top of that, our UFO is really getting brighter," Lola said.

"It just occurred to me that your imagination must help you burn up a lot of calories, Lola," Ella teased. "I hate to tell you this, but that's Venus. You know, the planet. The morning and evening star."

"That's perfect. I know Venus. She was out the first night I moved up here." Lola smiled at the thought.

"Wow!" Bridget eased herself into a chair and stared toward the heavens. "It's so big and so damn bright...I almost started to believe...oh, God...no I didn't."

"Not only does Venus have to do with love and fertility, it has to do with duality. Venus can be sweet, innocent, and intoxicatingly feminine or it can have a self-absorbed, narcissistic and destructive energy. I want to go with the feminine, love, and fertility part. How about you?" Ella asked. She looked from one friend to the other. Bridget seemed lost in her own thoughts while Lola was lighting a candle and filling their glasses with more of the Potion. So Ella stared at the sky and waxed on, saying, "You know what's so weird? I used to have a candle in the shape of an owl, and I would stand at my bedroom window and look up at the moon and the stars and say, 'Candle, candle, burning bright, make my spirit strong tonight.' I was so intrigued with the owl, the stars, and the moon back then. I guess I needed some extra help to keep me strong and to get me through. It's so funny. Looking up at Venus right now brought it all back. Things I had forgotten and don't do anymore. Wonder why our childhood curiosity and fantasy disappear when we get older?"

A pleasant silence filled the air, and Lola eventually broke it with a question that was pure Lola. "So tell me something. Can you get pregnant while you're on the Pill? I thought it was almost impossible."

"What? Of course you can get pregnant on the Pill," Ella said. "If you forget. Or if you think taking them anytime you want will magically protect you. You can't get lazy and skip a couple of days. And you can't ignore the directions and think everything will be just fine."

"Well, I got a urinary tract infection from doing you-know-what so much and was on antibiotics and I thought that's why I was feeling so tired and just not myself," Lola explained. "So I stopped the antibiotics thinking that would help. But I still feel tired, and my periods have been weird. You know, just some spotting."

"Sounds like maybe you should see a doctor," Ella said. "Do you have one?"

"I guess I should." Lola glanced at Bridget. "Hey, you. The clumsy knife-carrying Irish maiden. What do you think?"

"Huh, what? Sorry. I guess anything's possible." Bridget had only been half listening. Ever since Ella had mentioned Venus and fertility in the same sentence, her mind had been elsewhere. Bridget wasn't on the Pill. She had an IUD. But just like Lola, she'd had some spotting too. Bridget hadn't really thought much about it until now, because the spotting wasn't so unusual for her. Now she had to wonder.

FIRE

Day 2

*"I am more than just a granite rock for I hold the imprints
of All that have walked upon me, burrowed deep within
me, flown above me, and swum within my waters.
I carry the history of all these lives."*

~ Na'mow

September 15, 1996, Sunday Evening

Na'mow was aware that her Wild Ones, attuned to subtle changes in
vibration, felt "something" change in their natural surroundings
when the lightning torched the tree.

Na'mow witnessed those with feathers taking flight, the first to flee.

Witnessed the paws, hooves, and feet of animals large and small
standing in one moment immobile, and in the next, seeing their
stillness suddenly broken as Eru'tan began her frenetic twirling
dance…round and round the air circling, creating an intensifying
wind over the Mountain's terra firma.

Witnessed the growing fire reshaping the quality of the air.

Witnessed flames lapping at the trunks of huge trees, consuming
fuel not only from the treetops but also from the parched ground
overgrown with dried grasses.

Na'mow had been through this cycle of renewal many times in her past. Once again, she was the hearthstone to fire. From her past history, she knew that the wildlife often survived better than her human inhabitants did because their instinct proved a powerful motivator to flee danger. Of her human inhabitants, their unpredictability was both a strength and a weakness. Some fought, some ran for cover. The one shared emotion among her inhabitants was fear. But fire, much like life itself, was always to be respected, Na'mow knew, for it played no favorites.

Na'mow fretted at times like these, for in times of crisis, the young looked to their Nurturers of Life for a safe haven, for guidance in how to survive and how to adapt. Unfortunately, some caretakers fell short, which made Na'mow worry about how they would respect and care for her...their Home.

July 8, 1979

THE ROGUE

Looking down from her rocky outcropping, the lioness had studied the family for three days. She was now habituated to the brightness of the outside lights that flooded the side of the house and driveway, with the comings and goings of the humans. The big dog's powerful bark was no longer frightening.

At five that morning, the black Lab was the first one out of the deck's sliding glass door. The man, dressed only in boxer shorts, followed moments later. They stood together, relieving themselves at the driveway's edge. The man always scratched his balls after he emptied his stream. Then the black canine raced off following smells along the gravel road, urinating along the way, and only returning to the house after emptying his bowels in the tall grass between the aspens and junipers.

Amber eyes followed every move.

156

The next morning as the outside lights clicked on, the tall grasses and deep shadow between two bushy junipers provided perfect protection for felis concolor. Hunger gnawed in her belly. The dog was outside the brightness of the artificial lights and concentrating on the perfect place to defecate. The cat took two steps forward and then froze.

Bam! Bam! Car doors slammed. The lioness heard the car's engine roar and saw the car stop at the bottom of the drive to pick up the black Lab. And then they were gone, a wake of dust marking their departure.

The cat was undeterred. Now that her plans had been foiled, she continued her 25-mile territorial loop around the mountain.

The lioness started imitating human behavior patterns. Prey seemed more plentiful and active during daylight hours so she adapted accordingly. But this newfound boldness did not serve her well, as her usually covert movements became increasingly more overt.

Greg was on his knees tending to his cannabis plants when the hair rose on the back of his neck. He was being watched. There was no question. He stood up slowly, turned, and saw the mountain lion sitting just twenty feet away. Her tail slowly twitched from one side to the other. He blinked several times through bloodshot eyes. Then, the cat slowly and deliberately walked away, melding into the forest, leaving Greg to wonder if what he had seen was real or just a result of too much pot and not enough sleep.

Bullet's incessant barking woke Sam out of a deep sleep. He was spread out on his couch and fully clothed. It was 10:00 a.m. Surveillance on a cheating husband had kept him in Denver until the wee hours of the morning. He was exhausted.

"Bullet!" he yelled. "Quiet down, boy."

Bullet paid no attention. In fact, his barking grew more frantic. Scratching a day's worth of whiskers and smoothing out his mustache, Sam struggled into his cowboy boots. He opened the door and Bullet headed straight for Lady's barn, pacing manically and sniffing the foundation, the ground, and the encroaching grass.

"Bullet. What is it, boy?"

The dog responded by racing toward a small rock outcropping thirty yards into the woods.

Sam ducked into the barn. The horse was agitated in her stall and refused to be led out. Sam looked around and saw nothing that should've caused her nervousness.

"What the hell, girl?" He stroked her neck and whispered loving words into her face, and she slowly settled down. When she still refused to go outside, Sam left the top half of the Dutch barn door open and stepped back outside. The ground was damp from the overnight drizzle and a depression in the wet earth caught his eye. He recognized Bullet's paw prints with his toenail indentations, but dozens of others were very round and very huge and nothing like the dog's.

Sam swore out loud as he discovered the same muddy paw prints covering the barn's roof. His blood pressure elevated even more as a yelp off in the distance caught his attention, and he ran back to the house for his rifle.

Seconds later, Bullet bolted through the open door, an agitated mess. Fur from his right ear had been wiped clean, exposing pink skin.

"Bullet! Hey. Let me take a look." Sam examined the ear. It didn't look good, but at least there was no profuse bleeding. "All right. You'll be okay. But I need you to stay inside. You hear?"

He pointed at Bullet's pillow, and the dog curled up in a ball, whimpering.

Sam grabbed his cowboy hat, a loaded shotgun, and his rifle. He opened a beer, snared a lawn chair from the deck, and went outside to the barn. He got settled.

Yeah, it was a stakeout, for sure, just a little different than the one he'd been on the night before. Sam knew the lion would come back. As unlikely as this serial assassin was, he knew she'd come back.

July 12, 1979

NOT NOW!

The night was moonless. The lioness smelled mule deer, but she ignored them, quietly walking through the aspen grove on the western edge of her territory. The taste she had developed for dog made her salivate. She stopped, sat, and groomed herself in preparation for a kill. She had reconnoitered this dog's pen weeks before as she perfected her killing techniques on the smaller neighborhood canines and felines.

Now she was ready.

This particular dog was hugely muscular and savvy to outdoor living. His instincts were like those of a wolf, cunning and very aware of his natural surroundings. The dog sniffed the air as he patrolled the inside perimeter of his fence. At the northern edge of the pen, he stopped and stared directly at the lioness. Though the lioness remained hidden in the shadows, the dog barked fiercely. He then let out a barrage of booming howls that even made the cougar think twice about an attack.

Apparently satisfied with his warnings, the dog turned his back on the cat. He walked toward his water bucket on the opposite side of the pen and slurped thirstily.

The lioness saw this and pressed on.

The dried grass crunched under her feet. She slunk low and lifted each paw high before gingerly placing it back on the ground. She quickened her stride and stealthily cleared the six-foot high fence. The dog reacted too slowly, and the feline pounced heavily onto his back. Her powerful jaws clamped painfully onto the back of his head and neck. The dog roared with pain, struggling as the lioness's incisors sank deeper into his flesh and bone in her effort to crush his neck.

Her jaws embraced him in a death grip, and the more he fought, the more of his flesh ripped open from her protracted claws. The dog's loud yelping sounded pathetic as it transformed into a feeble rattling gurgle in his throat. The smell and taste of his blood intensified the lioness's madness. She proudly voiced her victory growls even as her jaws clamped onto the dog's head, patiently waiting for his life force to drain away.

"Oh my God! What the hell is going on with Laska?" Bridget cried. She jumped off the bed. "Dan!"

"I hear him! Get the flashlight." Dan grabbed his rifle and raced out the front door of the trailer.

He stopped dead, listened for a beat, and began walking cautiously toward Laska's pen. The yelping stopped, and Dan tried to calm his own breathing, at least enough to hear what he was most afraid of: the low-throated growling of a mountain lion.

His heart was hammering out of his chest as he fumbled with the safety release on the gun, shaking badly. He fired a warning shot over the pen as Bridget ran towards him, directing the flashlight beam into Laska's territory. The iridescent glow of the cat's eyes reflected back to them like those of the devil himself. Bridget held her breath. Time seemed to stand still. Eventually, the lioness dropped the ninety-pound dog, leapt effortlessly over the six-foot tall fence, and bounded towards the aspen grove. Then the serial-killing feline turned and did the unthinkable; she bolted straight toward the beam of light coming from Bridget's flashlight.

Dan froze, but Bridget didn't. She screamed: "DAN !...SHOOT HIM!...NOW!"

Dan raise his rifle, took aim, and fired. The crack of the shot echoed for miles; the plaintive cry of the lioness split the night and then faded.

The scene played out in a surreal fashion, blurring like the special effects in a disaster movie, and what took seconds seemed like an eternity. Then there was silence, a silence broken only by Laska's labored breathing.

"Laska!" Bridget shook off her momentary stupor and opened the gate. She ran to the dog and collapsed by his side. Sobs strained her throat.

"Oh, my God, Dan, he's really torn up and bleeding, A LOT! Get the truck...we have to get him down town to a vet. NOW!"

"Hang on." Dan readied the rifle and followed a bloody trail that led into the heavily thicketed pines. The blood increased with every step, but he dared not go too far. He took one step back and then another.

He called out to Bridget. "Bridge, stay there until I come over with the truck. And, for God's sake, stay alert. They always come back to claim what's theirs. Fuck!"

Dan turned and scrambled back to the trailer for his keys. They loaded Laska into the front of the truck, and Bridget held him tight.

"Oh Laska, poor baby, oh…" Bridget could taste the metallic tang that permeated the air around the bloodsoaked dog. She stroked Laska's head and whispered, "Don't worry baby, I'll take care of you. You're going to be all right. Please God, please let him live. Just let him live!"

She choked back a sob as Laska's tongue hung lifelessly out of his mouth. "I'm here. I'm here, Laska. We're all going to be all right. We just have to be."

Laska was lucky. There was no major organ damage; just a lot of puncture wounds and torn flesh that required a hundred stitches, an IV drip of antibiotics and sedatives, and at least a day at the vet's.

The next morning, Dan went into the bathroom where their bloody clothing was soaking in the bathtub. His stare transfixed on the clothes, sadness and anger waging an unrelenting war on his emotions. The image of his bloodied dog filled his head.

"I hope you rot in hell, you fucking lion," he said, the words a guttural whisper. "I hope you died in a pool of your own blood. Serves you right, you psycho killer. I hate you for what you did to my best friend. He'll never be the same. You zapped the life right out of him."

Dan did his business and roamed back to their bedroom. He looked at the clock and gave Bridget a small nudge. "Bridge. Hey. It's six-thirty. Aren't you supposed to be in Boulder by eight o'clock? First day on the job, girl. Remember?"

"Ohhhh shit, I think I'm going to heave!" Bridget tossed off the covers, clapped her hand over her mouth, and dashed to the bathroom. She slammed the door behind her.

"Bridge. Hey. You okay in there?" Dan stopped in front of the closed door and heard her retching. He leaned closer. Dan had never known Bridget to throw up, not even after half a bottle of Jameson. It never happened. She had a stomach made of iron and was damn proud of it. "Bridget? What the hell? What's wrong?"

⌒

Five seconds later, Bridget flung open the door with a wet washcloth pressed to her mouth.

"Guess what, Dan?" She pushed her mane of wild red hair away from her face, eyes rimmed red and tearing, and glared at him. "We're getting married! Oh, yeah, and you're going to be a father!"

Dan didn't miss a beat. He said, "I might be crazy, but did you just propose to me? And just in case you're interested, the answer is YES."

Bridget nearly knocked Dan down as she threw herself into his arms; her squeeze exploded with all the fear, joy, and need boiling up inside of her.

"I'm scared," she cried softly. "We can't have a baby now. Everything is so screwed up."

Dan led her over to the couch, gentle and caring. He wrapped his arm around her and said, "I don't know what you mean. I mean, look around you. Everything is perfect." He knelt down and cupped her chin. "Look at me."

He smiled so big that the wrinkles around his eyes deepened, and she couldn't help but let a small grin escape her face. "We're going to be fine. Hear me?"

"No house, no health insurance, and no steady income. You call that perfect?"

"You, me, and a little one on the way? Yeah, I call that perfect." He helped her to her feet. "Now you need to take a shower. You don't want to get fired your first day on the job."

Bridget stood in the shower and reflected on the irony of it all. She harbored some ingrained Catholic guilt about using an IUD that obviously hadn't worked. And now she was harboring some ingrained guilt about the fact that she intended to keep her last name once she and Dan were married. To hell with that; she was born a Jameson and she'd always be a Jameson.

Later that evening, Bridget got Lola and Ella on the party line and shared the news. If they were shocked, they kept it to themselves.

"I'm so excited for you guys," Ella said.

"Not me," Lola said. "I'm excited for me. I'm going to be an auntie all over again. Good job, Dan."

"Life is so weird," Bridget said. "First Laska was attacked and almost died. That was the worst night of my life. Then I proposed to Dan, and he says yes. That was the best morning of my life. Talk about an emotional friggin' rollercoaster. It's a shotgun wedding minus the shotgun, and that's only because they won't let me take one into the courthouse."

Her friends barraged her with questions. "So, are you telling your mom and dad?" Ella wanted to know.

"Hell, no, I'm not telling them. Not until it's all done and official. I'll tell them we decided it was going to be so damn complicated to deal with Dan's crazy family and all their issues that we decided to elope and save everyone the hassle. Some bullshit like that."

"So when and where?" Lola said. "'Cause we're sure as hell coming."

"Friday at three. We already scheduled a Justice of the Peace."

"We have to have a party," Ella said, getting excited.

"No, please don't do anything for us. We'll come home and spend a quiet evening planning our future. There's a shitload of stuff to figure out. Anyway, it's not like I can even have a drink to celebrate. Maybe we'll just, I don't know, 'officially' consummate the marriage." Bridget laughed. Ella laughed. Lola didn't. Not even a sigh.

"Lola? You still on the line?" Ella said.

"I'm pregnant too," she blurted out.

"Lola! What? You're pregnant too?" Bridget nearly screamed. "Oh, come on! Why didn't you tell us? And when the hell are you due?"

Lola bubbled joyfully. She said, "January. The worst possible time. I mean, don't you think it will be too cold for a little baby? And plus, I like all those warm weather outfits babies wear better than all the layers you have to put on them for winter. Oh well, I guess I can't change that now."

"Guess not," Ella said.

She was truly happy with anticipation. "This is so great. Now my two best friends will finally understand what it's like to raise a family on this crazy, wonderful mountain. And believe me, loving a child is so much more than you could ever imagine. It makes my heart swell just thinking about it. Our kids will grow up together, like an extended family. I'm so happy for all of us!"

"Oh, my," Lola muttered.

"What's wrong now?" Bridget asked.

After a long pause, Lola said, "Does being constipated have anything to do with hemorrhoids?"

January 1980

YES NOW!

"Yes!" Lola moaned. Then she barked, "No! No! No!"

These conflicting messages were typical of Lola and John's sex life in the last month of her pregnancy. John fought valiantly to understand his wife's vacillating and unpredictable desires, but it was not an easy task in her current state of mind.

They had a queen-sized waterbed, and it had been continuously shrinking as Lola's pregnant belly got bigger. It also sloshed up and down almost violently every time she moved, and all John could do was hold on for dear life. The bed was also a repository for so many pillows that Lola was more or less indistinguishable from them. A feather pillow supported her head, a small one fit under her belly, one rested between her knees, and another supported her ankles. Safe to say that pillows were Lola's best friends when it came to lovemaking.

The problem was, trying to get into a comfortable position was all but impossible in the bouncing bed, so John eased her doggie style onto the floor, with the fluffy bolsters piled under Lola's belly for support.

The good news was that John had become an excellent multi-tasker over the last few months, using whatever means possible to keep his wife satisfied despite an ever-evolving array of positions.

Today she was scolding him because his finger kept slipping off her little mound of joy just as she was about to come. And in Lola's state of mind, trading the Big NO for the Big O was not in John's best interest.

They often laughed that while John had became more masterful over the last few months, Lola had become lazier. She justified her sexual laziness because she was their unborn baby's home for nine months, and it was John's turn to crank it up to his full potential. She loved his full potential, and today things went just fine.

"I miss my body," Lola said, as John held her. "Nine months seems like an eternity."

"Come on. All the attention you've gotten. Don't tell me you don't love that?"

"I like the attention. I miss my body."

The hot pink bikini Lola had worn on her Hawaiian honeymoon a year ago was taped to the full-length mirror in their bedroom. It was a good reminder of how she had looked pre-Buddha belly and an even better incentive to get the baby fat off once their little one was born.

The baby was due in two weeks, and Lola was so ready to, as she liked to say, "pop the kid." She prayed to the Higher Powers, begged to the Lower Powers, and bribed the baby with promises for the future, no matter how unattainable they might be.

"Come out now," she pleaded, running a hand over her belly, "and your dad and I promise you riches beyond your wildest dreams."

"Yeah, right," John said. He got up and tugged on his jeans. "I'm going outside to shovel."

It was January, and the snow was piled high. Every day without fail, John shoveled out their cars and down the path to the road just in case the hospital was their destination.

Lola got up after he was gone and dragged the mini trampoline that she used for winter exercise in front of the bikini-clad mirror.

She stared at the mirror and jumped, an easy up and down motion, watching the bathing suit and laughing at the utter silliness of the scene.

And then it happened...her water broke. At first, she thought she had peed her pants. Then the water started gushing down her leg and onto the tramp.

Unworried, she said, "Oh, I guess John will have to clean that up tomorrow."

She stepped off the trampoline and looked at the bikini on the mirror. She smiled and said, "It won't be long now, old friend, until you're adorning this amazing body once again."

Then the soon-to-be mother yelled to John, "We're having a baby, Dad. Get in here." Then she went to the bathroom and cleaned herself off.

Before they left the house for the hospital, Lola pulled the bikini off the mirror and stuffed it into her overnight bag. "I'm not going anywhere without you."

March 1980

PICK ONE!

Outside, the early afternoon sunlight was blinding, but there was no heat in it. March had come in like a lion, and the wind was blowing and chilly.

Inside, the bar was dark, and there was an assortment of junk and odd artifacts hanging from the ceiling, filling every wall and spilling out of every nook and cranny. Not very classy.

The place was popular with the college crowd and hippies because the food was cheap and good, and it was almost impossible to beat the great prices on beer and well drinks.

And yes, it was indeed the "cheap but good" food that attracted Ella, Bridget, and Lola to the bar, and it didn't hurt that beer was twenty-five cents a mug.

Ella and Bridget had arrived at three-thirty as planned, and they weren't surprised that Lola was late.

Somehow their conversation had turned to the rogue mountain lion that had been terrorizing the mountain last summer, though Ella seemed to be doing all the talking.

"Do you know that lions can leap up to eighteen vertical feet and jump forty-five feet horizontally," she was saying in her most clinical voice. "There was a time fifty or a hundred years ago when a male's territory would range up to a hundred square miles. Not so much these days, not since their habitat began dwindling so drastically thanks to the influx of humans."

"Is that so," Bridget mused. She wasn't even remotely interested.

"Even today, you never see two males overlap in territory, but they say that two to three females can share his territory at any given time."

"Wow. You are a fountain of information."

"You probably didn't know this, but the way a male marks his territory is by urinating on piles of leaves, dirt, and sticks that he scrapes together in a pile. They actually call it a 'scrape.'"

"Who does? The lion?"

"No, silly. You and me. Scientists," Ella said, sipping her beer. "They also mark trees by scratching on them and peeing just like dogs do. Gary and I actually found a tree like that when we were hiking over the ridge from your property, and..." Ella stopped. She looked at Bridget and realized the memory she was revisiting. "Oh... God...Bridge, I'm so sorry I forgot about...the lion vanished after that. Thank God."

Bridget visibly shivered, sending a shockwave down her spine and through her now nine-month-plus swollen belly. "Okay, okay, gag me with a spoon, Ella. Enough of the cougar lecture. You're right, nobody has seen that damn cat since last summer and I, for one, am glad. Where the hell is Lola? I'm ready to scarf down some food!"

"Let's order. She can catch up when she gets here."

Lola arrived just as Ella and Bridget were getting their order of cheeseburgers and fries. Lola was carrying her baby in his infant seat, and she placed it on the table.

"Sorry, I'm late. Or I should say later than usual. Between the snowy road and nursing... ...well...I'm here and darn glad to be out of the house even though this place is so damn raunchy. I've been trying to eat healthy and get my bikini bod back, but the food smells heavenly. Could you two watch Baby while I go up and order?"

Bridget looked in disbelief at Ella as Lola waltzed to the ordering counter.

"Is she just yanking our chain or what? I really think she is mental. Baby? She's still calling him Baby? It's been six weeks and the kid's got no name. What the hell? Get out a piece of paper and a pen."

"And then what?"

"And then write 'NAME THIS BABY' in capital letters and put it on Baby's tummy," Bridget demanded.

"Are you sure? I mean, I know you and I agreed on an intervention, but this is the weirdest idea you've come up with." Ella sat on her hands as her tension mounted and then took a deep breath. "Okay. We have to be allies in this. Present a strong combined front, but..."

The pregnant Irish beauty grabbed the paper and pen and wrote "NAME THIS BABY" in huge block letters and laid it on the baby's tummy. Then she took another piece of paper, tore it into strips, and started writing boys' names as fast as she could. She put these in her cowboy hat and set the hat on the table.

When Lola returned with her tray of food, there was a rather unsavory hippie trying to put the moves on Bridget, and Lola got there in time to see Bridget jump up from her seat, point dramatically to her swollen belly, and yell at the guy, "Bite me. You think you could handle all of this? This baby's nine days overcooked, and I'm pretty much overcooked myself. So fuck off."

"I bet he has a small one anyway," Lola said as the hippie ran for cover. She took the paper off Baby and asked, "What's this all about?" Then she pointed to Bridget's hat. "Weren't you wearing that when I came in?"

"Glad you asked that very observant question," Ella said.

"I am observant as all get out when it comes to fashion, girls."

"Lola, shut your trap! Shit, my back is killing me and my legs look like tree trunks so don't piss me off any more than you have to," Bridget said. "My hat, as you might have noticed, contains pieces of paper with boys' names written on them."

Ella took over. "So stop chomping on your fries like you haven't eaten in ages and look at me."

Bridget took Lola's chin and guided it up to look at Ella. "Earth to Lola. Earth to Lola. Your best friends are intervening. We're surprised John hasn't been bugging you about the fact that his son doesn't have a name."

"Well, he has been so busy at work that he…"

"Damn, Lola, on second thought, don't name your beautiful boy. Just let someone else adopt him. They would give him a name in a hot minute. I'm about ready to give birth right here in this shitty bar with germs crawling all over me like I was a science Petri dish and…"

She suddenly ran out of words, and Ella took over again. She grabbed the hat and held it in front of Lola, waving her other hand over the hat in a circular motion. "Before Bridget here has a coronary, do us a favor and pick one."

Then, doing her best Lola imitation, Bridget said, "Trust in the universe and all things will be provided. Abundance flows into your spaced-out head because there is so much empty space to fill up. There are no coincidences, only mediocrity. No, I mean, synchronicity. This hat has been blessed by your invisible friends in high places and other flying thingies from Venus and beyond and is surrounded by the light of the white force. May the energies of weirdness and wisdom be with you, you la la princess, and may you choose wisely the name of Baby Boy Harte. It shall be done and done fucking now."

Ella grinned. Lola's mouth hung open. Finally, she reached into the hat, stirred the papers, and finally picked one.

"Read it," Ella excitedly exclaimed.

"Okay girls, I'll play your little game, but I am not going to settle on anything until I see all the names the Universe inspired you to write down."

Lola giggled as she went through the names. "Maximilian…rich sounding. Shane, Adam, Travis…Nah. River…now that's odd. Matthew…way too biblical, sorry. Sky…now that sounds Native American-ish and I can't imagine John's reaction. Ryan…nice. Kristopher…with a K; not sure about that. Jay…reminds me of a bird. Chad…like it. Jason, Justin, James…what's with the J names? Brandon…yeah, like that too. Ajax…you mean, like the cleaner? No way. Lance…you mean, like the thing a warrior carries? No can do. Zander…very cool."

"Ta dah!" Lola opened the last folded piece of paper. Her loud voice woke Baby Boy from his long nap. "Oh, you are awake, Baby. Today, as the girls are my witnesses…I name you…Dick."

Bridget and Ella both exclaimed, "There was no Dick in there!"

Lola looked back at the paper and squinted. "Jeez, I need glasses. You're right. It says…Nick. Well, it does rhyme with Dick."

"Get your head out of the gutter, Lola. You're a mother now." Bridget shook her head.

"Nick. I love it. It's a perfect name. Welcome to the world, Nick. Nick Harte." Lola removed him from his carrier, cradled him in her arms, and smothered him with kisses. "I love you, Nick."

She looked across at her special circle of friends, eyes misty, and said, "Ella, you were so right. I never imagined I had so much love in me to give to this little guy."

FIRE

Day 2

*"Friends capture our hearts in different ways,
that's why I never had one best friend but many
that added up to a community."*
~ The Circle of Na'mow Handbook – Hattie, Second Generation

September 15, 1996, Sunday evening

"Herb!" Ella screamed. "We have to get Herb off this mountain."

Gary was busy with Brice, trying to keep him grounded when everything around them was falling to pieces, but he gave Ella a nod as she headed for the door.

"Alena, I need you to stay put. I'm going to check on Herb," she told her fifteen-year-old daughter. "Make sure everything you need is in the car."

Ella didn't wait for an answer. She bolted out the door, sprang off the porch, and ran directly into the path of a small young coyote sniffing around the cars.

"Go. Scat," she shouted. The coyote danced away and then started following her up the road to their elderly neighbor's house. Ella shook her head. "Oh, for Christ's sake, all hell has broken loose up here. Not even the wildlife know what to do."

Ella bounded up the walk to Herb's front door, knocked once, and stepped inside without waiting for an answer. "Herb! Herb, where are you?" The house was quiet and dark, except for a lit hurricane lamp in the living room. "Herb? Oh, there you are."

She found him asleep in his rocking chair looking withered and lifeless. In his lap was a black and white picture of him and Betty, both much younger and both laughing for the camera. Ella tripped over an empty homebrew bottle that was scattered among a dozen others across the floor, and Herb's eyes snapped open at the sound.

Bloodshot eyes tried to focus on her, the trespasser in his home. A shiver ran through Ella's body as she recalled how many times her family had seen her in the exact same situation. The smell of alcohol tempted the addiction in her, and she stared at a line of airplane-sized liquor bottles lined up on the table next to Herb, all untouched...

Payback's a bitch, she thought, grabbing the bottles and dropping them into her jacket pockets. Herb obviously didn't need any more alcohol in his system.

The old man laughed and let out a sigh of relief when he finally recognized her.

"Oh, it's only you," he said wearily.

"My God, Herb, you're half crocked."

"Damn straight. If I'm going to die, I'm going to die happy, with my bride...and drunk."

"Yeah, well, that's not going to happen. I came to tell you that we have to get off this mountain. Remember...there's a wildfire raging out there," she said with a measured amount of sarcasm. "The plan was for you to follow me down to Dan's brother's place, but you're sure in no condition to drive."

"I'm not going anywhere, Missy. Betty would want me to stay. This is our home, and I intend to defend it to the end. Besides, I wouldn't mind joining Betty. You know, she keeps visiting me in my dreams. But today, I swear I saw her moving about the house," he said, shaking his head and weeping. "You know, my bride still keeps a close eye out on me."

"Yes, I'm sure she does, Herb." Ella wanted to scream at the top of her lungs, but the gallery of photos lining the dining room table brought her up short. Herb had created a shrine to his beloved wife: Betty as a little girl in 1927; Betty coming home from the hospital with Henry; Betty blowing out the candles on a birthday cake; the couple celebrating an anniversary. A life's celebrations captured on film. A lump formed in Ella's throat as she picked up a photo of Betty about the time the two of them first met. She held the photo closer, noticed the necklace hanging low on Betty's chest, and a shiver ran through her. How close they had become over the years. What a great friend. Betty looked so lovely and feminine with eyes that pierced through to Ella's soul, her heart igniting with an encompassing compassion for Herb's deep loss.

"Herb, Betty would want you safe. So…come on…it's time to go. You can ride with me, and Brice can drive your car down."

"What's Gary going to do?" Herb asked.

"He's staying with Dan. Dan's the only one in the neighborhood with power, and if the fire comes too close, they'll get out the back way. Come on…let me help you up." She reached for his arm, and Herb gently slapped her hand away.

"I'm not going to be some mamsy pamsy pussy and flee with the women. Tell Gary I'll go with him up to Dan's. I may be old, but I still have a penis and balls and most importantly, lots of homebrew!"

"NO WAY! I already had an argument with Gary about staying up here. It's too dangerous for someone…excuse me for saying this…as old as you are and…"

"What? Fragile? I may not be as spry as I used to be, but I have the wherewithal to know when to get the hell out and when I can weather the storm. It takes decades and decades of hard living to finally grasp that kind of wisdom. All of you up here are still in the infant stages of that. After that one Thanksgiving you had all those years back, hell, I thought the neighborhood had gone to the dogs! My God, Betty and I were amazed you all stayed up here. And look at you today, acting all grown up and, if I must say so, kinda like Betty. Fussing over me. I miss that."

"You know, Herb, you're a real piece of work. You really are. I'll have Gary and Brice come get you. I guess I'll let Brice stay with the men too, as much as I'll worry. He's got to grow up some time," she said. "Promise me no more drinking until they get here."

"Yeah, yeah, yeah, I promise. But grab a couple of dog biscuits out of that box by the front door, will ya? There's a young coyote I've been feeding. Think his pack left him behind, because he's been hanging around here keeping me company. He's almost taking those biscuits right out of my hand, we've gotten so friendly."

Ella wanted to lecture the old man about feeding the wildlife, but instead grabbed two dog bones and headed toward the door, shaking her head.

"I know what you're thinking," Herb said quickly. "And maybe you're right. But he and I are both short on family right now."

Ella opened the door and saw the small coyote standing next to the driveway waiting for a handout. She said, "So where's your family and all your furry friends, huh? You really do need to find your own kind, little one. They're the only ones that'll teach you what you need to know about surviving on this mountain. Not a guy with a collection of mini liquor bottles."

The timid animal cocked his head and came closer as Ella crouched down. She held out the biscuits, knowing better. But that was the thing about a wildfire. The creatures of the mountain sought solace in unconventional forms of companionship, just like humans did. Some relationships died, some thrived.

January 1981

THE BOMBERS

Betty steered her wheelchair frantically around the corner and barely missed the big grandfather clock in the hallway. She bumped the doorway going into the kitchen and hit her foot. She winced in pain. Then she cursed under her breath as she tried to navigate closer to the phone on the counter. She stretched up and out of her wheelchair and grabbed the phone. She collapsed back into her chair, stole a deep breath, and dialed up Ella and Gary, her closest neighbors.

Ella answered after the third ring, and Betty said, "Hi, Ella, it's Betty."

"Hey Betty, good to hear from you. Are you recovering okay from your knee surgery? Bet Herb is taking good care of you."

"Oh, I'm doing all right I guess, but Herb and I have a little problem and could use some help. Is Gary home?"

"No, I'm afraid not and I don't expect him for a couple more hours. He's out with the JJs. Why? What's up?"

"This is going to seem silly, but somehow Herb got himself locked in the bathroom, and I can't seem to get him out. I managed to get the doorknob off the door but it still won't open. Herb keeps yelling at me to take the hinges off the door but you know I still have this big cast on my leg so I can't stand up. I got the bottom one off, but that's as good as I can do."

"Oh, my word, Betty, you definitely shouldn't be trying to take a door off its hinges! Is Herb okay? How long has he been in there?"

"Well, let's see. He went in there to freshen up for dinner. That was about two hours ago."

"Two hours! Betty, are you sure he's okay?"

"Oh, yes," Betty replied calmly. "I think he's getting restless and I wouldn't mind getting in there and using the bathroom myself. But everything's fine otherwise."

"Okay, then let's figure this out," Ella said. "I'm stuck here babysitting three little kids, and they're all fast asleep at the moment, so I can't leave. Half the mountain is down in Boulder partying, but let me try Sam and see if he is home on a Friday night. I'll call you back as soon as I talk to him. Hang in there. Help is not far away."

Ella dialed Sam's house, and the cowboy picked up on the third ring. "Sam, thank God you're home. I need your help. Or rather Herb and Betty need your help. Can you run over to their house right now? They need help taking a door off its hinges."

"Why in the world would they be taking a door off its hinges now? It's after eight o'clock at night, for God's sake," Sam replied. "And besides I have a date showing up any minute now."

"A date? Well, we'll talk about that later. Herb is stuck in the bathroom, and Betty is sitting out in the hallway in a wheelchair. I'd go over there, but I have three kids asleep in the bedroom. Listen, just leave your door unlocked with a note. Is it Sarah? She'll understand."

"No, it's not Sarah. This is somebody new and believe me she won't understand. Tammy's a little temperamental. I haven't had a chance to break her in yet, if ya know what I mean."

"Sam, there's no keeping up with your love life." Ella smiled in spite of herself. "It'll only take you fifteen minutes and if this Tammy can't handle that then good riddance to her!"

"Well, I'm not exactly in it for her personality, if you get my drift," Sam guffawed. "Don't worry, Ella. I'm headed out the door right now. Sam Winston to the rescue!"

⌒

When Sam arrived at Herb and Betty's, he felt as if he'd been dropped onto the set of a slapstick comedy. "Now if that ain't some good old-fashioned western ingenuity, I don't know what is," he said to Betty.

Betty had somehow managed to get a six-gallon jug of homemade wine out of the closet and had dragged it over to the bathroom door.

Then she found a box of straws somewhere in the kitchen and spliced a couple dozen of them together. Then she'd run the home-made "hose" through the hole where the doorknob used to be so that Herb could share her alcoholic bounty.

Sam peeked through the hole into the bathroom. "Herb? How are you? Doin' okay in there?" Sam chuckled. "Nice skivvies by the way."

Herb sat on the edge of the tub with nothing on but his boxers, and one end of a straw was in his mouth. "Great! Never better!" followed by uncontrollable bursts of laughter. The Bombers were definitely in no pain.

"You all wouldn't mind if I get a picture of this, would ya? I'm guessing I could sell it to the neighbors so they can see how you turned a perfectly screwed-up situation into a party!" Sam doubled over with laughter. He finally managed to say, "Laughing this hard could hurt a fella."

"Ah…Sam. About the door," Betty said. "I've got to go something fierce."

"Oh, right."

Sam made short work of the door. Herb and Betty traded places. Then Herb pulled on a pair of pants and a shirt and insisted that Sam join him for a glass of their homebrew.

The cowboy grinned from ear to ear. "Alrighty. I guess it would be plain unsociable to say no."

Before they knew it, the grandfather clock chimed 10:00 p.m., and Sam jumped to his feet. "Oh hell! Is it ten already? How did the time get away like that? I'd better be headed back to the home front. I expect I might have a bit of trouble waiting for me there."

They said their goodbyes, and Sam took his time navigating the road back to his house. When he arrived, it was empty. Sam wasn't surprised. And he wasn't surprised to see his note shredded across the mudroom floor. He grinned. "Shucks! Tammy would have made a great nightcap."

178

January 1981

THE BABYSITTING CO-OP

Ella's kitchen was filled to capacity. There were seven mothers and nine children: herself and Brice, and several other women from the neighborhood, including Sharon, a single mom, and her son.

Since Ella was more or less desperate for an alternative to the daycare she was using in town, she had organized a meeting to discuss the possibilities of a babysitting co-op.

"Hey, everyone," she yelled above the symphony of voices. "Let's go into the living room and find a seat."

It took an inordinate amount of time before everyone was semi-happy and semi-quiet. But just as the room silenced, Bridget's son Michael chose to break free of his mother's embrace and tackle the unsuspecting child next to him. Much crying ensued from the hapless victim and from Michael, who at ten months refused to be contained. Bridget's love for him knew no bounds but her patience did. She apologized profusely to the other moms, knowing this would be the first of many apologies, and carried the screaming squirming Michael into the kitchen.

Ella introduced herself and asked that everyone do the same. When that was done, she handed out baggies full of white, blue, and red poker chips and explained how they would be used as tokens to be exchanged for babysitting, that a certain number of hours was assigned to the different colored chips. Then she handed out papers explaining how the co-op would work, medical release forms, and emergency contact forms.

"By the way, our wonderful neighbor Betty has volunteered to be backup in case of an emergency. So after all you mothers have a margarita in hand, Betty has something to share with us."

Blending margaritas took less time than getting nine kids settled down, and the cocktails seemed to be going down pretty easy when the 64-year-old reigning matriarch of the mountain stood up from her chair and clanked her glass. Everyone piped down when they heard the sound, even the children.

"Well, first of all, thank you to Ella for gathering us all together. This is very special," Betty began. "I thought this would be the perfect opportunity to tell you about 'arsenic hour' since we are witnessing it this very moment. Arsenic hour is the witchin' and bitchin' time of day, my dear ladies. It starts at five o'clock and ends at seven, more or less. As you may have noticed, your children are whining and squirming about that time in the evening because they have no idea what they want from you. Is it food, drink, a pacifier, a nap, some cuddling, or some playing? No idea at all. Also…don't forget your husbands get home sometime within that time frame wanting to be fed and nurtured. In other words, all hell is breaking loose."

Betty took a sip of her margarita and continued. "Back when our son was young, Herb would come home from work, have a drink, and sit down in front of the TV to watch the news. All he wanted was a few minutes without a clingy kid hanging on to him, so I'd invariably send our son outside no matter what the weather. That way, I could pick up a little, make dinner, pour myself a glass of wine and catch up with Herb. Now bear in mind that our son wasn't alone out there, because all the kids in the neighborhood were outside too. We called it the 'arsenic hour,' and creative magic is what those kids learned during that hour. They would build forts, have snowball fights, make snowmen, play cowboys and Indians, play hide and seek. Whatever it might be, it was good for their imagination. Plus they were physically active and not just lazing around watching TV and videos like kids seem to do these days. My time was also respected, which also seems to be sadly lacking in this day and age. So what I'm saying is keep the 'arsenic hour' in mind when your kids are old enough to understand the importance of adult time. Everyone will be better off for it."

Betty raised her glass, said, "Here's to arsenic hour," and took a long, slow sip of her margarita. Every mother in the room joined her.

December 1981

ELEPHANT TRUNK

"Dan, don't leave yet! I need you to add more wood to the stove. It's still only about fifty-eight friggin' degrees in here! Shit. We've been in this house for two years and I thought it would be a lot warmer than Big Pink. I'm freezing my ass off. And if I am, then our son must be too!"

Bridget was using the house for a baby shower for Ella and her new three-week-old baby, Alena, and the girls were expected any minute. The plan was for Dan to take Michael over to the Hartes' while the girls partied their asses off. At least that's how Dan saw it.

All well and good, except he'd just arrived home from a long day fabricating solar energy panels in town and was in no mood to leave again. There was some serious resentment going on here. He resented Bridget for making the time for her friends, and he resented the fact that Michael, all of ten months old, had taken over his spot as the number one man in the family. Dan loved his kid just as much as Bridget did, but she barely knew he existed these days.

His mood darkened even more when he saw his wife dressed in her Jordache jeans, tight wool sweater, and well-worn cowboy boots, and not a bit of it for him. Her red hair smelled of raspberries, and he longed to make love to her long into the night. And it wasn't just that. He longed for the carefree days before all this parent crap held him down in concrete.

"Sure hon, I'll get the fire going good and hot. Just wish you could do that for me," he said with mock sincerity. Bridget rounded the corner and shot him "the look."

Dan changed his tack. "I'll get the place warmed up as best I can, but you know it's below zero outside, right? Maybe you should cancel the party. Nobody in their right mind wants to go out in this cold."

"You know I can't do that. It's too late. I have over a dozen women and a three-week-old baby showing up in twenty minutes, and I want it like the fucking tropics in here."

"Well, I think I could warm up at least one of you, no problem." Dan ran his hand suggestively over his crotch and grinned his biggest grin.

"Yeah, baby. And that one had better be me!" She leaned in, gave his ass an appreciative squeeze, and planted a quick kiss on his mouth. Then she got back to business. "Okay, let's get it on!"

"Later then," he said, leveling his eyes at her with a look that demanded a commitment.

"You got it." She puckered her lips in a mock kiss.

Everyone arrived more or less on time despite the weather. Everyone except Lola, of course, which pissed Bridget off for a couple of reasons. First, the whole damn party had been Lola's idea to begin with, and second, she had promised to come early and tend bar. That wasn't asking too much, was it? *All I asked her to do is keep the blender running and the glasses full, because sure as hell everyone is going to need a good dose of the Potion tonight.*

Lola walked in thirty seconds later, and she wasn't alone.

"Lola! It's about time dammit! You promised you'd be here by…"

Lola waved a dismissive hand and pointed at the young and particularly good-looking guy by her side. "Bridget, I would like you to meet JD. He's our delicious entertainment for the night. JD, meet Ms. Impatient, Bridget. Don't worry, she's a lot more fun when she has some alcohol in her."

Lola flashed one of her award-winning smiles, determined to tease Bridget out of her annoyance. Then she said, "JD and I need a room to prepare him for his performance."

"No way. I need you to start mixing up some of the Potion for everyone," Bridget said. "I'll show JD where to go."

Lola batted her eyes. "Well, I really do have to help him prepare."

"Prepare? Prepare what? He's a stripper."

"Well..." Lola said as she dug into her purse and came away with a blue satin G-string made to look like an elephant with an artfully curved trunk. Lola looked at JD's crotch and then seductively up at his face. "Do you think you can fill this, dahling? I really didn't know what size to make it."

"What? You think you're going to be his 'fluffer'?" Fuck, damn! Lola, you're married, for Christ's sake!" Bridget shouted. "You're not helping him. I'm protecting you from yourself. Now get the blender churning! JD, use the baby's room, it's the warmest room in the house."

⁓

Lola had met JD at her yoga class two weeks ago. Turned out he was a dancer for an all-male revue. Lola having more charm than any three women that Bridget knew, JD told her that he would be happy to perform for her any time. For free. That was when Lola got her brainstorm.

"Let's really give Ella a baby shower she'll never forget!" was how she put it to Bridget the next day. "Let's get her a stripper. What do you think?"

Bridget looked at Lola like she had three heads. Lola was always outrageous but this topped it all. "Are you thinking about Ella now or yourself? Lola, if you had a three-week-old baby would you want a stripper at your baby shower? What I think is that this is the only way you can get to see this guy with his clothes off without pissing off John."

"Don't be silly. A stripper would be just the thing to get me over the whole birth ordeal and back to my normal self. Not to mention an inspiration for me to get back into shape!"

Bridget shook her head uncertainly. "Shit, I don't know. It's Miss Perfection we're talking about here. Ella's not you, Lola. She's wound a little tighter. God knows I would like to see her let go a little more. Well, I guess I don't want another boring baby shower any more than you do, so...okay, I'm game. Let's do it."

Bridget gave her friend a high-five and laughed when Lola completely missed her hand.

Bridget heard hooting and hollering as she walked from the kitchen into the freak show taking place in her dining room.

JD was in the middle of her dining room floor, bumping and grinding and shaking his ass off. Every woman on the mountain had been invited to the party, and when they heard about the entertainment, they all accepted. Well, all except the Jehovah's Witness lady down the road. Now they were all chanting and singing along with the stereo:

He's a brick _ _ _ _ house...
Mighty mighty, just lettin' it all hang out...

The room hit a crescendo of shouting, whistling, and clapping. The stripper whipped off his pants. With a practiced flourish, he began twirling them around his head and gyrating his hips.

His gaze came to rest on Ella, the guest of honor, and it wasn't a pretty picture. She looked tired and drained, and her face reflected a gray pallor. She held her Alena protectively in her lap, and the newborn "latched on" to her nipple. The baby closed her eyes, and Ella yawned.

At that moment, Lola moved over next to Bridget and gave her an elbow. She whispered, "JD couldn't fill out the trunk on his G-string so he stuffed it with some of Michael's little socks."

"He did what?" Bridget glared at Lola. "My baby's socks are in that sweaty-ass G-string? Are you friggin' kidding?"

Bridget shook her head and turned away. She caught sight of Betty taking a seat next to Ella and decided to join them. When Ella was done nursing, she laid the baby in Betty's outstretched arms.

"Ella, I know this isn't a very traditional baby shower, but believe me, it makes for a good story and sometimes, that's enough," Bridget heard the older woman say.

"She's right," Bridget agreed, pulling up a chair next to her friend.

Betty kissed Ella on the forehead. Then she gave JD a wave. "God help us," she whispered under her breath.

JD took Betty's cue and approached Ella with his best hip shimmies and pelvic thrusts. His elephant trunk was bouncing wildly just inches from Ella's horror-stricken face. The new mother glanced down at her engorged breasts and watched as her milk began to soak the front of her blouse. She looked over at Alena and thought forlornly: *Alena, you and I are going to need some serious therapy when this is all over.*

September 1982

GIRLS AND BOYS

Thirty-six hours of labor was what it took for Bridget's daughter, Shauna, to show up in the world.

Her redheaded mother had a near death experience, the kind that Lola had read out loud to her in some not-too-distant past. Bridget was so delirious at one point that she felt herself floating, leaving her body and watching the scene from the corner of the ceiling. Then she was traveling lightning fast through a tunnel toward the most brilliant light. The whiteness enveloped her…in an all-encompassing Love. Understanding coursed through her entire being, exploding in her heart. There had been no more pain, just bliss. It seemed so normal at the time. And then, poof! Back in her body again and torn apart by pain so excruciating that Bridget would forever curse the very thought of natural childbirth.

Thank God the doctors finally decided Shauna wasn't coming out and performed a C-section. By then, Bridget didn't care what they did to her; they could've cut her head off if it meant an end to her labor.

Bridget's doctor told her that she would need at least six weeks to heal, but Bridget didn't listen to him. Shauna was only three weeks old when Bridget decided to get back into the co-op daycare. She probably should have waited at least another week, but she wanted to send off Michael a couple of days a week so that she could have some alone time with the baby. First she had to put in her time to earn back some babysitting tokens, and she hoped she had the stamina for a room full of toddlers and babies.

With Michael, Bridget had been a ball of energy. She was so excited about her baby boy that she would sit and stare at him all night. Everyone thought she was crazy. They were right. She was crazy in love with him. So much so that she hated being away from him for even an instant. No one told her how absolutely amazing motherhood was going to be. Being a mother was like a portal to a whole other universe, a glimpse into something so wonderful that it made her heart hurt.

Yeah, three weeks was probably a little too soon, Bridget thought as the morning progressed. *What I wouldn't give to curl up with Shauna and take a nap right now.*

It wasn't a big group, only Brice, Nick, Alena, Michael, and Shauna, but it was still a serious handful. Especially Alena, who was only ten months old and needed all the attention a ten-month-old required. The boys, well, she just needed to keep an eye on them. They were already a rough and tumble trio, and Bridget could tell that just by the noise level.

The family room was not huge, but there was plenty of space for toys and mats and running. There was also a loveseat and a very comfortable couch, and Bridget took a moment to stretch out and get off her feet. Shauna was sleeping in a baby seat on a blanket right next to the couch, and Alena was crawling around, tasting all of the baby's toys as if each had its own flavor, and humming to herself.

Bridget had closed her eyes ever so briefly when some maternal instinct caused them to snap open again. She bolted to a sitting position and screamed just as the big red apple chime toy Alena was holding slipped from her little hands and landed squarely on Shauna's newborn head. Shauna's shrieking cries were like a knife though Bridget's heart, and she snatched the baby up into her arms.

The screams launched Alena into her own fit of panicked howling, and Bridget tried to console her as she examined Shauna's head, certain that her tiny skull had been crushed. Sobbing in fear and hugging Shauna to her breast, Bridget snatched the three-pound toy and hurled it across the room, screaming, "Fuck!"

The apple chime left a big dent in the wall and bounced to the floor, a cacophony of ringing that brought the boys tearing into the room.

Michael took one look at his screaming sister and demanded, "What happened to MY baby?" Michael really loved little Shauna. He felt like such a big boy when he was around her, and that's how he referred to her: HIS baby.

Brice had other things on his mind. He looked pointedly at Bridget and decided to enter into the dialogue in his own inimitable style. He said, "What was that word you just said?"

Nick wasn't interested in either Brice's question or why Shauna and her mom were so unhappy; he took one look at the scene, decided none of it applied to him, and went back in to the other room and the game he'd been playing.

It took a lot longer for Bridget to stop crying than it did ten-month-old Alena and three-week-old Shauna. And she really only calmed down after realizing that Shauna had only suffered a glancing blow and a little bruising.

When Bridget finally got herself under control, she fed the boys bologna sandwiches and Alena peas, carrots, and bananas. With their bellies full, eyes were heavy lidded.

"Okay kids, it's naptime. Today we are going to have a slumber party."

This led to a rousing, "Yip, yip, hooray!"

Unfortunately, napping didn't last nearly long enough by Bridget's way of thinking. The boys awakened first and started rolling around on the ground, giggling, and playing some make-believe game only they understood.

Bridget got down on the floor with them and whispered, "I'll let you watch cartoons until the girls get up, but only if you're real quiet. And then we can have Popsicles for a snack."

It proved to be a dumb thing to say, since the cheering that went up after hearing the words "cartoons" and "Popsicles" in the same sentence was all it took to wake up Alena. And Shauna wasn't far behind.

All Bridget could feel when she heard the girls flailing away in the cribs was exasperation and fatigue. She drew a deep sigh and said, "Okay, naptime is officially over. Michael, would you go get a new diaper for your sister? They're in the box in the kitchen."

"Sure, Mommy." Michael loved helping with HIS baby and raced off. While he was gone, Bridget took a moment to address Brice's question about the "bad" word she had used earlier.

"Nobody should use that word," she said. "I'm sorry. That wasn't okay for me to do. I know that you don't say that word at your house."

Brice looked at her with perfect seriousness and said, "Heck no. At my house we say Goddamnit."

Bridget smiled as sweetly as she could and patted Brice on the head. *Swearing in Ella's house. No shit.* The thought made her chuckle. *I wonder what else goes on over there behind closed doors.*

The boys congregated around the changing table as Bridget changed her cooing daughter's soiled diaper.

"Does she have a dick?" Nick yelled, trying to get a peek at Shauna's nakedness.

"What's a dick?" Michael looked up at his mom.

"A penis," Brice answered with absolute authority.

"Oh." Michael looked up at his mom to gauge her reaction and quipped, "You mean a tallywacker. Like me and dad have. She doesn't get one of those. She's a girl."

"Yeah, dummy," Brice said, giving Nick a shove.

Bridget bit down hard on her lip when she heard this exchange, and it took every ounce of her strength to keep from busting a gut.

"Let's not call each other names, boys," she managed to say. "Asking a question doesn't make you dumb. It makes you curious and interested."

October 1982

GOING GRAY

"Oh, my God! John, don't move!" Lola squealed. She grabbed his head and rolled him over in bed. John thought there must be a spider or some kind of bug in his hair. He hated spiders and hated even more the fact that it was his only phobia.

"OW!" A sharp sting caused him to grab Lola's hand in self-defense, but this didn't stop her from plucking a single gray hair from his head.

"Got it!" She held up her prize, ogling the gray strand as if it were made of solid gold.

This one gray hair was all Lola needed to set about organizing a "Going Gray Party" for her husband. John tried to object, but it didn't get him very far. Lola wanted a party; that's all that mattered.

And so it was. A date was set and invitations went out. It turned out to be a glorious and sunny October day with big fluffy white clouds gracing an azure sky. The first guests from town arrived right on time. The mountain folk who lived not five minutes away naturally showed up half an hour late. All brought food and drink and a serious party spirit.

Lola had decorated the dining room with brightly colored balloons, gray crepe paper streamers, and posters clinging to every wall. One near the entrance had a cartoon drawing of a frontal view of a turkey with the word "AWARD" written in large letters below it. "Going Gray" was written above it. The poem Lola wrote for John was penned in black magic marker on a poster-sized sheet of yellow cardboard.

"John, my dear, you've noticed hairs that are gray,
And pulled them by their roots to make them go away.

As you looked closer you started to pout,
So a question arises that causes some doubt.

What will you do with those pulled gray locks?
A solution I have is in this little black box.

To throw them away
Would cause some dismay.

So…treasure those locks
Right here in this box.

But if you decide not to pull and tear
There's another solution to hide the gray hair.

A hat or a bald cap will ease the pain,
Although really there shouldn't be any shame.

Gray hairs are a mark of distinction that makes you unique.
They're a mark that tells you that you are reaching your peak.

So please disregard all these silly funny jokes,
And consider these presents a humorous hoax!"

I love you,
Lola

An opened black velvet box containing one gray hair sat on a pedestal in the middle of the dining room table. A baseball hat and a nude-colored bald cap used by actors adorned opposite sides of the pedestal. The area surrounding the pedestal overflowed with gag gifts and gaily wrapped presents. A keg of Lowenbrau kept beer cups full. The Potion and margs were the women's drinks of choice. The kids drank fruit juice.

Much to John's surprise, Lola had asked everyone to come with their own special version of gray hair. There were gray wigs or hair spray-painted gray. Even the kids joined in.

One couple brought a wooden cane adorned with a bicycle ringer attached to it. A construction worker's gift was a tool belt filled with a pair of magnifier reading glasses, No-Doz tablets, Preparation H suppositories, adult diapers, Bengay, Tums, men's support socks, tweezers, Grecian Formula for Men, denture adhesive, eye drops for redness, arthritis cream, and a bottle labeled: Vitamin E for Enhancing the Purple Helmeted Soldier of Love.

Betty spied the belt and said to Lola, "You know, there's some damn useful stuff in that belt, Lola. You think John would mind if Herb and I take a few things home with us? I can see it coming in handy."

"I don't know, Betty. You might have to wrestle John for it," Lola said sincerely. And then they both broke up laughing.

A stream of kids raced up to Ella, and her son Brice posed the question they were all worried about. "Mommy, is this a Halloween Party?"

"No, baby. Halloween's not for three weeks."

"See, I told you," Brice said to his followers, and they all seemed so relieved.

"Dang, I was worried," Michael said. "That means we can still go trick or treating."

"Eat some food," Ella suggested. "Halloween's a long way off."

Not surprisingly, there was food aplenty. But the food, as good as it was, was not as popular as the alcohol, and that was going fast. When the JJs saw how low they were getting on tequila, they decided to make a trip back to their house for another bottle. Not ten minutes later, Lola noticed that there was also no more vodka for her world famous Potion, so she picked up the phone in a panic to see if they'd bring more vodka too.

She brought the phone to her ear and heard a woman screaming, "HELP! HELP ME! HE'S GOING TO KILL ME."

Lola slammed down the phone. "Damn party line! When are we going to get our own phone lines up here?"

She waited nearly a full minute hoping whatever the screaming was all about had gone away. No such luck. Even before Lola had the receiver to her ear, she heard the same voice screaming a similar refrain: "HE'S GOT A KNIFE. HE IS GOING TO KILL ME!"

"I hate party lines," Lola sneered and threw the phone across the room. Sam happened to be walking by at that exact moment and actually managed to catch the phone before it cracked against the wall.

"Whoa! Nice damn catch, Sam." Lola's eyes were as big as saucers. Then she shrugged her shoulders and nodded toward the phone. "Some woman. Thinks someone's about to kill her," she said.

Sam raised the receiver to his ear and listened calmly before saying, "Do you want me to call dispatch? I need you to hang up the phone so I can call the police."

The woman was still yelling, so Sam yelled back. "HANG UP THE GODDAMN PHONE SO I CAN CALL THE POLICE. DO IT NOW AND DON'T PICK IT UP AGAIN. NOW!"

It took Sam three more attempts before the woman hung up the phone. And then he called the sheriff's department and told them what was going on.

⁓

Sam waited forty-five minutes for the police to arrive. And when they finally showed up, it was a rusty brown Dodge Rebel with police lights and a shotgun mounted on the dashboard. Sam heard the deputy's radio even before he pulled up.

"You the guy who called?"

"I'm Sam."

"Billy." He climbed out. Sam thought he looked like a teenager. He had blond curly hair, longish sideburns, and a thick mustache just like Sam's. He was not in a uniform. Sam gave him a long stare, sizing him up.

"Yeah, yeah, I know. Guys in the department call me Billy the Kid," he said. Billy told Sam to leave his car on the road. He wanted Sam to accompany him down the lane to the cabin where the woman lived, explaining that if backup was needed he could tell them to look for Sam's car on the main road. "Seems like everyone around here has the same address. Hard to figure out who's who."

Sam thought the guy asking him to ride along was a little weird, but he climbed in the passenger side of the Dodge nonetheless. They turned off the main road onto a bumpy dirt road. They were losing light fast.

"We're considering this a domestic dispute. You know anything about these people?" the deputy asked Sam.

"Never met them. I know the woman was scared shitless on the phone. Neighbors on the same party line said the man must sleep all day and work at night because he takes the phone off the hook during the day. People say they can hear him snoring when they try to use the phone. The one neighbor has a whistle she blows into the phone to wake the bastard up."

"Sounds like a real piece of work," the deputy added.

The forest closed in around them. The sun hit the horizon. "Damn, it's starting to get dark. Always makes it more interesting."

When they saw the house, Billy said, "I'm not going to pull up too close. I'll leave the car in the driveway. Open your door, but don't go anywhere. Hear?"

"No problem," Sam said.

Billy squatted down between the driver side door and the running board of the car, and used the PA mic to notify the occupants of the house that he was with the county sheriff's department, responding to a call for help. "Come out with your hands where I can see them. Now!"

No one came out. Minutes went by. Billy looked at his watch and said to Sam, "I hope we don't encounter any gunfire. You might want to slip down a bit lower in your seat."

Sam did as the deputy suggested and said, "Where's your backup?"

"Don't worry. They'll be here soon."

The situation put Sam in mind of an old western where the posse seems intent on waiting the bad guys out, and when they finally come out it inevitably results in a shootout. He hadn't had this much excitement since his days on the force, and he felt a little unprepared for it without a badge and an unconcealed gun of his own.

Daylight faded. Billy used the car headlights to illuminate the cabin and the drive, and reached for his mic again.

"Occupants, come out of the house with your hands visible," the PA mic roared.

It worked this time. A muscularly built man walked out the door with his hands up in the air. He was dressed in boxer shorts. A petite woman followed close behind him. She was dressed in a tank top and shorts. Neither one of them wore shoes. Autumn on the mountain makes the days warm and the nights downright chilly. It was chilly now.

"What's the problem?" the man asked.

"A call of this nature requires that the man in question come out of the house to be interviewed and for the caller to go back inside and wait for an officer. You'll be interviewed separately. Ma'am. If you don't mind." The woman went back inside and slammed the door shut. The man just stood on the porch in his underwear, squinting at the car lights.

Billy ordered the man to approach the car with his hands in the air. The man walked fifty feet down the driveway to the car. Standing off to the side of the vehicle, Billy asked the man to put his hands high in the air and do a full rotation. The man obeyed and made a smart-ass comment about not being able to hide too much in a pair of boxers. The young deputy, speaking in a very normal tone of voice, began interrogating the man.

Sam listened, but not too closely. He was cold and stiff by the time a back-up patrol car arrived. His back muscles were seizing up and he couldn't move without groaning in discomfort. He was in cowboy boots and jeans but only a tee shirt. His body was as tense as a coiled spring.

The other vehicle, a patrol car, approached from the rear and blacked out its lights. Doors opened and closed. A female officer stopped when she saw Sam, knelt down, and asked him how he was doing. "I've been better," he said.

"It won't be long," she replied in a pleasant voice, and walked toward the house with her partner in tow.

The next thing Sam knew, the man was in handcuffs and the deputies were walking toward their car with a rifle and two handguns in their arms. Billy carried something wrapped in a towel. They placed the man in the back seat of the patrol car.

As Billy slid into the front seat next to Sam, he said, "That went well. In a domestic dispute case where weapons are found, we remove them from the home and take the man to jail for a cooling off period. The woman can stay in the house if she wants." Billy turned on the heat. "These October nights sure are cold up here."

Billy kept talking as they drove back. "I live east of town. We got some troubled ones in my neck of the woods too. I guess there's always one or two in every neighborhood."

"Ain't that the truth. Except I think our neighborhood has more than one or two," Sam laughed.

"By the way, I'm glad you didn't have to use your .38 special snub nose tonight, Sam."

"What the hell?" Sam stared at Billy, and Billy broke out laughing.

"C'mon, Sam, I'm a deputy. You think I didn't check you out before I came up to meet you out in the middle of God knows where? You're infamous in the department for the pranks you used to pull and your pissy attitude toward following the rules. Everyone knows you're a PI now and still have plenty of friends in the department. They told me you have a concealed permit and are partial to your snub nose."

"You're older than I thought," Sam said, giving Billy the once-over. "Smarter too."

"Don't worry, Sam. I won't blab your secret."

"I'll be damned." Sam grinned at the man sitting across from him. "So now that you know me so well, how'd you like to pull a little prank on a group of my friends?"

"No can do. Got to get this guy booked and fill out lots of paperwork. Bet you don't miss that part. Man, I need a strong cup of coffee right about now."

They turned onto the main road and Billy dropped Sam off at his car.

Sam sat in front of Lola's house debating whether to rejoin the party when a voice caused him to jump. "Hey Mr. Hero, would you like a drink? Thank God, you're not slashed up to pieces. I worried about you a couple times...you know...in between dancing and partying." Lola grinned ear to ear, handing him a beer.

He drank half of it down. "Glad to know you care so damn much," Sam scoffed.

"So, what's a macho man like you doing out here all by your lonesome?" Lola asked.

"Just watching and listening," Sam said.

"Oh, like a stakeout or something? I'm not in trouble, am I?" Lola teased. "Hey, I have an idea. How about you handcuff me and walk me into the house like a desperate criminal?"

"Lola, I'm a PI not a cop. I don't carry handcuffs."

"I have some you could use, but they're in the house. They're pink! Should I get them? It'd be a great prank to play on my guests."

"You're kidding, right? Don't think John would take too kindly to me handcuffing his wife."

"Well...guess you're right. Just wanted to rev up the party a notch. People are starting to head home and John's passed out in his favorite recliner snoring up a storm. Guess it's the gray hair..."

"Couldn't have anything to do with consuming too much alcohol," Sam added.

Suddenly the front door of the house opened, allowing the loud music to infiltrate into the crisp mountain air. The noise pollution increased as the partiers spilled out. Recharged by the cold, they sang and danced wildly on the huge wooden deck.

"Looks like everybody got a second wind and is staying around for the long haul," Sam observed.

"Oh, goody! C'mon, Sam, get your butt out of the car. You've got some drinking and dancing to do. And some storytelling. I want you to tell us all about savin' the day, you big hunk of man." Lola opened his car door, pulled him out and whisked him away into the mass of "gray hairs."

"Jesus H. Christ!" Sam muttered.

FIRE

Day 2

"We are the caretakers of this place called Na'mow.
Like those sisters who walked here before us,
we are intimately connected by our passion
for living in harmony with All that call it Home."

~ The Circle of Na'mow Handbook – Phoebe, First Generation

September 15, 1996, Sunday evening

Like fire, chaos doesn't discriminate. Anyone of any race, religion, or political belief, with or without morals or integrity, benevolent or evil can be consumed…for its essence thrives on the extremes, and the more that join its ranks, the better its destructive outcome.

The mountain erupted into chaos. The firefighters, police, and homeowners were being infiltrated by those who didn't belong, weren't there to save property and lives, and didn't have an emotional connection to anyone or anything that was of Na'mow. They were the looky loos, the media, and the weather chasers, all desperate for an escape from their mundane existence. To those who did belong, they were just in the way.

Tempers flared as the curious walked, bicycled, and drove around roadblocks and clogged the narrow mountain roads. Slurry bombers dropping their red retardant and helicopters releasing their huge water buckets barely missed these trespassers. Escape routes were congested, and the congestion did what no man could undo: it stole time when, with lives at stake, time was of the essence.

But even in the midst of nature's devastation and man's turmoil, one thing was certain: nothing was immune from the impending danger as the crown fires increased from tree to tree, the smoke impeded breathing for man and beast, and the usually clear blue Colorado sky turned an impenetrable black.

Summer 1983

WACKOS

Mountains lure people to their majestic beauty and ruggedness. A picnic, a leisurely walk, a day hike, or a weekend camping trip allow people to feel close to the natural world. Whether it's viewing a tiny hummingbird or a massive black bear, they feel small and insignificant in the larger scheme of the universe.

Mother Earth's bounty sustains them. She provides food and water for animal and man alike. She offers shelter, recreation, and natural remedies. She endows them with visual wonders that inspire awe. The mountain provides escape for the recluse and opportunity for those in tune with her enchantment.

City dwellers don't venture too far into Mother Earth's bosom for fear of losing sight of the path. Too much room, too many creatures, too big a sky, and too many trees scare them as they climb from the city's sterile starkness. Blinded by their brief bout with freedom, they believe themselves to be the first to have traversed a certain trail, climbed a certain rock formation, or experienced a certain magnificent view. They give little or no thought to the many who came before them. The Ancient Ones, the tribes, the adventurers, the explorers, the rebels against crowded living, the healers, the artists, and the lovers of solitude have long before them called the mountain their home. Strongly protective of her magic, they don't take kindly to those who don't respect Eru'tan's offerings.

Her beauty and her vastness also attract a less savory crowd: the mentally unstable and the illegal in particular. These lost souls search her out for comfort but never find it, and are left to wander deeper into their own darkness…on the path of the forgotten.

Mr. and Mrs. America loved the mountain and either hiked or jogged along its paths every day. Before work or after work, they found the time without fail to exercise within her natural beauty. This Saturday morning they decided to hike one of their favorite paths. It was a three-hour hike that followed a game trail along the meadow, through a grove of aspens, and into a stand of ponderosa pine. Then it traveled straight uphill and along a rocky ridgeline to the top of Twin Sisters. There, a 360-degree view of the entire area awaited them. Since thunderstorms were common after two in the afternoon, their plan was to be home well before then.

They set out at ten with plenty of water, extra food, and high spirits.

They had just left the aspen grove halfway up when Mrs. America stepped off the trail to pee and noticed several strange items scattered under a big tree, partially covered by a tarp. She remembered hearing a story from Ella about the old schoolteachers finding drug paraphernalia in the woods during the 1960s and '70s. This definitely fit that bill. But – it didn't look decades old. In fact it looked like someone had been here recently.

She looked closer. Protein bar wrappers had been thrown in a small fire pit along with cans of beer, empty boxes of decongestants, empty glass bottles, a small propane camp stove, and books on making hash, STP, and other drugs. A strong chemical smell wafted up to her when she pulled the tarp back.

She noticed empty burlap sacks piled up against a rock and suddenly the hair on the back of her neck stood at attention. She ran back to the trail where her husband was waiting for her.

"You have to see this," she said, dragging him into the woods. "It looks like a makeshift lab of some kind."

They didn't tarry, deciding instead to take a different path back home once they reached Twin Sisters.

"These wackos always think they're in some remote area far from civilization when, in fact, there's a subdivision only one-half mile away," Mr. America said when they reached the summit. "We'll just avoid the area for now. I'll tell the neighbors in case they see anything weird."

"It just irritates the hell out of me that they pick such a beautiful place to muck up. I hate the thought of God-knows-who using public lands for doing something illegal. I've never felt scared before up here, not even with all the wildlife roaming around. It's these unpredictable, random humans that frighten me." Mrs. America couldn't shake her gloomy mood, a mood which mirrored the now darkening sky. They heard thunder in the distance. "Let's go home before it starts raining."

Mr. America kissed his wife's cheek. He put his arm around her shoulders and they headed back.

Weeks passed. Mr. and Mrs. America started hiking less and jogging more because they thought it would prove to be less dangerous. It also fed their competitive juices.

Every time they went out, they tried besting each other as well as besting their own personal low times. Today was no different, not until they came out of a tight curve along a four-wheel-drive road and saw a parked car that caused them both to pull up. It was sitting in the shadows of two tall trees, in the exact spot where a man had committed suicide the summer before by running a hose from the exhaust pipe into his car.

"Damn! What's the deal with this spot? This just sucks. I'm not getting anywhere near that car after what happened last summer."

Her husband jogged toward the car, looked inside, and shouted back to her, "It's much worse than that." Then he turned quickly away, hunched over, and puked. Mrs. America started toward him, but he managed to shout, "Stay back."

He stumbled away from the car, and she took his arm.

"What's wrong? What is it?"

"I thought it was just dirt on the windows, but it's blood and stuff...and there's bullet holes. I'm surprised the windows didn't shatter," he mumbled. "There's two guys inside, and they don't look real good. We need to go to the nearest house and call the police right now!"

But they didn't stop at the nearest house; with adrenalin pumping through their systems, they ran all the way home. Then they called.

The police arrived thirty minutes later. They stopped at the couple's house, and Mr. America directed them to the car. Later, he led them to the location of the makeshift drug lab. Whether the murders and the lab were related, Mr. America didn't know. But it seemed likely. When he got home, he sat down and told his wife the story. Two young adult males shot at close range. Bullets to the head. They died instantly. The cops were surprised to see that they were not your typical "long hairs," but clean-cut, college-aged kids. The trunk of the car contained large burlap bags filled with freshly harvested cannabis.

"The killers didn't even look in the trunk," he told his wife. "The pot was still there. Under the car, the police found an empty envelope with $10,000 written on the outside. The envelope was empty. It was a drug deal gone bad."

When his story ended, Mr. and Mrs. America took a shower together, doing their best to wash away the physical and psychological dirt and grime. It was nearly impossible. The mountain was their sanctuary and now it had all the same problems as living in town. Irreverent outsiders had forever tainted the mountain's benevolence.

Spring 1984

DAMN KIDS

"Okay, line up for tick check!" Ella did a thorough job of combing through the kids' hair and looking under their clothes.

Mountain ticks were so bad this time of year and nothing to be taken lightly. You always found two or three of the nasty critters crawling on that beautiful soft skin, looking for the perfect place to latch their barbed mouths and eager to start sucking blood. There weren't many bugs to contend with living up here on the mountain: that was one of the nice benefits. But these disgusting ticks really made Ella cringe. She started with Brice, moved on to Michael, and ended with Nick.

"Oh, Nick! Here's one in your hair!" Michael and Brice crowded around, wanting to get a closer look.

"Let me squish this one," Michael shouted. "Can I?"

"My turn," Brice roared.

"Nope. Nick gets to do it since the nasty thing was on him," Ella said. She extracted the tick using a Kleenex, crumpled it up, and handed it to Nick. "Now squish him good and throw everything in the toilet."

When the deed was done, Ella herded them out of the bathroom. "You guys go downstairs and play till the girls get up. I'll give you a special snack then."

Ella looked at her mud-tracked floors as the boys headed down to the basement and couldn't help but sigh. *It's endless*, she thought. *You can clean and clean and clean and never get caught up.*

Ella grabbed her mop for the second time that day. "Thank goodness Alena finally went to sleep," she said to no one in particular.

Alena had been crabby all morning and running a fever, and Ella could only hope that it wasn't strep throat again. All it took was for one kid to get strep and you spent the next six weeks trying to chase it down with antibiotics, one kid after another. It was a nightmare breaking the cycle.

Ella's temples throbbed, and she couldn't wait for the day to end. She hurried down the stairs, hoping to find the boys engrossed in a game with their favorite matchbox cars, but she was in for a big surprise.

She started coughing the minute she hit the bottom step, and a wave of panic rose in her chest. Her first thought was smoke; her second was fire. Then she saw the three of them through the chalky mist that filled the air, their pants down with their little penises in their hands. They were urinating on the walls and on the doors and on the carpet, anywhere they happened to aim. Then she spotted the door to the wood stove standing open. That explained the gray dust covering walls, ceiling, furniture, and every inch of carpet.

"YOU DAMN KIDS!" Ella shouted. This sounded nothing like the usual restraint she so prided herself on, but that's how frustrated she had gotten. She pointed toward the stairs. "OUT!"

Lola pulled up in front of Ella's house, feeling a twinge of guilt about being so late, and not for the first time. She was turning off the ignition when she saw Brice, Nick, and Michael sitting glumly on the front steps. *Wonder what this is all about,* she thought, clamoring out.

"Hi, boys," she cooed. They looked like they were about to cry. Cooing didn't help. "What in heaven's name is going on with you boys?"

Brice looked up, his face the face of doom. "Mom kicked us out."

"She did what?"

"We made a big mess, and Michael's mom is helping her clean it up. We're in time out, I think for a long time," Nick told her.

Lola was suddenly inspired. She said, "I'll be right back. Brice, if your mom comes out, tell her I had to dash home for a minute."

"Where are you going?" Nick's eyes started to fill with tears again, and Lola gave him her sternest look. "You're in time out, young man, so you just sit right there until I get back. You hear me?"

Lola was back at Ella's front door in less than fifteen minutes. She knocked, cracked the screen, and held out a pitcher of The Potion. "Can I come in?"

Bridget answered thirty seconds later, and she was furious. "Goddamnit, Lola! You're a real fucking piece of work, you know that? Where have you been? And why the hell haven't you called?"

"Well, I, you know, I just…"

"Give me that pitcher!" Bridget didn't let her finish. She grabbed the pitcher from Lola's hand and three glasses from the kitchen. Then she headed for the stairs, calling, "Ella, we've got reinforcements."

Lola scurried after her. As she bounded down the steps, she called, "I'm really sorry. Ella, I…" Then she saw the damage that had been done to the basement and came to a screeching halt. "Oh my! What happened here? Damn, you two really do need a drink. And I think I might have to have one too. Damn kids."

August 1984

MEN AND TOYS

"If it doesn't make noise, they aren't interested! So much for the peace and quiet of the mountains. What a joke! Between their motorcycles and their guns and oh, don't forget their band, they couldn't hear a baby cry if they were sitting on it!" Bridget stormed toward the garage, her red hair flying back off her face, like a racehorse hitting her stride.

Dan and his buddies were leaving the next day for their annual Canyonlands trip; yes, it had become a tradition in a mere three years. They liked to refer to it as Bikes, Booze, and Bang. A week of camping, riding motorcycles, shooting guns, drinking like fish, and the telling of jokes so raunchy that only the male species could possibly find them humorous. The trip took precedent over everything, even family.

All Bridget heard as she approached the garage door was Dan saying, "I think it's bullshit that you think you get to call it up just the way you want, Greg. Total bullshit!"

The fiery Irishwoman threw open the door and announced her presence by shouting, "Is that so, Dan? That pisses you off? I thought you invented the rule about calling it up just the way you want and that's the way it is!"

"Hey Bridget, don't be so hard on my good buddy," Gary said, coming to Dan's defense. "He's a good guy."

"Is that so? Well, this isn't a damn frat house, in case you were wondering, Gary!" Bridget shouted. "Dan is a father and a husband, and that is supposedly his first priority. If you all can't keep that priority straight then you and your good buddy can start tucking each other in at night."

Then she turned on Dan and said through a clenched jaw, "The kids have to go to bed soon and the girls and I are starving. Are you about done playing with your toys for one night?"

That got everyone moving, though the guys just ended up sitting on the deck anyway, popping beers, finalizing the details of their trip, and toying with Dan's potato launcher.

"Who's got a lighter?" Greg asked, walking up to the railing with the launcher. "Let's get a little practice in while we're waiting for the food."

"Perfect timing, Greg." Bridget stepped out onto the deck with a tray of hamburger patties. "Why don't you make yourself useful and practice cooking these burgers instead?"

She nearly threw the tray Greg's way and then stormed back into the house. She slammed a cabinet door shut an instant before Lola could get her cornered.

"Bridget sweetie, why do you let yourself get so riled up by those boys anyway?" Lola said. "They're just big burly mindless Neanderthals put on this earth for our pleasure. The Goddess gave us all the smarts including cunning and conniving so we can look at them as pure entertainment for our enjoyment. Oh yeah, and they're suppose to provide, and protect us too so we can concentrate on being the divinely feminine beings that we were born to be."

"Are you fucking kidding me?" Bridget looked at Lola as if she were speaking Russian. "What drugs do you take to float above reality the way that you do, 'cause whatever they are I'm ready to overdose on them."

"You need a little attitude adjustment. As soon as we get them out of here tomorrow morning, let's just blow off the whole day with Jane Fonda, sunbathing on the deck, and maybe doing a manicure and pedicure for each other? I have a great new dancing tape. You have to hear it. It'll get your cells a-percolating."

Bridget was always amazed at how Lola diffused her frustration and got her to lighten up. "Okay. Okay, it's a date!" Bridget lifted her face toward the heavens and whispered, "Lord, please give me patience till then."

It wasn't to be. After everyone was gone and Bridget was looking at the mess in her kitchen, Dan made the mistake of walking up behind her, wrapping his arms around her waist, and nuzzling her neck. Then he made it even worse by saying, "I'm going to miss you, baby. Have you made my camp chili and trail mix yet?"

"What a fucking asshole you are!" She turned around to look at him, eyes blazing.

"But baby, you always make me food for the trip," Dan protested.

"Lola's right about you men being Neanderthals," Bridget replied. "You do remember that we have two adorable kids that call you

'Daddy' and want you to cuddle and coddle them as much as you do your goddamn mistress of a motorcycle? Hello? Have you even thought about helping me out with the kids? Like changing diapers or giving them baths? Like helping out around the house? Like vacuuming or scrubbing toilets? Like cooking a meal or two?"

Bridget shook her head. "The pathetically clueless look on your face just answered all my questions."

Dan made a recommendation. "Well, maybe if you started potty training Shauna, laundry wouldn't be such a big issue. I don't know why you don't just use those disposable diapers all the time."

The tray Bridget held in her hands slammed down hard on the kitchen counter, hard enough to send a vibration through Dan's head. In an unusually controlled delivery, Bridget said, "So, you want to make things easier on me, do you, sweetheart? Well then you'll be making your own goddamn tasty chili till hell freezes over and, believe me, that won't be any time soon...baby... I'm so sorry to say that you're going to be up all night cooking while I'm all cozy and snuggled up in bed dreaming of all the fun the kids and I are going to have when you're sleeping next to your drunk, stinky, snoring buddies. Oh, and do try to be quiet in the morning so as not to awaken your loving, devoted family. Good night...*baby*. Oh, I almost forgot, my big hunk of a man. I just changed the sheets in the spare bedroom. I know how much you like sleeping in freshly laundered bedding, so enjoy your slumber...*baby*. Sweet dreams and have a fabulous week away from us."

August 1984

JANE FONDA

Lola and Bridget dropped off their kids at the babysitting co-op house of the day and raced back to Bridget's house for their "girlie day."

They turned on Jane Fonda's workout video and rolled the small white Panasonic TV up to the sliding glass door leading out to the east deck. Bridget cranked up the volume. She and Lola were primed and ready to obey Jane's every command; her voice exuded a soothing, positive sensuality meant to inspire her invisible participants. The day was warm and dry. The blue sky reflected in the huge picture windows that lined the east side of the house.

Dramatic as ever, Lola was dressed in the latest fitness fashion: her leotard was striped, hot pink, cut high over her hips; she wore gray opaque leggings, dark pink calf warmers, and white high top sneakers. She had added a pink and gray striped headband. Her hair was pulled up into a high ponytail with a black scrunchie.

"Dang, girl, you are so in vogue," Bridget told her with a smile.

"These leg warmers are hot as hell for August, but I want to sweat the fat off these calves of mine," Lola replied, her posture a perfect mimic to Jane's.

Bridget's getup was a green version of what Lola was wearing, and she felt self-conscious standing in front of the TV.

"Glad the men aren't here to see this," she said. She was way out of her element in these foo-foo clothes and couldn't understand why a good pair of jean cutoffs wouldn't work just fine.

Both Lola and Bridget had gotten back to their pre-baby sizes – Lola a petite 5 and Bridget a healthy 7 - but now they were obsessed with getting firm and toned.

After ninety minutes of sweating like pigs, they changed into bikinis, intent on using the deck as their "pretend" beach. Bridget had already filled her kids' wading pool with water, and it had been warming up in the sun all day.

"Hey, get out here. The water's just about right," Bridget called.

She went in search of Lola and found her staring at the Clint Eastwood poster stuck to the door of the fridge.

"Don't you just love him? He certainly stops me from overeating. Every time I start to open the door in search of a snack, I stare into his eyes…and what can I say…I think 'bikini, thin, flat stomach.'" Bridget touched Clint's face tenderly. "I swear, I could ride him like there's no tomorrow."

"Clint just doesn't do it for me." Lola had Jim Morrison on her fridge and admitted that the Doors' lead singer made her think more about sex than not eating. Lola sighed and kissed the air.

"Sometimes, John catches me kissing Jim's thick, pouty lips, and it doesn't go over very well. I do try and make it up to him, however. If you know what I mean."

"What about Ella and her thing for Tom Selleck? Not sure I get that one," Bridget said in reference to Ella's fridge poster.

"She's into the Magnum PI thing, I guess. Who did what and where," Lola said with a shrug. "We, on the other hand, are into the pure primal sexuality thing."

"Clint's squinty eyes say it all, if you ask me," Bridget said. "The guy doesn't have to say a word to get his point across."

"So remind me of our affirmation," she said, turning to Lola.

Lola struck a pose and said, "We are beautiful inside and out. Mind alert. Heart open. Fat burning. Muscle building. We are beautiful inside and out."

"Lame," Bridget said, shaking her head.

"Oh, come on. If we believe, it manifests. I particularly like the fat burning part. Say it with me."

Bridget reluctantly complied and ended by saying, "Jesus Christ."

"Jesus Christ has nothing to do with this. It's all up to us and our intention to make this happen," Lola said. She thought about what she had just said and changed her tune. "Well, I guess Jesus could have something to do with it if He's the one you think makes stuff happen. I know He's the Christ Consciousness some people believe in, but I can't…"

"Christ, Lola!"

"Exactly," the brunette smugly replied. Then she turned her attention to the blender and announced, "Cocktail time. Just wish

Ella was here to join us instead of down in the city trying to save pregnant girls from the consequences of their ill-begotten actions. So what's on the menu?"

"I had a brainstorm," Bridget said, lining up the ingredients. "Since we're trying to build muscle and curb our eating, I'm making us "The Potent Potion." Just add vanilla protein powder to the regular Potion and voilà!"

"I kid you not, Bridge, that is divine inspiration." Lola clapped her hands and jumped up and down.

When their glasses were filled with the newly invented Potent Potion, they carried them out to the deck and submerged themselves in the wading pool. The conversation turned to men.

"Let's face it," Bridget said. "They've got it made when it comes to their regularly scheduled hunting and camping trips. I get a little sick of it, frankly. How often do we get away for a long weekend, much less a girls' night out? I'm sick of it."

"Chill out, Bridge. Here we are trying to have a girlie day and you're getting all riled up about you know who. Forget them," Lola said.

"Screw them. They'd have us by the balls, if we had any. How would we afford to go out even if we wanted to? We're fucking stuck here," Bridget said. Her eyes narrowed when she saw a mischievous smile spreading across Lola's face. "What are you smiling at?"

"I know how we can earn some extra cash," Lola said. "We charge for sex."

"What do you mean? Charge Dan and John for sex? Hell, Dan would kick me to the curb." Bridget laughed at the very idea of it.

"You just have to be very clever about the way you present it to him."

"I think the word is 'manipulative,'" Bridget said.

"Maybe." Lola shrugged. "But think about it. They get what they want – sex – and we get what we want – money. It's perfect."

They spent the next half-hour mapping out the rules of their sex for money scheme.

$20   Intercourse with nightgown on
$25   Intercourse nude
$30   Oral sex on wife
$10   Hand job
$20   Blow job (no swallowing)
$100   Blow job with swallowing (they knew their
       husbands would never pay it)
$1,000,000 Anal sex (never in a million years, but what the hell)

Everything else was negotiable including shower sex, masturbating each other, sex with toys, outdoor sex, chair sex, etc.

"The most important aspect of this little plan is that no one, and I mean no one, can know about the pact," Bridget said.

"On that we completely agree."

"Well, except maybe Ella. Who will just have a cow."

The Potent Potion was working its potent magic. Bridget put on some Motown and the girls sang along. They toasted their brilliant idea, the beautiful weather, living in a great neighborhood, their friends, their kids, Jane Fonda, and even their husbands.

September 1984

DEFIANCE

Snow fell steadily from the darkened sky. The good news was that it melted the instant it hit the warm pavement.

True, snow in September was not unheard of, but this storm caught everyone, including the weather prognosticators, by surprise. But Bridget and Lola were not about to let a little snow ruin their first Girls Night Out or GNO, as they called it. Their husbands weren't so accommodating.

"Can you fucking believe that he had the nerve to forbid me to go out? I thought he was just yanking my chain, but he was damn serious," Bridget said. "He said he was freaked out about me going to town in the snow. Like we've never driven in the snow before. So damn lame! Any excuse to ruin our first GNO. We didn't leave on a very good note. I screamed, 'Bite me, Dan!' and walked out. I talked to Ella, and she said Gary wasn't all too pleased either. Like meeting us after work was some kind of big deal."

"Oh, of course," Lola said. "It's okay if he and his buddies get together every friggin' Friday night to play their music at that lame coffee shop in town, but that's his response when she says she needs some 'friend time'? Well, to hell with him."

"That's what I told her." Bridget grinned. "She's meeting us there."

Bridget drove. Lola filed her nails. "So how's the sex for money thing going? Did you have the talk?" Bridget said.

"Oh, yeah. You?"

"I just cuddled up to Dan and explained how it would benefit us both," Bridget said. "The idea kind of turned him on. He said he'd just have go to the bank more often, that's all."

"John was speechless when I told him but...there's something so sleazy about it...men just can't say no. I have a sheet of paper with a list of the services and leave it on his pillow. He checks off what he wants, puts it on my pillow, and sets the cash down on my nightstand. I haven't refused him yet. I have a special place where I keep the money." She waited for Bridget to ask her where, and she did.

She said, "I can only imagine where that might be."

"See these shoes? They're my high-heeled 'Come fuck me shoes.' I hide the money in their shoebox. Every time I add a little money, I stare down at the shoes and say one of our affirmations."

"Dare I ask which of our many affirmations this might be?"

"I put the money in the shoebox and say, 'Walking in these shoes, I am an exquisite divinely inspired feminine being.'"

"Christ, Lola, what the hell does that mumbo jumbo mean?" Bridget barked.

"I'm not quite sure what it means. I just like the way it sounds," Lola admitted. "All I know is we look darn good. Time to switch from Mountain Momma to Party Princess."

"Hear, hear." Bridget slipped in a cassette of the Pointer Sisters, turned the volume up, and sang along: "Now I'm in the mood. He better JUMP, JUMP FOR MY LOVE!"

The duo parked as close to the front door of the bar as they could, shed their winter parkas, and replaced their boots with their dancing shoes.

"Look at you," Lola teased. "Wearing something other than your cowboy boots."

"Yeah, trying out some heels. Dan's always said I have beautiful ankles."

"And indeed you do," Lola agreed. "Let's go party."

They went through the front door and spotted Ella in the hotel lobby. Lola gave Bridget a jab in the ribs and said, "Holy crap, if anyone needs our affirmation about being an exquisite divinely inspired feminine being, it's you know who. I mean, shit. Look at her feet...Birkenstocks with wool socks."

They emerged a good three hours later. Bridget was stone cold sober. Lola was just slightly tipsy. Together, they squeezed through the narrow front door flanking an unsteady, pleasantly buzzed Ella.

"You're in no condition to drive...or talk...or anything, my drunk friend," Bridget said, commandeering Ella's car keys and thrusting them into her coat pocket. The three of them held tight to each other, trying to keep themselves upright while navigating what looked to be a good foot of new snow. "Where'd all this damn snow come from? It wasn't snowing that hard when we went in, was it?"

"I don't remember going in," Ella said.

"No, I don't imagine you do." Bridget used her body weight to pin Ella against the car while brushing snow from the side and roof with her forearm. It wasn't a very successful maneuver. She yanked the door open and managed to bring an avalanche of snow down on Ella's head. Ella didn't seem to notice. She crumpled into the back seat and started laughing. "Wow, what a night."

Lola jumped into the car as quickly as she could, changed into her boots, and buckled up her seat belt. Bridget performed a balancing act for the ages, changing from her dress shoes into her cowboy boots in a good foot of snow, and did so without getting her socks even a little wet.

"You comfortable?" she said when she saw Lola all settled into the passenger seat.

"Not really," was her response.

"Good. Because I need your help cleaning the snow off the car. Otherwise we're never going to get out of here."

"What about Ella?"

"It's a two-woman job, and you're woman number two. And the night's not getting any younger. Let's do this."

They set to work. The snow reflected in the fluorescent lights bordering the parking lot was swirling as if caught in some giant unearthly whirlpool. Huge gusts of wind pelted snow against everything in its path, obscuring any view of the cars sitting silently in the lot.

They set out, and the driving was treacherous at best. Bridget was white knuckled trying to see even a foot in front of the car. Not so Lola. She dropped her head back against the headrest and closed her eyes. Then she started complaining. "Oh, I wish we were home already. My feet are killing me. Those come-fuck-me-shoes are not so great for dancing. Maybe they should be just for fucking. Are your ears ringing? I can hardly hear a thing, and I'm starving."

"I'm starving too…and cold. Wish I'd eaten a big fat cheeseburger with all the fixings. Might have absorbed some of the alcohol," Ella said, clutching her coat. "At least the cold is waking me up some. That and my anxiety about getting home in one piece. Not to say, Bridge, that you're not doing a great job…it's just that Mother Nature is really pouring it on! And I don't think I'm getting much heat back here."

"She lives!" Lola responded.

Bridget was about to chastise Lola and Ella for their whining when the tires began to spin and the car slid sideways. Bridget pumped the brakes, and somehow the car came to a halt not three feet away from landing in the ditch running along the side of the road.

"OHHH CRAP!" Bridget slammed her hand on the steering wheel. "Lola, do you know how to put on chains?"

"Chains? For what? You mean for the tires? Hell, no I don't."

"Guess what, girlfriend, you're about to learn! Come on Ella, let's show her how it's done!"

Even after chaining up all four tires – which took nearly 45 minutes – the car still couldn't get the traction it needed to get up the long steep incline known to the locals as Bill's Hill. The tires just continued to spin and slide sideways.

Lola groaned, "Oh dear, what are we going to do now? Maybe we should just sit here until someone comes by."

"That's not being very proactive, my friend," Ella replied.

"Lola, its 2:45 in the morning. No one is coming by till Stanley shows up to plow the road at 6:00 a.m. We have to get home. We have to prove to the guys that we can't be stopped by a little blizzard. We need sand," Bridget said, sounding almost calm. "The good news is that there are sand barrels all along this stretch of the road. The bad news is I don't have a shovel. We'll have to scoop sand into our coats and carry it over to the tires, then lay down a path."

"Not MY coat! Bridget, I'm drawing the line, girl," Lola said with absolute determination in her voice. "John gave me this coat and he would never forgive me if I ruined it!"

Bridget rolled her eyes, but for once recognized the futility of arguing. "Good thing nobody gives a crap about my coat. Come on. Let's get this over with."

They found a sand barrel twenty yards up the road. After filling Bridget and Ella's coats several times and seeding a path in front of each of the tires, they were finally able to get enough traction to get to the top of the hill.

Bridget cranked the heat to high and focused every ounce of her energy on keeping the car crawling forward.

Ella played cheerleader, lending moral support and much-needed distraction. "You're doing a great job, Bridge…such a great driver… we all know you're going to get us home safe and sound." Ella whispered under her breath, "God willing."

Lola, on the other hand, was busy praying to the angels as snow sprayed up and over the hood of the car. "Oh great Venus, Goddess to all women, deliver us home safely. Angels surround us with your car-helpers. Ancient Ones attach your horses to our car and pull us to safety." She paused. "Let me think. Who else can I pray to?"

"I wish you could hear yourself, Lola," Bridget said. "You sound so silly. If I weren't so damn irritated, I'd find you hilariously moronic."

At long last, the car found its way to Lola's house, which brought a smug smile to her face. "See! All we had to do was pray to Venus and all my special friends. And here we are."

"Yeah, yeah, special all right," Bridget said. "Seems to me you forgot about the special friends sitting right next to you. The ones who put chains on our tires and hauled sand with their bare hands. You forget that your most important helpers don't hover around in the sky, invisible to all but you. Your fucking most important helpers can be seen and touched and held. They're called human beings. And they're made up of flesh and blood."

"Jeez, Bridge, you're a little testy…you can relax now, we're home. I have to admit that you guys had a lot to do with getting us home, too." Lola replied.

"Too?" Ella snapped back. Bridget glared at her front seat passenger.

Lola unhooked her seatbelt, twisted sideways, and reached out for her friends' hands, startling the hell out of Bridget. "We need to celebrate being alive! Ella, take Bridget's hand, please, and try not to scare her to death when you do so. Let's get some 'joie de vivre' moving through us with our own positive life force."

"Some what?" Ella and Bridget chimed simultaneously.

"Joy of living…it's simple to do…you know…the right hand gives energy and the left hand receives it…a give and take of energy in a continuous circuit…a friendship circle, so to speak. It's a way to connect on a whole different level. Come on! Let's end this night on a good note. We had such a great time together…well, at least until Mother Nature threw us for a loop…and even that didn't stop us from having an exciting adventure. So let's hold hands and give thanks for a great first GNO…and for each other!"

FIRE

Day 2

"Language is emotional."
~ White Sun

September 15, 1996, Sunday Evening

Just as dried grasses, trees, and wind fuel fire to either warm comfort or scorched memories, a tragedy fuels either a restoration of faith or a loss of it. Turmoil within the human spirit. It often comes as a surprise as to which direction a person chooses. No matter which choice is made, one thing is certain. People will seek out those who have had the same shared experience joining them together with hugs, tears, and expressions of comfort. Emotions laid bare.

⁓

"I love you. With no 'buts.' Just three words that heal the world. They should be spoken as they rise up out of your soul, gather momentum in your heart, and fill every cell of your body with blissful communion." Chimalis loved this quote of her mother's.

She first shared it with Phoebe and Martha, original members of the Circle's first generation, after her husband of twenty-two years had passed away. Phoebe shared it with Hattie during that horrendously dark time after Hattie's brother and sister-in-law were killed in a tragic car accident, leaving Hattie to shepherd her eighteen-year-old nephew into adulthood.

It was also a quote that Martha shared with Betty after her son left for college, a particularly difficult time for the empty-nester.

Who knows exactly when Hazel and Olive first heard it. When didn't matter as much as how. They all understood what Chimalis was saying, but they all struggled making it a reality.

"The problem with love is that it seems so conditional," Hattie said when the Circle gathered to celebrate Phoebe's passing in the late sixties. Funerals weren't the only reason the Circle got together, of course, but funerals often got the girls into a philosophical frame of mind. "I think I love you guys without condition, but that's really kind of nonsense. People turn on each other. It happens. And when it does, love goes right out the window."

"Love is part of the reason we don't turn on each other, Hattie," Olive said. "Love is why we accept each other's flaws."

"What flaws? I don't have any flaws," Hazel deadpanned. She looked at Betty. "You?"

"Not me. But love is why we accept Olive's and Hattie's flaws," Betty said without batting an eye. They laughed and drank and toasted dear Phoebe.

"I will say this about Phoebe," Hazel said with a tear in her eye. "If anybody knew how to heal the world, it was her. She was the first woman besides my mother who ever said, 'I love you.' How special that was to me."

"How special it was to all of us," Olive said, reaching out and taking her friends by the hand. "And, she, Martha, and Chimalis gave us the Circle to boot."

ELLA

Gary, Brice, and Herb took up residence at Dan's. The plan was for Alena and Ella to crash at Dan's brother's house in town along with Bridget and her kids.

Ella hated not having control and leaving her "boys" with Dan. It was a huge deal for her to surrender "her" troops to the macho group congregating at Dan's place. They'd be out of her reach and she worried about that. Even though Ella counseled people professionally, every bit of that training went out the window when it came to this crisis.

Ella's mind was swimming with all the could'ves, should'ves, and would'ves. She worried about everyone, friends and family alike, though probably Lola more than anyone. Then she stopped herself and repeated over and over again: "Be kind to yourself. Be kind to yourself so you can be a source of strength to others that need your help."

"Mom, why are you talking to yourself?" Alena laughed.

"Because I'm trying to remain calm and stay positive, that's why, and having a heck of a time doing so."

"No kidding," her daughter teased.

"Saying it out loud helps." She stared at the bottleneck clogging the road ahead and snarled, "DAMN IT! Look at these assholes on the road. It's hard enough to navigate when there isn't a damn wildfire raging."

Ella honked her horn at some loser who had stopped to take photos of a giant plume of smoke exploding off in the distance. Then she honked again.

"Good way to stay to positive, Mom," Alena mocked. "I'd honk again if I were you."

"You know, Alena, it's really easy to be calm and spiritual when everything's going your way. It's a whole other story when you're running for your life," Ella said. She looked over and grinned at her daughter. "I always thought it would be a great research project to take a group of cloistered monks and set them loose in New York City. See how good they do when they have to find work, pay rent, and deal with a few million people. Fat chance."

"Are we still trying to be positive here?" Alena sassed.

"So it's not working, okay? I'm just so worried about all the men, Brice is going to need some counseling with what he's been through," Ella said dramatically. "And then there's getting you to school tomorrow and getting to work on time for an important meeting…"

"Does it make you want to drink?" Ella's daughter boldly asked.

"Yes. But I've come too far to go backwards. But yes, goddammit, it does," she answered honestly.

"You won't," Alena told her. "You're too strong for that."

Ella glanced across the seat at her. "Thanks, hon. I needed that."

They finally reached the bottom of the mountain, and Ella pulled the car off Baseline and onto a side street. The car's front tire bumped hard against the concrete curb, causing an avalanche of framed photos to cascade onto Alena's shoulders and fall in her lap. Alena laughed, but her mom didn't. She said, "Sorry Alena, but I'm about to cry."

"Look at this," Alena said excitedly. The frame she held in her hand was worn but beautiful. Its filigreed metal showed off a faded black and white photo of Alena's great-grandparents, Oma and Opa, when they were youthful, slim, and full of vigor.

"Mom, I guess Opa died pretty young. I overheard Grandma and Grandpa talking about him one day. I guess he was an alcoholic too. 'A mean drunk' was how Grandpa described him," Alena said, staring at the photo. "Grandpa said that Oma raised him pretty much by herself."

"She was one strong woman, Alena," Ella said.

"Is that why Grandma and Grandpa were so concerned about your drinking? Still are, I guess. Because of Opa?"

"Alena, I never knew that about Opa! No one ever mentioned that to me. Not ever!" Ella said, her surprise genuine. "You know, Oma showered me with love when I was young. Always did. The emerald necklace I wear is hers. And sometimes I can see her and feel her around me. I miss her and wish you had known her too."

"But I have seen her, Mom. In my dreams," Alena said excitedly. She pointed to the photo. "Looking just like this...I just had no idea who she was!"

"What? Seriously?" Ella looked across at her daughter, shook her head, and smiled. "The universe works in mysterious ways, doesn't it?"

"It sure does."

"Listen, I want to talk more about this with you, baby, but we'd better keep moving. I have to call grandma and grandpa as soon as we get to Will's. If they see this on the news, they'll be worried sick."

She reached out and touched Alena's cheek. Held her gaze. "My God, this is just too much, isn't it? I'm frazzled and you must be feeling the same way, hon. My emotions are ready to explode. And we find this photo."

"Pretty heavy all right," Alena agreed.

"Maybe what we both need is a good cry. So come on. Let's just let it out!"

And so they did. Sobbed, laughed, and sobbed some more. "I keep telling myself that letting it all out is healthy."

"Okay then, let's get healthy," Alena quipped.

This caused them both to laugh, and this time the laughter won out. They wiped away their tears and smeared makeup and shared a weak smile.

"Ready?" Ella asked.

"Ready!" Alena yelled.

The duo arrived at Will's house minutes later, tired and drained, but glad to be free of the frenzied and smoke-filled environment on the mountain.

They were both in their pajamas when Ella's phone rang. It was Sam.

"Got an idea for you," he said. "Why don't you and Alena come by my Aunt Hattie's farmhouse tomorrow and spend some time with Lola. Grab Bridget, and the three of you can spend some quality time together. Sure know Lola could use it."

"How's she doing, Sam?"

"No doubt she'll be better once she's surrounded by 'her girls.'" Sam replied, and he was dead serious.

"And John?"

Sam's voice quivered and cracked. "All I can say is that our little filly is really going to need you and the whole doggone neighborhood. That's the damn truth!"

BRIDGET

All the way down the mountain Michael continued to protest about having to evacuate with the women and children. Bridget understood his position. She felt exactly the same way. Leaving her home, her mountain and her husband fought against every natural instinct she had. Stay and fight! That was her drive. Forget the easy way! Forget the best way! I will do it my way! That was exactly what brought her to her knees before. It haunted her now. Regardless, nothing short of protecting her children could have moved her off the mountain.

Truth be told, Michael was more pissed about being stuck with a bunch of women than he was about having to evacuate from the mountain.

"Michael, I know how you're feeling and I know you're mad, but I want to share with you what I've learned about control. Shauna, this is for you too because it will come up again and again in your life. You can't control everything in your life. Understand that there is a Greater Power in the driver's seat and that sometimes shit

225

happens when it's supposed to happen, regardless of what you do. At the time you might think it sucks, but it all works out in the end and it can be pretty friggin' amazing." Bridget felt somewhat hypocritical. While she firmly believed in what she was saying, she knew that she was still a prisoner of wanting to control life by sheer force.

"God, Mom. I get it, I get it!" Michael yelled. "But I'm not going out to somebody's house I don't even know and hang out with Shauna and Alena. I have a big science project that I'm working on with Ted and it's due this week. He said I could stay with him and that's what I'm going to do!"

Tears of fear and frustration started to welled up in Bridget's eyes as she fought to hold them back. Her mind was consumed with the prospect of losing her house again to fire. *I don't know if I can do it again...start over. This can't happen twice damnit! No fucking way! How much can one person take? This will NOT happen!*

"Duh...Mom! Did you hear me?" The car erratically swerved as Bridget barely missed hitting a squirrel. "Jeez mom, trying to kill us?!" Michael said.

"Michael, shut up! I'm doing the best I can to keep everyone and everything alive," Bridget lashed back. "And your father is NOT doing me any favors right now, staying on the mountain. Idiot! I can't help him if something happens. I'll be powerless!"

God, I've never felt so scared in my life. Just when I thought I finally had my shit together. Bridget's tears fell in earnest. There was no hiding it from the kids. She clapped her hand to her mouth, suppressing the sob escaping from her throat.

Shauna glared at Michael. "Give it a rest, Michael. Mom's trying to take care of us. Can't you see that?" Shauna reached forward from the back seat to put her hand on her mother's shoulder. "It's okay Mom, remember what you told us when the house burned down, that we'd be okay? And you were right, we were. We'll be okay this time, including Dad." Shauna began to feel stronger and less afraid as she comforted her mom.

"Mom, I'm sorry, don't cry. I'm not trying to be a pain. Can you please just drop me off at Ted's so I can finish my project this week?" Michael's tone softened. Her anger he expected; her tears were scary.

"Okay okay, I'm just so damned wor…Michael, just make sure you call me before and after school. I need to know you're safe."

LOLA

John's partners arrived at the hospital with all of the necessary legal papers for someone in his situation. John had given his ex-wife power of medical attorney, but Lola didn't give a damn about that. She sat there pretending to listen to the details of their conversation when all she cared about was John recovering from his massive stroke and coma.

When they were gone and the paperwork was all in order, Lola met Nick back at Intensive Care, and they hugged for the longest time.

Nick was a bundle of contradictions. He knew how serious his dad's condition was, but a part of him refused to believe something like this could happen. His dad wasn't that old. He exercised. He ate pretty well. Yeah, he worked too many hours and pushed too hard, but who didn't?

Nick wanted to spend the night at the hospital with his mom, but when one of his best friends' family showed up and offered to take care of him, he accepted.

"Are you okay with that, Mom?" he asked Lola. "I feel like I'm deserting you."

"You're not deserting anyone," she said. "Get some sleep tonight, and we'll figure things out in the morning, okay?"

When Nick was gone, Lola stared at the exoskeleton of machines surrounding her ex-husband: tubes, wires, bags of clear fluids, and machines humming, pumping, and beeping made up the white noise in the room. The rhythmic beat of the machines lulled Lola's eyes shut and transported her to the land of her dreams, where a circle of women held hands as they danced around a fire, chanting in an ancient tongue. Lola's heart felt its vibration…the melody was that of the death song…being carried upward on the fire's thermals only to captured, amplified and transformed by All That Passed Before. She was shocked awake as doctors and nurses checked and rechecked the equipment and John's vital signs. Lola sat by his side, stroking his right hand and talking to him about anything and everything except the most important thing of all…her pregnancy.

Sam tiptoed in. "Hey. How ya doin'?" When Lola didn't answer, he said, "I called Dan's brother's house. I remembered you said Bridget and Ella were staying down there. I left them a message. Hope that's okay."

"Thanks, Sam. I know everyone is just trying to get off the mountain and have their own dramas to deal with, but I do want Bridge and Ella to know what's going on." She gave Sam a hug. "And I know you've got your own family to deal with, and I want you to go take care of Dolly and Scout right now. Okay?"

"I'll be back in the morning. Promise." Sam said this knowing that by then, Bridget and Ella would have found a way to be with their friend. Lola would need them. She wasn't the kind to survive this kind of thing alone.

When Lola was alone again, alone with the man she loved even when they weren't together, she bent her head and pleaded with forces more powerful than the earthly realms that John would survive unscathed. She bent over his bed and kissed his cheeks, his forehead, and his lips. She rubbed his forearms and nibbled his fingers. "Please come back to me," she whispered.

Her knowledgeable, skilled hands massaged his legs and feet, trying to bring warmth into the coldness. Breathing in his "John" scent made her whimper. She brushed his hair off his forehead and stared longingly at one stubborn curl that refused to be tamed.

John felt so cold, so distant, and so motionless that as night descended, so did her hope.

A nurse came in and fashioned the recliner chair into a makeshift bed for her. "Get some sleep if you can," she whispered.

Lola nodded her head, but she couldn't stand the thought of sleeping so far away from him. So she climbed ever so delicately into John's bed, holding him, and believing she could will him to come back to her just by her touch.

Abandonment's neon light illuminated the dark corners of Lola's psyche, and she longed for the company of her friends: Ella and Bridget, who had always been there for her, and Gaia, who was so adept in showing her new ways to look at situations good and bad. Lola had no idea where Gaia was, but she prayed Ella and Bridget would come to her rescue. They were family. They had always counted on each other through good times and bad…a part of each other's history.

Lola tried to concentrate on this thought as she lay next to John, tossing and turning, hoping that when she awoke this terrible situation would all be a bad dream.

But it wasn't.

February 1985

GAIA

"Cabin fever" was not a term often used by the residents of Na'mow. In fact, if they used it at all, it was always uttered in disgust.

Here was the problem. Winter snow had been dumping on them since early September and showed no sign of letting up. It was February and everyone was damn tired of the cold. They'd had enough of shoveling, plowing, chaining up their cars, and adding an extra twenty minutes to their drive into Boulder every day.

Driving was a hassle. Exercise was a problem. Such things as snowshoeing and cross-country skiing, normally a family affair, were too dangerous to do alone. Packing on a few extra pounds over the winter was not uncommon. Too much fattening comfort food was the generic excuse. Crock pots smelled of stews and thick soups.

And then there was the problem of staying warm. People had begun to worry about having enough wood to last through this endless winter, and had resorted to piling on layers of clothes to conserve fuel supplies for their stoves. Not much of a tradeoff.

Ella had taken to going to yoga class during her lunch break, and today she'd even penned it into her daytimer. She was always back at work in plenty of time and felt exhilarated afterwards. She liked the slow, methodical movements. She liked the repetition. She liked the challenge of going deeper into each movement. She could truly empty her mind, focus on her breathing, and hold every pose with purpose. And besides, she was really good at it. She was very flexible, almost to a fault. In the old days, her grandmother had called it double jointed. The doctor she went to after injuring her knee while skiing called it instability. Because of her loose, overly flexible joints, she lacked the strength to hold her bones firmly in place. Not a good thing. She was in fear of dislocating her hips or knees if she didn't strengthen the muscles surrounding her joints. Thus, her love of yoga.

There were also two added bonuses. The meditative state of yoga often conjured up images of her deceased grandmother Oma, whom she loved dearly. Now she looked forward to visualizing Oma's face more and more during her routines. The image always brought Ella comfort and confidence. The second bonus was that she had stopped twirling her hair when she felt anxiety. She used her breath instead.

As she was walking into class today, a bright yellow index card stuck to the bulletin board at the entrance caught her attention. The message written in a deep purple magic marker read: *Single, spiritual woman looking for a place to rent in the mountains.* The woman's name – Gaia – was scribbled next to a phone number. Ella was excited.

She grabbed the card and headed into class. If it was the same Gaia she'd met in passing over the last few weeks, she'd tell her about the rental cabin next to her house.

Two weeks later, Gaia was officially a neighbor.

Three weeks later, Lola, Bridget, and Ella decided they'd had enough with cabin fever. It was time to get together sans children and husbands.

"We can use the cottage," Ella informed them. Gary had taken Brice and Alena to see a Care Bear movie and promised he would take them out for pizza afterwards. The kids were thrilled to have dad all to themselves, but not as thrilled as Ella was to have her "girl time."

That was all the encouragement Lola and Bridget needed. They showed up at Ella's early, which wasn't unusual for Bridget but unheard of for Lola. Both couldn't wait to get out of their houses to gossip and gab about everything and anything that didn't include kids or husbands. All they wanted was to act like silly girls for a few hours.

Ella greeted them with two surprises: a new alcoholic beverage – a Bartles and Jaymes Wine Cooler in fruity flavors – and her new renter. "The wine cooler is to remind us that spring is right around the corner. Don't you just love their commercials? Made me go out and buy some just for this special occasion. Let's drink to springtime."

"Hear, hear!" Bridget said, bottles clinking together in a toast.

"Shall we go over to the cottage? I have a new renter," Ella said.

"Well, hopefully this one will last longer than your last one," Lola teased her as they climbed the step to the cottage porch. The door swung open even before they knocked.

"Girls, we have another female on the mountain. Meet Gaia," Ella said. "And she's graciously invited us into her new abode."

"Hello. Welcome." The new mountain resident turned out to be a woman who looked like a gypsy in her flowing skirt, billowing blouse, and jewelry with funky weird signs on it.

They went inside, and Ella introduced everyone. Gaia literally stared at Bridget when she heard the redhead's name.

"Bridget? Bridget Jameson? Detroit, Michigan? I know you. I know your family," Gaia announced.

"Say what? I don't think so. Believe me, I wouldn't forget someone like you," Bridget said, her eyes playing over Gaia's wardrobe.

Because Lola was dressed pretty much like Gaia, she coughed and twirled and held out her hands as if to say, "Yeah, we both look great, don't we, Bridge?"

"Come on, Bridget. Take a guess," Gaia said. "You sat in front of me in homeroom. Nancy Johnson. I used to help you with your biology homework. My dad was a Baptist minister and my mom ran the choir. Who, by the way, weren't crazy about the fact that I changed my name. My grandmother was the only one that understood. She was always thinking outside the box. You know, she lived right here on this very mountain most of her childhood. She was a great storyteller. Always said I'd fall in love with the mountains. She was the one who encouraged me to get out of Detroit and find out what the West was all about, just like all of you. She died not too long ago and I decided to venture out here. I'm sure she's watching my every move! First thing I did when I got to Boulder was to come up here. Hiked around the lake. Was looking out for any 'For Rent' signs but didn't see any. Then…the Great Creator had a different plan…set in motion this very moment in time in this exact spot."

"Huh? You're not talking like the Nancy Johnson I knew. But, oh, my God. Now I remember. You were in all the Honors classes and a …" Bridget tried to find the right word.

"A nerd. You got it," Gaia finished her sentence.

"Well…yeah. I do remember that you wore lots of homemade jumpers and blouses with Peter Pan collars. And a silver monogrammed circle pin," Bridget said.

"Never went anywhere without it."

Bridget was shaking her head and smiling. "And let me think. Oh, yeah, and penny loafers. But I'll give you some style points for those. Everyone wore penny loafers. I think I even had a pair."

"See, we weren't so different after all."

"Yeah, but your hair was short and brown back then, with chunky-looking bangs. For God's sake, no one wore those doofus-looking bangs. I still can't believe it's you."

"Yep. Let my hair grow and permed it. These days, I streak it with Sun In. Just spray it on and presto, sun kissed. And no more glasses. Got contact lenses and love them."

"Wait a minute. Hold on." Bridget took Gaia by the shoulders and stared into her eyes. Then laughed. "Yep, it's really you. It's those weird-colored amber eyes. I'll be damned. And now we're neighbors."

"And that's not all. I've got a surprise," Ella said. "Gaia does Tarot readings, and she's volunteered to do a reading for each of us."

Lola tapped Bridget on the shoulder and mouthed, "Ten on your woo-woo scale. Looks like you're moving up."

Lola clapped her hands and giggled. Bridget frowned.

Right from the get-go, Gaia fit right in. How could she not, with the spirit of her grandmother guiding her? She could drink and laugh with the best of them. And when she placed a beautiful violet velvet pouch filled with her tarot cards on the dining room table an hour or so later, even Bridget didn't complain too loudly.

They all took their places. Gaia said a quiet prayer and then reverently opened the pouch. "If you guys are ready for this, I'll do two readings for each of you. The first will match your astrological sign. The second will be a one-card reading of what happens to be really important to you right at the moment. I do the regular Tarot spreads but I like to do these one-card versions that are sort of frowned upon by great Tarot readers. I like the spontaneity of the one-card throw," she said.

"Sounds exciting," Ella said.

"And since you're our host, we'll start with you, Ella," Gaia said.

Gaia matched Ella's Taurus sign with the Hierophant card. "The Hierophant often contains secret knowledge or something hidden," Gaia explained with a deep breath. "There is no 'I,' only the 'we.' Tradition and conventional beliefs lead to balance and conformity. You teach others how to be in community with the group. Team playing is important to you until you learn to embrace positive self-expression. You respect rules in moderation. Strict adherence to beliefs, however, stifles your soul. Know when to break free and change. Be confident in your own decisions. Your lesson is respecting yourself so that you may help others. You are the teacher."

"Wow, is that right on or what?" said Bridget, who became Gaia's next subject.

Her astrological sign was Cancer, which produced the Chariot card.

When Gaia looked up and saw the apprehension and anxiety written all over Bridget's face, she said, "Bridget, take a deep breath. Be open. Try not to control this process. I sense you're holding on too tight."

Gaia reached across the table and took Bridget's hand gently in her own. When she did, tears spilled involuntarily from the corners of Bridget's eyes. Uncharacteristically, the redhead let them drip down her cheeks, trusting her old classmate far more than she ever expected.

"Okay," she said, taking a deep breath. "I'm ready."

"The sign of Cancer," Gaia said, "is represented by the Chariot. We see that emotions are felt but often controlled, to be used for a higher purpose. So too do you control your emotions, Bridget. The charioteer controls the horses and directs them where to go, how fast to go, and knows their final destination. The horses will carry you to your final destination just as your emotions will help you to understand how to conquer your goals. Rein in your anger and face your fears head on. Believe in your abilities, and you will overcome life's most difficult challenges. Only then will you be successful. Only then will you lead."

Bridget was so overcome with the tenderness with which Gaia spoke that she wept, openly and unembarrassed. They all reached out to her, holding hands, and forming ever stronger bonds, here with this new woman in their lives.

After a moment, Gaia focused on Lola, and she leaned forward as Gaia began to talk. No one at the table was surprised to learn that the Star represented Lola's Aquarius sign.

"The Star will light your way even when you are lost. Lola, I feel that you are already in touch with this part of yourself. You light up the world with your childlike wonder. Look to the heavens for your guidance. Your intuition already leads you to trust the universe for all things. Have faith in that power and believe it will always illuminate your path, but do not rely solely on its guidance. You have to accept responsibility to make good decisions and work hard to understand not only your divinity but also your humanness. Use discernment."

When Gaia was done, Lola picked up the card and held it to her chest. This, naturally, led to some good-natured teasing. "Step away from that card, you star-stealer," Bridget said, grabbing the card and giving it quickly back to Gaia. "Keep it safe. And check your pouch before you leave tonight. I can see that our friend has her eye on it."

"At least she didn't kiss it or hang it on her fridge," Ella retorted.

"Well, now that we've gotten all spiritual, I have to admit that I need a cigarette," Gaia said. She glanced at Ella. "Do you mind?"

"Not at all. Why don't we all go outside?"

They carried their drinks out to the front porch, and Bridget used the opportunity to tease her old classmate. "So, Gaia, you've apparently picked up a couple of vices since our days in high school."

"I admit it. Tobacco and pot. And I have to say though that my Tarot readings are clearer after I smoke. I can't explain it. Just is."

When Gaia finished her cigarette and drinks had been replenished, the women took their places at the table again and Gaia prepared them for their next one-card readings. She handed the cards to Ella and said, "Take your time shuffling. And if it's easier, just spread them face down on the table and mix them all up. Remember that the cards need to be infused with your energy so that the appropriate one comes to the surface. So shuffle them well."

The girls were quiet and respectful as Ella shuffled the deck. When she was satisfied, she cut the cards. Then she selected the top one. They all stared at it.

"The Five of Cups. The card of Disappointment and Regret," Gaia said calmly. Out of respect, Bridget and Lola lowered their eyes when they saw the look of dismay that spread across Ella's face when she heard this. "Sadness fills your soul for choices past and present. It may seem hopeless until you reprioritize and re-evaluate. Open your eyes and see that change is inevitable. Change for the good."

Gaia came to her feet. She circled the table, knelt down in front of Ella, and looked into her eyes. But it wasn't Gaia that Ella saw. It was her grandmother Oma, and her rheumy eyes penetrated to her core and the gentleness of her voice pierced her sadness with these words: "Understand that change will happen, Ella. It will open your heart to happiness. You will be happy."

Ella blinked out tears as Oma faded away and Gaia's face came into focus. She didn't know what to say to this. She bit down on her lip and nodded, but the dismay continued to line her beautiful face. Finally, she pushed the deck over to Bridget. Bridget was slow to accept the cards, and when she did she took a long time shuffling, seemingly uneasy about turning over a card after hearing what Ella's had revealed. Eventually, she did.

"The Five of Worlds or Pentacles. The card of Setback," Gaia announced in a low voice.

Bridget heard these words and could not control the tears. "Fuck. What the hell is wrong with me? I'm such a crybaby tonight. This is ridiculous." She got up and stomped into the kitchen for a tissue. Everyone waited patiently. Eventually, she came back and slid into her seat. "Sorry," she said.

"I think I need to explain something," Gaia said, looking around the table. "The messages behind these cards may seem like doom and gloom, but the end result is growth. It can and will lead you to a higher calling if you believe. It will set you back on the path you chose before you entered this life. Don't ever lose sight of that. Ever!"

Gaia paused and let her words settle purposely into their consciousness. Then she gazed across the table and said, "Bridget, would you like me to continue?"

Bridget nodded yes, and Gaia took up her explanation. She said, "Focus on your spiritual development for it will carry you through the challenges of material loss. Once again your emotions come into play. Hold them too tightly in check or let them run amok, and the outcome will be the same. You will be blinded to the danger of your material and financial security. As you are humbled by loss, you will fight and gain personal success."

As before, Gaia took Bridget's hands in her own and looked directly into her eyes. She said compassionately, "You are a strong, courageous woman."

In the silence that followed, Bridget saw a thick mist fill the room, a mist that seemingly swallowed everything and everyone in the room. She felt lost. Then she saw a man's hand beckoning her to follow. Trusting him, she stepped into the fog and felt the relief of his touch. But just as suddenly, the man disappeared, and Bridget was left holding a feather.

From afar, she heard Gaia calling her name softly and shook her head, clearing her mind and returning to the comfort of Gaia's teeny living room. Her eyes opened, and she realized she was holding the feather from the band of her cowboy hat. How and why she wasn't sure, but it somehow felt right.

Now it was Lola's turn. She didn't shuffle the cards but spread them out on the table, mixing them together thoroughly. Then she confidently turned one over.

"The Fool," Gaia said, identifying the card. "Light and wonder shine forth from you like an innocent child. Spontaneity feeds your soul. Your fearlessness in trusting others may lead you into danger because you believe in the goodness of all. Do not let another take control of your being. You march to a drummer that is not of this world. You must bring yourself down to earth in order to protect yourself from too many distractions. Live and learn in the present moment so that you can make excellent decisions for yourself in the future."

The instant Lola heard the word "drummer," she was transported to another place, a place far away, and the drumming of the Ancient Ones filled her ears with a familiar rhythm.

Lola returned only when Gaia circled the table and placed her right hand on the crown of Lola's head. "Lola," she said, holding Lola's gaze. "Learn to be present and trust your gifts and abilities."

Gaia arose and ended with: "So be it!"

In that moment, the smell of roses seemed to permeate the air. Lola caught the scent and inhaled deeply. Seconds passed. A full minute. Then Bridget came to her feet and retrieved her parka from the front hall. From the front pocket, she pulled out a flask filled with Jameson. She came back, saying, "Gaia, we need some shot glasses. All of you can continue drinking this girlie wine cooler crap, but I need something stronger to clear my Irish head…and friends to share it with."

"You got it," Gaia said. She retrieved four shot glasses from the kitchen and lined them up on the living room table. Bridget took her flask and filled them to the brim. The girls each took a glass and faced her. She held hers high and said, "There is an old Oscar Wilde saying that one of my crazy Irish relatives loved to quote. Goes like this. 'Moderation is a fatal thing – nothing succeeds like excess!' Slainte!"

They drank. Bridget slammed her glass down and said, "Okay, now I feel like myself again." She poured another and downed it in one big swallow.

She slapped Gaia playfully on the shoulder and said, "Okay Gaia, now that you've revealed our deepest woo-woo shit, I, for one, want to know what the hell happened to you."

"Reveal yourself to us," Lola said, waving her hands like a sorceress.

"I've moved around a lot, I have to admit," Gaia said.

"Depending on where the universe called you, right?" Ella teased.

"Exactly." Gaia took it well, smiling broadly. "I was born and raised in Detroit, just like Bridget. As I said before, my Dad is a minister and my mom works with the choir, so needless to say they disowned me when I decided to drop out of Stanford after only two semesters. I was so burned out. I had been overachieving in school since I was five years old. My roommate introduced me to pot and dragged me to some New Age seminars and all kinds of metaphysical stuff...like a channeler that communicated with dolphins."

"Now that's one I wouldn't mind trying," Lola admitted.

"It was pretty cool," Gaia said. "And there were things like astral projection and drumming. You name it, I tried it. It was the first time in my life I was doing something I wanted to do. I loved helping people reach their potential in the unseen realms, and I loved blowing their minds when they saw it happen."

239

Sedona was home before she moved to Boulder, where the mountains beckoned to her. She talked about vortexes, the divine feminine energy, Tarot, yoga, Native American rituals, animal totems, and her love of drumming.

"I'm really a Jill of all trades, if you want to know the truth."

But she was much more than that. A gentle but powerful energy radiated from Gaia's heart chakra; her amber-colored eyes, by far her most striking physical feature, drew people into her personal space like a magnet and separated her from every other New-Ager in Colorado. Little did anyone know, but Gaia was very much in control of the people she let into her space. Without even knowing it, Lola, Ella, and Bridget had all been permitted into her sacred bubble, and now they were feeling the effects.

"Why do I keep getting whiffs of roses? Do you smell that? And it seems like it's much stronger now." Lola twitched her nose like a rabbit.

"Actually, a lot of people catch the scent of roses when I do my 'thing.' The vibrational frequency of roses is the highest of any plant, and its scent helps to raise our own frequency to a higher level. To me…it means that all the people in a room are 'in tune' with each other and that the truth is being spoken," Gaia said with a gentle smile. "We should all feel very blessed."

Everyone sniffed the air and nodded in agreement. Then Bridget sneezed and effectively broke the spell.

Ella said, "My grandmother Oma loved yellow roses. She used to say how much joy and beauty they brought into her life. So we'd always buy her yellow roses for her birthday. It was a wonderful tradition."

"I love roses too," Lola interjected. "Especially white ones. They remind me of the alluring whiteness of angel wings."

Bridget was crying and mumbling, "fuck this shit" under her breath. Everyone stared at her and waited for her to explain. Eventually she did.

"I don't know if I can hang out with you, Gaia. I can't seem to get my crying under control," she finally managed to say. "My grand-mother on my dad's side had this pitiful patch of ground that she grew roses in…peach-colored ones. My father has an old black and white photo of her standing next to a rose bush full of blooms. I love that photo. Grandma said the peach color symbolized gratitude… and it was a challenge to grow that color. The bush reminded her of all the hardships her family had to overcome and to give thanks every day."

Bridget wiped her nose. "Dad keeps that ragged old photo on his nightstand and I never realized why until now. Shit, the smell just got stronger. It's like being in a damn perfume bottle. I need some fresh air."

All the women followed Bridget outside, and it was Ella who asked, "Do you ever read your own cards, Gaia?"

"Oh, yes," she said with a smile.

"I was just thinking it might be a great way for us to get to know you."

"Thank you. I'd like that," she replied.

The prospect of this and a cold wind coming in off the lake got everyone back inside except Gaia. She was comforted by the spiral and stars carved on the door. She rubbed her grandmother's silver pendant nestled safely between her breasts. It bore the same symbol. She was grateful she had been guided to this place, the birthplace of her grandmother's fairy tales. She belonged here; it just felt right.

"Thank you, Nana," she whispered as she tugged open the front door.

Ella opened a fresh round of wine coolers. Bridget swigged Irish whiskey straight from the flask. And when everyone was seated again, Gaia shuffled the deck and turned a card over.

"Ah, the Queen of Cups," she said. "The Queen of Cups is highly intuitive, empathetic, psychic, and surrounded by an ethereal ambi-ence. She mirrors back to others lessons they need for their own

241

personal growth. Like water, she flows through the seen and unseen worlds effortlessly. Art, music, nature call to her. Balance between her heart and mind is needed for her to see clearly. She is a healer."

"Cool," Lola said, as a gust of wind rattled the windows and sent a bitter cold draft through the house. Lola shivered. "Oh God, the wind! Yuck! It's going to be a long, noisy night and I'm not talking about the party."

"Batten down the hatches." Ella folded pieces of newspaper and stuck them between the windows and the sills to stop the rattling.

"Oh, come on. It's just a little wind. It can't be all that bad," Gaia said. "Can it?"

March 1985

100 MPH

Gaia felt as if someone was trying to shake her out of a restless dream and into consciousness. A loud CRACK sounding exactly like a rifle shot snapped her out of her theta wave state and into full awareness. She sat bolt upright.

The cabin trembled with each gust of frigid, ominous wind. Her feet hit the cold, carpeted floor and sent a shudder up her spine. She looked at the clock on her nightstand and realized it had stopped at 2:35 a.m. She tried the lamp switch, but the electricity was obviously out.

Gaia trudged into the bathroom, lifted the lid, and peed. She flushed. The water drained from the bowl, but didn't fill up again. She jiggled the handle, but to no avail. She tried the shower and was greeted with three plaintive gurgles and then silence. Gaia hurried into the kitchen, picked up the phone, and was greeted with a dial tone. "Thank God." She called Ella.

"Ella, sorry to call so early, but nothing's working."

"That's because the power's out," Ella answered calmly. "So's the water, because the pump runs on electricity."

"Damn. So I guess that long hot shower isn't happening," Gaia said mournfully.

"The good news is that you have a gas stove so you can heat up some snow to sponge off with," Ella suggested.

"That's not exactly what I had in mind." Gaia grimaced.

"And, don't flush…"

"Already did," Gaia informed her. "So what am I supposed to do when I really have to go, which is probably what's going to happen in just a few minutes?

"That's what the outhouse is for, Gaia," Ella said, grinning to herself. "And on days like this we're very thankful we have it. After breakfast, I'll have Gary shovel a path for you to the outhouse. If you need to go out there before that, be sure to take some toilet paper with you. But don't leave it in there because the mice love it."

Gaia was right. She felt the urge not ten minutes later. She threw on layer after layer of clothes and coats, buckled up her boots, and set out. She bent her head and trudged through a good two feet of snow. Visibility was almost zero. She grimaced, pulled the hood of her parka tightly around her face, and realized she was staring at the source of the loud crack responsible for waking her up this morning. A beautiful old juniper, probably three feet in diameter, had been snapped in half like it was a toothpick.

"Oh my God!" The words were hardly out of her mouth when a blast of wind roared across the mountain face at what felt like 100 MPH. The gust knocked the wind from her lungs and sent the toilet paper roll flying from her hand. She fell to her knees, gasping for breath. Panic set in. She began crawling toward the outhouse, desperate to get inside and for more reasons than the obvious one.

Once inside, and with no time to latch the hook and eye lock, she ripped her pants down and squealed in shock when the ice and snow on the seat bit into her skin. She clenched her teeth against the discomfort and whispered, more pleading than prayerful, "Okay Mother Nature, I rejoice in your beauty and power. There's no need to convince me any further."

That's when she noticed the piles of paper, leaves, and cloth stuffed in the corners and heard the slight scurrying that could only be the mice Ella had mentioned.

Hurrying to finish her business, Gaia murmured, "Oh, I just want to get out of here!"

As if in answer to her prayer, another horrific gust threatened to lift the outhouse off the ground. Gaia's fertile imagination flashed on Dorothy and the Wizard of Oz at the exact moment the outhouse door shrieked in protest and was ripped from its hinges, flying through the air as if powered by its own engine.

Gaia screamed, and then shouted, "I am out of here! Where's that toilet paper!" Remembering that she had dropped it in the snow, she grabbed the doorframe and pulled herself up. That's when she saw Gary peering around the corner with his shovel in hand.

Gaia hardly blinked. "Believe it or not I am soooo happy to see you. Do you have toilet paper with you because I am about to use my scarf."

Gary grinned conspiratorially. "There's a bunch of it in the tree out here. God must have delivered it just for you."

"Gary, this is NOT funny," she said through chattering teeth. "Can you please hand me some toilet paper?"

He pulled some damp squares of paper off the tree and said, "Watch out for the pine needles. They're damn sharp. Especially in tender places."

"God, I hope the power comes back on soon," Gaia moaned. She pulled up her pants.

With a short hoot, Gary yelled back, "Don't count on it. It could be days." And he walked towards the house eyeing the woods for any trace of the door.

June 1985

FRIDAY AFTERNOON CLUB

Party time. Lola, Bridget, Ella, Gaia and their friend Sharon were gathered along with two or three thousand other people outside the Grand Hotel. The Grand was located at the base of the foothills – a beautiful view, had the girls been interested – but the eclectic crowd had all of their attention.

Friday Afternoon Club was a Grand Hotel tradition, but Gaia was the only one among their group who knew anything about it since she'd been doing palm readings on weekends for the hotel guests. "Gaia, thank you so much for telling us about this. I can't believe they do this every Friday, and we never heard about it before," Bridget said.

The vibration of a bass beating out a Motown rhythm was enough to get their blood pumping with excitement. Lola was already moving her feet, and they were all chatting with the ferocity of five prisoners suddenly freed of their winter doldrums.

The grounds were set on sixteen acres. The festivities included two outdoor bars, several beer stations, volleyball courts, a dance floor filled with people, and a stage where a band none of them had ever heard of was holding court. On top of that, it was bordered by a gorgeous creek and towering cottonwoods.

"I told you we were wasting our time at that other place," Bridget said, the other place being a bar someone had recommended in town. "I mean, free tacos are great but who cares when there's this kind of party waiting for us."

Lola had ordered one Long Island Iced Tea with five straws. "Here's our drink, girls. Hold onto your hats, because it's a stiff one." She batted her eyes and raised the glass. "I like my drinks like I like my men, good and stiff. Happy June, everyone!"

Ella looked puzzled. "Are we all drinking the same drink?" The four other women stared at her in disbelief, knowing they were all on tight budgets. "Would I be breaking some rule if I ordered my own, 'cause I could really use it."

After two or three Long Island Iced Teas, the girls were drawn in different directions – some to the dance floor, some to booths filled with art, some to the various men who couldn't seem to take their eyes off them – and Ella and Gaia found themselves arm-in-arm after two or three hours of drinking and dancing and general exploration.

"I'm fading fast, Ella," Gaia said. "What time is it?"

"Nine o'clock," Ella said, peeking at her watch.

"I've been doing readings since two this afternoon," Gaia said. "I better get myself home."

"Are you okay to drive?"

"I'll be fine. Been drinking just water for hours." Gaia waved goodbye and walked in the direction of the parking lot.

By this time the band had stopped, but the buzz of conversations, giggling, and piped music still drifted through the darkness. Ella expected to find the other girls hanging out in front of the stage, but the dance floor was deserted. Now there were two thousand partiers milling around, trying to get inside the hotel to listen to tunes and to shake it up. After all, it was still early.

Worry turned to panic as Ella strained her neck and stood on her tiptoes to get a better view. There were so many entrances and exits to the place that finding three women in this mess was going to be nearly impossible. Ella wrung her hands in worry and whispered, "Where, oh where, can those girls be?"

She spent nearly twenty minutes searching the grounds before she inadvertently found them in the hotel bathroom, chatting and giggling like three teenagers on Prom night.

"Where have you guys been? I've been looking…" Ella paused in mid-sentence when she saw what looked like a badly tended garden on top of Lola's head. "What's in your hair? Is that grass? It looks like straw or leaves or something really organic."

The other three burst out laughing, and Sharon said, "Ella, we're so glad you're here. We need your help. Get over here and help us clean this stuff out of Lola's hair." She turned to Lola. "Our good friend was rolling around in the hay with a member of the opposite sex by the look of it."

Ella looked at her disheveled friend. "Lola, do I have to remind you that you're married with a son? You're just asking for trouble."

"Oh, come on. It's just innocent flirting." Lola demurely sipped her drink through a straw; the girls looked like a group of baboons, grooming her for bugs and separating hair from organic matter. An Afro took shape, and not a very attractive one at that.

Bridget finally threw up her hands in frustration. "Fuck. I'm done," she announced. "The good news is that while you were rolling around in the grass with God knows who, I met the coolest guy who couldn't stop telling me how fabulous I was. And you know what? I have to say I really enjoyed the attention! I didn't have to talk about anybody but me. Imagine! I need more conversations like that. Repeat after me, girls. We are fucking fabulous!"

"Are we?" Ella asked, not quite believing it. "Bridget, not you too. This is how it all starts…always so innocently and then bam…you're in lust…and then you think you're in love…then you 'accidentally' have a love child. I hear it all the time from the women I counsel."

"It's just a little fun. And I like having someone think I'm fabulous, even if it's only for this one night." Bridget smiled mischievously. Ella groaned.

"Okay, I'll buy it. We are all fucking fabulous!" Sharon cheerfully repeated.

"Oh my. I may be fabulous, but I don't look it at the moment," Lola said, staring at herself in the mirror. "What the hell was I thinking?

I need waterproof mascara and better hairspray. Anyone have any Binaca?"

July 1985

WOMB ROCK

Womb Rock anticipated their arrival. It had become a favorite picnic spot for the women and their children. The kids called the woods around the rock Alice in Wonderland and why not; they believed in magic, and the place really was enchanting.

They believed in fairies and elves, and it all seemed so plausible at Womb Rock.

This was a place meant for kids, or adults pretending to be kids. Which was exactly why Bridget, Lola, and Gaia decided on a night of camping, less kids, husbands, and the intrusions of home and endless chores.

"I didn't realize it would be such a short hike. It's close. I thought we would be hiking for miles." Gaia stopped and gazed up the mountainside.

"We aren't there yet. We have to go straight up from here." Bridget pointed. "It's hard to get your bearings surrounded by all these amazing rock formations. But Womb Rock is special. Believe me, you'll know it when you see it."

Gaia called the mountain an herbal treasure trove. As they climbed, she told them of the aspirin-like qualities of aspen bark. She was surprised to find that in the shadows of the aspens osha was growing upwards of six feet tall. Its roots were used for colds and headaches. She told them about the currant bushes, the yarrow, the mullein, and the Indian paintbrush. She explained the properties of bedstraw, mullein, and a dozen other varieties of flowers.

"The Indians had a use for everything," she said, jumping a small stream and studying the quartz that littered the mountainside.

"We're here," Bridget announced suddenly. They had reached a small level clearing surrounded by monolithic rock formations and groves of fir, pine and aspens. She tossed aside her pack. "And this is a great spot for our tent and a campfire."

Lola demonstrated her approval by twirling around and around and making herself so dizzy that when she stopped she had to cling to a fir tree for support. "Damn, I love the outdoors."

Gaia stared at two imposing rocks that millions of years ago had crashed into each other. Between them was a triangular-shaped opening big enough for a person to walk through. The rocks exuded a personal intimacy, and she immediately felt connected to the divinely feminine nature of their appearance. "This place is so amazing."

"Can you believe this opening?" Lola called to her from below. "Just like a cucha. I just love it!"

"I can only imagine what a cucha is." Gaia shook her head.

"Oh, I'm sure you can guess. I made it up 'cause I liked the sound of it. It's my cute little name for va-jay-jay." Lola trotted back and forth through the rock opening, and all Gaia could do was shake her head and grin.

That's when they heard Bridget say, "Oh, gross me out!"

She was laying out their tent, and the musty odor that rose from it made the three of them hold their noses.

"So obviously Dan didn't air this sucker out after his hunting trip," Lola suggested.

"No shit," Bridget said. "And you better believe he's going to hear about it from me."

Gaia asked permission to smudge the tent to clear out any negative energy and to infuse it with new positive energy. When she was done explaining, Bridget shrugged her shoulders and said, "Be my guest. But Dan's still going to hear about it."

When the tent was set up and Gaia had finished her cleansing, Lola wanted to know more. "So, do you get any special vibes from this place, Gaia?" she eagerly asked.

"Just look around you. The whole meadow is surrounded by herbs used for childbirth."

The next five seconds were dedicated to staring blankly at Gaia before Bridget finally said, "Cut to the chase, Gaia. I, for one, don't know what the fuck you're talking about and from the look on Lola's face, neither does she." Bridget had a way of saying things that often caught people off guard, but by now Gaia was wise to her brusque style and actually found it endearing.

"You asked for it," she said, smiling. They started touring the area and moving from one plant to another.

"The first thing I notice is the uva ursi. I think you guys call it kinnikinnick. It's like a lush blanket covering this whole area. Makes you want to lie down in it. Besides being used for urinary tract infections, the Indians used it to normalize the womb after childbirth."

"No shit." Bridget found it hard to believe.

"Do you think it's a coincidence that it's growing at a place called Womb Rock? I think not." Then Gaia pointed to all the raspberry bushes bordering the kinnikinnick patch. "The berries are a food source, of course. Everyone knows that, right? But the raspberry leaves were also used to make a tea the Indians used throughout pregnancy and during childbirth. The effects baffle scientists even today, but the tea helps to strengthen and tone the uterus. It can also relax and normalize contractions during childbirth."

"That is so cool," Lola said.

"And look at all the wild rose bushes. The leaves and petals were also made into a tea to lessen labor pains and anxiety. I also noticed some junipers right below here; they would have used juniper berries for tea during and immediately after childbirth. Womb Rock is aptly named. With the wind blowing through the opening, I can hear a soft moaning. The whole area has such a very feminine vibe, don't you think?"

"Absolutely," Lola said. "Let's all take off our shoes and walk through the opening. I do that every time I'm here, and it always feels so powerful. Like a rebirth or a cleansing."

Lola took Gaia's hand and led her to the opening. When Gaia entered, she inhaled deeply and felt an electrical charge that sent a tingle from her head to her toes. She whispered, "Yes, Mother Earth, I feel your presence. Thank you for showing yourself to me today."

Then she smiled at the girls and said, "Thank you guys for bringing me here. I wish Ella could have joined us."

"Well, you know Ella. She has a little harder time putting her foot down with Gary than Lola and I do with our men," Bridget said.

They walked back to the tent, casually picking raspberries and popping them in their mouths. "No wonder the bears love this place," Lola said.

"Funny you mention that," Gaia said. "Did you know that kinnikinnick is also called bear-berry? Crazy bears apparently love to eat it even though the berries taste horrible. They know there's something medicinal about it, even if we don't. And the osha we saw growing in the aspens is called bear root because they eat the root when they're sick or wounded."

"Big Bear Medicine! Gotcha," Lola said.

"Well, we don't have to worry about bears," Bridget said matter-of-factly. "I'm packin'."

"Packing what?" Gaia asked.

"My .38 special," Bridget said as if nothing could be more obvious.

"What a minute. You brought a gun?" Gaia was flabbergasted.

"Gaia, I know you think you have all sorts of magical powers in the air here, and I know you believe you have helpers from other galaxies protecting you. Good. No problem. In fact, Lola thinks that too, for Christ's sake. But those things aren't going to be much help when a bear thinks you might be a tasty meal and decides to maul you to pieces." Bridget was enjoying herself, and both the other girls knew it, so they let her ramble. "Now, you and Lola smoke some pot, relax, and enjoy the experience of being in the Rocky Mountains. Stare up at the stars and think about which star or planet you came from. Just know that Bridget 'Sure Shot' Jameson is here to protect you guys from the creepy crawly things that go bump in the night. Wow, that just reminded me. I need to get me a shot of Jameson. The whiskey, that is."

Dusk. A changing of the guard. Creatures of the day gave way to a wave of night hunters. A symphony of rustling sounds rose with the lessening of the light. Evening touched the air with a tincture of pine, and the sweet smell of grasses and herbs retreated with the sun.

"I love this time of night," Bridget said. "I just love the transition. There's a certain energy, don't you think? A certain suspense and magic."

Bridget stopped short. Her ears picked up the echo of some distant sound, a branch breaking perhaps, or a rock breaking loose from the mountainside. And then it was gone. She listened a moment longer, then shrugged her shoulders and raised her glass. She said, "Girls, I would like to propose a toast. To 'Living, Loving and Learning' as Dr. Buscaglia has proclaimed it." Then she spread the fingers of her other hand into a Vulcan salute. "Live Long and Prosper."

Gaia and Lola both cracked up, and Gaia finally managed to say, "Have you been into that pot already, Bridget? Because that sure doesn't sound like the whiskey talking. I think you've been infused with magical thinking, oh ye of rational thought."

It was just then that the night exploded with a heart-wrenching CRACK!! It sounded like someone or something crashing through the woods. Bridget jumped to her feet yelling, "Make some noise, girls, and lots of it! If that's a bear, it should scare it away. Come on! Yell, sing, anything!"

They didn't get a chance to. Just then, a large black bundle of fur burst through the trees. Lola and Gaia screamed. Bridget didn't. She yelled, "Son of a bitch! That dog almost gave me a heart attack!"

When Lola finally caught her breath, she said, "Oh, look at that! It was a bear after all." The "bear" was Ella's Labrador retriever – whose name actually was Bear – and he was standing in front of them with his tongue hanging halfway down his legs.

His owner showed up a moment later, panting like a woman who'd just run a half-marathon. "Ella! Damn, girl, you made it." Lola threw her arms around Ella's shoulders, and Gaia and Bridget joined in. "What happened?"

"Sorry guys, if I scared you. I had serious FOMO not being here with you. Gary is furious with me."

"Screw Gary. Hell, you almost got yourself shot, girl," Bridget said. She wasn't really as pissed as she sounded. More worried. "You can't come crashing through the woods in the dark like that! What about a little 'YOO HOO' or something?"

"I know, I know. I wasn't thinking. The FOMO got the best of me. I was just so determined to be here with you guys."

"I don't mean to interrupt," Gaia said, grinning, "but what the heck is FOMO?"

"FEAR OF MISSING OUT," the girls all chanted at once, and a wave of laughter rolled over their campsite.

"Here! I have a peace offering. Vodka!" Ella held out the bottle to Lola.

"Oh my! I think it's going to be a long night." Lola unscrewed the top and took a whiff.

With nothing but straight vodka and whiskey to drink, it didn't take long for the girls to find a good excuse to crawl gratefully into their tents and fall into an inviting slumber. Too bad it didn't last. They'd been asleep for a mere two hours when Bear started barking.

"God damnit! Shut him up!" Bridget hollered from her tent, thinking this was exactly why she hadn't brought Laska.

Bear's barking may have woken them up, but Lola's piercing squeal got them all up and out of their tents. "Oh my God, I think aliens have landed! They finally came and found me. I knew they would come to the mountain someday."

"What the fuck has gotten into you, Lola?" Bridget emerged from the tent with her gun in hand, only to look skyward and gasp. "Holy shit! This gun ain't gonna work against that."

The sky to the north was alive with bright and swirling lights, and Gaia was wide eyed with joy and amazement. "Wow! I can't believe it. It's the Aurora Borealis!"

"What?" Bridget was too confused for words.

"The Northern Lights, silly. Do you know how rare it is to see them this far south?"

"I guess not, since I don't even know what the Northern Lights are." Staring at the amazing spectacle, her three best friends by her side, Bridget realized that she was going to have to revise her scale of woo-woo.

Late August 1986

IPECAC

"Are you missing something?" Mr. and Mrs. America asked Lola when she opened her front door.

Jason was Sharon's three-year-old. Actually, Jason was three and a half, as he was quick to point out to anyone interested enough to ask. At the moment, he was standing in front of the couple, his eyes averted from Lola's intense stare.

"We found him a half mile down the road walking all by himself. He said he was going to work. Can you believe that? He's on his way to work. What a crackup. We were jogging by your house and saw the neighbors dropping their kids off. Assumed he belonged here." Mr. America nudged Jason toward the door as if the kid had cooties.

"Gotta go." Both joggers looked at their watches, punched their stopwatches, and ran off without another word.

Lola didn't even question Jason. What could she say?

She sat Alena, Shauna, Jason, and two newcomers to the co-op in front of the TV and popped in a video: the original *Pinocchio*. The five kids were immediately engrossed.

Lola was the only co-op mother who consistently allowed her brood to watch videos, and they loved it. More importantly, she loved it, because it gave her a few minutes of peace and quiet. She looked up at the clock. *Thank God,* she thought. In two hours, two of the little rug rats would be off to kindergarten, and that, at least, would help with the chaos. Lola was not a big fan of chaos, especially when there were kids involved.

After lunch, the bus picked up the kindergartners, and Lola put Alena, Shauna, and Jason down for a nap. She wasn't as strict as some of the other mothers when it came to talking during naptime. Lola didn't really care what they did as long as it wasn't destructive, and as long as they didn't bother her.

I'm so sick of kids, she thought. *Especially with Nick in school all day. Nobody better have another baby, because I've changed my last diaper.*

Lola was sick and tired of the co-op. She and John rarely needed a sitter, because they rarely had a night out, and when they did, it was usually work related. *Life used to be a lot more fun before all this damn adult...wife...mother... responsibility got in the way.*

The phone rang, and with it went Lola's pity party. It was JD, the stripper from Ella's baby shower. For better or worse, Lola had kept in contact with him ever since his mountain debut. "Hey, Lola, I got you four tickets for next Saturday night's Chippendale show. Bring the girls and make a night out of it. What d'you say? I don't want to hear any lame excuses like you can't because of your rug rats." He laughed, thinking he was much funnier than she did.

"Boy toy, that's the best news I've had all day. I'm so sick of kids and an absentee husband!"

"What kids?"

"The kids I'm babysitting. I have…well, it's too hard to explain, especially for a single guy with zero responsibility. Thank God they're down for a nap right now." Lola heard a noise. "Maybe I spoke too soon. Hang on a minute." She walked into the bedroom and saw all the kids standing up in the middle of the room, with little golden gel caps stuck in their hair and all over their clothes and littering the floor.

"What the hell are those?" She looked closer. "Oh my God! It's my Vitamin E. Did you eat these?" Jason started crying.

Alena said, "No way." Lola plucked one off of her sweater and noticed bite marks. She ran back to the phone and said to JD, "I've got a fricking disaster here. Hang up! I've got to call Gaia."

"But what about Saturday night?"

"Pencil me in. I'll call you later."

Lola was shaking as she dialed Gaia's number. "Oh, please be home." Alena, Shauna, and Jason stared up at her like zombies. They didn't dare touch the Vitamin E covering their faces, hands, and clothes, not after the scolding Lola had just given them.

Gaia answered, and Lola blurted out her dilemma. "Do you have Ipecac?" Gaia asked calmly.

"You mean the stuff that makes them throw up? Think so."

"Just to be safe," Gaia said. "Get their systems cleaned out." Uncharacteristically, Lola mouthed a silent "fuck" as she hung up.

She was not too thrilled about spending the rest of the afternoon with puking children, but's that what she did. She bribed them with animal crackers, and they took their Ipecac with a minimum amount of tears.

Lola took them outside to do their business, and then inspected the results to see who had swallowed the most. Naturally, Alena, who was nearly as cautious as her mom, had swallowed the fewest, while Jason, all boy, had pounded down a good two dozen. Well, big surprise, Lola thought.

When the three were bathed and wearing clean clothes, they got their animal crackers and another video while Lola lay on the couch with cucumber slices over her eyes and a Vitamin E mask on her face.

The phone rang, and Alena, always willing to please and very accommodating for her four and a half years, answered. She put down the phone after listening for ten seconds, took a cucumber off Lola's right eye, and said, "He wants to talk to you."

"Who's he?" Lola asked. Alena shrugged her shoulders and sat back down in front of the TV.

"Hello?" Lola hadn't moved, and she held the phone away from her ear so as not to get Vitamin E oil on it.

"Did you pick up my dry cleaning? We have a charity event to go to Saturday night with my partners." Not a lot of warmth in John's voice.

A bolt of anger caused Lola to rip the cucumber slice from her other eye and jump to her feet. "Why don't you start with 'Hi, honey, how's it going?' Do you even care? Do you know I have a house full of kids today? Do you know I just made them all throw up and then washed them up, re-clothed them, re-fed them and now I'm re-entertaining them! You better be home by dinnertime WITH dinner, and I'm not talking about pizza!"

"I told you I am working late every night this week," John said, completely unfazed. "I'm working on that big case. I already told you that...about a dozen times."

"But I need you," she whined. "You have no idea what I'm going through."

John wasn't sympathetic. He said, "I can't help you, Lola. This case starts next week, and I still have a ton of work to do. Call one of your girlfriends."

"Sure, John, I'll just do that. I'll call all of my girlfriends because we'll be going out Saturday night!" Lola paced back and forth.

"But I expect you to go to the event with me. It's important, and I want my beautiful wife by my side Saturday night."

"Yeah, and I've been needing my handsome husband too. But you'll adjust to being alone. I have. Oh, and dear, don't forget to pick up your own fricking dry cleaning!" Lola slammed down the phone so hard the kids looked up from their movie.

She inhaled three deep breaths, twirled around, jumped back on her couch, replaced the cucumber slices on her eyes and sighed, "Chippendales, here I come!"

"Chip and Dale? You mean Alvin and the chipmunks? Do you have one of their videos, Lola?" Alena asked innocently. When Lola heard this, she nearly laughed herself off the couch.

September 1986

HEADLINES

Danger was the furthest thing from Bridget's mind.

This was all about an evening of fun. Little did she know.

The Chippendale's show last Saturday night had been such a blast that when Sharon told them about the all-black male review at a club in Denver, she, Ella, Lola, and Gaia couldn't wait to go. None of them had ever seen a strip show before last week, and, after tasting what it was all about, they couldn't wait to see another one.

Bridget spent the majority of the drive venting.

"I'm so fucking sick of Dan's shit," she fumed. "He and his loser buddies sit around our house all weekend drinking beer, shooting guns, and talking gear head crap like that's all there is in the world! Dan doesn't even know he has a wife and kids anymore. Now that asshole, Harvey, has started bringing cocaine up. Dan can't handle that stuff at all. He gets so emotionally abusive on coke that he's just not himself. He doesn't seem to notice how badly it affects him. Honestly, I can't even leave the kids with him if his friends are around. It's not safe. Thank God Betty offered to watch them for me tonight."

"If I know Betty," Ella said with a grin, "I just bet a part of her wishes she was coming with us tonight."

That was six hours ago. Bridget gazed out the window barely hearing the chatter going on in the car. It was late, well after midnight. She was tired and reflective. They were all lucky to be alive as far as she was concerned.

She pictured the headlines:

Five Women Hospitalized – Violence erupts in a neighborhood bar on the east side of the city. Racial Conflict cited as cause for the disturbance. Five White Women Attacked and Beaten – The attack came at the hands of a group of black women while attending an all-black male review. The women stated that they had no idea that going onto the stage and touching the dancers was not allowed. Their injuries are not critical, but all five women remained in the hospital overnight for observation.

Bridget snapped out of her reverie in time to hear Lola exclaim, "That one with the pink bow tie around his neck was just so choco-licious! I just couldn't help myself. I had to wrap my legs around him!"

Sharon joined in. "Oh yeah, and trust me. He loved that sandwich thing we did with him. He couldn't get enough of us! If Ella hadn't thrown up on the floor, I don't think those women would have gotten so pissed off. Well, maybe we were a little in their face with the dirty dancing."

Ella huddled miserably in the corner of the back seat. "I'm telling you, someone put a drug in my drink," she moaned. "When I told the waitress, she thought I was accusing her. That's when she started screaming at us, calling us a bunch of lying white bitches and that we needed to know whose turf we were on. God, we were so full of ourselves. I can understand why they were so pissed. Breaking rules we didn't know even existed. Acting like we owned the joint. I would have been pissed too."

Bridget finally spoke up. "Damn, ladies. We're fucking lucky to be alive! Gaia, thanks for getting us out of there when you did. I was ready to start showing them some of my Irish." Gaia was the only sane and sober one among them, and she had gotten them out through the back door in the nick of time. "I know this is going to sound weird coming from me, but there must have been some of Lola's angels looking out for us tonight."

"Did you girls see that line of men waiting to get in after the show?" It was like Lola hadn't heard a thing. "Too bad we had to leave when we did. That could have been a lot of fun."

All heads turned to look at Lola, and Gaia said what they were all thinking: "Is she for real?"

Summer 1987

WATERFALL

The mountains of the Western Slope shed their winter snow, and by June the spring runoff had begun in earnest. Streams and rivers raged, and the lake at the base of Na'mow swelled.

The waterfall at the lake's edge was a hidden gem. Few flatlanders even knew it existed. But the citizens of the mountain visited it regularly during the summer, knowing it would dry to a trickle later in the season.

The girls and their kids hiked there as often as possible. The path they favored meandered through aspen groves and stands of fir and juniper, and finally ended in a steep downward climb into a shadowed ravine. Hot and sweaty from exertion, the coolness of the shady trees and the even cooler waters of the pool at the base of the waterfall were a welcome respite to them all. Everyone traded their hiking clothes for bathing suits and plunged unabashed into the frigid water. The kids squealed with delight, and the adults made themselves comfortable.

Ella found great enjoyment and comfort from this place. Her peripheral vision seemed to catch movements that others missed: a little flickering as the sun hit the splashing water and reflected prisms of light everywhere. Shadows taking the forms of animals and impish elves. A gust flirting with the treetops.

She and Sharon sitting on the big mossy rocks lining the pool and keeping watch. Lola tossing one kid after another into the water. Bridget and Gaia laying out blankets and towels and snacks galore. Who could ask for more?

Suddenly, a golden eagle's magnificent cry echoed from the treetops, and everyone followed the sound. Dragonflies hovered over the water. Butterflies of every color danced above bergamot plants, gorging themselves on the nectar of the frilly purple flowers. A colorful western tanager flew from tree to tree as mountain chickadees foraged.

In the beginning, the children seemed to have endless energy. But after an hour or so, they made their way to the refreshments and wrapped sun-warmed towels around their wet bodies. Gaia told them stories of water spirits, sprites, fairies and elves, of Peter Pan and Winnie the Pooh, and of a wonderful world where all lived as one.

Eventually, heavy-lidded eyes gave way to sleep, and the campsite grew quiet. Gaia lit a votive candle and placed it on a mat in the center of a large blanket. Then she retrieved folded pieces of paper from her backpack.

"Can we make a circle?" she asked the women.

The five of them came together on the blanket, sitting cross legged, and forming a tight circle around the candle. They held hands, and Gaia said, "As you stare into the flame of this candle, please just let your imaginations run free. Let the flame ignite and spark a primal stirring within your being. Now close your eyes and feel the power in the center of your core. Feel the earth supporting you and grounding you as you sit here and become one with the flame. Don't forget to breathe. Take in the elixir of life. Share your energy with the circle. Feel your blood pulsating throughout your body..."

Bridget exploded in laughter.

"Bridget?" Ella said.

"I'm so sorry, but I just couldn't hold it back any longer," Bridget confessed. "You know this woo-woo stuff...I mean, I admire you Gaia, but I really think it's all a load of crap!"

"Really? Is that why you tear up every time I do a reading?" Gaia said calmly. "Bridget, something is trying to get through to you, and it's touching you at your very core. Humor me and just try and flow with this little meditation. Will you do that?"

Bridget looked around the circle, at the faces of her friends gazing back at her. She felt Lola's and Ella's hands in hers. Eventually, she stole a deep breath, nodded in Gaia's direction, and said, "Okay."

"Thank you," Gaia said softly. "Now please close your eyes and picture the candle's flame in your mind. Everyone with me?"

When no one spoke, Gaia continued in a low voice. "Ignite the Fire of illumination of your unconscious mind. Breathe. Go deeper within. Imagine. Listen to the pulse of your Spirit. Breathe. You are sitting here at the edge of the waterfall's pool. You hear something. You might smell it. Breathe it in. Listen. Watch for it in your mind's eye. It's so close. It brushes up against you. Slowly open your eyes... have soft focus. Now pick one of the papers out of the pile. Don't open it. Hold it in your hands."

Gaia waited until each of them had chosen her paper, and she took the last of them. "Now close your eyes. Repeat after me: 'This animal's essence will be honored by me. I will receive its message. It is a mirror, a mirror reflecting back to me my life's challenges at this very moment. My choice is to open my eyes and see.'"

When the quiet whispers of her friends fell to silence, Gaia said, "Open your eyes. And now your paper. You don't have to share your animal totem with anyone. In fact, it's better that you hold it sacred only for you."

Ella was first. She stared at the words written on her paper, and tears filled her eyes. It read:

> COYOTE
> The Trickster
> Accept the love of your pack.
> You are avoiding something you don't want to look at in your own life.
> You are too smart to lose everything you hold dear.
> Enjoy the simple pleasures of your life.
> Smile and laugh often.

Ella closed her eyes and drew a deep breath. Next to her, Bridget very cautiously opened her paper. It read:

> BEAR
> Formidable appearance, protective of family, stands up to fight
> You are too quick to anger and overly confident.
> Your inner strength will stand up against challenges on all levels.
> Learn to be a gentle giant in words, actions, and deeds.
> You will survive.

Bridget read the words again and then held the paper to her chest. She saw Lola reading her paper and heard her chuckle.

> HORSE
> Beautiful, grace in motion, endurance, stamina

Because of your free spirited nature, you may surrender
too much of who you are and let others control you.
They ride you into danger.
Sometimes you need to buck a few people off your back.
Use more caution when you feel your joy and playfulness
of life.

Lola smiled across the circle at Gaia, and then glanced at Sharon. Sharon didn't believe in any of this New Age nonsense, but she opened her paper slowly nonetheless.

MOUSE
You are "mousy" and timid. Stop hiding. Face your fears.
You can nit pick, become judgmental, and be overly critical.
Get out of your routine so you don't become boring.
Use discerning curiosity.

Sharon continued to stare at the words while Gaia took a deep breath and looked skyward. Then she opened her paper and turned her eyes on the words.

DEER
Sensitive, gentle, aware.
You sacrifice too much for the greater good and lose
your individuality.
You are aware of the hidden.
You teach others to open their hearts to love their lives.
Learn to receive from others.

A sense of peace seemed to sweep over the circle, and Gaia explained that the smoke of the candle would carry their intentions, prayers, and wishes to the heavens and make them come true, and she finished just as the kids began to rouse.

"What's going on?" Alena asked.

"We've been meditating," Ella said. "Want to join us?"

When the kids were all seated with their respective moms, Gaia said, "Okay, everyone, you kids too, think of a wish or a prayer." She waited. "Everyone have it in their mind what they want? I'm going to blow out this candle and the smoke will rise higher and higher, and then sometime soon that wish or prayer will be answered."

When they were done and the smoke had dissipated, Michael lifted his face to his mom and asked with as much seriousness as a seven-year-old could muster, "Mom, will that really happen? Will my prayer be answered?"

Bridget looked at his solemn little face and replied, "Did you wish for something big?"

"No," he said. "I prayed for the witch to go away."

Lola and Bridget exchanged a glance, and Lola shook her head and grinned. Bridget knew exactly what she was thinking. She was thinking that this woo-woo shit was certainly trying to become a part of her everyday life, and she didn't like it one bit.

Nonetheless, she looked at Michael and tenderly asked, "What witch, Michael?"

He said, "The witch that lives in the cave on the other side of the lake. She comes in my dreams."

Bridget squatted down and looked deep into Michael's eyes, her heart aching at the look of anxiety she saw there. "Tell me what happens in your dream, honey."

Her son's lower lip quivered and tears welled up in his eyes. "You should know, because you go there too. So does Nick's mom and Brice's mom."

"Michael, it's a dream. There's no way for me to know what happens in your dream."

Michael took a deep breath. "Mom, she's really, really scary. Her face is all black and blue, and she only has one eye. Her hair is all messed up with tangles and sticks and stuff in it. One time I saw her teeth and they were all red like with blood or something." Michael shuddered. "It's always winter out when you guys go over there. There's a rope swing that goes over the lake, and a deer is always waiting to take you to the cave. One time, I snuck into the cave without any one seeing me. I was so scared. I didn't want to do it, but I had to. It seems like you were washing something in a big pot. I think it was a blanket, but it looked like the shirts dad wears when he cuts firewood. You know, the ones that look like a checkerboard." Michael looked up at Bridget to see if she believed him.

Even as Michael was talking, Gaia had drawn close. And now she leaned even closer and said in a voice that was both soft and sure, "He's talking about the Cailleach, the Goddess of Winter."

Bridget's eyes widened, and a distant memory surfaced in her mind. "Oh, my goodness. Cally Bear!" she exclaimed. "My grandmother used to tell me about the Cally Bear, especially when it was really cold and snowing. I would get so mad because I couldn't go out and play, and she compared me to Brighid, the Queen of Summer. I guess Brighid was always fighting with Cally and trying to get her to go away. She said I looked just like Brighid with my fiery red hair, always shaking it back and forth to bring light and warmth into the day. I had forgotten all about that!"

"That's so cool," Gaia said. She looked down at Michael and shared her warmest smile. "In Ireland, which is where your ancestors are from, they call a white blanket of snow the Cailleach. In their stories, the Cailleach looks just like your witch."

"Really? You're not making it up?" Michael said hopefully.

"You bet, buddy. I can show you a book I have about it. The Cailleach is just part of nature's cycle. You like to ski and sled and have snowball fights, don't you?" Michael nodded enthusiastically. "Well then, if it weren't for your winter witch we'd never have cold or snow and you wouldn't be able to enjoy those things. If it weren't for her, you wouldn't have any snowy fun at all."

Michael's face brightened, and he turned back to Bridget. "You know what, Mom? I think I got my wish. The witch isn't so scary anymore, not if she brings the snow. I'll just try not to look at her face next time."

Everyone laughed when they heard this. Bridget tousled her son's hair and gave him a fierce hug.

FIRE

Day 3

"Change and choices spiral around each other and end in a dance that can come at a high personal cost. Consent to your life as the earth endures you by yielding, by evolving, by nourishing"
~ The Circle of Na'mow Handbook – Martha, First Generation

September 16, 1996, Monday morning

By Day Three of any wildfire, you've either escaped or been destroyed.

The Plains tribes were a mobile people. They carried their homes on their backs. They moved with the seasons, with the fickle nature of their food supply, or with the even more fickle nature of Eru'tan.

These indigenous inhabitants didn't pour foundations or build walls of wood or brick. It wasn't that certain locations in their migrations didn't hold a special place in their hearts. Many did, Na'mow among them. But what they held closer to their hearts was survival. And if this meant fleeing in the face of a wall of flames, they weren't sentimental about it.

White men liked to put down roots. They liked solid walls. They liked a permanent source of water. They liked a church with pews.

They liked the security of a town with a general store. They liked a system of laws and someone to carry out those laws.

Fire was something white men chose to fight. It wasn't a lack of respect for Eru'tan exactly, but it was certainly a lack of understanding.

"Eru'tan is not sentimental," Chimalis told the First Generation of the Circle. "If you choose to stay in the face of a wildfire, don't blame her if it goes bad."

The members of the Second and Third Generations of the Circle learned to define what "bad" meant. Losing your house was bad. Losing a loved one was very bad. You could rebuild a house. There was no bringing back a man, woman, or child lost because you were too slow to pack your bags and get out or too pig-headed to think you should.

LOLA

Sam showed up at the hospital early.

On his way in, he talked to Ella and Bridget to see if and when they planned on meeting up with Lola. Both were dealing with their own fair share of complications, especially with the fire – kids, work, evacuation – but both said they would be with her as soon as possible.

Nick came to the hospital on his way to school. He'd spent a sleepless night at his friend's house and looked small and frail with his backpack slung over his shoulder. Lola met him in the hall outside John's room.

"Hey. How you doing?" Lola was determined to put up a strong front for their son, no matter what, and she wrapped him in a strong, maternal hug.

"I don't want to go in there, Mom," Nick confessed. He tossed a furtive glance in the direction of his dad's hospital room. "I just want to remember him like he was before the stroke."

"It's okay," Lola told him. "Go to school. Be with your friends. If there's any change, I'll call you. Otherwise, we'll get some dinner together later tonight in the hospital cafeteria. Mrs. Jenkins said you can stay at their house as long as you need to."

They hugged for the longest time. Then Nick hurried out. Lola didn't blame him. She went into the bathroom in John's room and threw up, except there wasn't much to throw up. When the dry heaves passed, she got to her feet and stared into the bathroom mirror. She ran her hand over her forehead, stopping to stare at her widow's peak. She mumbled, "Some kind of sick cosmic joke," and then a bout of sobs consumed her. Her hair was pulled back into a messy ponytail, her eyes were dark and sunken, and she looked like she had aged twenty years overnight. Clothes hung on her frame. Zombie-like, she shuffled back into the room and dropped into the chair next to John's bed.

Sam knocked, and then moved silently into the room.

"I had a helluva time getting in here. There's a bunch of new nurses, and every one of them ready to turn away anyone but family. I lied and told them I was your brother." Sam walked over to John and touched his lifeless hand. "Any change?"

Lola shook her head. "The doctors said there's too much damage. They don't expect him to wake up. I'm hoping for a miracle. It just doesn't seem fair...such a smart guy...so athletic. I never had a chance to tell him...about...about the baby." She broke down again, sobbing almost uncontrollably. Where all the tears came from, she honestly didn't know.

Sam put an arm around her shoulders. "What have you had to eat this morning?"

Lola shook her head again. "Nothing."

"That does it. You're coming with me. John's in good hands here, and you're going to shower, eat, and get some fresh air. And you and I know exactly why, don't we?" Sam helped her up. "I'll meet you in the hall."

Lola leaned over John's inert body and covered his forehead in little kisses. Then she backed away, turned, and closed the door quietly behind her.

They walked in silence to the parking lot, and the silence continued as they started away. "I know it's hard to put a foot in a closed mouth, Lola, but you are scarin' me with your silence, girl," Sam finally said. He patted her hand. She grabbed his and held on.

"All those years, lost. I could've been better to him, Sam. Tried harder to understand what he was going through, working so hard to provide for us. Sam, he loved me just the way I was. Am. And I just let him slip away without a thought about his feelings. It was all my fault. It was always about me. Always about me..."

"If you don't mind me saying, darlin', it takes two. But in your case, there were two or three others that hitchhiked that road called crazy with you, and there was nothing and nobody going to stop you till you hit a big concrete wall or ran out of gas. Lola, every path has a few puddles, and you got wetter than most," Sam said with an enormous amount of understanding. "But promise me, no regrets. Nothing you can do about it now. And besides, everything you've gone through, every step, every misstep, all of it has made you...all of you...stronger in the end. You need to gather up all that strength, Lola."

August 1987

DENNY'S

Sam looked at his watch. It was 2:00 a.m. He talked to himself the way he always did when he was trying to stay awake. "This is the part of the job I hate. Sitting around in the middle of the night waiting for someone to do something stupid. I'm going to give this another thirty minutes, then I'm calling it a night. If she's really having an affair, this won't be the only night."

Suddenly, Sam sat bolt upright, stared out the window at the hotel exit, and whistled under his breath. "Not exactly who I was looking for but, what…do…we…have…here? Things are about to get a whole lot more in-tur-es-tin.'"

He picked up his binoculars just to make sure his eyes weren't deceiving him. "Yeah, it is. Lola."

Lola and a man "not her husband" strolled arm in arm out of a heavily landscaped side exit of the hotel.

Four hours of sheer boredom had suddenly been interrupted by a new turn of events that finally got his adrenalin pumping. He turned the key in the ignition, and the engine quietly purred to life. Curious, he followed Lola and the man who was "not the husband" as far as the local Denny's, brushed his thumb and index finger over his mustache, and said the words out loud. "Denny's. At 2:00 a.m.? Damn."

Sam watched as Lola and "whomever" walked into the Denny's and greeted a table of four other night owls.

"DAMN! OH, HELL!" Sam unbuckled his seat belt and headed straight for the front door. He approached the most boisterous group in the restaurant and recognized Bridget's raucous laughter before seeing her.

"Ladies," Sam announced. He smirked at Lola, glanced blithely at Bridget and Sharon, and managed to completely ignore the three men sitting at the table.

"Sam?" The girls giggled as if it were the most natural thing in the world to see him at Denny's at two in the morning. The guys didn't share their nonchalance. They looked distinctly uncomfortable, eyes darting from one to the other as if the cat were suddenly out of the bag.

"Whatcha doin' out so late by yourself, Sam? Did your new girlfriend dump ya?" Sharon slurred her words, clapping and laughing almost uncontrollably.

Sam anchored his hands on the table and whispered, "Nope. I'm on a job. I was hired by a man to investigate his wife's extracurricular activities."

The girls exploded into drunken, sloppy laughter as the smell of whiskey and beer wafted unpleasantly up Sam's nose. He noticed that the guys were definitely not laughing.

The one named JD looked at his watch and said, "Well, I guess I'm out of here. It's getting late." His buddies agreed wholeheartedly.

One of them bent over as he slid out of the booth and gave Sharon a deep penetrating kiss, and ended it with a big slurping smack of his lips. "Call me when you get home and tell me a bedtime story."

"You betcha, baby." Sharon gave Sam a sideways smile and a wink.

The other one, obviously Bridget's companion, hardly gave her a glance, and Bridget was thankful. Then he turned at the last second and mouthed, "Call you tomorrow." Sam slid in next to Lola. "Which one of you lovely ladies has the privilege of driving everyone home this morning?"

"Morning?" Lola asked. "Oh my, that's right. Time flies when you're having fun!" Sam had never seen the girls like this. He was searching for the words to describe it, and all he could come up with was irresponsible. *Dagnabbit! Just plain ol' irresponsible,* he thought.

Once again Sam asked, "Who's driving?"

Sharon's arm shot straight up toward the ceiling and her hand waved frantically in the air. "I am. I am. It's my turn." Her eyes were glassy and bloodshot. Mascara was smeared underneath her lower lashes. She was not a pretty sight.

"Yeah, right. I can smell the booze on you from across the room! Ladies, it's your lucky night. Sam Winston, chauffeur extraordinaire at your service." He removed his cowboy hat, placed it over his heart and slightly bowed.

"Ladies, if you would follow me," he instructed. They followed him out, even if a little begrudgingly. "This is a very good idea, you realize. You don't want to risk getting in ANY MORE trouble."

Their heads snapped in unison in Sam's direction, but he merely whistled a tune through a big shit-eating grin.

When they were inside his car, he said. "Seat belts fastened?" and then laughed. "And if any of you girls are thinkin' about pukin' you'd better give me plenty of warning. I do NOT clean up anyone's 'too much fun vomit'! Got it?" He gave them one last disapproving look. "And one of you was really going to drive? Wow!"

Lola looked at Bridget and sweetly but smugly said, "I didn't know chauffeurs were of such privileged status as to ask personal questions of their employers?"

"Well Miss Lola, I ain't juz no reg'lar showfur, I'm also your pers'n'l bodyguard and con-fee-daunt."

"In that case, the plan was to sit and drink coffee until we sobered up a bit. Maybe even have a greasy spoon breakfast."

"Sobered up a bit? Why, you sweet things, you. Why should I believe that when it appears your judgment is lacking in some other areas of your life?"

Bridget finally broke her silence. "Shit Sam, we're just out having fun with some friends. Nothing wrong with that! Come on. How much trouble can we get into at Denny's for Christ's sake?"

"How about getting in a heap of trouble at a certain unnamed hotel at the base of the mountain?" Sam glanced over his right shoulder and looked straight at Lola.

A suddenly sober Bridget squeezed Lola's hand hard and sat bolt upright. "Sam, just who the fuck hired you?"

Late August 1987

DENIAL

Ella was hung over again. Two drinks had turned into who-knows-how-many. Again. She was talking to herself, and it wasn't pretty. "I hate sunup. Mostly I hate what follows sunup. Definitely my least favorite time of day." First there was the sun, which hurt her eyes no end. Then there were the kids. Always the kids. Fixing their breakfast, fixing their lunches, brushing their teeth, combing their hair. And God knows what else. Every morning her head pulsed with the same dull ache, and every morning she said the same thing. "Tonight, I promise. Only two and then I'll feel better. I know I will."

She yelled up the stairs. "Brice, hurry up. You're not even dressed. You won't have time to eat anything before the school bus gets here."

"Where's my black shirt?" he yelled back in frustration.

"It's dirty. You know that. Pick another one. And hurry up! We're really running late!"

Ella hustled into her room and grabbed the first thing she saw out of her closet. How she dressed didn't even register on the list of things she cared about. Her hair and makeup weren't much of a priority either.

"Look at the bags under your eyes," she said, staring at her reflection in the mirror.

A loud crash snapped her out of it and sent her running. She found Brice in the laundry room surrounded by a pile of dirty clothes. Next to him was a shattered bottle, shards of glass strewn everywhere, and a clear, odorless liquid flooding the floor.

"It's not my fault! I was just trying to find my black shirt. How was I supposed to know that was a liquor bottle in there?"

Gary walked through the doorway at that very moment and a look of anger and disbelief lit his face. "Brice, get dressed NOW! Get your sister and go wait for the bus. I am not going to say it again!"

Brice didn't need any more encouragement than the sight of his dad's fists clenched at his sides, and he scurried up the stairs yelling for Alena to get her butt moving or they'd both be late.

A red-faced Gary bent over and picked up a piece of the broken vodka bottle. He held it up in front of his wife's face. "Ella, what the hell is going on? Was this in the clothes hamper?"

Ella attempted to swallow down the panic that had been rising through her chest and up into her throat since the moment she walked into the laundry room.

"How should I know?" She mustered all the defiance she could into one look and glared at him. "I can't keep track of everything that goes on in this house! And right now I have to leave for work."

Gary caught his wife by the forearm as she attempted to shoulder her way past him. "Ella, we're going to talk about this. This isn't the first time a bottle has shown up somewhere it didn't belong. I'm not stupid! There's a problem here and we have to address it. Honey, look at me. I'm worried about you. I'm your husband and your friend. I want to help you. Don't you understand that? Please, Ella, talk to me."

"Honestly, Gary, you're making a mountain out of a molehill. I'm stressed out. That's all. I get to listen to the worst kind of misery and mental illness all day long and then I come home and deal with you and the kids and every other damn thing in this house," she said, her mind whirling. "Tell me this. Where were you when Bear died last week? Huh? Were you here to see him struggling to stand up out of his own urine or hear the rattling in his chest as he took his last breaths? No. You were at some...some conference. It was just me and the kids watching our dog die. I was the one that had to be strong for them. I was the one who took our poor Bear to the vet to be euthanized and watch the life flow out of him."

She was rambling. The words came out of nowhere, but she didn't try and rein them in. They were her only defense. "I loved that dog! Do you even know that the small pewter container on the dresser contains his ashes? Did you thank me for taking care of our children's emotional needs when the shit hit the fan? Answer me, damn it! I thought as much…No, nothing, zip. Well, nobody is taking care of my needs but me. So what if I have a couple of cocktails at night to take the edge off, I don't want to hear about it from you! You got it? *Honey?* You want to help me? Look at all these dirty clothes. Try doing the laundry once in a while." Ella shook free of his grasp. She averted her eyes as she moved past him, grabbed her car keys, and headed for the door. "Thanks for all your concern, but I don't need it. I'm fine, just fine."

"Do you think the kids think you're fine?" Gary shot back, but the banging of the front door as she stormed out was his only answer.

Fall 1989

AFFAIRS OF THE HEART

Bridget and Lola watched the soccer game from the safety of the sidelines.

"Thanks so much for being my chauffeur today," Bridget said. She pulled the hair tie out of her hair, shook loose her ponytail, and laid back in the cool grass.

After ten seconds of prolonged silence, she rolled onto her side, propped her head up on her hand, and saw that Lola had her eyes closed. She gave her a nudge. "Earth to Lola. Is anybody home? You there? Hey, listen, I know it was a pain for you to pick up Alena and Shauna and then rush out to get me after work. Damn car! Dan said he'd have it fixed yesterday but I guess it wasn't a priority for him. Anyway, thanks for pickin' and takin'. I owe you one."

"What? Huh?" Lola's eyes opened and slowly focused back on the present. "Pickin' and takin'? What's that?"

The redhead laughed. "That's what my mom always called it. Who's pickin' and who's takin'?"

Lola was still only about half there, and Bridget said, "You okay?"

"I was just thinking how boring things have gotten with my life. I think it's because I do bore pretty easily. This thing with JD. I mean, the edge and danger are both gone. That and all the coke he's doing are killing our little dalliances." Lola let out a long deep sigh. "I get so jealous hearing about you and Steve."

Bridget made sure the kids were out of earshot and lowered her voice.

"Lola, I really don't know what the hell I'm doing. It's just crazy. I feel so guilty sneaking around behind Dan's back, but I can't stop. Dan and I haven't connected on ANYTHING for such a long time. All he wants to do is hang out with the guys and drink beer."

"Hey, I get it. I mean, we're all going through a rough patch."

"But Dan is a total ass to the kids and me. I mean downright mean. Ever since I started working full time, we hardly see each other. And when we do, all we do is fight. Same fight, over and over. I want him to be more involved with the family, and he wants us to kiss his ass! And I have to tell you, I truly hate sitting in an office all day while Dan works whatever schedule he wants." Bridget was nearly a year into her job with the software company, and Dan was doing sales for an alternative heating company that was just getting off the ground. "I'm really sick of his lack of motivation and crappy attitude about everything. I swear if I have to keep doing it all I'm going to lighten the load. Steve, on the other hand, is the highlight of my life. He's so appreciative of everything I do for him, just little things. He always makes me feel so beautiful and…special. You know? I can't explain it, but he's like a drug. I'm even addicted to his smell. I never knew that I could surrender so completely to a man. Hell, it's like I have no will of my own and don't really care."

She and Lola exchanged a knowing glance. "Hey, don't raise those perfectly plucked eyebrows at me. Yeah, me. I know, surrender is not usually in my vocabulary. It's like riding a kick-ass roller-coaster, scared as crap one second and delirious with excitement the next. God, I have tremendous Irish Catholic guilt about it, but that doesn't stop me. I mean, what's wrong with me? With us?"

At exactly six o'clock, soccer practice ended but the boys were still brimming with energy. They ran over, and Nick more or less shouted, "Joey is having a birthday party at his house right now and we want to go."

"Is that okay, Mom?" Michael blurted out.

"What? No way, Michael," Bridget said. "Time to get home. It's a school night and Shauna and Alena are exhausted."

"And besides, you both have homework, if I'm not mistaken," Lola added.

"You never let us do anything!" Michael shouted. "I hate living in the mountains!"

"We always miss out on all the fun!" Nick said, picking up their mutual protest.

Just then, Joey's mom walked over and said, "It's kind of last minute but Joey wants to have a few of his friends over for burgers and cake in the back yard. I told him I would do it, but everyone has to leave by eight o'clock. Can the boys come?"

The two mountain mothers understood how frustrated the boys felt being isolated from their friends in Boulder, and seemed to come to the same decision at the same moment.

"Okay, okay. But we have to call Ella and make sure she's okay with Alena staying out for a while. I'm sure it will be okay," Bridget said. "You guys go ahead and walk with the rest of the boys to Joey's. We'll pick you up there in a little bit."

"Hey, girls!" Lola called to Shauna and Alena. "You want to go out for pizza?"

There was a "Yippee!" from Shauna and an "Oh, yeah!" from Alena. And then Shauna went a step further and asked, "Can we have a cola too?"

"No, but I'll consider a lemon lime soda if you don't nag us." Bridget smiled.

"Come on, Mom," Shauna pleaded, though it sounded a lot like whining to her mom.

Bridget said, "It's that or milk, take your pick."

"Okay. Lemon lime soda." Shauna took Alena's hand, and they skipped gleefully across the field.

October 1989

LETTING GO

Red wine usually accompanied a delicious Italian dinner or was served as a relaxing elixir after a long day. Not tonight. Tonight it was meant to calm Lola's frazzled nerves. She was on her fourth, waiting for John to return from yet another late night at the office.

The door opened ten minutes later, and John was clearly surprised to see his wife up and awake. "Hi honey. What are you still doing up? It's after eleven." He leaned over and gave her a quick peck on the cheek.

"I've been trying to have a conversation with you all week but you simply couldn't find the time," she said with an edge in her voice. "So here I am. Waiting."

"For the hundredth time, you know how critical this case is that I'm working on."

"Yes, but you don't realize how critical this conversation is," Lola said in a thoroughly sarcastic voice. "Oh, honey, my sweet overworked baby, you've had a long day at work. Sit down. Relax. Have some wine. And while you're at it, top off my glass."

John didn't bite. He was too damn tired. "What's up? You max out your credit card again?"

"No honey, nothing that serious." Lola's teeth were clenched tight as she offered him a toothy, disdainful smile. "I'm pregnant."

"Holy shit, Lola. Are you sure?" John stared at her. "Hell, we've only had sex a couple of times this fall, and I'm pretty sure I used a condom when we did."

"Which doesn't mean I'm not pregnant. I am. I've decided I'm going to give this little soul another chance to pick out the perfect parents, metaphysically speaking."

"What the hell are you talking about? You mean adoption?"

"No, termination. I'm going to let that precious soul return to its Source and have another chance at coming into this world…with another couple."

"Hold on a second. I have a say in this too, Lola," John said emphatically.

"No, actually, you don't. You haven't had a say in my life for years. We've been living separate lives for who knows how long," Lola said, her words touched with alcohol. "Let's face it, John. You're never home and you never make Nick or me a priority when you are home. I'm invisible to you. I've tried to create a nice home environment for the three of us, and you're never home long enough to enjoy it. You accept invitations to stuffy social events knowing damn well that I don't fit in with those kinds of people. And you think all of my interests are trivial."

Lola started to cry. "John, what happened to the adventurous you? What happened to the adventurous us, for that matter? We don't have the spark anymore. I'm lonely. You're never home. You're a fantastic provider, but I need more than that. I want the John Harte I crashed into on the road that day."

John didn't respond to any of this. He sat down next to her and waited until she stopped crying. Then he said, "Are you really serious about not having the baby?"

All Lola could do was nod.

"Well, if you terminate this pregnancy, you terminate our marriage too." He struggled to his feet. "I'm tired. I'm going to give Nick a kiss good night."

"That's it? No pleading to save 'us'? You, the lawyer, putting up no argument? You might've persuaded me in a different direction if you just would've fought for 'us'! Can't even give me the satisfaction of a good old-fashioned verbal sparring? So…it's too late…such a damn shame…for 'us,'" Lola disappointedly replied, still wanting the attention she desperately craved.

John turned to walk away and then paused. "I love you, Lola. I'll always love you, but I won't be able to forget what you're about ready to do and I'll remember every time I look in your face. I'll be reminded of the potential that could've been. All I ever wanted was to provide for you and Nick, to keep you secure. You're the most unique, loving, and kind person I've ever met. You make me laugh harder than any person I know. I love the way our bodies fit together, and I regret all the times I've come home too damn tired to make love to you. But I know how I am and my career is also important to me. I'm afraid I can't change for you right now, and I realize you can't change for me either. I'm sorry, Lola. You're the best thing that ever happened to me. We have an incredible boy who knows he's loved, and I want to keep it that way. I have to let you go and you have to let me go before we start to resent each other. I'm so sorry. I am so damn sorry."

John wiped at the tears spilling down his face. "I love you, but I just can't cherish you the way you want me to."

"Why? Why now, John? Why tell me all this now?" Lola wanted to know. But she didn't wait for an answer. "The hardest part of letting you go is knowing you have the potential to be the best husband and father and lover a girl could ask for, and you choose not to be those things. That's the thing. You're not an asshole. I can't even justify hating you. You're just absent in my life. Absent in my mind, body, and soul." She shook her head and drank. Then set the glass down hard. "This just sucks. I wanted you to at least yell and scream and carry on, but John the lawyer has to have a logical argument, even for this. I only wanted some goddamn passion! And I wanted it from you! I truly thought you were my soul mate. I wanted this to work so badly. I'd even consider a goodbye love session but your energy would stay in my aura for nine months and right now I don't want anything…your essence…this baby… screwing that up for nine months. Missing you is something I'm already used to. It will just be more permanent."

They both smiled through tears and hugged each other tightly. When John pulled away, he looked at Lola and said, "You had my attention until the nine-month-hanging-out-in-your-aura thing. Honestly, Lola, I never did understand all your metaphysical mumbo jumbo. Here's what I do know, even if I'm in or out of your aura, I'll continue to take very good care of you and Nick. You can count on that."

They talked and cried for an hour. Then they walked into Nick's room together and kissed their son goodnight. John grabbed his pillow and migrated to the guest bedroom. Lola curled up in their bed, sobbing. She rolled over and ran her hands over his side of the bed. It was cold and empty. She decided that if they were never to make love again, then by god she was going to make it the best fuck ever.

She still worried about getting him out of her aura, but then she figured that Gaia would have an answer for that. "Oh, poor John. He'll be stuck with my energy for months."

Lola felt a sudden flood of loneliness and scurried into the guest room. She slipped under the blankets, and John welcomed her with a deep kiss. He threw his boxers on the floor and embraced her nakedness. Their eyes locked. She lightly stroked him. His index finger strummed her engorged pleasure mound rhythmically. Lola tried not to moan as their eyes took in each other. As if on cue, they stopped and embraced. The kiss started slowly. They were holding back, wanting the lovemaking to last as long as possible.

John kissed her neck tenderly, and she shivered. He slid down between her legs. Wet. He looked up at her and smiled. She smiled back. His tongue worked its magic, and she cried out. It was only then that he entered her.

She inhaled the intermingling scent of Aramis and sex. He intertwined his fingers in hers, lifting her hands above her head as he slowly rode her into a mutual ecstasy. Not a word was spoken. Memories and emotions of what had been but would never be again were revealed and held like a delicate bubble between them.

<hr />

The separation was amicable. Lola stayed on the mountain. John found a condo not far from his job in town. Nick lived with Lola during the week and John on weekends, but they were flexible depending on schedules. Their son actually thrived on the arrangement. He loved his town time with his father; after all, for the first time in years, John devoted entire weekends only to him. Nick was also only minutes away from a growing circle of Boulder friends. After John joined the country club, Nick took up tennis and golf and used the pool almost every time he was there. He was a natural athlete and loved the competition. John bought him a top-of-the-line mountain bike, and the youngster rode pretty much anywhere he had to go.

Things weren't quite so good on the mountain. Nick started to feel isolated even though he had his mountain friends. His taste for city living had been whetted, and his appetite for it kept growing.

As for John, he continued to push his law career to the limit. He'd found a passion, and he excelled at it. The money was good, and he made sure Lola and Nick were well taken care of.

Lola, for her part, excelled at a different sort of career...searching for passion. And she was willing to go wherever the search took her.

December 1989

CAUGHT

Bridget looked around the table as her father warmed up for his third Irish toast, interrupting everyone's dinner. She noticed how much older both her parents seemed to have gotten since their last Christmas gathering. Their hair was more gray now than brown; when had that happened? Their wrinkles were deeper; were they really that old? And her father's mood was definitely not mellowing with age; no surprise.

Her brothers, on the other hand, never changed. James was the oldest. He was big and brawny like her dad. Patrick was the youngest. He had a much slighter frame and was the spitting image of their mother.

Looking around the table, Bridget realized how much she had missed them. Seeing them once a year was hardly enough, but that didn't mean that she missed Detroit, not even a little bit. Did she miss her dad's toasts? Well, that was debatable. Still, she raised her glass again while his booming voice filled the room.

"May you live a long life
Full of gladness and health,
With a pocket full of gold
As the least of your wealth.
May the dreams you hold dearest,
Be those which come true..."

The words came to a halt mid-sentence. Bridget had been watching out of the corner of her eye as Michael stole a dinner roll off Shauna's plate – not a good move since bread of any kind was her daughter's favorite food next to the mashed potatoes – but there was no time to intercede. Shauna was already retaliating, giving Michael a good shove and demanding her roll back.

Their grandfather's face darkened, but his rebuke was aimed at Bridget, not the kids.

"Bridget, are these the kind of manners you're teaching these children? You were raised better than that." Then he growled at her kids, his glass still raised. "Knock it off and show some respect or you'll find my hand on your backsides!"

That was enough to stop the kids dead in their tracks, but it caused Dan to come to his feet. Oh, no, Bridget thought. All of Bridget's worst fears washed over her; how often had she told people that she was more afraid of her own dad than she was of dying some terrible death.

But Dan surprised her. Instead of going off on his father-in-law and risking the ire of his brothers-in-law, he raised his glass and finished Joseph's toast, saying:

"And the kindness you spread,
Keep returning to you."

Then he said, "Here's to you, Joseph."

Dan drank. So did Bridget's dad. If anyone else noticed Dan's insincerity, it didn't show. Then, Bridget's mother was clamoring to her feet and rescuing the moment as only she could. She said, "Bridget, honey, let's start clearing away these dishes while the men go relax. Shauna, you can help us."

Shauna immediately started to protest, but one look from her mother shut her up.

"You get the first taste of the pumpkin pie and no one will know," Bridget whispered to her. She gave her daughter a wink and a nod, and Shauna skipped smugly into the kitchen.

It was midnight when Bridget made her call back to Boulder. She had carried the phone to the back stoop, needing every bit of privacy she could muster. Even then her eyes kept flashing toward the kitchen. She was freezing, stamping her feet and pacing just to keep the circulation flowing. Her breath seemed to freeze even before it left her mouth, but the discomfort was worth every intimate moment.

She didn't see her dad stumble into the kitchen, rubbing his eyes with one hand and his stomach with the other. The kitchen light was on, and he couldn't figure out why. "Somebody must think we're drowning in money or something," he muttered to himself. He was opening the refrigerator door and reaching for the milk carton when he heard Bridget creeping through the back door, her voice whispering, "I adore you too. Miss you."

She laid the phone back in its cradle and found her dad staring at her, jaw set and eyes blazing. His daughter nearly leaped out of her skin, her eyes wide and her heart about to explode through her chest. "Dad, what are you doing up?" She tried to keep the tremor out of her voice, but failed miserably.

"Who the hell are you talking to at this time of night, Bridget Jameson?" Joseph's glare was as icy as the coldest Michigan night, and so was his voice. "I asked you a question."

"I was talking to a friend in Colorado, wishing them Merry Christmas."

"And what friend might that be?"

"Well…Umm…my friend Lola. You remember Lola, don't you?"

"Really? Your friend Lola? 'I adore you. I miss you too'?" Her dad wasn't that gullible. He said, "Look at me, daughter! How dumb do you think I am? You may not answer to me anymore, but you sure as hell have to answer to your husband and to God. How the hell do you face God every Sunday morning with your soul stained? I assume you'll be going to confession in the morning and God help you if you die before then. And as for your penance, your husband may very well take care of that! If you had stayed here in Detroit with your family where you belong, this would never have happened. Not with your mother and I watching. Better life, my ass!"

Bridget started crying. She shook like a leaf, both from cold and shame. Joseph's tone softened slightly when he said, "My God, daughter, what are you doing to your life and your family? You're playing with fire here. Don't you know that? You're going to hurt a whole bunch of people, yourself included."

He took her by the shoulder and looked her squarely in the eyes, leaving no room for doubt or argument. "You are my daughter, and I trust in God Almighty that you will do the right thing."

December 1989

FAMILY NIGHT

The decade of the eighties was coming to a close.

Ella saw this as a major complication, so she pre-wrote a bunch of checks with 1990 scribbled in the line reserved for the date. She had no intention of writing in the wrong year and having to void a check. It was a waste of money, and they didn't have the money to waste.

This was also one thing she could mark off her list before her parents arrived. They were spending two weeks at the house over Christmas, and all Ella's attention would be on them. She looked forward to it and dreaded it all at the same time. Brice and Alena knew they would be flooded with gifts. Gary would hardly even notice because his routine would be unchanged. So it was up to her to keep everyone happy. Her and her alone.

Two nights into their visit, she packed everyone into the car and went into town to the Coffee Shop, Gary's home away from home when he needed a music fix. Tonight he was jamming with a bass guitarist named Jake and a singer and keyboard player named Michelle.

They were singing Dylan's *Lay Lady Lay* when Ella, the kids, and Bob and Shirley, the in-laws, walked in. They found a table and ordered coffee for the adults and hot chocolate for the kids. Between songs, Gary introduced them to the coffee shop's patrons, and then he invited Brice to join them on stage.

"My son plays a mean guitar," he told the crowded room. "Brice, do you want to come up here and show us your stuff? Grab a guitar."

A thoroughly embarrassed Brice trudged over and climbed the stage. He was checking out a couple of his dad's guitars when Gary called out to the audience, "Any requests?"

"How about *Blowin' in the Wind*?" Bob called.

"You're kidding me, right?" Brice looked over at his dad. "I don't play that kind of song. It's for old people."

"Hey, guy, watch who you're calling old," Michelle said with a grin.

Brice wasn't grinning. "Yeah, maybe you should look in the mirror," he sneered.

"Brice. How dare you!" Ella jumped up, immediately tripped over the leg of a chair, and sent a coffee cup crashing to the floor. That was all Brice needed to see; now his embarrassment turned to humiliation.

"Nice, Mom." He walked right past her, shaking his head, and mumbling, "I'm not picking you up again."

"What in the world does that mean?" Shirley said, her eyebrows knotted in confusion.

Gary set his guitar aside and rushed to Ella's side, helping her to her feet, and smelled alcohol on her breath. "Oh, my God, Ella! Are you okay?"

"Fine. Just a little embarrassed," she answered.

The party was over. Gary said, "You need to go home. Give me the keys." He turned to find his father-in-law. "Bob, can you drive everyone home?"

"Sure, I can drive everyone home, Gary, but what are you going to do?"

"Shut up, Robert," Shirley said quickly. "Just take the keys. Let's go."

They made their exit in silence, and not a word was spoken the entire trip up the mountain. When they got home, Bob and Shirley huddled at the kitchen table while Ella ushered the kids to bed. When she finally appeared twenty minutes later, it was only to announce how tired she was. "It's been a long day. I'm going to bed."

"Not so fast," Shirley said. "When will Gary be home? We want to have a family talk."

"Mom, I have no idea when Gary is coming home. I guess when he feels like it," Ella muttered.

"Well, maybe it's better we talk to you alone then. We know there are some problems here."

"You mean problems like everyone else in the world has?" Ella wanted a drink, not a family chat with her disapproving parents.

"Your son is out of control, your daughter won't even talk to you, and your house is a mess," her father said, waving at the burned-out light bulb over the kitchen table. "You look like holy hell. Gary's never around. It doesn't look to me like you can take care of yourself, much less anyone else. Honestly, I don't know exactly what's going on in your household, Ella Louise, but you have to straighten up and pull yourself together!"

"I thought you said you wanted to talk, Dad. This is just another lecture on all the ways your daughter doesn't measure up," Ella said, her own disgust mounting. "I don't need to hear it right now. Okay?"

Shirley put her hand on Ella's arm. "You know we love you and only want what's best for you, but your father is right. You need to snap out of this."

"Snap out of this!" Ella clenched her teeth together hard enough to make them crack; she had lived with their constant criticism for as long as she could remember, and it never stopped. She was about to head for the bottle she'd hidden in her closet when the kitchen door opened, and Gary popped in, a model of false exuberance.

"Oh great, I'm so glad you're all still up," he said, tossing his jacket aside and setting a snow-white cake box on the table. "I brought home your favorite New York cheesecake, Shirley. You know, it's really great to have you both here again. Christmas wouldn't be the same without you."

Bob arched his eyebrows. "Really? That's sort of hard to believe since we've seen you for, what? Maybe ten minutes total since we got here."

"Bob, I am sorry you feel that way," Gary said. This was not the time to unleash his thoughts. "It's just been a busy week."

"Yeah, busy. But not with your family." Bob refused to be pacified. "It's Christmas vacation, for Pete's sake."

Gary changed tactics. He turned to his wife and said, "Ella, why don't you get some forks and plates, and I'll cut the cheesecake for us. Would anyone like me to put on a pot of decaf?"

"Or how about champagne? Let's make it a celebration!" Ella nearly shouted. All three of them showered her with looks of stunned disbelief, and she tried backtracking. "Hey, I was just kidding. It was a joke, everybody. Just a joke."

"We don't know what the hell is going on in this household," Bob said, his eyes traveling from Ella to Gary and back again, "but there are clearly some problems, and we're here to help if we can."

"Gary, honey, we are just very concerned about all of you," Shirley chimed in. "Ella is not herself. And for that matter, neither are you. We just want to understand why."

Gary put his arm around Ella in a show of support, while still trying to rein in a flood of emotions. "Thanks for your concern, but we're capable of handling things ourselves."

"Mom and Dad, I'm fine," Ella added quickly. "I just need a little break."

Shirley's eyes suddenly brightened. She clasped her hands together, illumination filling her face. She said, "Well, if it's a break you need, I have a great idea that will be a win-win for everyone."

"What's that?" Ella wasn't sure she wanted to hear it.

"Your dad and I can take the kids back to New York for the second week of their Christmas break. That way the two of you can get a little peace and quiet and spend some time together. And this will give you the break you need, Ella!"

Bob patted Shirley on the back. "That's a hell of an idea, Shirley." Then he looked at the astonished couple. "Sounds like we have a plan. We can tell the kids in the morning."

March 1990

PLAYING DRESS UP

Every conceivable "going out dancing" outfit was draped over the furniture in Lola's bedroom. Dresses and blouses hung over the chairs and table in the living room. Shoes and boots lay on the floor of the hall.

Sharon, Lola, and Bridget were dressed in their bathrobes and were playfully searching through the mounds of clothes, trying to decide what to wear.

Each of them had brought something to trade or borrow, because, after all, the best part about going out was the before-party primping. It also didn't hurt that a little friendly advice might help avoid a fashion faux pas. The good news was that none of the girls gravitated toward the same style, so fighting over garments was never an issue.

The scene reminded Lola of eager bridesmaids getting ready for a wedding.

Their hair was done but their makeup was not.

The coffee table was the only piece of furniture clear of clutter, and a blender full of The Potion sat off to one side. Birthday presents and a bottle of Damiana were neatly displayed in the center.

The front door opened and Ella and Gaia waltzed in, both dressed with an understated sense of fashion. Frumpy almost.

"You guys aren't even dressed yet," Ella said, though not in the least surprised. She gestured in Gaia's direction. "Ladies. Our birthday girl."

The women shouted, "Happy Birthday, Gaia," and Lola presented her with a drink.

"This is a special recipe made just for you on your birthday. We call it the Booty Potion. We had a hard time coming up with a theme for your little party, since most of your woo-woo magic and all the otherworldly stuff you're so versed in is over our heads, so we thought we'd try to come up with something that would be meaningful to you, even if it was only quasi-woo-woo."

"Like whites pretending to know Indian stuff. You know, quasi-Indians," Sharon said, trying to be helpful.

"Well, sort of," Lola said, waving Sharon off. "But remember, we don't intend any disrespect to you, or, you know, any belief system or culture or…"

"Spit it out, Lola," Bridget said.

"We just wanted to make it our gift to you…a unique mountain style of feminine all our own. A birthday for you to remember."

"And that includes the three of you in bathrobes?" Gaia quipped.

"See! That's what I'm talking about. Something you'll never forget. It's already working," Lola said proudly.

The group moved clothes out of the way and sat down. Lola loaded a pipe and said, very ceremoniously, "We are going to pass the pipe and have a blessing. And we want you to know that we've really done our homework for this blessing."

"Sure we have," Bridget said sarcastically. "Light the pipe."

"We pass this pipe filled with your favorite substance with a single purpose: to make you happy. And, well, let's just say happy for now."

Gaia took a toke and coughed. "This stuff is strong."

Gaia passed it to Ella. Ella looked at it as if it might sprout claws and passed it on to Sharon, then to Lola, and finally to Bridget. Each handed her gift to Gaia while holding the pipe and reading her part of the blessing.

"From us," Ella said, nodding to Sharon. It was a beautiful red top and very revealing. "This gift symbolizes the East and the power of red. May you grow strong and be blessed by the wind."

"Well, I…" Gaia got two words out before Bridget jumped in and said, "Zip it, girl. You have to wait until we're done before sharing your insightful comments."

"Oh, sorry," Gaia laughed, and ripped open Bridget's gift. It was a pair of black fishnet stockings and a very short, very sexy black dress. "Wow!"

"Representing the West," Bridget said. "May the stars shine on you, even when it's raining."

Finally, Gaia held up yellow panties and a white Wonderbra from Lola. "Yellow represents the South and white the North. May you grow old with a smile on your face."

Gaia stared at the ensemble and found herself speechless, maybe for the first time in her entire life. Lola said, "It's your birthday suit, girl. Put it on."

"But I'm already dressed," Gaia protested.

"Not quite." Bridget led her into the bedroom to help her change. "I'll give you a hand."

"What am I? A walking compass?"

Lola, Ella, and Sharon crowded into the bedroom and watched the transformation taking place. Lola said, "You of all people should know the colors of the four directions, Gaia. It's symbolic."

"Same with the pipe," Ella said. "So the smoke will carry your blessings up to heaven and make them forever true."

"It's the only woo-woo shit we could come up with," Lola admitted, and Gaia rolled her eyes.

"Yeah, right," she said.

The outfit looked surprisingly sexy and fashionable on her. She put on the ballerina-like shoes Ella had brought over and executed a graceful pirouette.

"You look like a million bucks," Bridget said. "What do you think?"

Gaia looked at herself in the mirror and said, "Got to admit. I like it."

All eyes turned toward Ella. "Now your turn," Bridget said, grinning mischievously.

Ella held her hand up in front of her, trying to ward them off. "NO, NO, NO."

"Yes, yes, yes," Sharon said.

They explored the many piles of clothes, everyone picking her favorite, and guided Ella back into the bedroom carrying armfuls of clothes and shoes. And then they went to work.

"I want a mirror," Ella said when the makeover was complete.

"We aren't done with you yet," Lola announced. "Where are the hair sparks? Do you want red, purple, or blue? Purple, I think. They'll really stand out in your blonde hair…and add some volume too."

"Purple hair sparks? Are you crazy? Okay, purple it is."

When her hair was done, they stood Ella in front of the mirror, and her jaw dropped. "I can't go out looking like…Wow, I look hot!"

"Hell, yeah, you do," Bridget said.

"Must be the…" Ella was still staring at her transformation. "I think I'll have another Booty Potion."

Everyone finished getting dressed. The makeup took the longest since the alcohol proved makeup-application-challenging. Lola cranked up the music and shouted, "Get your booties moving, girls."

They danced, sang, laughed, and paraded. Bridget eventually looked at the clock and was shocked at the time. "Holy shit! It's nine o clock. We better get moving. Who's driving?"

Sharon said, "I know! Let's call Sam. He can escort us down and chauffeur us back." The girls burst out laughing, and Bridget nearly spit out her drink.

The laughter got everyone dancing again. An old Beatles tune came on, and they all started singing, "She loves you, yeah, yeah, yeah..."

"What's in this drink?" Gaia shouted. "I'm starting to tingle in the South."

Bridget grinned from ear to ear and held up the bottle of Damiana. "The Goddess for the Goddess."

Gaia's eyes widened. "Damiana? The Mayan love elixir?"

"I wondered why I was looking so damn sexy tonight." Ella grabbed the womanly-shaped bottle from Bridget and never missed a beat. She ran a hand over the bottle and laughed. The Beatles gave way to Genesis. "I've never seen such a provocative bottle. Hard to miss it on a shelf."

Lola set the tone by turning off the lights and replacing them with the flame of a big pink candle. Sharon snatched it away from her, held it high above her head, and started moving her hips in a slow, provocative fashion. The rest of the girls grabbed candles and joined in.

In the darkness, the flames animated like tiny fairies gliding through the air. The song ended, and silence followed. Gaia reached for the conga drum that Lola kept in the corner and began a hypnotic, rhythmic beat. As the power of the drumming increased, so did the frenzy of the "Candle Dance."

The girls gave way to its spell. They formed a circle and moved in unison.

Damiana was working her magic.

Labor Day Weekend 1991

FUN HAS ITS PRICE

The trip to Mexico was not planned. A travel agent friend of Ella's told her about a great weekend deal to Puerto Vallarta for three nights and four days. September was the rainiest month in Puerto Vallarta and therefore one of the best months for low-cost tourist deals. Airfare and hotel were only $383. The plane departed Thursday morning and arrived back Sunday evening.

Ella told the girls about it on Monday and everything was booked by Tuesday afternoon, including the babysitting arrangements. Gaia, Sharon, Ella, Bridget, and Lola were thrilled; the kids and their fathers were not.

Unfortunately, it didn't go as planned. Or maybe it went exactly as planned. With too much alcohol, too much partying, and too much overindulgence. In the end, there is always a price to pay for having too much fun, and it hit Ella the hardest.

Fantasy, such as it was, was replaced by reality the minute Ella walked into her house four days later. Brice greeted her at the door. He didn't smile and was talking with a weird lisp, like he had peanut butter stuck to the roof of his mouth.

Gary grabbed her suitcase but didn't give her a hug or say, "Hello," or "How was your trip?" or "We missed you." Probably because he didn't miss her, and probably because he was still upset that they had agreed to let Alena stay with her grandparents in New York for the school year. Basically, it was Ella's decision. She rationalized that the change would expand her daughter's circle of friends and her view of the world, but it was also a matter of decreasing the tension in the house. Ella wasn't fooling herself.

Gary gave her a wide berth as he walked past, and a wave of physical and emotional rage swept over Ella. She aimed it in Brice's direction. "You're talking funny. What's the matter with you?"

Brice tried to escape but she grabbed his arm and hauled him back.

"Open your mouth." Ella used two hands to force her son's mouth open, but Brice clenched his jaws. "Brice, I said open your mouth!"

Her grip tightened, and she didn't seem to notice how much she was hurting him.

"Let him go, Ella." Gary burst into the room. "I said let him go. You're hurting him."

Ella stood her ground. "Brice Allen, did you pierce your tongue? Answer me. Now!"

Brice nodded, but he refused to open his mouth. Ella turned on Gary and literally shoved him against the wall.

"He's only thirteen. You gave him permission? You signed the consent form? Without consulting with me? His body is still changing…growing. What kind of shop would even consider piercing the tongue of a child?" Her voice trilled with rage and venom. "You cowards. Both of you. You went behind my back. You're both cowards."

She turned away, completely deflated, and stared out the window. Snowflakes drifted down from the sky.

"From sand to snow in one day. It's only September!" The beautiful sputtering of white pushed Ella closer to the edge. She was beyond furious.

"Come on, Mom. Every musician I know has one," Brice said. "It's only my tongue. Don't be such an uptight prude."

"Don't you talk to me like that! Are they only thirteen?" Ella swung around, and Brice took a quick step back. "And I suppose every musician you know drops out of school, does drugs, snorts up, chugs alcohol, and bangs the groupies too? I deal with those kinds of people every day. They're losers! Your father and I brought you up better than that." Gary's eyes widened, and Brice hung his head. "Is that your plan? To screw up your life just so you can fit in?"

"So what if I do," Brice retaliated. "I'm smarter than you think. You don't even know me. I know what I'm doing. And you're over-reacting. I know what moderation is. Which is a helluva lot more than I can say for you, you hypocritical lush."

Ella's hand was already in motion, and the slap caught Brice flush across the cheek, instantly turning it a bright red.

Brice's hand went to his cheek, and he stared at her, completely in shock. "I hate you, you bitch. I wish you never gave birth to me. No wonder Alena wanted out of here. You suck! I was happier when you were away."

He ran to his bedroom and slammed the door.

"My God. You just hit your son." Gary shook himself.

"Don't just stand there," Ella sneered. "You're his father! He's your uncontrollable, disrespectful son. Do something."

"I think you've done plenty. You have two kids who can't stand to be around you." Gary pushed himself away from the wall, his hands clenched. "What the hell, I can barely stand you myself. You're not the woman I married. You walk in the door and start acting like a raving lunatic. So just for the record, how many drinks did you have on the flight home? Because you know what, you reek of alcohol."

He stared at her, distain flooding his words. "Well, here's a newsflash for you, Ella. Your vacation is over and now you have to take on your roles as a wife, mother, and social worker again. Well, you've already screwed up the mother role; try not to screw up the rest."

He paced, trapping her in the hallway. "God, it just blows my mind that it's always about poor Ella. Your parents didn't show you

any affection. They never thought you were good enough. Blah…
blah…blah. Funny how the things that piss you off about your
parents are the same things that piss your children off about you.
Why don't you just run back to your girlie friends? Hell, I bet they
were glad to be rid of you. You and your neuroses. Talk about
someone that needs help. Look in the mirror. You've become such
a self-absorbed bitch that it makes me cringe!"

Gary's venom was unyielding. "By the way, we did just fine
without you and your critical attitude. In fact, Brice and I bonded."

"By getting his tongue pierced? You call that bonding?"

"A tongue piercing isn't the end of the world, Ella. Brice is just
spreading his wings and trying to find his way. It's harmless. You
treat him like he's in jail and you're the warden. He's exactly like I
was at that age. We'll reel him in if he needs it. For Christ's sake,
woman, you were more of a rebel growing up than he is, except you
never got caught. Ease up. I'm sick and tired of all this arguing."

The phone rang. "Get that, will you? I'm going upstairs to talk
to Brice," Gary said.

He headed for the stairs. Ella reluctantly answered the phone. It
was her mother, calling to tell Ella how well Alena was adjusting
to New York living. She had new friends, new clothes, and a new
outlook.

"Never a dull moment," was how her mother described Alena's
new world.

Ella gripped the phone, fuming. Her mother rattled on and on,
hardly taking a breath, and never once asking her own daughter how
her trip went or how her life was going.

Ella listened, feeling joy for her daughter and utter despair for
herself. And her despair deepened as she watched Gary and Brice
leave the house. Gary had his arm around Brice's shoulder. They
were laughing.

A week passed. Gary and Brice avoided Ella like the plague. She hated going to work and hated coming home. She hadn't spoken to any of the girls except Gaia since her return, and that was just to make sure she was feeling better. Gaia had spent a good part of their vacation sitting on the toilet with some sort of intestinal problem. Three days after they got home, she gave up on her homeopathic remedies and opted for a prescription from her doctor. Venturing too far from the cabin was not in her plans for a while.

Saturday morning, Bridget, Lola, and Sharon came by and the four of them congregated on Ella's front porch and talked about how things had been going since returning home.

"Well, look at you?" Bridget said. "Pretty casual for a Saturday."

Ella was barefoot and still dressed in her oversized flannel nightgown even though it was noon. She looked haggard.

"You don't look so good yourself," Ella replied. Actually, they were all a sight for sore eyes in one way or another. Bridget had been a special target for the Puerto Vallarta mosquitoes, and their bites had left her covered in hard crusty "zits." She had flesh-colored Calamine lotion dotting her scabs to remind her not to pick at them. She been plagued by a low-grade fever and body aches ever since she got home from vacation. She, too, had gone to her doctor to make sure she didn't have Dengue fever or some equally appalling affliction. Her doctor also removed a few deeply embedded cactus spines from a fall Bridget had taken.

"Yeah, a bit of a mess," Bridget admitted.

But then they all were. Sharon had been diagnosed with phytophotodermatitis. Her lips swelled four times their normal size and a rash on the front of her thigh was sore as hell.

"My doc said he'd seen a lot of it with college kids returning from spring break in Mexico. He jokingly calls it, 'Lime Disease.' Told me not to suck on limes in the sun. You know how many of those suckers I grabbed off the margarita glasses?" Sharon said. "'Lime Disease.' That didn't make me feel any better."

"You look like Donald Duck," Lola told her.

Sharon was wearing a very wide brimmed hat and was slathered with sunscreen. She'd lost weight because getting food into her mouth hurt so much. "Not a diet I'd readily endorse," she said. "And besides, I miss my junk food."

Lola's only complaint was her peeling sunburn. Her skin looked caramel colored in the places that had already shed the burned skin. "I refuse to complain," she said. But that was Lola. She refused to allow a single bad memory to creep into her consciousness, and the girls decided not to remind her.

"I don't know if leaving on vacation was worth all the crap," Ella complained. "I come home to an out-of-control son and an indifferent husband. I have cactus thorns appearing out of nowhere after that fall I took and my thighs still hurt from that damn coral cutting my leg when we went snorkeling. I could have died from a staph infection, especially in such a tropical environment. Death might have been an easier solution than a family that wishes I weren't around."

"God, could you be any more depressing? You're alive, but it looks like you're not doing too good of a job at staying that way. We all went through our fair share of shit down in paradise," Bridget said. Then she favored Lola with a mocking glance. "Well, everyone but Lola, that is. The gods blessed her and provided her with a Mexican God, a slithering phallic symbol called a snake, a tanned body, and great photos of the trip."

Ella was the only one who didn't laugh.

"Hey guys, I'd like to stay and complain, but, believe it or not, I've got to go to town to finalize the paperwork for a new job I just got," Sharon said, trying to sound matter-of-fact, but looking extremely guilty.

"What new job? Where? Down in town?" Bridget barked three questions in a row.

"No, not Boulder. It means moving to Colorado Springs," Sharon confessed. "I start in two weeks."

"And when were you going to tell us? I mean you had every opportunity in Mexico to spill the beans." Ella was clearly distressed.

"Well, I didn't want to jinx it. I'm going to be the office manager for a chiropractor down there. He's a friend of mine from high school and recently divorced. It's his ex-wife's former job. Come on. It's not that far away! And, besides, Mexico was a great going away party. Don't you think?"

"No! Mexico was not a great going away party. It sucked down there and it sucks up here!" Ella spouted.

"Ella, really! Yeah, Mexico kicked our asses. Get over it," Bridget said. "I mean, Jesus H. Christ, you're the professional here, but you sure as hell aren't acting like one. If you ask me, you're fucking depressed or something. It's noon and look at you. Hell, girl, you've got cottonmouth breath and bed head. You're barefoot and wearing an ugly sack of a thing you call a nightgown. No wonder..."

Ella's eyes were wet, and her tears brought Bridget up short. Then she said, "Oh, come on. I'm just jerking you around. I'm talking tough love. We love you, but...what the hell are you thinking? We're concerned..."

"Screw tough love," Ella growled. She gathered her nightgown around her and stumbled back into the house. Seconds later, she reappeared and raced down the steps toward the women. "Hold on a second," she growled.

Her eyes turned an icy blue, wild with anger, as she grabbed Bridget's shoulder from behind and began her verbal assault.

"Friends? You call yourself friends? Here you are giving me a loada crap about how I'm living my life, but what about you? Talk about acting irresponsibly. Bridget, you're acting like you're single, seeing a man behind your husband's back. You're married, for Christ's sake. Do you have any idea how that feels? I just know Gary is sneaking around my back with the bitch Michelle, coming home later and later, never touching me. I feel like I just don't matter, not to him, not to anyone.

"But what really pisses me off is that there's always justification to soothe your guilt...about how Dan doesn't want to work...or isn't motivated enough to find a good-paying consistent job...yaddy dah. Isn't loving and adoring his wife good enough? And then money, or should I say the lack of money rears its ugly head and gives you the excuse you need to complain and act out even more. At least he and your kids...at least they love you. And this is what they get in return? Infidelity? I don't know how much more of it I can take!"

She was just getting wound up and turned on Lola. "And you, your promiscuity is out of control. Where's your dignity and self-control, for God's sake? Is sex the only thing that you ever think about? I'm not getting any and can barely stand to listen to your amorous liaisons. Nobody wants me! And now you, Sharon, leaving? I'm surprised you didn't just disappear without saying goodbye!"

Lola's face reddened with every word. She finally took a step Ella's way and faced her head on.

"Okay, so we're talking truth now, are we? Well, you can point the finger at us all you want, Ella, but what about you? You talk about dignity and self-control! Alcohol has become your lover, making you feel good and numbing you out to the reality of your life. So don't give us this high and mighty attitude. You're no different than us." Lola stole a deep breath. "I swore I'd never be like my mother, and now I'm really no different than her. Believe me, it's made me more sympathetic toward her. What kind of void was she trying to fill going from man to man? Maybe we should all be in therapy or something, but you know what? For now, doing what I'm doing feels too good to stop. I'm not 'there' yet. And what scares me is that by the time I am 'there,' I may have lost everything near and dear to me."

Lola hung her head for a moment, then looked up. "It's pitiful, I know. But I, for one, am glad we are in this together." She reached out to Ella. "Come on, Ella. No matter what, we need each other. Friends survive the good and the bad together. Looks like we're all in the same boat."

"Yeah, a boat ready to sink," Ella sarcastically retorted.

"Shit, let's hope we're smart enough to have our life jackets on when we start to go under," was the only reply Bridget could utter.

Dark clouds gathered, obscuring the sun. They hugged, but the clouds remained.

October 1991

DECEIT

Gary pulled up in front of the house. *Damn*, he thought, seeing Brice bolt across the road toward the waiting school bus. Brice pulled up short when he saw his dad's car, his backpack jostling uncomfortably over one shoulder. Brice had a confused look on his face. "Hey Dad," he called. "Did you forget something?"

Gary hated to lie, though he'd been lying for so long now that it came second nature, but he played dumb. "Yeah, son," he said, trying to grin. "Seems like I'm always forgetting something."

Brice nodded, then shook his head. "Mom said you had to go in to work early today. Too bad you had to come back."

"Yeah, I had some papers to grade before school. Got halfway down the mountain and realized I'd left some of them here." Gary tried making the lie sound normal, but his mouth was dry, and the words came out clunky and self-deprecating. He nodded toward the school bus. "You better roll, man. The bus driver's not going to wait all day."

Gary's plan was falling apart fast. He'd hoped Ella and Brice would already be gone so he could get a quick change of clothes and head back down to town.

They were usually out of the house by seven. Gary glanced at his watch. It was 7:13. Maybe the bus was just running late.

He went inside. Ella was sitting at the kitchen table. She was still in her nightgown. There was a bottle of vodka open in front of her. A glass was half full. She looked like death warmed over.

"Holy Jesus, Ella!" The words tumbled out of his mouth. He went on the defensive. "What do you think you're doing?"

Ella looked at Gary with red-rimmed, swollen eyes. "Getting home a little late, aren't you? Or is it early?"

"I didn't call you last night because the band ended up playing really late and I didn't want to wake you. I crashed at Brad's house because I was just too tired to drive up the mountain."

His wife pressed her hand against her forehead, trying to keep her head propped up. "Are you fucking her?"

She said these four words as if the entire world were build of sand, and the tide was already washing everything away. The inevitability stung.

"What? Nice language, Ella. Now you have a foul mouth along with being a sloppy drunk. You've been spending a little too much time with your best friend." He nodded toward the vodka bottle.

She filled the glass. Stared at the clear liquid and screamed, "ARE YOU FUCKING HER, GARY?"

November 1991

GASPING FOR BREATH

Bridget had gone out dancing with friends and was thankful Dan was on the Western Slope, hunting elk. He wouldn't be home for a few more days, and Bridget was just fine with that.

The drive up from Boulder was dicey at best in the snow, and the car lost traction more than once before she finally got to the babysitter's house.

It took another ten minutes to get home. She pulled into the driveway, hit the brakes a little too hard, and skidded to an abrupt stop.

Michael and Shauna moaned and groaned as she guided them inside, and it was nearly one by the time she got them in bed.

"Holy crap," she said when she looked at the clock in the kitchen. "I'm going to be dead tomorrow."

Thoughts of her husband and their freezing house were not flattering. The kid's bedding had even been chilly to the touch, and that really pissed Bridget off. "Shit, it's cold in here."

She and Dan had an ongoing battle. He didn't believe in turning on the furnace until mid-November. He liked to joke that it would make them all tough, but the truth of the matter was that he was just damn cheap.

It broke Bridget's heart to see Shauna huddled up behind the wood stove just to keep warm or Michael wearing three layers of clothes. For Christ's sake, that's just not right.

It wasn't like Dan was paying the bills. All his fucking money went to his damn toys. The new rifle he bought for his hunting trip was a perfect example, and the thought of it got Bridget pacing.

"Shit, girl, you gotta calm down. You had a helluva good time tonight, and that's the memory you should be taking to bed with you." Bridget grinned. "But first things first. Get a fire started to take the chill out of this igloo of a home."

Bridget stuffed the box of the stove full of wood, got it started, and hoped to hell it would still be warm in the morning.

Then she realized she'd left in such a hurry that she'd forgotten to put food in Laska's bowl. "My baby must be starving."

Laska wasn't a house dog. He slept in his huge pen. Even the lion attack all those years back hadn't changed that. As his arthritis got worse and his hind legs grew weaker, Bridget tried to get him to sleep inside, but Laska loved the snow, loved being out in the fresh air, loved the sounds of the mountain.

Bridget put on her heavy boots and gloves and went outside. She poured dog food into a bag, filled a bucket full of warm water, and headed out to the pen. Her headlamp led the way as fluffy flakes of snow gently fell from the blackness. A mound of snow came to life as Laska shifted in his snowy insulation.

"Hey buddy, your momma's finally here. Sorry I'm such a moron. Here's some chow and fresh water."

Laska raised his nose from under his thick furry tail and the accumulated snow fell from his massive head and neck. His ears stood at attention and his nose sniffed the air. He struggled to stand, and his legs gave way on the ice-hardened snow. He yelped with pain.

"There, there old boy, let me help you." Bridget reached under his belly and helped him up. His tail wagged, and she let him slobber all over her face.

"Look at you. You still have that twinkle in your eye, don't you, big fella? You hungry?" She held the dog food under his nose, but he ignored it, continuing instead to nuzzle her hair and neck.

"I love you too." A flood of memories washed over her. Bridget liked to call him Houdini the dog, because there wasn't a fence he couldn't jump or a harness he couldn't escape. They'd fixed a dozen holes in the fence around his pen over the years, but Laska was an escape artist. "That's right, big boy, nothing could stop you. Though not so much these days."

The dog's hindquarters quivered, and he collapsed to the ground.

"Are you sure you don't want to come in where it's nice and warm? Sure would help your joints."

Laska had always been a "talker," but Bridget noticed he did less and less of it these days. But tonight, he growled and groaned and let out a series of little barks as she playfully roughed up his fur, her guilt making her play with him longer than usual.

As Bridget headed toward the gate, she noticed the gap in the fence and smiled back at Laska. These days she worried more about what could get in, because he certainly didn't have the strength to get out. She'd fix it in the morning.

"Love ya, boy. See you in the morning." Laska perked up his ears, listening to her words and sniffing the air.

Ten minutes later, she was burrowing under the covers of her bed and searching for her own warmth. She spent a pleasant moment thinking about Steve. What a blast they'd had dancing the night away. Yeah, the "high school" sex they had in the back seat of his car was cold and uncomfortable, but it was better than nothing. Knowing they could get caught at any moment added even more intensity to the act, leaving them feeling like crazed animals being driven more by instinct than heart and soul.

That was her last thought before drifting off.

In her dream, Bridget was gasping for breath. She was wildly and uselessly clawing at some unknown horror, on the verge of unconsciousness. Her hands went to her neck, and she grabbed at the cord that was strangling the life from her, knowing she had only seconds left if she wanted to survive.

She tried screaming: "Where is it? What's happening? No! No! NOOO!" Her screaming melded with the incessant, desperate howling of a coyote, escalating her terror and confusion and launching her out of her nightmare and into full consciousness.

She sat bolt upright in bed, only to discover that she was still choking, choking because there was only smoke filling her lungs and coughs wracking her body.

Fire! Oh, my God! It was her one, clear thought, and adrenaline pounded through her veins. She threw off her covers and screamed: "Michael! Shauna! Get up! Get up! Now!"

Bridget's vocal cords burned as she scrambled out of bed and groped toward the hallway. Tears streamed down her face, blinding her in the dense smoke.

She burst through Shauna's door. Shauna's sleeping form was outlined in a warm glow of orange light shining through the window; the light came from the flames on the roof and nearly drove Bridget to her knees in fear.

"FIRE!" Bridget screeched as Shauna opened her eyes, oblivious to the drama. Shauna saw the flames. The panic caused her to inhale deeply, and the smoke caused her to choke. Bridget yanked her out of her bed. "Come on, baby."

They ran into the hall where they found Michael standing with a thin quilt covering his nose and mouth.

"Heard howling…woke me…hear it?"

Bridget heard it too, but gave no notice. She grabbed Michael and propelled her children down the stairs. They burst through the front door into the frigid night.

November 1991

DISCOVERY

Lola couldn't believe that two years had passed since her divorce. She couldn't believe she was broke. Not flat broke, but close. Sure, John paid for child support but every cent of her settlement was gone. Poof! Vanished right before her very eyes.

She was in denial about pretty much all the bad choices she had ever made, but her finances were not one of them.

Her finances sucked and having a roommate hadn't .1elped much.

JD had moved into the mountain cabin with Lola three months ago, but his money situation was always tenuous. JD spent most of his time looking for ways to make a quick buck. His latest was a clever but illegal pyramid scheme running rampant in town. The people who got in early had apparently made tens of thousands of dollars in a matter of a month. JD convinced Lola to invest the last thousand dollars of her emergency fund just about the time the con men blew town and left the state. The $1,000! Gone! Just like that!

JD may have been a genuinely nice guy, but he was naïve as hell, just like Lola. It made for the spaciest of relationships. Yes, they had a few things in common – their metaphysical musings, their sexual appetite, their undeniable playfulness – but the relationship fell short in the reality department.

Money, or the lack thereof, was a huge issue. Confusing lust for love was another. And then there was the issue of drugs. Lola was a recreational drug user. JD was a habitual user who liked his coke and anything else he could get his hands on. Lola overlooked his overindulgence because she liked falling asleep next to a warm body.

That morning, a thousand dollars poorer, Lola came out of an extremely erotic dream to discover JD's hand between her legs and moving in unison with her now undulating pelvis.

He whispered, "Slowly, baby, ever so slowly. Stay on the edge for a while. I want this to last all morning. Look at me." She fluffed her pillow and looked down at his semi-soft member.

"This is all for you," he whispered, trying to get himself hard. He wiggled it at her. "He's all yours."

"Let me help you." She tried to place her hand near his, but he grabbed her wrists and pulled them over her head. "No baby, this morning is all about you."

"That's news to me. I thought all along it was always about me." She laughed. He smiled adoringly at her.

JD held her wrists, kissing and nibbling her neck and brushing his mouth across her face. Lola wanted to kiss him deep and hard but he continued to tease her. And then, he jumped up and hurried into the bathroom.

When he returned, he held an open bottle that smelled of menthol. He poured the fluid into his hands and rubbed them together, then took her hands and did the same. "It's menthol to heat up the skin."

Lola certainly didn't need to get any hotter. Their moaning became louder as the heat from the liquid worked its fiery magic. Lola grabbed his butt with both hands and held him down hard on her as she arched her back and whispered, "I'm coming. I'm coming."

Tears ran down her cheeks as he interlaced his hands with hers in a gesture so tender she cried openly. She felt way too vulnerable and realized that as soon as she opened up unconditionally to a man and let go of her mind, body, and soul, she would also let go of him. JD had to go.

"Think I'll take a shower, baby," he said after holding her for ten minutes. "You can go back to sleep, if you feel like it."

"I just might," Lola said. She lazed around in bed listening to the shower run and then decided to join him. When she opened the bathroom door, JD wasn't in the shower at all. He was sitting on the toilet with an empty syringe in his hand. His foggy, drug-induced journey was already beginning, and he was only startled enough to drop the syringe. Lola didn't say a word. She picked up the syringe, holding it as if it might have cooties, and carried it into the kitchen. Catching him in the act, she realized, was a godsend and made getting him out of her life all that much easier. Sadness was the only emotion that would hold its grip on her heart because he was, despite his flaws, a nice, funny, and tenderhearted person.

Then a light bulb went off in Lola's head. There had been suspicions that JD had moved from coke to heroin, and now Lola knew they were true. And she knew her $1,000 had gone for drugs, not a pyramid scheme gone bad. He had been lying all these months about hunting for a job, and their sex lives had gone from a trickle to nonexistent over the last month because of his growing impotence and lack of desire.

JD had moved on. And now she would be moving on without him.

The sound of running water finally stopped. JD floated out of the bathroom softly humming to himself. "Listen, baby, it's not what you think," he said with a smirk. "I found that syringe under the baseboard heater when I dropped an aspirin on the floor. You said yourself that the previous owners had rented this house to some druggies in the early seventies."

He fell into a chair, nodding off like someone had flipped a switch. The humming came and went. Lola didn't say a word. Robotically, she went about the house gathering JD's belongings. There wasn't much: a few cassette tapes, an armful of clothes, and car keys. She removed her house keys from his key chain. She went into the bathroom and gathered up his toiletries from the vanity. She pulled out a scrunched-up piece of paper towel, and several used syringes tumbled to the floor. Lola jumped back, a chill running down her spine. *Oh, my God! What if Nick had found these?*

JD roused himself long enough to see his stuff piled near the front door and to hear Lola talking on the phone to his former room-mate. "JD needs a ride out of my life and a place to crash," she was saying. "Bring a friend to drive his car down the mountain. He's in no shape to drive and I want him out of my life NOW. How dare he bring shit into my life like this! I believed every one of his damn lies but he can't lie to me anymore."

JD tried prying the phone out of her hand, mumbling, "She's kicking me out. She doesn't get how much I love her. She doesn't get how much I need her."

Lola pushed him aside and said into the phone, "Listen, John is dropping Nick off in a couple of hours, and I don't want any evidence of JD around here. Too bad too, because Nick really liked him. But he screwed up that relationship too."

"When did he tell you?" JD's friend asked her.

"Tell me? He didn't tell me. I caught him red handed. He was shooting up in my bathroom."

"No, I'm not talking about that. I'm talking about AIDS. You both need to be tested. Didn't he tell you?" Then the friend said, "Shit."

"WHAT DID YOU SAY?"

October 1991

SHATTERED

Gary's long pause told Ella what she already knew was true, and she responded by throwing back half the glass of vodka.

"I'm not doing this with you. You hear me?" Gary snatched the glass and bottle from his wife's hands.

"Is that because you are too busy doing it with Michelle?" Ella snapped back with glaring eyes full of rage.

"Leave Michelle out of this. This has nothing to do with her. This is about you and your drinking. I've had it! I can't take it anymore. You refuse to be helped. As much as I've tried to talk you into treatment. Tried be understanding..." Gary threw up his hand. "Oh hell, Ella, I'm leaving you. I'm not going to live my life like this anymore. There, I said it. You want to drink yourself to death, go ahead. But I'm not going to watch you do it. I'm moving into town, and I'm taking Brice with me."

Ella didn't respond to this. She mumbled, "You haven't touched me in so long, I can't remember the last time. Is it better with her?"

"What? Don't ask me questions like that. You're pathetic. God. Okay, okay. I'll play this little game of yours. Who would you rather be intimate with? You? Who are either hungover or too drunk to stay awake to even fake romance? It's like doing it with a sack of potatoes. Your mouth always tastes like cotton. Your breath is always stale. Your mascara is always smeared. Your sapphire blue eyes, once the most soulful eyes in the world, are always bloodshot, glazed over, and out of focus. And look at your clothes. You dress like...I can't do this...I just can't."

"Does she swallow?" Ella formed a big O with her mouth.

"Jesus, I wish you could hear yourself. You've become someone I don't recognize...or even want to know. If only your parents could see you now."

Suddenly his wife bolted toward him, knelt down, and fumbled to unzip his pants. "I can do it. Is this what you want? I can do it. It's been a long time, but I can do it."

Gary slapped her hands away and grabbed her chin. "Don't! Get up! Sit at the table. We need to talk."

An hour passed as the two of them hurled accusations and blame back and forth in a verbal tennis match that got more ugly and more brutal by the minute. "Don't tear our family apart, Gary. I beg you." Ella was scared and consumed with grief.

"Don't worry. You've always got your bottle and your girlfriends to keep you company. I doubt you'll miss Brice and me for a moment. I just pray you find your way."

The phone rang. They stared at one another, their verbal sparring so rudely interrupted. Gary struggled to his feet and picked up the receiver.

"Hello?" He listened for five seconds, and then said, "Yes, this is Gary Foster. What about Brice? Is something wrong? Is he okay?"

Gary's voice rose with concern.

"What is it?" A wave of panic drove Ella to her feet and she began pacing. "What is it?"

Gary held up his hand, silencing her. "It's the school principal," he mouthed.

"Okay, I understand," he said into the phone grimly. "I'll be there in forty-five minutes."

He hung up the phone and faced his wife. "Brice just got suspended from school. They caught him smoking a joint. I'm going down there."

"I'm coming with you!" Ella fired back. "I told you last month that this was going to happen. After you let him pierce his tongue. Didn't I? But would you listen? NO! It's always me that's the problem, the one that's wrong! It's never the rest of you! You're having an affair and our son is doing drugs, but I'm the problem? Fuck you, Gary. You can move in with your lover if you want, but you are not taking MY son. I will fight you for Brice!"

"Yeah, right, Ella," Gary said with derision. "You won't even fight for yourself."

November 1991

DEVASTATION

Laska was standing on the front porch howling as Bridget, Michael, and Shauna wobbled from the burning house. Disoriented and hacking, they tried freeing their lungs from the smoke of the fiery monster that was once their home. The acrid smoke followed them down the porch stairs like a demon stalking its prey. Laska stopped howling and tried to follow, but his legs wouldn't hold him. Bridget clutched his collar and tried pulling him along. Michael and Shauna stopped to help.

"No! Get your sister away from the house, Michael," Bridget screamed. "Go!"

Bridget mustered all her strength, but she couldn't get Laska to budge. Suddenly his collar gave way, slipping over his head and sending Bridget tumbling backwards down the stairs and into the snow.

She scrambled to her feet and took a step toward the porch, but the burning inferno drove her back. Laska lay immobile, his imploring eyes opened wide, fighting for breath in the overwhelming soot. All Bridget, Michael, and Shauna could do, huddled together beneath a thin quilt, was shout his name over and over again, urging him to move.

"Laska! Come on, Laska. Come on, boy! Come on!" Laska's ears perked up when he heard his name, but his eyes closed and he struggled to raise his head. With his muzzle pointed skyward, smoke and fire consuming him, he let out one last soulful howl before the flames engulfed him.

"L...A...S...K...A..." Bridget wailed. Her kids screamed. But their voices were drowned out by the crashing, shattering sound of glass raining down around them as one by one the windows exploded out of the house.

A distraught Michael broke from his mother's grip and raced toward the raging fire, screaming Laska's name.

"Michael! NO!" Bridget sprang after him.

Michael was halfway up the stairs when the heat brought him up short and stole every ounce of his breath. For a brief moment he was paralyzed, and in that one moment the front door collapsed in flames onto the porch and buried Laska underneath it.

Michael didn't have time to scream. He felt his mother gripping his arm and pulling him to safety just as the porch collapsed and sent burning timbers flying.

Bridget dragged her kids down the slope away from the house. Wrapping her arms tightly around them, she threw back her head and released a primal howl of anguish, sounding so much like Laska one would have wondered whose voice it really was breaking through the destructive roar. The howl turned to painful, wracking cries that rose from the very depth of her being. Sobbing, Bridget slowly turned her children around and walked away from their burning home for the last time.

"I'm here," she said to her kids through the cries. "I'm here. We're going to be okay. I promise. I love you guys. I love you."

Michael and Shauna clung desperately to her and she to them.

317

The first couple of days following the fire Bridget racked her brain to find a way to contact Dan. It was futile. He never called when he was hunting. She had no idea how to find him.

Maybe it was a good thing, because Bridget wanted to kill him for his negligence. The batteries on the smoke detectors had died last summer. She remembered the night because she had to wake Dan from a dead sleep at five in the morning, and get him to pull out the tray and batteries to silence the incessant beeping that had woken everyone else up. Those battery trays had been sitting open for four months, waiting for him to drag the ladder into the house and replace them with the ones Bridget had bought that same week. No matter how many times she reminded him, he never made it a priority. Knowing how close they had come to death, she held Dan responsible.

On the other hand, she thanked God for Laska. The dog had saved them. Somehow, he had used the last of his strength to drag himself from his pen to the house and to rouse them with his barking.

Bridget's grief and anger over losing such a faithful companion were unbearable. The memory of his eyes looking at them from that burning porch haunted her. It haunted the kids too. They cried for him every night when they went to bed. And when Shauna said, "I miss his slobbery good night kisses, Mom," Bridget wanted to die.

November 1991

WRATH

Few people had ever witnessed the "Wrath of Lola." And those who had wished never to be subjected to it again. Lola floated above most earthly concerns on ethereal realms that protected her from the reality of accountability. Then came AIDS. The potential of this horrifying reality roared into her humanness.

JD's bodily fluids had combined with hers for years, months, days; and once again this morning. Nothing could transcend the reality of that.

JD curled into a fetal position on the couch as she hit him over and over again with her fists. Spitting venomous words and screaming, "I fucking hate you. I wish you were dead. Where's the coke or heroin or whatever you're shooting up? Let me help you. Let me help you die. Everyone will believe you overdosed. They probably expect it."

She drove her fist into his side. "AIDS! AIDS! You cocksucker. You not only jeopardized your pitiful, meaningless life, but mine. Don't you get it? I actually love my life, you sick fuck. It's a matter of life and death...life and fucking death. I don't want to die like this. Not from AIDS. Not now, leaving Nick without a mother. I know what that's like. You fucking asshole. This can't be happening to me."

Snot ran from her nose and tears streamed from her bloodshot, swollen eyes. She stopped hitting him, struck suddenly by the actuality that her bodily fluids might contain the AIDS virus. Appalled at the thought, she found herself hating her own body for the first time in her life and ran outside into the frigid weather.

She looked up into the falling snow and screamed to her Creator: "How could you let this happen? Why didn't you warn me? I thought you loved me and protected me against harm. You always gave me signs in the past. Why not this time? Why, God? Why didn't you hit me over the head with a two by four? Why didn't you warn me?"

Even as Lola's earth-shattering wail echoed off the ridge, she abruptly stopped crying. And then she heard it: the howl of a coyote echoing her own cry. And then she understood.

"Oh my...oh my...oh shit...I get it...you just did."

December 1991

SHARED EMOTIONS

Gary moved out, and Bridget and her kids moved in.

Ella was glad. Glad not to be alone in these trying times. But she was finding it increasingly difficult to put on a happy face.

She was so tired she could barely stand up. She was not sleeping well, and knowing that she needed to be there for Bridget and her family only compounded this lack of sleep. She busied herself in the kitchen, putting away the breakfast dishes and trying unsuccessfully to block out the crying coming from the next room. The anger, fear, and grief emanating from that room were palpable. She could feel herself being sucked in, contaminated by the sheer force of the emotions consuming her friend's family.

The answer was only a matter of inches away, there in the cupboard over the refrigerator. Her hands began to shake as she reached for the handle, shook even more as she reached for the bottle of vodka hidden there.

She uncapped the bottle and took a long, deep swig, rationalizing as she always did: *I know it's only ten in the morning but the only way I'll be able to help these people is if I remain calm and reasonable. It's just a little crutch to make me strong for them. There's nothing wrong with that. I'm doing it for them…to help them.*

December 1991

CHARITY

Bridget had taken to talking to herself; or more like, fuming to herself. Her favorite place was in the car where the words echoed off the dashboard and she didn't have to worry about anyone thinking she'd lost her marbles.

"I guess Karma had its way with you, Dan, didn't it? I can't imagine which would be worse: reliving the terror of the fire over and over again or pulling into the driveway at midnight and seeing only the stark silhouette of a chimney, totally unaware of the circumstances and wondering if your family was dead or alive. That's what you got, Dan. Confusion and bewilderment. Serves you fucking right. If you'd only thought about contacting someone while you were gone or just checking in to make sure we were okay, you would have been spared that experience. No, not you, Dan. And not me either. I was destined to have a front row seat for every shitty drama life could throw our way, up close and personal."

The weeks that followed the fire blended into a series of indistinguishable moments for Bridget. Everything seemed to have a surreal quality to it, like being in a foggy haze. The one exception was the kids. She needed to be strong and positive for them, and she promised herself that she would never let them down no matter what God threw at her.

Bridget parked the car in front of Ella's house and climbed out. For good measure, she clenched her fist and shook it towards the sky. "Do you know what it's like to be human, Omnipotent One? Fuck no! We're flesh and bone. And in case you were wondering, our hearts feel emotions. And right now I have all the emotions I can handle: love, grief, sadness, emptiness, anger. You name it, I'm feeling it."

She opened the back door of the car and stared at three large garbage bags full of clothes people had donated to them, and all she could think was: *Does anyone really know what it means to lose everything? To not even have a pair of shoes or underwear to call your own. And who knew you couldn't get any personal identification without having any personal identification. What a circle jerk that is! I'm just thankful that Mom still had my original birth certificate and was able to overnight it to me. Thought I was going to have to kill some city administrator.*

Bridget groaned as she lifted one of the bags and carried it inside. What a scene she had created at the social services office. She was astonished and dismayed by how generous and caring people could be for someone they didn't know and had never heard of before. It gave Bridget hope for the human race.

The truth was, accepting any form of charity was almost impossible for Bridget. If it hadn't been for the kids, she would have sent it all back. That, and her dad's words ringing in her ears. "So daughter, you're too good for charity. That's nothing but your false pride talking to you now."

Donations came from so many sources that she couldn't begin to keep up with the flood of clothing, toys, and household items people were sending. Bridget was so grateful to Ella for extending her home to her family. Being able to stay up on the mountain, with the same friends and the same routine, was good for the kids. And what was good for her kids – the friends near at hand and some semblance of a routine – was good for her too.

She and Dan needed to figure out their future, and it didn't look pretty. Bridget shrugged away the thought.

The hardest donation for Bridget to accept came from a local company that adopted them for Christmas. The company's employees had unanimously decided to forgo their office Christmas party to help a family in need. Just thinking about the kindness and generosity of those fine people brought a lump to Bridget's throat.

The night the company's representatives came to Ella's house to present Bridget, Michael, and Shauna with dozens of wrapped Christmas gifts and a check for $2,000, she couldn't stop the tears from flowing. Here were these perfect strangers embracing her and her family and bringing true meaning to the word "giving."

How do you repay such generosity? It weighed heavily on her heart. So did the guilt and anger she felt surrounding the decisions she had to make.

The only thing Bridget could figure out was that she had failed to close the damper on the wood stove, which resulted in a chimney fire that ignited the roof of the house.

Dan blamed her. She blamed him for not replacing the batteries in the smoke detectors – a decision that cost Laska his life – and for failing to get homeowners insurance for their house.

His rage was equaled only by her fury.

Dan procrastinated on everything she felt was important, including the attention she and the kids deserved, health insurance for his family, and something as basic as homeowners insurance.

They had truly lost everything they had worked for. And, at the top of that list were their love and respect for each other. Anger was their only bond.

And that's where their conversation that morning had led them. Dan was actually trying to convince her to clean out their old pink trailer and move into 300 square feet of misery while he figured out how to rebuild the house.

"Dan, there's no fucking way this family can move into that damn trailer trash heap! Did you not hear what Ella said? If Social Services got wind of it, they would snatch these kids away from us in a heartbeat. We're going to move into an apartment in town. For Christ's sake, can't you think about your family's well being for once?" she fumed. She paced. She glared at him with hateful eyes. "Rebuild the house? With what? We have no money. Are you fucking kidding me? You're a goddamn fool and that makes me an even bigger one for still being with you. I've fucking had it...I'm taking the kids and moving to town. You can live wherever you want as long as it's not with me!" Bridget's normally beautiful green eyes were black with rage and intention, causing Dan to retreat a few steps to gather his defenses.

"Bridget, I will never forgive you for burning down the house! Did you hear me? Never!" His face turned purple as he screamed at her.

"That's it? That's all you have? It was a fucking accident, Dan! I didn't spend the last year ignoring the damper like you did the smoke detectors and the insurance. Take some responsibility for our loss. Everything could've been replaced if you'd only given a shit! Now, we all get to live with YOUR choice!"

"Oh yeah? You think Laska could be replaced? You're to blame for his death. You, and no one else," he sneered. "So go ahead. Go ahead and move to town. I'm not leaving this mountain for you or anybody! Just remember when people ask: YOU left me and gave up on being a family!"

The next day, Bridget visited the burned-out hole they used to call "home." She walked over to the hearth and chimney, fell to her knees, and wept.

The voice she heard clawing its way into her bruised and battered mind belonged to her grandmother, and with the words came the embrace of an unseen force of love and compassion.

"My child, do you not understand your purpose? Brighid, the Goddess of so many faces? Is it not a wonder that you live at such an elevation, Brighid, the Goddess of lofty ideals and elevations? Home is this mountaintop, and you brought witness to the flames of infinite height. You, the Mother Goddess of fertility and midwifery, and the protector of children. You, the 'Bright Flame,' the antithesis of the Cailleach ushering in the first Green of Spring and bringing the promise of abundance and beauty to the naked whiteness of winter. The trinity exists within you – maiden, matron and crone – but you have sought out two others to help complete this in you. The colors of white, black, and red – of ashes, smoke, and flame – are you, Brighid. You are the personification of the eternal flame... beautiful, a face framed by your mane of untamed curls of red and a blazing personality fighting for the matrilineal lineage of All that is Woman."

Bridget raised her head. She opened her swollen eyes and saw her great-grandmother standing before her. Her clothes were tattered, her face dirtied, and her hands calloused. But her posture demanded reverence and admiration. "The common people are your ancestors, and you, as the Goddess Brighid, stand for All common folk. Yet you have chosen to remain separate. Brighid of this time and place, you must be careful not to destroy yourself with the eternal flame that rages within, or you will destroy all you hold dear. We knew right from the start that you were too hot to handle," her great-grandmother said, as a smile formed on her lips. "And that is why you were born under the water sign of Cancer, so that your fire could be cooled."

The vision evolved, and the Women of the All embraced Bridget, arms holding her close, whispers encouraging her to use the fire within to illuminate her soul. But Bridget fought back, struggling against them, and breathing out an angry flame that extinguished them into the gathering mist.

Her altered state continued as she shook herself and shouted, "Fuck you all. Just leave me alone. Do you really think I believe this shit? I am just trying to fucking survive! This must be some kind of sick karmic joke!"

And then she suddenly came awake, blessed with an indescribable amnesia, for only her soul would hold the memory of the vision.

With the amnesia came calmness, a calmness that surrounded her as she took from her pocket several small vials. Into them, she scooped several handfuls of ashes from the only standing remnant of her house, the stone fireplace. She held the vials high and said, "This hearth was our home. Bless those who lived here."

December 1991

REPRIEVE

The HIV test results took a week.

Lola decided to use all her metaphysical knowledge to make the results come back negative. She lit candles to enhance spells, chanted, prayed, and meditated. In the end, however, she just pleaded with the higher powers to heal her.

Promises were made to be more careful, less promiscuous, eat organic food, volunteer at the hospital, anything at all to change her fate. Depression reared its head. Her answering machine picked up unanswered phone calls. People stopped by to see why the social butterfly was not flitting around. She told people she had the flu and was very contagious. A note to that effect was unceremoniously pasted on the front door window.

John agreed to take Nick for the week after she explained her "flu" symptoms. When he drove up to get his son and saw Lola's appearance, he practically ran out of the house for fear of catching whatever it was she was suffering from. She looked like a sallow-skinned, alcohol-guzzling, cigarette-smoking middle-aged woman who had lost her life to hard luck.

Lola's self-loathing had consumed her over the past two weeks, but what scared her most was what happened the night before she got the test results. She was sitting in her bedroom and staring out the window when an apparition from an age long past materialized right before her eyes. What she saw was a long line of starving Indians walking through the snow, their tattered blankets wrapped tightly around them, the wind whipping the ends into the air like broken and battered bird wings. Impoverishment showed as much in their demeanor as it did in their rags. They had lost everything: their land, their health, and their families, but most importantly their dignity. Battered victims with their heads hanging down, shoulders slumped, eyes blank. A never-ending line, thousands upon thousands of the living dead trudging toward their fateful destiny. Some too weak to stand, others too weak to help.

Lola watched as a mother carried her young son in her arms, tenderly talking to the boy, soothing, cooing, and despairing. The mother aimed her gaze directly at Lola, her eyes beckoning Lola to join the walk of her people. Lola broke down in tears, feeling one with the mother, their bond the ugly knowledge that they were just waiting to die. Walking directly behind her was an old man, the very one who had appeared at her parents' wreckage site years ago. His eyes held hers. His voice rasped, "You've heard of the cycle of life, haven't you? Death. Transformation."

The hooting of an owl shook Lola from her trance. She sat bolt upright and stared out into the open space beyond her cabin. The apparition was gone, but not the weight of its dark message. She clamored to her feet. Feeling the need for comfort and protection, she ran to the drawer where she kept her special turquoise necklace. Special because Sandy had given it to her upon her arrival in Colorado. It symbolized "new beginnings." Lola slumped empty handed to the floor, the owl's haunting voice seemingly mocking her. The necklace was gone. Her life was over.

⌣⌒

The phone call came early the next morning. Lola practically collapsed when she heard the results were negative for HIV. But her joy was short lived when the caller explained that she would have to be tested again in six months to make sure she was still negative. Sobbing with relief and dread, she called Bridget. The moment her redheaded friend answered, the words spewed out of Lola's mouth. She held nothing back and only paused when Bridget managed to get a word in.

She said, "Slow down, Lola. You're talking too fast and crying too hard for me to understand you."

She went through it again. The AIDS scare, the future retesting, her financial disaster, and the loss of her necklace.

"And I thought my life was 'up in smoke.'" Bridget laughed at her own joke.

"Oh, Bridge, I didn't mean to dump all this stuff on you when you, of all people, really have absolutely nothing."

"Fuck you very much Lola for making me feel shittier than you." She chuckled knowing Lola meant no maliciousness. "But I think I have a solution. Not just for me, but for you."

"Thank God, Bridge, I didn't know how I was going to get out of this mess all by my little ol' lonesome."

Bridget rolled her eyes and continued. "You know that Steve is a realtor, right? He told me a client of his has a huge house that's big enough for you and Nick, me and the kids and it's for rent. And the rent's damn cheap."

"But I don't have any money," Lola confessed. "Not a red cent."

"Here's how I see it. You rent your house for a pretty penny because it's beautiful and perfect for someone who wants to be in the mountains. You'll have enough left over from the rent to pay for half the cost of this new place. The kids want to be in town anyway. We'd be closer to everything, including you finding work. The best part is that it's been vacant for two years and the owners aren't going to make a fuss about the rent; they just want it occupied. Steve said it's barely outside the city limits and surrounded by ranches. It's 4,500 square feet, has a barn, a pond, and people already board horses there. I'd love to have you be my roommate. And by the way, you'll test negative in six months too. I just know it. What do you say?"

"I say yes," Lola said. And then, as an afterthought, "But really, Bridge, why is the rent so cheap?"

FIRE

Day 3

"Child, my dear, dear child...look at me...see me...see us. You're so young to go through so much pain right now, but you will survive."
~ The Circle of Na'mow Handbook – Hazel, Second Generation

September 16, 1996, Monday morning

When the mountain wildfire started on Saturday morning, the plumes of smoke could also be seen from the flatlands, well east of the Flatirons. Thunderheads briefly huddled over the high peaks, then dissipated into fluffy fair weather clouds scattering throughout the turquoise sky. Half an hour later, concentrated black bursts of smoke billowed up from behind the peaks, integrating into the mixture of clouds and creating a gray swirling palette in the sky. Flatlanders looking westward wondered if they were seeing clouds or smoke.

Watching the mountain wildfire from a distance didn't alleviate any fear or panic. In fact, the anxiety spread from person to person just like the flames from tree to tree, and increased as smoke infiltrated the unadulterated air surrounding Boulder. Hours later, the smoke traveled even farther toward the eastern plains, like a runaway freight train as the wind picked up speed down the mountain's sheer rock face.

As the smell of the impending disaster filled the air, many people found solace in the busyness of daily routines. By engaging in mundane activities, they tried to push away the mounting feelings of trauma and grief.

Evacuees who sought shelter in Boulder were surprised to learn that people far removed from the tragedy were often just as traumatized as they were. As for the lucky ones, they would find safe comfort in the embrace of calm and loving arms.

IN TOWN

The century-old farmhouse was about twenty minutes from town.

Sam put an arm around Lola's shoulders as they made their way up the walk to the front porch. The door swung open before Sam had time to knock, and a spry, elderly woman stepped out and gave Sam a warm embrace. This was his Aunt Hattie, and her stature and feistiness always reminded Sam of Barbara Stanwyck in "The Big Valley."

"Aunt Hattie, this here is Lola. The one I told you about."

Hattie stuck out her hand. She had a firm grip and a warm smile. "How do you do, Lola? Welcome."

"She's going to be needin' one of your deluxe breakfasts...no coffee...but lots of milk. Her stomach's been a might uneasy lately so she might need more time at the table for digesting." Sam had barely made his introductions when a dog barreled out the door and started jumping up and around the couple. Sam settled him down and said, "And you already know this rascal."

"Hey, Scout." Lola ruffled his ears.

"Got him and Dolly off the mountain right quick – the first night of the fire. You'll get real used to seeing him around."

"Yes, you will," Hattie assured her. She held the door open. "Let's go inside."

Sam led them into the kitchen and pulled out a chair for Lola. "Here, Lola, sit down. I've got Dolly to check up on."

Sam went back out, and the dog followed.

"I'm so sorry about your husband," Hattie said. "Well, I guess he's not your husband anymore, but I'm still so sorry."

"Thank you. I feel so lost," Lola admitted, surprised at her own candor around a woman she'd just met.

"Well, let's start by fattening you up some," Hattie said. She bustled around the kitchen like a steam engine picking up speed, and her nervous chatter made up for Lola's silence. Lola was just glad to have some female company.

After breakfast, she took a bath in an old claw-foot bathtub. She even put on a little makeup but skipped the mascara, knowing she still had tears to shed.

"My Lord," Aunt Hattie exclaimed when she reappeared in the kitchen. "When you first walked in, you looked like you were rode hard and put away wet, but now you're pretty as a speckled pup under a little red wagon."

"Thank you, Aunt Hattie. I feel much better. And now I know where Sam gets all his country sayings from." Lola laughed, her fondness for the woman growing with every passing minute.

They heard footsteps out on the porch, and then Sam appeared at the window. He motioned Lola to come outside. "Got something to show you."

Lola pulled herself up and went, mainly because she didn't have the strength to argue.

"Now, that's the Lola I recognize," Sam said. He looked Lola up and down, then led her toward the corral and the beautiful palomino watching their approach. "You remember Dolly, don't you? She needs some exercise and someone new to do it. You ride, don't you?"

"What? I got all cleaned up for this?" Lola shook her head. "Are you crazy? I'll smell like a horse."

"You'll smell like the outdoors," Sam corrected. "And you can always take another bath."

"But shouldn't we be getting back to the hospital? What about John?"

"I gave the nursing station my cell phone number and Hattie's home number if John's condition happens to change. We'll head back in a bit. Come on, let's take a ride."

They went into the corral, and Sam helped Lola into Dolly's saddle. Then he led them both out into the open pasture away from the view of the foothills smoking in the distance.

Lola's brown wavy hair, straight posture, and her ease in the saddle made for one beautiful sight. "I haven't been on a horse since I was a little girl. Totally forgot about it until just now," she said to Sam. "My dad had a friend that owned some acreage outside Las Vegas. I must've been about twelve. Dolly's smell and that leather scent of the saddle brought it all back."

The air was crisp, the breeze slight. Lola filled her lungs and cleared her mind. She looked over the plain, thinking of its vastness and how alone and lost she felt, how insignificant.

Sam led horse and rider on a well-worn path toward a grove of huge cottonwoods and a small, rambling stream. The smell of decomposing leaves and the sound of running water conjured up old, ancient memories, and Lola let her imagination wander.

"You know, there used to be Arapaho encampments all along this small river basin. This farm belonged to Aunt Hattie's husband's family. His ancestors were friends to those Indians," Sam said. "They had a mutual respect for one another and for this land. I used to spend a lot of time here. Lots of good memories."

They stopped by the water's edge so Dolly could drink and graze. Conversation between them flowed as naturally as the water. They shared stories and memories, hopes and fears. Eventually Lola remounted Dolly, and they prepared to go.

"I think you can ride back without me leading you," Sam said. He took Lola's hand before relinquishing the reins. He said, "Lola, you're ready to take control. You let Dolly know where you want to go but be clear about your intentions. She needs precise signals from you."

"I don't know, Sam." Lola looked worried.

"You can do it, Lola. Courage is being scared to death and saddling up anyway." Dolly whinnied in agreement as Sam walked away, heading back to the farmhouse.

As Lola trotted by Sam, she exuded an untamed confidence only found by having a good friend to talk to…a friend that just listened.

Before they left for the hospital that afternoon, Hattie pulled Sam aside and suggested he put in a call to Ella and Bridget and invite them to spend some time with Lola at the farmhouse. "I've lived long enough to know when a woman needs some female companionship, and this is most definitely one of those times."

Sam smiled tenderly at his aunt, "I'm one step ahead of you. Already did."

"Somebody must've raised you up right," Hattie laughed.

Then Sam and Lola drove to the hospital, and spent the afternoon talking to doctors about John's condition and questioning nurses, hoping for signs of improvement. Nothing had changed. Lola spent an hour at John's bedside before kissing him goodnight and returning to Hattie's place. When she saw Ella, Bridget, and their girls, she broke into tears and ran into their arms. Sam watched the scene and then said to his aunt, "If that ain't a sight. Guess we were both right about a girl needing her gals."

"Why don't you girls all come inside," Hattie called to them. "We'll have something to drink and then I'll rustle up some dinner."

They congregated in the kitchen while Shauna and Alena explored. "The older I get, the earlier I eat," Hattie said, stirring a pot on the stove. "You know all those early bird specials at restaurants? That's just so they can make money off us old folks. We need lots of time to digest our food before we head to bed before 9:00 p.m., you know. Otherwise the gas could blow us clear over into the next county."

The old woman had a belly laugh that reminded everyone of Bridget's laugh. "So, I'll have this dinner ready by five-thirty. In the meantime, maybe these young ones can feed the chickens for me." Hattie looked from Shauna to Alena with a gaze as warm as hot milk. "Can you do that for me?"

"Sure can," Shauna said. Hattie gave the girls some feed and pointed to the yard. "The rest of you can help with the potatoes and corn."

Bridget cleared her throat and said, "I don't mean to be rude, Mrs.…"

Hattie was already shushing her with a raised hand. "You can call me Aunt Hattie just like Sam and the rest of the world," Hattie chuckled.

"Okay, Aunt Hattie. I'll just get straight to the point. I've had one helluva day and was wondering if you had any whiskey?"

"Good God, child, a woman after my own heart. Sam, you know where it is. Bring us the good stuff. None of that rotgut. There's a bottle of Jameson in the back I save for special occasions. Glasses all around."

"None for me," Ella said.

"Nor me," Lola added.

No one questioned why Ella wasn't drinking, but none of them were quite sure why Lola wasn't, except for Sam. He gave her a wink and a nod and refilled her milk glass.

Dinner was delicious. Homemade chicken and all the fixings and a beautifully lattice-crusted apple pie for dessert.

When dinner was over, Sam took Scout, Alena, and Shauna outside so they could spend some time with Dolly. The ladies all congregated in the living room where Hattie held court, and the talk was private and personal and more meaningful than any of them could have imagined.

FIRE

Day 3

"Seeing with focused eyes doesn't allow for peripheral vision. Gazing with soft eyes allows us to open to sacred mysteries."
~ The Circle of Na'mow Handbook – Hattie, Second Generation

September 16, 1996, Monday afternoon

If anyone thought the fire would die down overnight, they were sadly mistaken. In fact, the profusion of dried fuel from downed trees, parched underbrush, and scorched shrubbery increased the power of its annihilating force, and the change could be heard and felt even in the blackness of night.

Erratic winds shifted continuously within the fire zone, causing great concern among firefighters, law enforcement, pilots, and residents.

Eru'tan looked on. The wind had a purpose. It moved over the earth like a great hand pushing the elements. The heat of the fire drew it in. The wind reacted to changing currents high above even as it pushed the fire down one slope and across the face of another. Together, wind and fire had a purpose. They culled the weak from

Na'mow's slopes and made them fertile for new growth, new life, and the inevitability of change.

The mountain was impervious to the fire.

The fruits of its soil, however, all that grew above ground and reached out to the sun, was not. What survived was meant to survive. What died gave birth to the new: aspen trees, new grasses, new groundcovers, blooms no one had seen since the tall trees blocked out the sun.

It worked. It may not have struck the inhabitants of the mountain as pretty, but it worked.

ON THE MOUNTAIN

Anyone who lived in the city, any city, might ask why the men of the mountain refused to evacuate their homes and their land when the fire was so out of control. They could hose down roofs, exterior walls, and porches, but that really ensured nothing, not with the power of this blaze. Yet they stayed. The mountain was their home. The mountain had opened its arms to them and shared its bounty. They had to do whatever was in their power, even if it proved futile.

Most slept in their own beds, then returned to Dan's house to regroup and lay out their plans for the day.

No house was safe. Not really. No one could let down his guard and nerves were starting to unravel. Some men looked unrecognizable as beards three and four days old covered their faces, wrinkles appeared deeper, and eyes grew increasingly more bloodshot. Smoke permeated skin and clothes.

They monitored the comings and goings of the slurry bombers dropping their retardant and helicopters dumping their huge buckets of water. They stayed in touch as best they could with firefighters trying desperately to create firebreaks across the mountain face, but they realized how futile this was proving to be as the blaze jumped over those lines in a hurried fury to devour more of the landscape.

They heard a report of the fire racing up a nearby gulch flanked by a steep-sided ridge dense with vegetation, grass, and fallen timber. They heard weather reports predicting a possibility of a wind shift. This was not good news. If the wind shifted, the fire would rapidly blow up the gulch, travel through the middle of the subdivision, and burn out the entire residential area. Total devastation of every property would be a real possibility.

They were told that a limited supply of slurry was available for the rest of the day. Those in charge were going to stop all drops in the main fire area and focus on the fire line between the back burn area and the neighborhood. The retardant would be splattered next to a winding roadbed that served as the main escape route for any resident still braving the fire. They heard a hopeful report that helicopters were standing by to put out hotspots that might jump the fire zone. Thank God water was readily available from the lake.

Brice had been given an important task. His job was to make periodic trips on Dan's ATV to the jeep road where the deputy sheriff had set up a command post. Any updates were immediately relayed to Dan, Gary, and the rest of the men.

Herb was pacing nervously at the foot of the driveway when he saw Brice heading his way. Herb was half panicked over the fact that he had left Betty's wedding ring in the top drawer of his dresser back home.

Brice brought the ATV to a halt, sensing something amiss. "Herb, you okay?"

"I need your help, Brice," he said hurriedly.

"Sure. What's up?"

Herb explained about Betty's ring. "It's the one keepsake I can't bear losing. I need a lift back there."

"Can't do it, Herb," Brice said. "The deputy told me to stay put, because they're going to conduct a back burn. We don't want to get caught in that. And even if they weren't, I would have to ask my dad. And I know what he would say. He'd say, 'Forget it.'"

"I understand your concerns, son, but I just couldn't forgive myself if I lost Betty's ring. I can't believe I left without it." Herb's voice turned to pleading. "What do you say? It won't take long. We'll be back in a jiffy. Please!"

Brice felt pity for the old guy. He really did. "Okay, but we're going to have to go off road, because they'll be stopping everyone on the road." Brice tossed his thumb in the direction of the passenger seat. "Hop on and hang on tight. I don't need you falling off this thing."

The going was slow. They worked their way across private lands and over some very challenging terrain, trying to remain undetected by prying eyes and the binoculars of law enforcement and firefighters.

They were a quarter mile from Herb's house when a wave of total darkness enveloped them and clouds of noxious smoke caused Brice to hit the brakes. Seconds later, a wall of intense heat stopped them dead in their tracks.

IN TOWN

Lola walked into the living room of Hattie's farmhouse and found herself staring at a shadowbox hanging from the wall.

It was filled with arrowheads neatly arranged in concentric circles. Sitting on a table below the box was a reed-filled basket that contained beautiful feathers, several colorful stones, a deerskin beaded medicine pouch, and two weathered, leather-bound journals.

Photographs of Hattie's ancestors covered the rest of the tabletop, and Lola felt herself drawn to the one of a woman in a long worn dress and bonnet. She was holding a shotgun by her side and managed to look both feminine and menacing in the most compelling way.

Lola lifted the photo carefully from the table and looked at it more closely. She didn't hear Hattie enter the room, only her voice, gentle and proud.

"My mother," she said. "She was sick of coyotes taking her chickens, so she declared war on them."

"She looks like the kind of woman I'd rather have on my side," Lola said with a smile.

"Oh, indeed you would," Hattie agreed. "We all learned to shoot at a very young age, and those varmints were our prime targets. Nothing personal, but our livelihood depended on it. We learned to fend for ourselves back then, and that's the God's truth. Heck, I got a loaded shotgun in my bedroom closet to this very day, and you'd better believe my aim is still darn good."

"That I can believe," Lola said. She pointed in the direction of an old leather pouch that looked as if it had seen better days, yet still radiated the craftsmanship of its creator. "It's beautiful. Kind of reminds me of the ones our friend Gaia gave us some years back. Mind if I hold it?"

"I don't mind at all," Hattie said, laying the pouch in Lola's hand. "The Indians that lived around here were always a good lot to my husband's family. Mutual respect is what got both sides through. His mother used to tell us stories about Indians trading away their most beautiful belongings just for a bit of food; those were hard times. Who knows how many of them starved to death? But there were good times too. She had stories about playing with the Indian kids and the friendships she made that brought tears to my eyes."

Hattie pointed to the arrowheads arranged in the shadowbox. "Those were found on my family's first homestead, the place where Sam lives now. We found plenty of them down here too."

"What about this? Is it a medicine bag?" Lola said, gesturing at the unusual-looking leather bag.

"Think so. Yep. My father found it up on your mountain at our old homestead. You know, Sam's place now. It was hanging from a branch apparently," Hattie explained. "At first, he just left it, thinking someone would surely come back for it. They never did. Finally, he took it down. Said he'd keep it safe. No one's ever opened it up. Pa forbade it. Said it was someone's hopes and dreams in there, so it was for the owner's eyes only. Every so often, I'm tempted. But then I hear Pa's voice, and the temptation goes away pretty darn quick."

"Someone's hopes and dreams." Lola felt a tear run down her cheek. She touched her turquoise necklace and thought of the pouch she had safely tucked away in her purse. Yes, all three of them treasured this small, wonderful gift that Gaia had given them and the significance of it was never lost on them. The pouch had become a permanent companion. Ella's was in her toiletry bag and Bridget had hers in her cowboy hat in the front seat of her car.

"What are you guys up to?" Ella and Bridget walked in and Lola waved them over.

"Hey, come and look at what Hattie is showing me. So cool," Lola said.

"Oh, wow!" Ella was drawn immediately to a photo of a group of women with wide smiles and necklaces with matching silver pendants hanging low on their chests; it was a portrait of Betty, Hattie, Olive, and Hazel taken decades ago. "Oh my God, I've seen this picture before, Hattie. At Herb's place. In the makeshift altar he built in Betty's honor."

Ella set the photo aside and allowed her fingers to run over the cover of one of the worn leather-bound journals and the spiral emblem embossed there. "And I've seen this emblem before too. Hattie. What is…?"

Hattie smiled and held up her hand. "Be patient, my dears." She gestured at the journals. "Those are about my journey…with my friends."

"Your journey?" Bridget asked.

"Just like all of you. I'll get around to telling you all about it before you leave here. But first you'll have to tell me about your own journeys. Bet that's some good storytelling. And I have a feeling you'll be very surprised at how much we have in common!"

341

They were interrupted at that very moment when Sam hustled back into the house with Scout at his side. "Nasty out there," Sam said. He switched on the television and turned on his scanner. "Let's catch up on the weather and see what's going on with this infernal fire of ours."

"I just hope everyone is safe up there," Ella said. "I feel so stupid letting Brice stay up there with the guys."

"Hard letting go, isn't it," Hattie said, as the wind rattled at the windows and night blackened. "Sam's told me you all have a very special neighborhood up there. Always has been. Even he knows it, and he's a man."

This got a smile out of the women despite their worry. "I know exactly how you feel. To feel like you belong to something bigger than yourselves, something more significant than just a life with a mundane existence. I know what it's like to love the land. You can lose yourself in its dirt. When you know every tree, each rock, the nests of birds, the dens of animals, the game trails, the name of all its flowers and shrubs, and the sounds that pass over its landscape. You become a part of its history. And you always will be."

"I know exactly what you mean," Bridget said to her.

"You create footprints of memories of a love so encompassing you'd do anything to protect it."

"I love how you put that, Hattie," Lola said.

"And when you find a community like you all have and a group of people that feel the same way, it just magnifies the feeling. It doesn't happen often. But when it does, it's because you've been called. You've been called because the mountain knows it can trust you to be its guardian."

Hattie looked from one woman to the other. They were crying.

"Land's sake! Now I've gone and done it. I put you all in a mood with my rambling on." The wind continued to blow and clouds gathered in the sky. Hattie gazed out the window and jumped to her feet. "I know there's a mighty fierce wind blowing but let's go outside. What do you say?"

"I'm game," Ella said.

"Count me in," Bridget said.

Hattie lit a couple of hurricane lamps and headed toward the door. "Ella, grab a couple of shawls from that coat tree. There's a chill in the air tonight. Bridget, take one of these lamps and Lola, go get the girls. The more the merrier. We're going to do something about that godforsaken fire up there on that mountain. It's time for a rain dance. And let me tell you, timing has everything to do with the outcome of a rain dance."

"Yes, it does," Sam said, shutting the door behind them.

They were back inside a half-hour later. Bridget had retrieved her leather pouch from her car and felt better once it was in her hands. She took Shauna upstairs, and Shauna was asleep as soon as her mother tucked her in. Bridget lay down beside her. She played a dozen worries through her head: her family, her home, her friends, and the amazing job opportunity that had been proposed to her that afternoon. The job was everything Bridget imagined a job to be: the responsibility, the incredible salary, the prestige. The only downside was that she would have to move to London, and she wasn't particularly excited about sharing this news with Dan.

As Bridget drifted off, she touched her hand to her neck and wrapped her fingers around the familiar bear necklace that always seemed to calm her. She slept, deep and dreamless.

～～⌒⊃

The bedroom Hattie had assigned to Ella and Alena was just large enough for two twin beds. A handcarved wooden chest matched the design of the dresser and the bedposts. White lace curtains hung to the sides of a long vertical window.

A well-worn wool carpet cushioned Ella's footsteps as she inspected her surroundings. Delicately painted glass lampshades sat atop brass bases. It seemed to Ella that she had stepped back into history. The room was so warm and inviting that her shoulders finally began to release the tension of the day. If only the feeling could have lasted.

She heard footfalls on the stairs, and they were moving swiftly. Sam, she thought by the sound of it. She heard a soft knock, and then the door cracked open.

"Ella?" Sam peeked into the bedroom.

"Sam. Hey, come on in. What's wrong?"

"I've been listening to the scanner and talking to a couple of my buddies up on the mountain. They initiated a back burn earlier, and it didn't go so well."

"Oh, no."

"They're telling everyone to evacuate." He hesitated, and Ella saw him bite down hard on his lip.

"What is it, Sam?"

"Brice and Herb are missing."

"What? Oh, my God. What do you mean, missing?"

"I'm trying to get more information but it's pretty chaotic up there. I'm so sorry."

"Sam…"

"He'll be okay. He's a smart kid. And he'll keep Herb safe too." Sam put his arms around her shoulders. "I'm going up there. I'll be back as soon as I have news, Ella. I promise."

Ella looked at the open door. She felt her heart pounding deep inside her. Not Brice. Not her baby boy. *My God, help me. I need help. I need hope. Something. My heart…Oh, God, I can't take much more of this. You've got to be kidding me.*

Ella paced. Tried catching her breath. Tried calming herself. Tried picturing Brice as safe. She couldn't. All she could think about was the patient who had killed herself last week, a second one who had overdosed, and how her luck lately didn't bode well for Brice's safety. All she could think about was her family on the brink. Her home in flames. Her son missing.

Ella's knees gave out, and she sank to the bed. She wanted to call for Bridget or Lola, but they had both been through so much, especially Lola.

Ella reached for her coat and dug into the pocket for a Kleenex to wipe her moist eyes. Instead of tissue, she discovered two small, airplane-sized bottles of vodka. She wrenched them out and stared at the clear liquor inside. She thought of all the reasons not to take a sip, but her control melted away as thoughts of Brice, alone in the woods, fire closing in all around him, clouded her thinking.

She clamored to her feet and hurried into the bathroom. Its window had a perfect view of the foothills. It was too dark to distinguish between clouds and plumes of smoke covering the sky. All she could do was imagine the worst, so she hastily opened the small bottles.

Alena raced into the bathroom calling for her and saying, "Mom, there's a phone call for…"

Ella tried hiding the empty bottles from view, but her fingers lost their grasp and they tumbled to the floor.

Alena gasped as her mother ran past her, out of the bedroom, and down the stairs.

FIRE

Day 3

*"Na'mow is the landscape on which our fate lies,
and we accept it with joy and gratitude."*
~ The Circle of Na'mow Handbook – Olive, Second Generation

September 16, 1996, Monday late afternoon

Permanence is an illusion, and this truth becomes glaringly obvious in a natural disaster, especially a wildfire. Even for the massive granite mountain Na'mow, change happens, albeit over millions of years. Nonetheless, it happens.

Fire has its own methods of change; they are incomparable to a flood's. A flood transforms the landscape with the same raw materials that were present when it began. A fire not only transmutes everything in its path but can also obliterate it, wiping it off the face of the earth and vanquishing it into the ethers.

Fire transforms, and this one was no different. This wildfire would leave scars both seen and unseen.

The first inhabitants on the mountain were the Traveling Tribes, nomads, who didn't really fit the definition of settlers. They settled insofar as the communion they created with the mountain, but they never feared picking up and leaving. They didn't fear it, because they didn't see it as leaving. The spirit of the mountain always traveled with them. The communion was eternal.

The settlers who came later and built with logs and stone loved the mountain in a different way, though with no less fervor. They desired permanence. They just didn't really understand that very little was permanent on the mountain. You either changed with the seasons, the weather, and the moods of Eru'tan, or you eventually packed your bags for the bright lights of the city.

The Traveling Tribes believed in destiny. So did the settlers who built with logs and stone. Again it was a matter of definition. The Tribes believed that both the "seen" and "unseen" forces played a hand in their fate, which was often shown to them in visions and dreams. These other dimensions were an integral part of their reality…and they knew not to interfere. The settlers who built with logs and stone believed they were in charge of their own destiny, manhandling their fate with force.

Fire had a way of making the first inhabitants, the Travelers, look smart. Fire had a way of making the settlers who built with logs and stone look stubborn.

ON THE MOUNTAIN

A back burn had been ordered by the commanders and initiated by the fire crews. Firefighters ignited the windward edge of the hill that flanked the gulch. They used drip torches and two-gallon tanks filled with a mixture of diesel and gasoline. A lighted wick dripped burning fuel onto the ground.

The back burn process started a ground fire, which traveled downwind and moved toward the hill that flanked the gulch. The purpose was to consume all the combustibles in the entire fire zone in advance of a wind shift. Then, if the wind did shift, there would nothing left to burn. In effect, a preemptive strike.

The idea was to maintain full control of the burn, but that didn't happen. The fire was in control one minute and out of control the next.

Deputies informed any residents still on the mountain to evacuate and to do it quickly, because they could no longer ensure anyone's safety. Hungry flames threatened houses and prepared to run up a ridge and down into a fuel-laden gulley. There would be no hope of saving structures if it followed its current path of destruction.

Humans like ants scurried about trying to protect what was theirs.

"You've got thirty minutes to evacuate," the deputy sheriff told Dan and his group. "Sixty max. Don't mess with this, Dan. Get moving. The fire crews have already pulled out and are heading toward the command center."

No one said a word about Brice and Herb. Everyone but Gary and Dan headed for their cars. It was time to go.

Gary watched them go. He had a gut-wrenching decision to make. His only option at this stage was to escape via the four-wheel-drive road where they had moved Herb's SUV earlier that day. Gary had hoped to find the old man and his son waiting for him over the ridge, but he didn't. His panic and fear were close to redlining. The fire was creeping eastward and lapping at his neighbors' properties.

From their vantage point behind Dan's house, he and Gary saw fire trucks on the secondary road and small smoke trails coming up in several spots along the road. Each smoke trail got bigger and spread out until they all merged into one line of smoke blowing toward the top of the hill. The smoke cloud grew steadily and finally hit the ridge. The smoke cloud was gigantic and obliterated everything. At this point, the pair strained to see, even with their binoculars.

A few minutes later, it looked like a bomb exploded. A giant black tornado swirled 360 degrees outward and upward and moved against the wind. It generated more power than the wind, and Dan and Gary lost sight of most of the neighborhood below. Slurry bombers circled the area and lined up for their drops. Two helicopters buzzed in and dropped water at the edge of the smoke to put out hotspots and protect homes. Smoke and blackness covered the ground.

The helicopters and their bucket brigade continued for nearly three hours by Dan's count, and by now he was counting almost entirely on his hearing, the drones of helicopters and planes sounding like something straight from the depths of hell.

When the smoke parted momentarily, their worst fears were realized.

"Oh my God, we've lost houses," Dan muttered.

All Gary could think about was his son and Herb. He hoped to God they were nowhere near the fire, but his gut told him differently. When the worry was too much to bear, he turned aside and threw up. Threw up until there was nothing left in his stomach, and a bout of the dry heaves started.

There was nothing Dan could do, so he gave Gary his privacy.

Watching the fire move away from his house was no consolation. Dan knew that the fire had breached the eastern side of the subdivision and traveled up to the ridge. At this point, it could easily crest the top of the ridge and work its way down toward Boulder. Who knew how many homes stood in its path and how many of these homeowners were friends of his.

Dan was staring down the slope of the mountain when he saw one flank of the back burn blow up bigger than anyone could possibly have expected. He glimpsed a burst of flames crossing the road and heading toward the main command post. He could imagine surprised men and women scrambling to get out of its way and cars clogging the road's main artery. The chaos that surely ensued was inevitable. Crown fires jumped far forward of the fire's front line, greedily consuming acres and acres of heavily forested terrain.

Dan felt completely helpless, so he bent down at Gary's side and consoled his friend in his hour of grief.

_____

Candi and Greg completely miscalculated their escape.

Their SUVs were packed with few sentimental items because their most important concern had to do with their illegal marijuana business: the plants, the harvested product, and the bundles of hundred dollar bills.

Greg crammed his Subaru with as many plants as he could, hiding them under an old wool army blanket. The pungent cannabis odor permeated the car even with the windows half way down. Now the wildfire's smoke began seeping into the car, and Greg resorted to a bandana around his nose and mouth that really didn't help much.

"Let's get out of here. I don't give a rat's ass about these damn plants, Greg," Candi shouted. "My car is stuffed and the smell is making me sick. We should've left hours ago. This is stupid! It isn't worth dying over. We have to leave NOW!"

"Stupid? There's still room in your car. We still have tens of thousands of dollars of product left in the house. It would be like just burning cash..." The words stuck in Greg's mouth when Candi began hacking and coughing so violently that she bent over at the waist and began dry-heaving.

"Hey babe, you okay?" Greg asked.

"Don't...want...to die." The billowing black cloud settled over them like a thick blanket, blinding them.

"We gotta go!" Greg grabbed his wife's arm and guided her to her car.

Candi managed to get the engine started and turned on the headlights. She knew the car was in the driveway pointed toward the main road, but she was too disoriented to drive away. Greg headed for his vehicle and disappeared into the darkness. The rumble of the fire sounded like a runaway freight train seemingly powered by a tornado force wind, headed on a collision course with the couple.

Candi's eyes burned and teared as the soot and charred debris floated all around her. The roaring intensified, hurting her ears. Paralyzed, she held on tightly to the steering wheel trying to ground herself to something tangible. The tops of the trees flared up toward the sky, sending small burning missiles downward, pelting the ground hard. She doubled over with uncontrollable coughing. Each lungful of polluted air seared her throat and lungs, the pain unbearable. Swallowing was impossible.

A juniper straight ahead burst into flame, illuminating the drive, and she saw Greg crawling on his hand and knees trying to feel his way through the darkness to his car. Candi squinted; she could see him doubled over and coughing uncontrollably.

"Greg!" Another resin-filled bush ignited. Greg's body collapsed, his hands grasping at his throat.

The noxious mixture was thick with soot and organic debris, assaulting all of Candi's senses until she was consumed in an oxygen-deprived, smoke-filled coffin. Death came quickly.

Dan and Gary saw it. Not the details, but enough to know what was happening.

They found it almost impossible to take their eyes off the fast-moving inferno. It mesmerized them with its dancing orange and blue light show.

Suddenly, Dan grabbed Gary's arm as two huge explosions lit up the skyline, sending out two thick black mushroom clouds of smoke.

"Candi and Greg's place! Oh, fuck," were the only words Gary could manage.

Reality was too close for comfort. Gary closed his eyes. Dan wept with unrestrained emotion.

FIRE

Day 3

"Millions of women touch me igniting the passion for living in the harmony of the divinely feminine. So many woman, yet so intimately connected."

~ The Circle of Na'mow Handbook – Chimalis, First Generation

September 16, 1996, Monday evening

The fire was deceptive, especially under the direction of Eru'tan. And Eru'tan liked to churn things up with the duality of her inherently fickle temperament.

For an hour or so, she directed the wind to settle down, bolstering false hope to all those present. Then, without warning, she amped up the wind's velocity, inciting fear and hopelessness within man and beast.

All knew that within a day or two, she would tire of the heat and welcome the onset of winter with open arms. The wheel would turn once again, though this was certainly the last thing on the minds of those trying to escape her current mood.

For Na'mow, this was nothing new. She had seen Eru'tan play with fire before, and this was no different. Eru'tan always moved on, because Eru'tan had a schedule to keep. A schedule that the natural world followed…communing with the rhythms and cadences of the universe.

This communion Na'mow knew as the divinely feminine.

It was, therefore, not surprising that the mountain was responsible for teaching White Sun and her daughter Chimalis much about honoring the divinely feminine.

Things the mountain has known since the beginning of time have never been secret or hidden. That is not the way of Na'mow. White Sun loved to say, "Na'mow is an open book. Open to those willing to observe and listen. Open to those willing to be still, wonder, and fill their hearts."

The mountain's first lesson in the divinely feminine was perhaps her most obvious: the cycle of death, rebirth, and renewal, the Infinite Life Circle. "The tree, the flower, the shape of the stream, the change of the seasons," White Sun would say. "And closer, the butterfly, the cub, the fallen deer. The old woman, the infant, the rising and setting of the sun. All gifts of Eru'tan, all reflections of Na'mow, all manifestations of the Divine Mother."

The mountain didn't favor the divinely feminine. The mountain didn't play favorites. But the mountain understood strength, recognized courage, and rejoiced in change, growth, and the inevitable transition of Life.

This was always a prime subject of conversation for the Circle. They had a rule, one Chimalis suggested the very first time she, Phoebe, and Martha gathered. Embrace the Wisdom of Woman. Restrain neither laughter nor tears. Never fear speaking from the heart. Never fear rejection. Never fear failure if it alleviates ignorance. Know that the mountain knows. Believe that the mountain believes. Just as the Circle knows, believes, and loves.

IN TOWN

Lola rested her head in Hattie's lap. The older woman's caring hands stroked Lola's hair, pushing it away from the tears.

The sadness that Lola felt could no longer be contained in her body. Shudders of grief rippled from her heart and out her extremities. The Ancient One's feminine essence seemed wholly present in Sam's aunt, and this tenderness…this nuance of the heart…made Lola feel safe and secure.

Lola closed her eyes. Sleep rescued her, then enveloped her with a dream as powerful as life itself.

John stood next to her on top of a huge butte. They talked about their lives. After reaching some telepathic agreement, a huge eagle carried him off. Lola watched as bird and man climbed higher and higher in the sky. John seemed happy in his freedom. Moments later, Lola heard a baby cry. The baby was lying on the ground surrounded by scores of women who were singing the most beautiful lullaby. The baby suckled at each woman's breast before they set the child in Lola's arms. Suddenly, an old hag ripped the baby out of her arms, yelling at the top of her lungs that she alone had the power to decide life and death. Everyone vanished. Lola was left crying for help.

She woke with a start and struggled to sit up. She heard the last notes of Hattie's soothing lullaby and gulped for air, completely disoriented. Hattie embraced her.

"I'm pregnant," Lola said, expelling her closely held secret. "I'm pregnant with John's baby…and I don't know what to do about anything. I'm all alone, and I'm so so scared."

"I know, I know." Hattie held her, stroking her hair. "You were talking in your sleep. And from what I could gather, you're doing some deep soul searching. Lola, look at me."

Hattie gripped her shoulders. "You have strength you haven't even tapped into yet. Be strong for your son; he's hurting too. You may have to make the most difficult of decisions on your own, but no matter what you decide, you will be embraced with the love of your friends and family. They...I mean, we are here for you. Believe it, sweet child."

"Thank you, Aunt Hattie. Thank you." Lola blinked away her tears, and they both turned in the direction of the footfalls sounding from the stairs.

It was Bridget. She was dressed in a flannel nightgown and visibly shaking.

"Come and join us," Hattie said. "You okay, child?"

"I just looked out the window. I thought I was hallucinating, but I saw an orange glow creeping down the front side of the mountain heading straight for Boulder. Shit...the fire was nowhere near that far east when we left. I don't have a good feeling about this. Dan doesn't answer the phone. Most of our men are up there," Bridget said, pacing the length of the living room. "God knows how many other people stayed up there. Christ, I don't even know the number here for my parents or Michael to call. Can't find my phone charger. I totally forgot to call them and now I don't want to be asked questions I don't have answers to. They must be worried sick."

Bridget heard Lola's low whimper and took a seat next to her. "Hey, you. How you doing?" Bridget didn't wait for an answer. She reached out with her strong hands and began to massage Lola's feet and legs. With each motion, Bridget felt some of the immense tension Lola was holding in her limbs disappear under her fingertips.

As if on cue, Ella ran into the living room frantically waving her arms and describing exactly what Bridget had seen.

"This is just crazy. And my son's up there. Lost and alone. And Herb...I'd never forgive myself." She took a seat in an old rocking chair that creaked with every movement and filled the room with a distracting white noise that no one seemed to mind. The whiteness of Ella's newly brushed teeth contrasted with her weepy bloodshot eyes and swollen nose. She looked like hell. She looked forlorn and helpless.

"I thought you all went to bed. Thank God you're still awake."

Hattie shared her warmest smile. "Well, this isn't very good news, is it? And it would seem like there's nothing we can do about it but worry. Worry ourselves sick. And that won't do," she said firmly. "All worry does is divide the mind between what has passed and what's to come. It makes no sense to start tracking tomorrow's problems since you don't have tomorrow's strength yet. We have the strength to deal with only today so I suggest we get our minds on a different track. How about telling me about your friendship? Right from the get-go."

They all looked at this remarkable woman and marveled at the depth of her question and the sincerity of her insight. "It's so nice you're all so close. Like family," Hattie continued. "Women need each other to share the joy and, like now, especially now…the pain. Well, one thing's for sure. You look like survivors to me, yessirree."

This made Bridget chuckle, and Lola shuddered. Ella just stared, her eyes wide.

"I guess we are, now that you put it that way, Aunt Hattie," Bridget said.

"And I bet you have some tall tales to tell. What else do we have to do but talk ourselves out of this dadgum worry? So indulge an old lady. And don't leave out any of the details. Not a bit of the sex or the gore or the craziness. Who's first?"

"That's exactly what I need." Lola wiped her eyes, blew her nose, and smiled. "Okay, I'm game. But you have no idea what you're in for, Aunt Hattie. And neither did we. Come on, girls, I have to get my mind off John, the fire, and whatever other crap is trying to smother the life out of me. We all have to share in the telling of it. And I think we should title it, *To Hell and Back*."

"That sure as hell sounds appropriate," Bridget said. She held her hand out to Ella, and Ella pulled her chair up close. "To hell and back?"

"To hell and back it is," Ella muttered.

"It started when we either left the mountain and/or left our minds or maybe both…and found our way back to it," Lola said. "It's a story with ghosts, woo-woo, sex, jealousy, loss, food, and mud. Hell, just about everything a good movie has in it. And we are the stars."

"Hell, yes, and the survivors," Bridget added.

"God, I hope this doesn't make us feel worse than we do now," Ella said.

"Yeah, because it's bad, Aunt Hattie. Really, really bad. But at least we lived through it…unlike…" Lola couldn't finish the thought. So she let herself cry again.

"Uh-oh," Bridget said. She put an arm around Lola and reached out for Ella's hand again. "Come on, Lola. If we made it this far, we can make it through a little storytelling. But I have to say, it's going to take some whiskey for me to lay raw all the so-called S. H. I .T. we've seen go down."

Bridget jumped up. "I'll bring a shot for you too, Aunt Hattie."

"Make it a double!"

"Tea for me," Ella called. "Hot, hot tea."

"And me," Lola said.

"You girls will make it through this," Hattie told them as Bridget rummaged in the kitchen. "Your friendship will help you through it. Guaranteed. My friends and I went through the good times and the bad times just like all of you. Women have been banding together to cope with life's ups and downs since the beginning of time. I'll make you a deal," she said as Bridget served up whiskey for Hattie and herself, and tea for Ella and Lola. "Once you're done telling me how you survived up on that mountain, I'll tell you how my friends and I did too. It's all in these journals."

Hattie reached for the journals sitting on the table under the shadowbox and laid them on her lap. "Land's sakes alive, no one but the Circle has ever set eyes on these writings or even know that we, the Circle, exists."

She looked from Ella to Bridget and then to Lola. "But it looks like Na'mow and Eru'tan are ready for some new members. And I do believe they have chosen the three of you."

"Na'mow? Eru'tan?" Ella shook her head. "I don't get it."

"Me neither, but oh, do I need a good bedtime story," Lola beamed.

"Please don't tell me it's got woo-woo in it?" Bridget exclaimed.

"A bit of woo-woo and a lot of wisdom," Hattie said. "And believe me, all of you are going to need it! So tell me everything!"

February 1992

TO GOOD TO BE TRUE

It was getting dark as Bridget heaved a sigh, dropping the last box from her car in the middle of the living room.

Never in a million years would she have pictured herself living in a house like this. When Steve first brought her and Lola out to look at it, her mouth hung open with disbelief. It was just too nice. From the crystal chandeliers and the white marble kitchen counters to the stained glass windows, the library with floor to ceiling built-in bookcases, the piano room, two gas fireplaces, and a reproduction of an old cook stove in the kitchen, it was an elegantly appointed contemporary colonial house built just four years prior.

The house was situated on a fifty-acre ranch atop a mesa, complete with a pond out front and a sweeping circular driveway that reminded her of the opening scene in the TV series "Dallas." There were horses boarded in a large barn. There were outbuildings and fenced corrals. There was a small unassuming bungalow connected to the main house by shared rooflines, a breezeway, and a huge deck; Bridget took this to be the original homestead, and she was right.

"This place is just too nice for me. It's just not me with all the incredibly elegant touches. It's a house I'd be hired to clean, not live in!" Bridget admitted to her roommate.

"You're kidding me, right?" Lola looked at Bridget like she was a complete idiot. "Not me. I was meant to live like this," she chirped. A huge smile filled out her face. "You need to get over it, Secondhand Rose. Eight hundred bucks a month to live in this luxury? This is karma making it up to us for all the shit we have been through. We deserve this!"

When Bridget considered the alternative of living in a one-bedroom basement apartment in Boulder with her two kids for $750, she had to admit this was a no-brainer. She just couldn't get rid of the nagging feeling that if it seemed too good to be true, it probably was too good to be true. Bridget didn't consider herself a superstitious person. But two weeks ago as they were sitting in the breakfast place signing the lease, her excitement quickly turned to horror as she watched the news of a plane crashing into a mountain in France. It felt like an omen or a warning; cries of anguish and disbelief rose in waves through the room of diners as the broadcaster announced that most of the crew and passengers had perished. People all over the world felt the same sickening pain. What that plane crash had to do with their new house, Bridget didn't know, but she swore it didn't feel quite right.

For now, she tried shaking off all the negative vibes and surveyed the chaos of the boxes surrounding her. Thank God the kids were staying on the mountain tonight because it would give her and Lola a chance to get some of this crap organized. But first things first. A drink and a toast with her new roomie.

"Lola, where the hell are ya?" she bellowed through the huge empty house. "Let's chill out for a few minutes and have a drink." Bridget bounded up the enormous curved staircase to the second floor yelling, "Hey, girl, whatcha doing?"

She walked through the master suite into the master bathroom, both of which Lola had claimed as her own. Her logic was good. There was a giant Jacuzzi with a sweeping view of the Flatirons that Lola was sure Bridget would never use or appreciate, and she was probably right.

"There you are. I should have known."

Lola was arranging and rearranging all her toiletries, perfumes, and lotions into neat little rows on the expansive counter top with a focus that only an Aquarius would have for such a task.

"Glad to see you are taking care of the most important things first!" Bridget snapped, given that most of the heavy lifting had been left to her.

"Well, I have to be organized before the kids show up tomorrow," Lola replied defensively.

"You're right. This will definitely make things easier than getting the kitchen unpacked and organized," Bridget retorted. She forced a smile. "Come on, roomie. Let's have a toast to new beginnings."

"Oh, yes!" Lola's eyes lit up. "I think a glass of wine and a long soak in this beautiful tub will be just the thing to finish up this grueling day."

Afraid of an uncouth reply, Bridget bit her tongue and turned for the door. She whispered, "Count to ten, Bridge. One...two... three..."

She got no further, quickly forgetting her annoyance as she moved down the stairs to a completely dark first floor. "Now that's weird. I know I left all the lights on. I wonder if we blew a fuse or something." She flipped on the light switch closest to the bottom of the stairs and to her surprise, all the lights flooded back on. "God, I hope there isn't some fucked-up electrical circuit problem in this house. That's all I need is to burn down another house."

"Stop!" Bridget cried out in her dream. Her head flew off the pillow, her heart pounding in her chest, her breathing ragged. "Damn. What the hell kind of dream was that?"

She glanced at the clock and couldn't believe it was already two in the morning. Didn't she just go to bed? She didn't hear her bedroom door opening, but a sudden draft of cold air alerted her to a presence in the room. She automatically reached for the gun on her bed stand, but it wasn't there. Of course it wasn't there; all of her guns had been lost in the fire. Damn! She felt her body coil in preparation for an attack when she heard Lola's squeaky, timid voice.

"Bridge, I'm scared. I had a bad dream. And on top of that, I'm freezing. Can I climb in bed with you?"

"Jesus Christ, Lola! You scared the crap out of me!" The wind howled and beat against the window.

"I'm sorry. But I had the worst dream. There was a train crash right out there on the highway..." (she pointed to the north) "...and all the people from the wreck were trying to get into our house. They were all screaming and scratching at the doors with broken arms and legs. One person didn't even have a head. They looked like zombies! I was so scared!"

"Wait a minute." Bridget shook her head, stunned by what she had just heard. "How could you and I be having the same dream?"

"What?"

"There's no freaking way. And I'm definitely not mentioning the woo-woo scale," she said, hugging herself. "Lola, did you leave your window open?"

"I told you. I'm freezing," Lola whimpered. "Why in the world would I open any damn windows?"

"Feel that wind!" Bridget jumped off the bed. She flipped on the light at the top of the stairs. She peered down the staircase and saw that the front door was wide open and banging in the wind. She raced down the steps and realized that every door in the house was open. Five sets of French doors banging wildly in the wind.

"Holy Mother of God, what the hell is going on here? Lola, get your ass down here and help me."

They raced around the huge house closing doors and securing locks. Then they searched every room in the house. It was frightening and exhausting.

It wasn't until they were back upstairs and huddled in Bridget's room that Lola said, "You told me you locked the doors when we went to bed. I would've done it if you didn't feel like it. All you had to do was ask me."

"Lola, that's a load of crap! I checked all the doors right before I did the dishes, put the food away, turned off the fireplaces, and turned out all the lights, even though I didn't fucking feel like it!"

"Well then how do you explain that shit show we just saw? Huh?" Lola replied, ignoring the obvious barb. "I'd say we are dealing with a ten on the woo…"

"Don't even start with that…" Bridget did not feel like getting into it with Lola. She was dead tired, and Lola's accusation hit too close to home. The last thing she needed was to relive the blunder that caused the fire in her own house.

"Good night, Lola," was all she could say as she stumbled back to bed.

Bridget had barely started to settle into that weird theta wave sleep state that she loved so much when Lola crept into her room on her hands and knees, whispering, "Sshhh…don't make a sound or turn on the lights."

"What now?" Bridget growled.

"SSHHH!" Lola put a finger to her lips. "There's someone parked out by the barn next to my car. I saw them get into my car and look in the glove box. Now they're just sitting there with their lights off. Oh, my God, what should we do?"

The brave redhead crawled from bed and into Lola's room, where they had a better view of the driveway. *Well, at least she didn't make it up*, Bridget thought, staring at the car. "Isn't that the same kind of car that JD drives?"

"I don't know. It's too dark to tell." Lola clutched Bridget's arm.

"I'm going downstairs and turn on the floodlight out by the barn." Bridget pulled Lola off her arm and stood up in front of the window. Lola all but knocked her down dragging her back to the floor.

"No, you are not! Do you want to get us killed? We don't know who that is and we're out here in the middle of nowhere in a house where the doors won't stay closed. Maybe whoever that is broke in and opened the doors to scare us before they come in to do God knows what." If it was possible to shriek while whispering, Lola had just perfected the technique.

"Well shit, I'm not going to just sit here all night looking out this window! I'm either going to go out there and ask them what the HELL they want or I'm going to bed," Bridget sneered. "You decide."

"Bridge, you can't. I'm scared. We need help. I know, let's call Sam. He'll help us."

"Lola, it's three in the morning, Sam is not going to come down from the mountain, not at this time of night."

Lola already had the phone in her hand and was dialing Sam's number, which she knew by heart. Forty-five minutes later, they watched through the upstairs window as Sam pulled into the driveway and approached the dark car. A few minutes later the car drove away, and Sam knocked on their front door.

"Ladies, you really owe me for this one. It'll be daybreak in an hour and a half, and I expect a killer breakfast after I take a short nap."

"Who was it? What did they want?" Lola stammered. She grabbed Sam and pulled him into the house.

"That was your friend JD. Said he went to your house and found someone else living there. They told him that you had moved out here but he wasn't sure this was the right place so he decided to wait it out."

"JD? Oh, Bridget, you were right. That was his car. I don't know whether to be relieved or more scared. Is he stalking me? What does he want with me? I told him I hated him and I wanted him to die." Lola paced and babbled. "Oh, no. Now what should I do?"

"I had a little talk with your friend; my advice to him was that if he really loves you and wants any kind of chance to even be your friend, he'd better get himself straightened out. That you would never speak to him again if he wasn't straight," Sam said pragmatically. "A good friend of mine went through the same shit and came out the other side, so I gave JD his number and told him he might as well try talking to someone who would understand 'cause it sure wasn't gonna be you. I also told him that not only am I your self-appointed guardian angel and fiercely protective of you, but that your new roommate here is inclined to shoot first and ask questions later. He was lucky I got here before Bridget came after him." Sam gave Bridget one of his slow sensuous winks. "Now I'm going to hit your couch for a couple hours."

"Oh, Sam," Lola cried with true regret ringing in her voice. "Bridget's gunless, and we don't have a couch yet."

Lola's eyes invited him upstairs with her, but Sam didn't bite. He said, "Good Lord, I reckon I'll just make acquaintance with the floor before all my poor judgment gets stuck in my pants. Sweet dreams, ladies."

⌐

At the end of their first week together, Bridget was feeling a lot better about living with Lola. The house still had some weird quirks to figure out, but things had started to settle into a routine. Not much forethought had gone into developing a schedule when they had lived with their husbands. It just sort of evolved through time. But now, a scheduled routine was essential. The roommates mapped out agreements for things like cooking, doing dishes, cleaning, and buying groceries. They decided that every Sunday night they would plan the kid's meals and divide the cost of the groceries in thirds, with Bridget paying for Michael and Shauna and Lola footing the bill for Nick.

Their schedule for cooking and cleanup depended on which kids were in the house. Because Nick spent more time with his dad than Shauna and Michael did with Dan, Lola only had to fix dinner twice a week, which suited her quite well.

All three kids thought the new house was "way cool." Their only complaint was being a good twelve miles from town and their friends. But much like the mountain, they could use the freedom provided them by the extraordinary open space to entice their friends to come and stay over.

At one of Michael's wrestling practices, Bridget overheard a parent talking about a litter of puppies that was soon to be given away, and she made inquiries. Then, against her better judgment, she went to see the puppies. Of course, she came home with the cutest little Aussie mix the kids had ever seen, and they fell immediately in love with her. The children named the pup Trixie.

Lola was not as thrilled. She had never had a dog herself and decided that they were way more trouble than they were worth. It was so much more fun to give biscuits to the neighbors' dogs than to have the constant interruption of a dog jumping on you, barking, and needing discipline. And that was not the worst of it. It was as if Trixie knew Lola had a problem with the whole arrangement, because Lola was always the target of the dog's destruction. Panties, shoes, scarves, belts, purses; nothing of Lola's escaped Trixie's powerful desire to chew.

Lola was sure the dog had it out for her even though the space cadet never felt the need to pick up or put anything of hers away.

Bridget harbored a secret delight that fate was finally forcing Lola to clean up her shit. Her house back on the mountain had always been an explosion of whatever expression she felt that day, and now things were changing thanks to an eight-week-old puppy. Hallelujah!

Lola arrived home at 5:30 on the night of Trixie's eight-week-old birthday. She hurried into the kitchen, gagging and pinching her nose. "Oh my God! What is that awful smell?"

Bridget was standing at the stove making dinner. She sniffed the air like a hound looking for a scent. "I don't smell anything but these Sloppy Joes I am making."

Lola cautiously removed her finger and thumb from her nose. "That's weird. I just smelled the most horrible smell. It was so bad my eyes burned."

"Did you fart?" giggled Bridget.

"I did not fart! Besides, my farts don't stink." Lola tossed her mane for effect.

Now it was the kids' turn. First Nick. He scampered into the kitchen with the same complaint. "UUGGHH! What's that rotten smell?"

Bridget sighed. She put down her spoon and turned off the burner. "Where did you smell this really rotten smell?" she said with a touch of sarcasm.

"Right by the stairs." He pointed to the entryway.

Then Shauna. She'd been on her way to the basement – a 1,500 square foot slab of concrete – to practice her rollerblading, a very serious avocation for a girl from the mountains where there weren't a lot of places to work on her chosen sport. "Mom," she called. "Something smells really bad downstairs. Like when we found all the dead mice in Michael's closet!"

And finally, Michael, who called down from his room on the second floor: "What the heck is that smell? What's the deal? Does Trixie have diarrhea or something?"

"Shit! I hope it's not the septic tank backing up," Bridget said. She opened the door to the hallway bathroom, fully expecting to see raw sewage backed up in the sink and toilet. *Hhhmmm...Nothing. Not even the slightest odor.* She headed towards the foot of the stairs and: *Wham!* It was like hitting a wall of blinding stench. Bridget slapped a hand over her mouth and nose and retreated to the kitchen where three sets of eyes looked at her expectantly. She sucked in a lungful of clean air and shook her head in confusion.

Then she marched outside to where the leach field was located, sniffing heartily all the way, and smelled nothing, not the slightest whiff of anything foul. She ran back inside and headed into the basement. As she put her foot on the first riser, the lights began to flicker.

"What is the fucking problem?" Bridget screamed.

Then it was gone. Vanished. No smell, no flickering lights, nothing. It was as if it had never existed.

"This is crazy." All five of them gathered at the foot of the stairs, eyes wide with astonishment.

Lola broke the spell. "It's simple. Obviously somebody farted. We just don't know who," she said. Then, in her search for comic relief, looked from one child to the next and added, "Do ghosts fart?"

No one answered the question so Lola continued. "Well, everyone, I do believe we have some paranormal activity happening in this house." She eyed Bridget as she talked on, "This ridiculously cheap but beautiful rental. I've read about spirits expressing themselves by screwing around with door locks and electronic equipment, but farts...that's a new one to me. Seems like we've taken up residence in a haunted house, kids. Now that makes for some interesting gossip."

"Cool," Michael said.

"Hope they don't fart too much," Alena fretted.

"Wait till I tell Dad," Nick added.

"I'm gonna kill Steve! A good deal, huh?" Bridget fumed.

March 1992

NEVER CRY WOLF

Bridget gave Michael a choice for his birthday. He could have an afternoon party with twelve kids or he could have a sleepover with six kids.

Michael was overjoyed. He decided on the slumber party because the fun factor was high, and he and his friends could stay up all night running around the great big new house creating mischief. He was annoyed that Shauna got to have her friend Lillie over for the night, but figured it would probably keep her out of his hair. Michael invited Brice, who was three years older, but Brice declined. The truth was, he didn't really feel like hanging out with a bunch of twelve-year-olds, and he sure didn't feel like spending the entire night with them. The birthday boy may have been a little bummed about that, but he understood. He probably wouldn't want to hang out with his younger sister and her friends either if the tables were turned.

Michael planned the party like a real event planner. Everyone was to arrive at three Saturday afternoon. They would play outside and in the barn until it got dark around six. At 6:30, they would have pizza, brownies, and root beer floats. This, he decided, after informing his mom that nobody liked birthday cake anymore. After opening his presents, they would all settle in to watch scary movies; Michael chose "The Shining," "Gremlins II," and "The Addams Family." How could they go wrong?

Bridget bought an assortment of junk food – caramel corn, Cheetos, and chips with onion dip – and went healthy with apples, oranges, and bananas. The healthy stuff made Michael laugh, as if his friends would eat anything healthy at a birthday party.

The guests arrived on time and were ready for action. But before they got started, Bridget laid out the rules for them. "Rule number one: no one for any reason is to go out on the pond. Does everyone understand me?" A nodding of heads followed. "I want to hear you say yes. Every one of you."

The pond out front was a big danger because the ice was starting to get thin and unstable. For kids, it was a huge magnet. They always snuck out there to slide around on the ice. The water wasn't very deep, but deep enough for a kid to drown in if he or she happened to panic. Bridget had threatened them with their lives a million times, but it didn't seem to make a difference. She made Michael promise he would not go out there during his party, telling him it would be his last if he did.

"Rule number two, nobody leaves the ranch. See that fence line out there?" She pointed out to the edge of the pasture. "That's as far as you can go. Fifty acres ought to be enough even for you guys. And last, but not least, rule number three." The boys started groaning and Michael shot her daggers with his eyes. "Have fun!"

The boys barely had time to throw their gear in the house before Michael was dragging them out to the "way cool" barn. Climbing on the rafters was the first order of business. Twenty feet above the ground was a great place for a game of chicken and dare. Nick and Michael were daredevils by nature, having grown up on the mountain where fun was dependent on your imagination and willingness to take risks. Some of the other guys, however, were not quite so excited about the game. It was just too plain scary and dangerous. Of course, none of this faction wanted to come across as wimps, so they compensated by calling the game stupid and boring. Michael finally got tired of arguing, so they broke out their slingshots.

"You know what these are for, right?" He pointed at the pigeons roosting in the rafters of the barn and loaded his sling with a rock the size of a quarter. He let it fly. The rock missed the pigeons but hit the roof with a loud *bang*, and there was an immediate flurry of wings and squawks and flying feathers. Everyone cheered.

There were three slingshots among them, and they all took turns. The score was boys two, pigeons zero, when Bridget came out to check on them.

She peeked in the barn and almost had a heart attack. "What the hell are you boys doing?" she yelled as a third pigeon hit the floor, still frantically flapping its wings. Bridget felt sick seeing the dead birds, her fury manifesting in a face as flaming red as her Irish hair.

"This is sick and disgusting. This is what we call animal abuse, killing for no reason but your own fun! I should kick your twelve-year-old butts for this. All of you out! Get out of this barn. NOW!"

Bridget collected all three slingshots and pointed to the front lawn. "Find something to do with yourself that requires a little more imagination and a little less stupidity."

Then she charged towards the house, thinking: *Thank God the horses were out in the pasture. I can't imagine what might have happened if they had tormented them. I can't wait to tell their parents about this one. Ugghh.*

Lola poured the redhead a glass of wine and told her with unusual clarity, "Bridget, boys will be boys. Sit right here and calm down. Then we can talk about what to do with them. It will do no good to get your bowels in an uproar."

"You're right," Bridget said. "I'm ready to kill those kids. It makes me sick what they did, without even a thought. Like some wolf pack mentality."

The words were no sooner out of her mouth when the front door flew open and Shauna and Lillie raced in, screaming in fear.

"MOM! Jimmy fell through the ice!" Shauna called. "Nick and Michael are going out to get him. We told them not to!"

Bridget sent her chair flying and nearly knocked the table over jumping up, as she and Lola raced out into the early dusk surrounding the pond. Michael and Nick were crawling out onto the ice and were halfway to their friend by the time they got there.

"Michael and Nick!" Bridget screamed at the top of her lungs. "STOP! Right there. Don't move! Shauna, go get me your jump rope. Fast as you can."

Bridget told Michael and Nick to inch their way back to the shore, one at a time. Then she called to Jimmy. "Hang on, Jimmy. Just hang on. I'm coming to get you."

As soon as Michael and Nick were off the ice, Bridget inched her way out. When Shauna got back with her rope, Bridget said, "Give the rope to Michael, Shauna. Michael, toss it out to me. Right into my hands, buddy."

Michael gave the rope a toss, and Bridget reached out and caught it. Then she turned all of her attention to the boy shivering in the water.

"Jimmy, I know you're scared, but grab on to the rope. The water isn't that deep right there…you can touch the bottom. So help me out…good…see…you can stand…that's right…" She slid one end of the rope in Jimmy's direction, and he grabbed it. "Good. Now just jump up a little to get yourself moving, and I'll drag you over toward me. Jimmy…keep looking at me…you're doing great…you're safe now."

The boy was soaked and freezing as Bridget and Lola brought him and the others into the house. After Bridget was sure that everyone was okay and changed into warm dry clothes, she sat them down in front of the TV.

The whining started almost immediately, and of course it had to do with food. "We're STARVING, Mom," Michael pleaded.

"Too bad!" Bridget snapped. She put a tape of "Never Cry Wolf" in the VCR. "You'll watch this and you'll watch it with your mouths closed. Remember rule number one?" she asked. "This should help refresh your memory!"

She fast-forwarded the tape to the scene where Tyler, the main character, falls through the ice in an Arctic wilderness lake and spends several agonizing minutes trying to resurface. It was a hair-raising scene, truly frightening. Tyler eventually makes it out just as the last of his air expires. Bridget played the scene over and over for an entire hour until the boys nervously fidgeted and the girls started to cry in their misery.

Satisfied that the youngsters got the message, Bridget fed them dinner.

After another couple of viewings, the boys persuaded her to switch "Never Cry Wolf" for "The Shining." Amazingly, the tape went blank right when the boy started chanting "Red Rum, Red Rum."

Now their complaining was ceaseless. How could such a thing happen!

Bridget rewound the tape and played it again. It happened again. She put in a second movie and it did the same thing. "What a pain in the ass," Bridget groaned. "Kids, I've got bad news…"

The power went out at that exact moment and plunged the house into darkness.

"Enough already!" Bridget yelled out to no one in particular. Then…poof, the power clicked back on. All the children freaked out and jumped closer together. The chorus of complaints and whining was overwhelming.

By this time, Bridget had had all she could handle for one day. "Guys, I think it's time to call it a night."

"No way!" Michael yelled at her. "It's only ten o'clock. You said we could stay up till midnight!" Like a silent applause from an observing audience, the lights began to flicker on and off. Everyone but Michael hushed. "Jesus, Mom, you said you were going to get dad to check out these screwed-up lights. This totally sucks!"

"What did you say? Michael, this is NOT my fault," Bridget said as calmly as possible. "You need to chill out, and you guys need to get your sleeping bags out and have fun the old-fashioned way. Tell your own ghost stories."

"I want to go home," Jimmy said suddenly. Clearly he'd had enough excitement for one day. He jumped up. "I'm going to call my dad and ask him to come and pick me up."

Bridget didn't argue. And all Michael could do was groan; who could blame him. Jimmy's dad showed up half an hour later, and two other boys joined the exodus. The other three burrowed into their sleeping bags, but the party was pretty much over by then.

<hr />

The next day, Bridget checked out both movies before returning them to the video store. Both played without a glitch. "Figures," she said.

Michael was standing behind her, hate spilling from his red-rimmed eyes. "You ruined everything! You've ruined my whole life. Dad's right. It was all your fault the house burned down, and now we're living out here in this crazy house. My friends think you're a freak. You totally embarrassed me. I'm not even going to school on Monday, and I'm going to go live with dad!"

"In the friggin' pink trailer? Right," Bridget retorted. "Michael, get over it. Life's a bitch sometimes."

Michael stomped off. He stopped at the top of the stairs and looked down at his mom, his voice filled with malice. "Yeah Mom, and like Dad says, 'Then you marry one.'"

February 1993

SQUARING HER SHOULDERS

Bridget hated getting up at five in the morning. She wasn't an early riser by nature, though life had caused her to be over the years. Funny how kids and work did that to you.

Bridget had a huge presentation to give this morning at the office, and she was determined to practice it before anyone else got up.

She had been working for an up and coming technology company since the fall of 1989. She had been promoted five times in four years. She was now the director of marketing and operations, and had her sights set on a vice president position.

In four hours, she would be standing in front of the company's executive staff proposing an entirely new program that would take the company into markets they had never been able to penetrate before. Profitable markets. Bridget knew the program would require signing contracts with several new vendors and had a significant budget tied to it. All of which meant it was going to be a tough sell.

Bridget ran through her presentation a second time, and then poured herself another cup of coffee. She stared out the window as the first signs of dawn etched across the horizon; she may have hated the mornings, but sunrise was always special in Colorado. Very special.

The last year had been tough: the fire, her separation from Dan, taking on a new roommate. Michael and Shauna finally seemed reconciled to the fact that Bridget and Dan were not going to be together anymore. Michael had taken it the hardest. He resented Steve being in his mom's life now. And for the longest time, he blamed his mom for every negative thing in his life. Some of their battles verged on the epic. It was better now. Not perfect, but better. Michael had finally come to terms with the fact that his mother wasn't trying to hurt him, only that his life had changed and that he didn't necessarily like how it had changed. *Guess that was part of growing up*, Bridget thought. The problem was, she didn't want her kids growing up, at least not as fast as it seemed to be happening.

It would be another twenty minutes before she had to wake them up and get them ready for school. Which brought up another issue that needed to be dealt with. Not only did Bridget have to get her kids up and out the door, but she had to get Nick up as well. Lola took it for granted that since Bridget had to be up anyway, there was no reason they should both be miserable. So, through some unspoken agreement that had been created by Lola's default on her responsibilities, Bridget had assumed the task of getting Nick dressed, fed, and on his way to school every day.

At first, Bridget wasn't too concerned about Lola's crazy friends and unconventional lifestyle; she slept late, worked nights, and partied hard. But after a year of people crashing at the house, late night gatherings that lasted through half the night, and Lola's sleeping in till almost noon every day, Bridget had become resentful. And what was worse, Lola's laissez-faire attitude had begun to rub off on the kids. *They're starting to get as flaky as she is with their chores.*

Bridget never knew who was going to be in the house when she woke up or how long they planned on staying. A bunch of wackos and freeloaders! This was no way to be raising three kids, and the day of reckoning had come for Bridget.

She looked at the clock again after practicing her presentation for the third time.

"Five till six; time to get the show on the road."

She went into the bathroom. Squaring her shoulders at her reflection in the mirror, she caught a quick glimpse of her life flashing before her eyes, of all the dimensions her life had held so far. It surprised her to think about how many unique experiences she had been blessed with and how glad she was for all of them. "I guess you can have it all in this life," she said to herself. "You just can't have it all at the same time."

March 1993

ZAHAR

Lola's life certainly had changed after moving in with Bridget. She rented her mountain cabin to a young, financially stable professional who paid her a hefty sum every month. She supplemented her newfound money stream with her new gig as a belly dancer. All those years of taking lessons were finally paying off. So were the seamstress skills she had learned from her mother. When other belly dancers saw the beautiful designs Lola was sewing for herself, they enlisted her to make outfits for them. The money was good. Most of her jobs were private parties and word of mouth was her only advertising. Because Lola made it clear that her dancing was a legitimate business and not a front for a hooker, affluent housewives booked her for birthday and anniversary parties as eagerly as men did for their bachelor parties.

People loved her, and of course Lola loved being the center of attention. Best of all, it was not unheard of for her to make $500 in a single night.

Business was slower on weeknights so she danced at the local Moroccan restaurant. Her current boyfriend was the restaurant's bouncer. His name was Tye. Tye enforced the club's hands-off-the-dancers policy. Tye was one of the reasons Lola got home so late every night and why she could never drag herself out of bed to see Nick off to school.

One Friday night, after the show was over and Lola had thoroughly entertained a rowdy group of 200 Italians visiting from New York City, she used the restaurant bathroom to change into tight-fitting jeans, a turtleneck sweater, and a down parka. Like Lola, Tye had survived an AIDS scare and both had demanded proof that they were "clean" before engaging in sex. They always used a condom. Fucking each other was their obsession and his van was their motel. The glow of the nearest lamplight dimly illuminated the inside of the van, and Lola found the setting oddly erotic.

It didn't hurt that Tye was over six feet tall and an ex-model. During his younger years he had a lucrative job in New York City, but drugs destroyed all that. Clean and sober now for three years, he swore to Lola that she was the love of his life.

"Zahar," he whispered, pushing Lola's hair back to kiss the nape of her neck. "I want you."

"Show him to me," Lola pleaded, fumbling with his zipper. Their sex took a different turn every night, and tonight it was Lola's turn to take the lead.

Twenty minutes later, they were both in the throes of a violent orgasm, Tye groaning loudly and calling out "Zahar, Zahar," when a sharp banging shook the van's back door and a bright light shined through the window.

"Open the door, Tye. Open the goddamn door! I know you're in there," a woman's shrieking voice demanded.

"Oh, shit," Tye moaned. As fast as lightning, he threw a sheet over Lola and pulled on his clothes.

"Tye! Open this door right now, you cheating bastard."

Lola looked at Tye, her eyes wide with disbelief, and yelled, "You're married?" That, she suddenly remembered, was the only question she'd forgotten to ask him when they started "van dating." "You asshole."

Lola was trying to get her clothes on under the covers and creating quite a tangled mess. She managed her bra and panties, grabbed her jeans and sweater, and escaped out the driver side door. The banging was still echoing throughout the alley as she turned and ran smack dab into Sam. Unfortunately, the flash of recognition came a second too late, and by then she had kicked him right in the nuts.

"Sam? Sam!" Lola leaned over the figure moaning in the gravel.

Sam managed a look and muttered: "Lola?"

"Oh my! Oh my! I'm sorry, Sam…but I have to go. I didn't know he was married. You can't tell her who I am. Please, Sam. Oh my! So sorry. Sorry…" Lola ran around the block and only came back to get her car when she saw the van leave with both Tye and his wife inside, screaming at each other.

There was no sign of Sam, and she didn't see his car. She opened her car door, dove into the front seat, and tried to slow her breathing and the rapid flow of adrenalin. She leaned her head back against the headrest and had a word with the universe. "Why me? I was careful. So damn careful. Married! Never even crossed my mind. Another note to self. Ask if they are married. Universe, I guess you need to guide me…better."

A bloody hand grabbed her from behind and clasped over her mouth. The back seat intruder was breathing hard.

"Listen very carefully to me." Sam's ragged voice steadied. "You owe me."

Lola tried talking through his hand, and his grip tightened. "Lola, you kicked me in the balls."

She murmured, "Sorry, Sam."

"First the wife who hired me slapped me across the face when she found out you got away, then the husband punched me in the nose just because I was spying on him. This after being kicked in the balls by my good friend." He loosened his grip.

"Really sorry, Sam."

Sam leaned back, exhausted and disgusted. "Thank God I got paid upfront. I'd have to expose you if I pressed charges against them for assault, so I'm going to save your ass again. The wife told me she thought it was some floozy belly dancer working with her husband, and so it was. Well, I can tell you that Mr. Cheater won't be working there again, not if his wife has her way. I had no idea you worked at this dive of a restaurant, doing your exotic dancing thing." Sam drew a deep breath. "Well, guess what, exotic dancer, you're going to do Sam a big favor. I'm the best man in my buddy's wedding next month and had no idea what to do about a bachelor party. Now I know. We'll have the party here, and you, young lady, will be our entertainment for the night. No tips allowed. I know you'll be as charming as ever. As far as I know, none of my friends have ever laid eyes on a belly dancer up close and personal-like, so they'll have something to look forward to. And come to think of it, neither have I. So it will be a night we'll never forget."

Sam released her and fell back in the seat. Lola looked back and nearly had a heart attack.

"Sam, oh Sam, I'm sorry. Oh, you look like crap and ohhhhhhh... you're bleeding all over my upholstery. Jeez, I just had the car detailed." She grabbed a bunch of tissues out of the console and handed them to him.

"By the way, who the hell is Zahar?" Sam asked, holding a wad of tissue to his nose.

"Why Sam, that's my stage name."

"Jesus H. Christ," Sam replied. "Why am I not surprised."

June 1993

LIFE IS HARD

Turning forty was very uneventful for Ella. And that was the way she wanted it. She accepted the birthday wishes of friends and family, but made it clear she was in no mood to party.

Bridget and Lola felt guilty about it nonetheless, so they schemed to celebrate the summer solstice as a way to get her to join them in town. Besides, they knew Ella was lonely and still was finding way too much comfort in drinking her vodka alone.

Like any good alcoholic, Ella often made rules for herself regarding her drinking. "I will only have one drink and sip it slowly to make it last for hours." "I will only drink on the weekends." "I will never drink alone." "I will never drink and drive." "I won't drink hard liquor." "I will get a glass of water every time I want to drink and drink it out of a beautiful crystal glass." "I will only drink wine and at dinner." "I will never drink again."

Of course, Ella broke the rules as fast as she made them, and then chastised herself for doing so. It was a losing battle. But that thought brought up another rule. "Never admit that it's a losing battle."

As she drove down the mountain for her weekend with the girls her dog, Red Dog, sat in the seat next to her. Ella promised herself: Only two drinks a day while she was with them.

"Darn it! Why can't I hold my liquor like Bridget? The girl drinks like an Irish sailor. Why can't I just…just hold it together and not make a fool out of myself? What's wrong with me? I just have to try harder."

Ella's self-pity manifested itself in a flood of tears. Red Dog immediately reacted. He swung his head her way and started licking her face, his rough tongue tickling her nose and neck, causing her to laugh.

"Crazy dog." She playfully swatted him away and concentrated on keeping the car in her lane. "You know me too well, don't you, boy?"

And Red Dog did. He knew just what to do to comfort Ella and intuited her moods like a seasoned psychologist. He was five years old and had been part of the family since shortly after Bear died. The kids named him Red Dog because he was a golden retriever who was more red than gold. The name was practical and caused strangers to chuckle over the simplicity of it. Red Dog made up for his undisciplined quirky nature with his sweet disposition. He loved Ella unconditionally, and she him. Many a time she woke up out of a drunken stupor with his warm body next to hers. He never judged her drinking and licked her mercilessly as soon as she opened her bloodshot eyes. They were best friends and bonded by their unmanageable behavior.

~⁓~

"Where's Trixie?" Ella asked Bridget as Red Dog sniffed the kitchen floor looking for freebies. "I thought Red Dog would have a playmate this weekend."

"Oh, hell, I forgot that your boyfriend was coming with you," Bridget teased Ella as she knelt down on the floor to get smothered by a big slobbering tongue. "Trixie and the kids are up on the mountain with Dan. That pup is wearing me out. I thought Dan could let her go crazy in Laska's old pen. Besides, Michael needs to learn some responsibility when it comes to taking care of her. This weekend is just for us girls."

Lola sauntered in wearing a wreath of baby's breath and yellow flowers and carrying three more wreaths exactly like it in her hand.

"Gaia dropped these off earlier. Aren't they amazing?" she said.

"Where is she? I thought she might be here," Ella said.

"She's conducting a ceremony at a retreat center west of here. She's going to try to manifest getting done early so she can join us," Lola explained. "Per her explanation, the yellow flowers are called Chase Devil or St. John's Wort. Gaia said it was to ward off evil... you know, chase the devil away. In the old days, the people would hang sprigs of it over an entryway. So...beware...wooooooo." Lola placed the headpiece over Ella's blonde hair and gave her a big squeeze.

"So glad you can share your belated birthday with us. I've missed the hell out of you, girl," she said.

"Get your ass over here for your welcome drink," Bridget said. She held up a frothy margarita glass and handed it to Ella. Then she placed one in Lola's hand.

"Margaritas? What happened to The Potion?" Ella asked, taking a quick sip.

"We're going Mexican," Bridget said. "This is our version of a solstice fiesta. Later on we'll build a small bonfire and smoke copious amounts of Mexican reefer."

"Which will no doubt add some Druid authenticity to the entire celebration," Ella said, sipping her drink and grinning.

"You better explain the wreath thing," Bridget said to Lola as she adjusted the foreign object on her head, "'cause I'm feeling a little ridiculous right now."

"Well, you know how much Gaia dislikes this place and is always telling us to protect ourselves from the 'bad vibes' here. The wreaths are meant to do just that, protect us from...all the bad stuff lurking around and waiting to destroy our happiness and..."

"Okay, thanks so much for the depressing explanation," Bridget interrupted. She pointed to the patio. "Let's sit outside as the sun goes down and experience the solstice. The actual solstice isn't for a couple more days but it's our intention that counts, right?"

"So right you are, senorita." Plate in hand, Lola opened the door and was immediately knocked flat as Red Dog made a mad dash past her. Her drink and burrito went flying, and the flower circlet flew from her head. Red Dog ignored the drink and snatched up the circlet and the burrito.

"Red Dog, that was not polite," Ella called to him.

"I knew there was a reason I bought these plastic glasses and plates," Bridget yelled from the other side of the kitchen. She was already making Lola another drink. "Someone always has some kind of mishap when the three of us get together."

Ella helped Lola up, and Lola pointed at Red Dog. "Look at that crazy dog. Talk about a kindred spirit," Lola said, laughing. The golden retriever had somehow managed to get the wreath stuck around his neck but, true to form, was far more interested in finishing off Lola's burrito.

The three women settled into chairs around the unlit pile of wood, sipping their margaritas and munching chips and salsa. Time flew by as Lola entertained them with stories of her outrageous escapades. Bridget bitched about her discontent with men in general, and Ella desperately tried to pace her drinking, an ever more consuming effort that scared her no end.

Eventually, she began to relax, and her mind drifted off. *What a perfect evening,* she thought as the sun began to set. *Surrounded by your best friends and the boundless beauty of nature.*

It was a magnificent thought wrenched from her consciousness by a loud pop.

"Shit! What the hell was that?" Bridget jumped up out of her chair and looked to the west.

"It sounded like a big gun going off," Lola said.

"You're damn straight it was a big gun. That was a rifle," Bridget clarified.

Ella turned white as she stood up and looked around for her dog. "Red Dog! Red? Where are you, boy?" Red Dog hated gunshots, and his first instinct was to run to Ella for protection. But not this time. This time he was nowhere to be found.

They all three started yelling his name. Bridget jogged toward the western boundary of their property, and Ella and Lola followed. When they didn't find the dog, they split up and searched the property from the pond to the barn and back again.

"Find anything?" Ella yelled to them.

"Nothing," Lola called.

"What the hell?" Bridget said, as they headed back toward the house, heavy hearted and emotionally exhausted. "This makes no sense."

The moment was torn apart by the sudden ringing of the kitchen phone. Bridget raced inside, and Ella and Lola huddled within earshot. All they could hear was Bridget's rising voice.

"Yes, yes, the dog is a friend's... I know you've warned us about dogs chasing your cattle... The dog was chasing a calf...? CATTLE MUTILATIONS? WHAT THE HELL...? YOU SHOT THE DOG...? DEAD?" Bridget's reddening face exploded with expletives neither of the other women had ever heard expressed. "YOU JUST LEFT HIM OUT IN YOUR FUCKING PASTURE? YOU FUCKING ASS-HOLE. I DON'T GIVE A SHIT ABOUT YOUR LEGAL FUCKING RIGHTS. THAT DOG WAS MY FRIEND'S BEST FRIEND!!!" The phone almost broke in half as Bridget slammed it down.

She turned and walked straight to Ella, tears streaming down her face, and wrapped her arms around her. "Oh, Ella. It's Red Dog. He's..."

"Dead. Shot. I heard," Ella said.

Ella wanted to crumple to the floor, unexpected pictures of Bear flashing through her mind, but she didn't. Instead, she gathered all her strength and said, "We have to bring his body back here. We have to bring his body back right now. We can't leave him out there."

"We won't," Bridget said. She hurried into the kitchen and grabbed three flashlights. Then she went outside and found her daughter's old red wagon.

They set out just as dusk was falling and found Red Dog on the rancher's property, not an eighth of a mile across the property line. The bastard's bullet had struck him right behind the front legs. He had bled to death. A big tuft of cow hair was stuck to his teeth. The flower circlet was still around his neck, and reminded Ella of a funeral wreath.

"He said he didn't know what kind of animal was chasing the calf because of the wreath. Said he'd never seen anything like it before," Bridget said as she tried to get the flowers over the dog's head.

"Leave it on, Bridge," Ella said. She managed to chuckle through her tears. "It just seems so fitting. He was such a goofball. He deserves flowers for his burial. So much for warding off evil." She leaned over and kissed the top of Red Dog's head. "I'm going to be strong. I just never thought I'd lose another dog so soon. Another one that understood me better than anyone. My...best...buddy." She broke down.

Her friends lifted the dog into the wagon and they turned for home.

Back at the house, Bridget called Gary to say that Ella needed him. Again, it was a one-sided conversation that Ella and Lola were privy to.

"No, Gary, she's not. Red Dog was killed," Bridget curtly answered. "She'd like you to meet her up on the mountain so you and Brice can bury him...Yes, right now...! Gary, I'm so sorry... Okay, I'll tell her..."

When Bridget hung up, clearly touched by Gary's unexpected show of compassion, tears formed in her eyes.

"What did he say?" Ella was desperately trying to hold back the pain and sadness she was feeling and having very little luck doing so.

"He said, 'Tell Ella, not to worry. Brice and I will be there for her. I know how much she loved the dog and that I did too...and...that I've missed her.' Then he broke down and sobbed. I'm such a softy when a man cries. God, Gary crying." Bridget wiped away her tears.

"I've missed you too, Gary," Ella muttered. She crumpled to the floor, and Lola joined her, gently rocking her in a loving embrace.

Bridget straightened her posture, stomped over to the counter, and roughly grabbed the three flower headpieces. She stormed outside, threw them on the pile of wood in the fire pit, and lit the fire.

"What the fuck do you want from us?" she screamed to the sky. "Can we never be without heartache or sorrow? Can't you just leave us the hell alone! We just want to be happy! Just give us that! Come on, what's it going to take?" Bridget fell to her knees. She pummeled the ground with her fists, furious. Lifting her tear-soaked face toward the fire, the smell of smoke panicked every cell in her body and made the bile rise in her throat. She dry-heaved until her stomach hurt. Then she sat back on her heels and tried to focus her eyes at the growing fire. She didn't know where the ancient circle of women came from, but they were dancing rhythmically to a beat rising in her head, their colorful tribal dresses swaying. Bridget looked closer. She recognized her own face. And then, she recognized the faces of her friends, separate and yet one. She tried to speak, but there were no words.

Gentle hands touched her shoulders. Suddenly, Lola and Ella were beside her. Bridget was desperate to describe what she had seen, but both women seemed lost in their own trance-like world and no words formed on her tongue.

And then she heard a voice; it was close and soothing. It belonged to Gaia, and she was standing behind them. She wrapped her arms around the three women and said, "You are in the hands and hearts of the Ancient Ones who are here to teach, love, and comfort you. They are your true family leading you toward your destiny. Life is testing you to see if you are worthy to be a part of the sisterhood."

"Are you kidding me? Life is testing us? Fuck! Then we're in a heap of shit because none of us are very good with tests!" Bridget hissed. "And in case you haven't noticed, we're all just hanging on by a thin unraveling thread."

"Then thank the Great Creator for that thread," Gaia whispered into the ethers.

October 1993

JEALOUSY

Beauty and the beast lived side by side on the mesa.

Beauty fed the eyes and soul with magnificent views of the foothills and the snow-capped mountains behind them, offering an astonishing silhouette for sunsets as brilliant as they were breathtaking.

That glory, however, came with a price. October was a month of transition, a clash between the lingering warmth of summer and the crisp coolness of the approaching winter. This was the time of year when the raging Enchantress of the Warm Wind challenged any early signs of the Cailleach's awakening. Winds uninterrupted by trees and buildings raced unabated down the mountainside and across the valley, sweeping in full fury across the top of the mesa. With winds gusting from 80 to 120 mph, anything not nailed down was at risk from the beastly enchantress.

Small children, the frail elderly, and stray dogs could be picked up and literally blown away. Lawn furniture was tossed around like child's play. Trees suffered terrible injury enduring the wind's brutal power. The battle between The Enchantress of the Warm Wind and the Hag of Winter would play out over and over from now until spring.

Bridget hated this time of year, not the season itself, but because winter followed. She was listening to Steve rambling with one part of her brain and complaining about the weather with the other.

"Bridget, why can't you answer me? I want you to live with me. Do you love me enough to share my home with me? It's a simple question. Yes or no?" Steve demanded, eyes flashing his impatience.

The redhead clenched her teeth together as another fierce gust battered the side of the house. On days like this, the toilets had whitecaps in them big enough for a miniature surfboard to float across the bowl, or so her kids said. She didn't want to be having this conversation. They'd already had this conversation, like twenty times. *Shit, all I want to do right now is have a little Sunday afternoon delight and maybe a nap before the kids get home.*

"Steve, you know how much I care about you. We always have a good time when we're together, but I can't move in with you. I'm still legally married to Dan and it would be too disruptive and traumatic for the kids. I just can't do that to them. We've talked about this before and my decision hasn't changed."

"Yeah, yeah…right…the kids," Steve replied. "They're used to disruptive and already past being traumatized. You're separated for Christ's sake. It's always about the kids. You know I think they're great as far as kids go, but I just want more of you and the only way to get 'the more' is if you live with me. The family thing is not my gig. I admit that. But I can put up with it. It seems like everything is more important to you than me, than us. If it's not the kids, then it's your job. I think you even love that damn job of yours more than you do me."

Bridget fidgeted, trying to figure out how to temper her response in a way that wouldn't alienate him. *Just stay calm, Bridge.* "Steve, I don't want to lose you, but it's not like we're talking about a hobby. It's my job. I have a family to support. I can't just ignore that. Why can't you understand that?"

"Dammit, Bridget! I've been more than understanding about all the shit in your life. You, however, have not done the same for me. When do you support what I want? I keep getting pushed further and further down your priority list. You didn't even mention anything about my birthday and it's tomorrow. I thought we'd celebrate this weekend, but it looks like I fell off your radar again!"

"Shit! Oh my God! Steve, I'm so sorry. With all that damn traveling last week, I completely forgot. Hell, I hardly know what day it is anymore." Bridget looked at him, her brow furrowed. "Is that what this is all about? Your birthday?"

"No, Bridget. That's not what this is all about! I love you! I'm in love with you! You rock my world, baby, but I need some attention too, and I'm sick of waiting. I've planned my life around you. Which is funny, since you've never planned yours around me. What a sucker I've been. Living in a fantasyland. Got to hand it to you, Bridge, you did a helluva job making me believe my fantasy could come true. What a bunch of bullshit!"

Damn, he keeps saying he loves me and, God, that love word just keeps getting stuck in my throat. It's so hard for me to say it to anyone... love...shit.

Seeing the pained look on her lover's face, Bridget surprised herself by taking a page out of Lola's playbook. She seductively batted her eyes while stroking the inside of his thigh. "How 'bout we go upstairs right now and I give you the attention you deserve? Will that make you feel better, baby?"

Steve did his best to resist her advances, because he was still pissed. But when Bridget ran her hand inside the top of his jeans, fingers seeking to stroke his already hardening cock, he gave in. "God, Bridge, I so love you…I…"

A deafening crash put an end to the moment and sent a dramatic shudder through the house, knocking a picture frame off the wall behind them.

"Jesus friggin' Christ!" Bridget jumped up and screamed at the same time. "Fucking wind!"

She scrambled to her feet and ran to a window, still shouting. "I hate it! It never stops! It's relentless!"

Poor Steve barely got his pants zipped up when the front door crashed open and nearly shattered the transept window in the top of the door. Dan and the kids burst into the hall. *What the hell were they doing here?* The kids were screaming, "Mom! Mom! Dad's hurt!"

Bridget rounded the corner, and there was Dan, holding the side of his head, blood gushing profusely between his fingers and down his arm.

"Oh, my God! Dan, are you all right? What happened?" She raced to his side, cradling his face in her hands and tenderly stroking his bloodsoaked hair away from his face.

"I…I think I'm okay. Shit! God, that hurt!"

"What the hell happened?"

"Got hit by a tree limb the size of a Volkswagen. Never saw it coming."

There was a war raging outside, and the wind was winning. When a wave of sticks and gravel catapulted through the open door, Bridget turned to close it. She couldn't do it. The door was pinned to the inside wall, and the wind had every intention of keeping it there.

"This is a fucking nightmare!" she bellowed over the wind. "You guys have to help me! Don't just stand there…NOW!"

It took three adults and three tries before there was a sufficient pause in the wind to get the door closed. Even then, the three of them had to throw their full weight against the door before Dan could engage the deadbolt.

When it seemed the door would hold, Dan sank to the floor, breathing hard, his head still bleeding. "Son of a bitch!"

Bridget continued to fuss over him long after the bleeding had stopped, holding the ice pack on his head for him. The cut wasn't as bad as it looked, and she treated it with a butterfly bandage. That did the trick.

The kids were rustling around in the kitchen looking for something to eat when Steve announced to anyone who might care that he was leaving. Bridget followed him out.

"I'm really sorry our afternoon was ruined. Sometimes things just happen, you know?" She stared deeply into Steve's eyes and only saw hurt and anger.

"Yeah, Bridge, I can see how things just happen to you. You introduced me to Dan as 'a friend' of yours and Lola's? Really? Your friend? What the hell was that supposed to mean?"

"Steve, I know you're probably mad but the whole situation was so uncomfortable and I didn't think we needed any more drama. Please understand."

"There's no probably about it and I think I'm starting to get the picture with crystal clear understanding. Why don't you call me when you can make the time, since I'm only a friend? You pursue me for a while because I'm done with chasing after you. I am so done!"

Steve turned abruptly and walked away. Bridget called after him, "I'll call you after the kids are in bed. Promise."

Steve didn't look back, and Dan was pulling on his jacket when Bridget walked back in the house. A mass exodus. "I've got to get going too," he said.

"Why don't you stay and keep the ice on your head a while longer. I'll put together some dinner for all of us."

"No, thanks. I've had enough of this place for one day." Dan ruffled the kids' hair as he passed through the kitchen and headed out the back door.

Bridget was suddenly playing mom again. She improvised a dinner of grilled cheese and tomato soup and served it on paper plates. She sat with the kids and made small talk before asking why their dad had brought them back early that day. Michael shrugged and said, "He said something about a hot date coming up to the trailer for dinner. Guess he didn't need us around."

What? A hot date? Bridget could feel the heat rising on her face. When it began to burn uncomfortably, she jumped up, gathered the dishes, and carried them to the sink. The jealousy she was feeling manifested in anger. "You tell your inconsiderate father that the next time he wants to change the plans he'd better call and ask me first!"

"Not my job, Mom," Michael muttered. "Sorry."

As if to accentuate her son's painfully astute observation, a horrific blast of wind made the whole house shudder and creak on its foundation, and Bridget realized the shoe was suddenly on the other foot.

December 1993

THE SCARF DANCE

A glimmer of red rhinestones flashed in the dim light of the flickering candles that lined the mantle and decorated the Christmas center-pieces on tables throughout the huge house.

Middle Eastern music played softly in the background. People were dressed in their winter best. They drank hot chocolate with peppermint schnapps and eggnog spiced with rum.

The owners of the house were determined to host a holiday party with an exciting, exotic flair this year. As the guests arrived, a butler greeted them, taking their coats and escorting them inside. But this was no ordinary butler; he was clad only in a skimpy loincloth. With his bulging biceps and huge calves, the young man looked like a Playgirl centerfold. And he was not the only one. The male caterers were dressed in like attire, and the female help looked like "I Dream of Jeannie" clones. The odd mix sparked conversation and peals of laughter.

A low, exquisite lighting added an aura of mystery to the celebration, and a huge Christmas tree, exquisitely decorated, served as the room's biggest and most eye-catching centerpiece.

Food for every taste was available throughout the house and alcohol flowed freely. Incense filled the air with evocative scents.

After an hour or so of revelry, there was a sudden pause in the music. The sound of a spoon chiming against a crystal glass replaced it. All eyes rose to the balcony of the main room where the host and hostess looked down on them.

"Ladies and gentlemen. We hope you're all enjoying yourselves tonight. We're delighted you could join us in celebrating the holidays," their host called. "We have a special treat for you tonight, a bit of exotic flair to spice the evening. We present to you...Zahar."

The music rose again, filling the house with intrigue, and the lights dimmed. The dancer known as Zahar moved into the room, her face veiled, her candy apple red gown a perfect match for the season. Anklets of tiny bells tinkled as she danced, slow and captivating. Her jewel-encrusted bra shimmered wildly in the candlelight, her midsection adorned with a huge ruby red rhinestone, jewels hugging her hips as they moved with hypnotic sensuality. The filmy fabric covering her legs opened and closed, offering tantalizing glimpses of perfectly sculpted thighs. Her hair sparkled with tiny diamonds. Her eyes flashed.

No one spoke. Time stood still. The dancer held them in her palm.

The rhythm of the zils accentuated the melody and the snap of her hips. The music pulsed. The dancer worked the crowd with back bends and shimmies. As the tempo of the music rose, so did the enthusiastic clapping of the crowd. She had them.

Her hips, arms, hands, and head seemed to move independently of one another, blending into a fantastically frenzied finish. Applause exploded. Cheers echoes off the walls. Zahar bowed, but only for a moment.

A long silk scarf suddenly materialized from her wardrobe. The music slowed, yet its power grew. The scarf began moving, and Zahar moved with it. Like two competing waves, scarf and dancer floated around the room, intermingling with the crowd, enticing them to join her. The room went eerily silent. As if by magic, a single line of people formed behind her, reverently following her. Around the Christmas tree she circled, her feet gliding to an ethereal melody.

Before the dancer knew it, they were chanting, "Zahar, Zahar, Zahar," as she rose stair by stair to the balcony, and the music ended.

"Show your face to us," the host called, his glass held high. "Let us see you."

Zahar did so. She removed her veil, batted her long lashes for dramatic effect, and smiled widely. Breathtaking.

Glass breaking on the tile floor far below broke the spell. All eyes turned to the tall, handsome man whose drink had crashed loudly to the floor. He stared at her, and she at him. Recognition registered in the man's eyes. Zahar stood paralyzed.

~~~~~~

It was midnight before Lola could extract herself from the gathering, and she could not get out of there fast enough. The gated neighborhood was quiet except for the revelry in the house. Cold air enveloped her face as she pulled her coat tighter around her neck. The snowflakes looked bigger and fatter than just minutes before. Stopping on the sidewalk, she noticed the moon peeking through the thickening clouds and knew she was going to have a hard time sleeping tonight.

She opened her car door and climbed behind the wheel. She was fumbling with her keys when a man's voice sounded in her ear. "Zahar? Is that what you call yourself?"

She cried out. She was scrambling for the door handle when the voice said, "LOLA, it's me. John. Wait."

Lola stopped, her breath catching in her throat. She slammed her hand against the steering wheel and turned around to face him. "WHAT ARE YOU DOING SCARING THE BEJESUS OUT OF ME? HOW DID YOU GET IN MY CAR? I THOUGHT YOU WERE A CRAZY KILLER. PEOPLE HAVE TO STOP HIDING IN MY BACK SEAT!"

John opened the door and moved into the front seat beside her. "Then maybe you should lock your doors."

"Zahar," he sneered. "You're kidding me, right?"

"I thought I saw you in there. Then I thought it was my imagination playing tricks on me," she explained shakily.

"Exactly my thoughts. A belly dancer? Really Lola, that just blows my mind. Where's Nick?"

Lola and John stared at each other. John felt an unexpected wave of affection that nearly derailed his anger, but he pushed it aside. This was not about them. It was about Nick.

"Where's Nick, I said. While you're out gallivanting till all hours of the night? Answer me! Where's my son?"

"Home."

"Home? You mean alone? It's nearly midnight." Now he was genuinely pissed. "He's a kid. What if something happened? What are you thinking?"

"John, he's thirteen. Kids baby-sit for other kids at that age. You're being overly protective. Anyhow, Bridget and her kids are there too."

"But what about when they're not there? And in that wacky place you live in. He's told me all the stories. Would you want to be alone in that spooky place…and leaving him alone so you can feed your ego by belly dancing in front of a bunch of salivating assholes? That's just wrong. You need to get a *real* job or I'm going to have to take custody of Nick so that he has a stable environment to grow up in. He's a teenager and needs supervision."

"Wrong? How dare you tell me my job is wrong? It's my job. I make more money belly dancing than waitressing. A lot more. I work my butt off supporting Nick and myself, and he wants for nothing. And I love it, and people love me. Hell, Nick really doesn't even know what I do. He just knows I work weird hours. You can't tell him. You can't take him. I'm a damn good loving mother…" Lola started sobbing, thick mascara running down her cheeks.

John reached out to comfort her and stopped himself. "It's not just Nick's safety I'm worried about. It's yours too. People get the wrong idea. Find something else, Lola," John said in no uncertain terms. "You've got to have more skills than just dressing up like a genie and dancing like a sex fiend."

Lola straightened. "You enjoyed my dancing just like everyone else. Admit it. I was fabulous."

"That's not the point. You have to find a more legitimate job with daytime hours so that our son is not alone all night long, or else."

"You're acting like my husband. You're not my husband."

"No, Lola, I'm acting like a concerned father and a responsible adult!"

"Do you ever have any fun, John? I mean, seriously. You know what I think? I think you really need to get laid," she said, knowing she had crossed over the line.

He glared at her. Then he scrambled out, slammed the door, and disappeared into the night.

January 1994

INTERVENTION

Ella's last day on the job was actually one of the best days of her life. She just didn't know it yet.

She sat across the desk from her supervisor Karen, staring down at her hands, her long stringy hair obscuring her face. All she could think about was how cracked and ragged her nails and cuticles were. *Whose hands are these? They sure can't be mine.*

Ella felt disconnected, like she was watching a movie that had absolutely nothing to do with her whatsoever. The growing silence in the room finally caught her attention and snapped her back to the present. She tried focusing her bloodshot eyes on the person in front of her, but with minimal success.

"I'm sorry, Karen, what were you saying?"

"I was saying that this is the third time this month we've had this conversation. I was saying you've missed work five of the last fifteen days without notifying me, and the days you do show up, you show up late and looking like one of our homeless people. Hell, girl, when was the last time you washed your hair or even got it trimmed?"

"I know, I know, I haven't been myself lately. Just give me a little slack, will you? You know better than anyone else that I'm going through hell. My husband wants to divorce me and my own kids aren't even living with me. It's just about killing me…my own children. How'd this happen to me? I mean, really?" Ella shook her head. She couldn't hold Karen's look. "Just give me a little time to put my family back together. God, I miss them…if only I…I…"

"Ella, look at me," Karen said. "I'm not only your supervisor, but I am also your friend. Everyone here has always admired your work ethic and respected the caring and compassion you show your clients. We are so lucky to have you. You're one of our best social workers. That's the only reason you still have a job here. We've given you a lot of leeway the last several months, but you're becoming a risk to the well being of your clients and a liability to the organization. I've offered you counseling. I've offered you a leave of absence. But you've been unwilling to pursue any of those options."

Karen leaned across the desk, her eyes sympathetic. "I've no choice but to put you on a probation notice. Your performance will be reviewed weekly for the next ninety days. If you fail to meet the performance requirements I've laid out for you, your position here will be terminated immediately. I'm sorry."

Karen's voice cracked. She cleared her throat. "You need to sign and date this agreement before you return to work today, Ella."

Ella snatched the paper from Karen's hand and scrawled an illegible signature at the bottom of the page. Without so much as a backward glance, she stormed out of the room and stomped down the hall to her office. She slammed the door, caught the hem of her dress between the door and the threshold, and heard it rip as she stormed toward her desk. She collapsed in her chair and swore. *I hated this skirt anyway. So good riddance.*

She snatched a thermos from her briefcase and, without a second thought, threw her head back and guzzled down the entire contents: straight vodka. She wiped her mouth with the back of her hand, even as tears welled up in her eyes. She rocked back and forth in her chair, trying to convince herself it was just a string of bad luck that had screwed up her life. Things were going to work out. Like always, she would hold everything together. Everyone would see.

Ella's thoughts wandered to the day Red Dog was killed and the week-long binge the dog's death had precipitated. She thought about Alena abandoning her to go live in New York with her grandparents. She thought about Gary's affair, and how he had dumped her like yesterday's garbage. She thought about Brice storming out of her life and refusing even to come see her on the weekends. *What's wrong with all of them? How can they forget all I do for them, all I give them?*

And now my good friend Karen has gone and put me on probation. Some fucking friend, Ella thought bitterly. *Well, screw her. Screw them all.*

Ella fumbled through her purse looking for her emergency stash. She was reaching for the bottle when a knock on the door startled her. "Who is it?" she called out a little too loudly, slurring her words.

"Janice is here, Ella. Shall I send her in?" The torn piece of fabric from Ella's dress fell to the floor when the door opened a crack, and her receptionist stared at it. "What's this?"

Ella yelled, "Don't come in here!"

She jumped to her feet and plunged toward the door. She didn't get far. The chair rolled over the hem of her skirt and sent her toppling. She reached out for something to break her fall and swept everything on her desk onto the floor ahead of her. The crash resounded out into the hall, the receptionist and her client raced in to find Ella in a pile of debris, unconscious.

The next morning Ella awoke in a hospital bed and the first thing she noticed was the grim-faced doctor standing at the end of her bed.

"Where am I?" She knew where she was so she asked, "What happened?"

The doctor didn't waste time on niceties. "Your head is fine. We did a CT scan. There's no skull fracture or evidence of brain injury, but a concussion is likely. We'll keep you here another twenty-four hours for observation. We also tested your blood alcohol content. It registered .25%."

The doctor raised his eyebrows to see if she understood what he was saying, but Ella's face remained completely expressionless. Instead, she shifted her position and looked out the window, trying to escape his knowing look. "We did some blood work. The tests revealed elevated levels of serum GGT enzymes. I've ordered some more testing."

"Why?"

"My concern," he voiced, "is regarding potential organ damage from extensive use of alcohol. You have evidence of malnutrition and elevated glucose levels along with elevated serum enzymes. That suggests a potential for organ damage."

Ella had remained very still and silent during his monologue, but now pushed aside the sheets and tried getting up. "That will not be necessary! There's nothing wrong with me that a little rest won't cure. I want to be discharged from this hospital immediately! Right this very moment! Where are my clothes?"

A nurse was immediately at her side, coaxing her back into the bed and trying to keep her IVs intact. The doctor explained again that they needed to watch her for another night to ensure she didn't suffer any consequences from the concussion, sidestepping the detox implications. He reassured her that everything would be fine, that she needed to rest for a while.

"In the meantime," he said, brightening his face, "your husband is outside and anxious to see you."

Ella fell back against the bed. She was trembling all over and realized she didn't have the strength to stand even if she wanted to.

Her mind panicked, half afraid, half grateful that Gary was there to see her.

The next morning, Gary arrived as promised to take her home. He had been so warm and kind to her since yesterday that her heart welled up with unrealistic hope. She convinced herself that everything was going to be okay, even though she had a horrible headache and was terribly nauseated and anxious.

Ella looked across the seat at Gary and smiled, grateful that he was with her and not Michelle and believing he really cared about her. She felt happy for the first time in a very long time. And then the demons started in. *When I get home, a little glass of vodka will calm things down, and I'll be able to relax. Then Gary and I can talk about how much we've missed each other and how we're going to patch things up. I knew it would all work out for the better. I just knew it would!*

Ella closed her eyes as Gary drove up the mountain. He pulled over twice during the trip when the dry heaves caused his passenger to retch.

"I feel horrible," she moaned, and the feeling increased when she saw the cars parked in her driveway. "Who's here?"

Ella saw the trepidation in Gary's eyes, but she didn't have time to question him. She threw open the car door and puked in the gravel. Gary ran to her side and helped her up.

"Who's here, Gary?" she managed to say again.

"It's just some friends. They've been worried about you and wanted to make sure you are all right."

"I can't handle any company right now, Gary. Please go in and tell them to come back tomorrow. Please! All I need is you with me now. I just want to be alone with you."

"It'll be okay, Ella." Gary's heart cringed; his wife looked unrecognizable. "Let's go in and talk to them together."

Gary walked her slowly toward the house. Ella retched twice along the way, once on the driveway and once on the lawn.

Her fingers dug deeper into Gary's arm as they climbed the steps to the porch and walked through the door, and she nearly threw up again when she saw her parents huddled on the living room couch next to Lola, Bridget, and Karen.

"What are you all doing here?" she cried, looking at her parents in disbelief.

Karen spoke first. "Ella, we're here because we love you and care about you and we don't want to lose you."

Shirley piped up, "Ella, honey, we all just want to help you get better."

"What are you talking about? I'll be fine in a couple of days! You didn't need to fly all the way here from New York." Ella looked from face to face and finally turned all her rage and fear in Karen's direction. "Is this your idea? Some kind of intervention? I'll tell you what, if you don't like my work, then just fire me. But stay the hell out of my personal life!"

The room went very quiet. Even the howling wind seemed to take pause, waiting for what was next. Karen held Ella's gaze and clearly said the words: "You have been fired, Ella. We're here to talk about what you want to do next."

Reality caused Ella's knees to buckle, and gravity pushed her frail body toward the floor. Gary instinctively grabbed her by the shoulders and maneuvered her gently onto the couch. "It's okay, babe. Sit. Please. I'll get water and coffee for everyone. We have a lot to talk about."

And indeed they did. At the end of two heartbreaking hours filled with communal shouts, spats of rage and anger, whispers of grief and fear, and hysterical crying, Ella chokingly agreed to engage in the treatment program her friends and family were adamantly proposing. What scared her more than anything was the fact that, according to Karen, Gary would get custody of the kids since she had no job and seemed incapable of holding one.

"It has to be the Betty Ford Clinic," Shirley inanely insisted. "It's the best clinic in the country for this sort of thing. And besides, everything's already been arranged. Nothing but the best for our daughter." She patted Ella on the shoulder. "Thirty days and you'll be good as new." Then she looked at Bob. "Twenty thousand dollars is a small price to pay to have our girl back, right, Robert?"

All Lola and Bridget could do was roll their eyes, and it took every ounce of restraint not to lash out at Shirley's ignorance.

They nudged the older woman off the couch and wrapped Ella in their arms. "Our eternal friendship is at stake here and we won't let it go down without a fight," Bridget told her.

"We'll do everything we can to help you through this, Ella. You always grounded us into the rational. We'd be lost without you. You are not in this alone," Lola said. "This time we'll be the rock for you like you have always been for us."

The three began crying all over again.

Finally they yielded the floor to Gary, who had been uncomfortably quiet throughout the process, trying, not surprisingly, to sort through his own anger and obvious disappointment with his wife.

"Listen, Lola and Bridget are right," he said. "We care about you, Ella. We care about your well being. I care about your well being. And you have my promise that I won't file for custody of the kids if you make an honest commitment to this treatment program. If you make an honest commitment to getting sober. Will you do that?"

Ella didn't answer right away. Finally, she looked up at him and said, "What about the divorce? Will you continue with that?"

Gary swallowed hard, but replied candidly. "I don't know what to say about that right now, Ella. I really don't. Right now, you need to focus on yourself and your own healing. We can worry about everything else later."

August 1994

PORTAL OF HELL

Goosebumps appeared on Gaia's skin as soon as she crossed over the threshold of Lola and Bridget's rented house. Ella always felt "odd" inside its walls too, and even though it was late morning and the sun was brightly shining, she felt spooked and grabbed Gaia's hand.

"What's with the cobwebs?" Ella said, pointing to the doorjamb.

"Pretend everything's normal," Gaia replied.

Despite the challenge, both women put on their happy faces as Lola and Bridget welcomed them with hugs all around.

"How are you?" Lola asked Ella, squeezing her hand.

"Good," Ella replied with a smile. And it was true. Enough time had passed for Ella to be comfortable around the girls and not crave a drink. They still made The Potion, but hers was a Virgin Potion. So was Gaia's. Ella had convinced herself that the virgin variety tasted even better without the booze. As for Gaia, she had taken a toke before going in because she wasn't very fond of alcohol and wanted at least a little bit of a buzz.

This was the first time all four women had been alone together in many months. Gossip, stories, and lots of laughter made the hours fly by. Gaia pulled out her Tarot deck; time for a one-card reading. Each woman shuffled the deck. Gaia cut the cards and spread them out in a semicircle. Ella, Lola, and Bridget placed their hands over Gaia's, and she guided them over the cards. Then she stopped, picked one up and showed it to them.

"The Hanged Man. Creepy," Lola stated with hesitation. Despite the August heat, she shivered. Ella and Bridget both took a step backwards. Gaia cleared her throat and steadied her voice.

"Okay, let me gather my wits about me. I need to close my eyes and ask my guides to help me through this interpretation." Ella, Bridget, and Lola stood as still as statues and didn't utter a word for the first time in hours.

Finally, Gaia's eyes opened. "Come with me. You all look so worried. Don't be. It's really a great card. We need a big bed that will fit us all. And a room with a view of the mountains."

"What? Why?" Ella asked. She couldn't help herself.

They followed Lola into her room on the second floor. It had a queen-sized bed facing a huge picture window. "This is perfect," Gaia said.

"Perfect for what?" Ella asked again.

"We're all going to lie down on our backs and look out there." Gaia pointed at the view.

"If you say so," Bridget said dubiously.

They all followed Gaia's lead and lay down side by side with their heads hanging over the edge of the bed. When everyone was comfortable, Gaia said, "Ready? I want you all to imagine what the world would look like if you were hanging upside down. At first, it's scary. But then, you start to get used to it. Your entire perception of the world looks different. In most Tarot decks, this card is represented by a contented Hanged Man wearing a halo and dangling upside down from a tree with a rope around one ankle, usually his left."

"Why the left?" Bridget wanted to know.

"Because left represents the female intuitive side," Gaia answered. "Now, imagine being that guy. All you can do is just hang there, unable to escape."

"Escape from what?" Bridget again.

"Basically from yourself," Gaia said patiently. "Life passes you by and you just have to hang there, unable to participate. This topsy-turvy view is your new normal. You have to give up your power to control your destiny by becoming vulnerable and surrendering to the all-knowing Universe, which knows your fate. Going with the flow of life by just watching it go by. Patiently waiting for things to come to you instead of you rushing in, interfering, and trying to fix or change things the way you see fit and right."

Gaia gave them a moment, then said, "What are you seeing in this position? Just like the Hanged Man, you really can only see in front of you because trying to see what's behind you would take too much effort. Relax into this position, just be. Since you can't see behind you...in other words, into your past...just let it go. Calmly watch the images in front of you in the present moment, and just take them in. You can't act on them so you go with the flow of life. Feel the blood rushing to your head and nourishing your brain. Enjoy being with yourself and wondering about things you never thought of before. Let the thoughts illuminate and enlighten you. The universe is in control. You aren't. Surrender everything old that isn't serving your best interests. Rest inside yourself. Breathe. Know that everything will work out for your highest good."

She paused again, letting the words settle. "Go back to when you were born. Passing through the birth canal with great forces pushing down on you, you were born into this world upside down, trusting you would survive as you were set free from your very comfortable confinement of the womb. So too you will break free of everything holding you back, surrendering your need to control. The newness will feel uncomfortable at first, but it will propel you into the wisdom you need in order to know your destiny. Understanding your true nature, happiness will be yours with this new perspective on your life and the world. By quieting the chatter in your world, the true voice of your soul will be heard and felt. Your darkest hours will begin to dissipate as The Hanged Man brings forth transformation and rebirth."

Gaia closed her eyes and was silent.

The peaceful snoring of four contented women came to a sudden halt as the sound of yipping coyotes and an anguished dog's howl penetrated the serenity of the room. Bridget sat bolt upright, then flew off the bed.

"Trixie! I forgot all about Trixie."

Bridget's panic was contagious. They all sprinted down the steps. Lola grabbed a big can of pepper spray from the front windowsill. Everyone ran out the front door shouting Trixie's name. Feeling uncharacteristically brave, Lola held the can out in front of her like a gun.

They searched for a half-hour without hearing or seeing any signs of the dog. They stopped to regroup. Bridget was calling out orders like a quarterback when Gaia pointed into the setting sun. There, a large group of ravens was circling over a small ravine on the western property line.

"No!" Bridget started running. Lola and Gaia set out after her, knowing the sight their friend was sure to see would be more than she could bear alone. Ella couldn't move. She stood paralyzed, remembering too clearly when her own dog was shot almost a year ago now by that stupid, cowardly rancher. She knew Trixie was dead.

Four shovels dug in parched hard dirt illuminated only by the light of a half-moon. They made quick work of Trixie's grave. It was an eerie scene as they wrapped the bloodied and mangled dog in her favorite blanket and gently lowered her into the deep hole. They piled rocks for a grave marker. The women formed a circle around the grave and held hands.

"Such a loyal friend Trixie was," Gaia said. "Such a warm and wonderful companion she was for Bridget and Lola's household and all their kids. She will be sorely missed, even as her spirit looks down upon us with watchful, caring eyes."

"Thank you, Gaia," Bridget said, holding back her tears. "I can't think of anyone else I'd want to share this moment of sadness with than my three wonderful, loving friends. Thank you all for being here with me."

Then, to everyone's surprise, Bridget went on to talk about the Hanged Man card's message about moving forward and leaving the past behind. Then she just let go and sobbed. She thought about the kids and having to explain Trixie's death to them. They would surely think her the hypocrite after all her endless talk about keeping a close eye on a dog living in the country or on the mountain. She cried even harder.

The girls wrapped her in their arms and made their way back to the house. Lola made an extra-strong batch of The Potion for Bridget's sake, and Gaia retrieved sage smudge sticks and matches from her satchel.

"Girls, this is war!" she said angrily. "We have to take action now! It's time we smudge this house. We should've done this the first day you two moved in. Something is so wrong here. I don't know how the two of you can stand it. We've ignored it for too long – whatever negativity resides here needs to go."

She lit the smudge sticks and allowed the smoke to curl into the air. The pungent aroma filled the house. They ventured into each and every room, all of them reciting the affirmations Gaia had taught them.

When they got to the pantry where Trixie's bed and food bowl lay, Bridget broke down and shared her own interpretation of the chant, shouting, "Fuck you, evil spirits! Get the hell out of here. You've caused enough heartache. Leave us the fuck alone!"

"Damn, girl, I think you just reached a ten on the woo-woo scale," Lola informed her.

Gaia walked over to Bridget and very kindly told her that wasn't exactly what she had in mind, chant-wise.

"I suppose not," Bridget admitted, straightening her posture.

They continued on, moving from room to room, until Lola said, "Don't forget the basement. The kids love to hang out down there."

When they were done with the basement, Gaia said, "Anything else?"

"Just one more," Bridget said, leading them outside to the abandoned cottage that the owners had specifically told them not to go into.

"Not sure why," Bridget said, noticing that the lock wasn't really even closed completely on the outside door. The shadows of tree branches and their bodies danced against the side of the building in the lunar light.

Ella screamed suddenly and dug her fingernails into Lola's arm.

They all saw it. A rope noose hanging from the rafters of the cottage's peaked roof, eerily silhouetted by the moon's yellow light. A jagged piece of glass hung precariously in its frame.

"Holy shit!" Bridget proclaimed, peering up through the broken window. The girls gathered tightly together. "All this time, and we've never noticed that before."

Gaia relit their smudging tools, and Bridget kicked in the door. The hinges squealed and a wall of musty, hot stench filled their noses. Four bats burst through the door and nearly took their heads off. They were too scared to scream, but not too scared to let out a collective gasp.

They stepped inside, and a flutter of wings signaled the wild scurrying of a small flock of birds up in the rafters; the scurrying set the noose swinging.

"God damn!" Lola whispered. "This is too creepy for words."

"Come on," Gaia said bravely. "This place needs smudging more than anywhere else. Quick. Get in here. We need to say the affirmations with intention and in unison."

The girls obeyed. But their obedience only lasted until an owl burst through the broken window, swooped down on them, and darted out the door. It landed in a nearby tree and hooted.

The girls scattered. Ella was the first out, tripping over the threshold and scraping her knee. Lola was right behind her, screaming, "Oh my God, Oh my God," over and over again. Bridget and Gaia collided into each other, burning holes in their clothes with the fiery ash of the smudge sticks.

Bridget's stick fell to the floor and ignited a pile of dry leaves. The thought of fire loomed huge in her mind as she stomped the flame out. She sprinted out the door, silently whispering a Hail Mary for good measure.

The foursome met up at the front door, breathing hard, and debating the urge to fight or flee.

The owl resumed its hooting and the shadows became evil monsters taunting them.

"What the hell was that about?" Bridget asked, gasping for air.

Gaia looked at the women and proclaimed, "Hell is right. Girls, we've run smack dab into the Portal of Hell, and the two of you need to move out of this house: NOW!"

FIRE

Day 4

"Mornings are perfect for a 'dew bath,' which amplifies our senses and connects us to this great Earth."
~ The Circle of Na'mow Handbook – Betty, Second Generation

September 17, 1996, Tuesday morning

Eru'tan's power didn't come from the earth alone. It came from the heavens.

A fire scarring the slopes of a mountain, any mountain, no matter how beautiful and proud, was truly a small thing to the heavens. A blink of the eye.

Eru'tan didn't view fire as a source of concern the way humans did. Fire served many purposes; it was only one of Eru'tan's many tools.

White Sun and her people knew enough about Eru'tan to realize that her hand could not be forced. Change represented the one constant. The Traveling Tribes knew this and respected it.

White Sun understood that time was your only ally when the forces of nature turned on you. You could wait out a fire; the Traveling Tribes knew that. You wait. You don't fret or fear. You hasten to another mountain or another valley where the forces of nature are less severe. Then the winds change, the clouds appear, the skies open, and behold, the rains come. Or, in the case of the great fire charring Na'mow's slopes that late summer of 1996, rain, sleet, and snow.

And so it did when the Cailleach made a dramatic appearance early in the morning of the fire's fourth day, bringing with it a deluge of rain. The temperature dropped and the rain began to freeze. Six inches of sleet and the snow soon followed. And sure enough, the rain, sleet, and snow served to slow the fiery beast.

The smell in the air was unsettling, something no one could describe accurately…a smell of devastation…a smell that conjured up hopelessness, defeat, death. The firefighters, cops, and anyone else who had survived the night agreed…it was not a pleasant smell, not at all. This immediate world on the mountain felt off kilter, skewed, distorted, robbed of its natural balance. Everyone knew it was going to take a long time before the word "normal" could again be used to describe anything in the neighborhood.

What they didn't see, and what White Sun would have surely told them had she not been dead for a hundred years, was that this was normal. A new normal, perhaps, but normal in the eyes of Eru'tan, and normal for Na'mow and her millions of years of life experience.

ON THE MOUNTAIN

Dan and Gary spent a restless, unsettling night at Dan's house. They ate hot dogs. They took turns at the watch as night descended and the orange glow of embers and the blue-white hue of flames continued their onslaught on the eastern side of the subdivision, up the ridge and down toward Boulder. They still had no idea what houses had survived, but Gary didn't care. His only concern was for his son Brice and their friend Herb; it overwhelmed and consumed him, and Dan had to physically restrain him from driving into the fire to try to find them.

"I can only imagine what you're going through…but we can't be stupid about this. We have to keep ourselves safe…for our families' sake. Brice and Herb are smart, and I have to believe they're all right. That's all we can do right now. So…let me cook up some hot dogs. We need to eat. Then, we can take turns sleeping. That way if the wind changes, we'll have time to get the hell out of here. But Gary, there's nothing else we can do right now. All we can do right now is sit tight and wait. Promise me you won't go out there alone?"

Gary gave his word.

Their fitful slumber ended at 3:00 a.m. First Dan, then Gary. From the window, they could barely make out the orange glow. Snow covered the deck and big white flakes were falling like shadow diamonds from the sky. The beauty of the whiteness tugged at their hearts, a reminder of why they loved living on the mountain. Tears formed in their eyes as they took in the sight.

Dan embraced Gary in a hearty hug that only men who have survived a common battle could understand. The stillness of the moment was a gift of regeneration of their beings. Each man would need all his strength to face the aftermath of this firestorm.

IN TOWN

It was 5:00 a.m., and the snow had dampened the distant shimmer of the fire. Hattie and Sam were sitting at the kitchen table drinking coffee when the patter of feet signaled the sudden appearance of Lola, looking like a woman who hadn't slept a wink, which was no less than the truth.

"Well, lookie here. Another of us who apparently couldn't sleep," Hattie said, getting up to pull out a chair for her.

"Good morning." Lola set her purse and car keys down on the counter.

"Where d'ya think you're going at this hour?" Sam asked. He

sounded concerned. But then, this was Lola, and Lola had a special place in Sam's heart, even if he wouldn't admit it.

"I'm going to the hospital. I really need to see John…to touch him…kiss him…tell him that I love him…that I always loved him…and…"

"And…you need to tell him about the baby, Lola. Even if he can't hear you, you still need to tell him," Sam added.

"Oh, Sam, I still don't know what to do about that. And besides, what difference would it make saying the words?"

"It'll make all the difference in the world, child." Hattie lovingly touched Lola's hand. "It'll make all the difference in the world. Believe me. Both to you and to him."

"You want me to drive you?" Sam said. "Happy to."

"Thanks, Sam, I know you would. But I need some time alone."

"All right. I get that. I'm here if you need me." He got up, put his hat on, and headed for the door. "If you ladies will excuse me, I need to check on my Dolly."

The door had no sooner closed behind Sam when Bridget and Ella roamed in, Bridget wiping the sleep from her eyes and Ella yawning.

"And so our early morning party grows," Hattie said cheerfully. "I'll pour coffee."

"I couldn't sleep after reading the journals of the Circle's first generation and then yours too, Hattie," Ella said. "And besides, I can't think of anything other than my Brice up there on that mountain."

"I know Brice, Ella," Lola said. "And that boy's a survivor. He's smart and he's resourceful. He's going to be all right."

"That's true. Every word of it, Ella," Bridget said, taking a cup of coffee from Hattie and nodding her thanks. "Just so you all know, I made an executive decision. Not going in to work today. I have to be available if Dan needs me and I want to find out more about the Circle, and to be here with my girls."

"Oh, that reminds me," Hattie said, "some bigwig from your work called late last night and wanted me to give you a message. Hold on, I wrote it down. Something about a job in London."

Hattie passed the note to Ella, who passed it to Bridget.

"A job in London? What's up with that?" Ella stared at Bridget for an explanation. So did everyone else.

"I was going to ask you the same thing about these." Bridget slid the empty liquor bottles across the table. "Alena gave these to me. She's worried sick about you."

"And I'm worried sick about my son," Ella shot back. "Give me a break."

"Stop it. Both of you. This is no time to fight," Lola said sternly. "We need to be grateful for what we have right now. No matter what happens, we've always had each other through thick and thin, and we need each other now."

"Lola's right," Hattie said, putting her arms around Ella and Bridget and giving their shoulders a squeeze.

"Sometimes we have to be reminded of that. That we'd do just about anything to save our mountain and the ones we love. I may be finding that out a little late in the game, but reading the stories of the Circle helped. Seems like we're reliving our lives. No wonder we love being in your little cottage. There is so much female energy in there. And not just ours, but from past generations too," Lola said to Ella.

"I never thought of that," Bridget admitted.

"Gaia must have felt it too. She had to have been channeling some Circle stuff because she did some initiation thingy with us," Lola said. "Wish I knew where she was. She reminds me so much of your Chimalis, Hattie."

"I should have known Betty was part of the Circle," Ella said. "She helped us transform from girls to women, but she never said a word about anything unusual having gone on in that cottage." Ella looked at Hattie and smiled. "God, you guys really knew how to keep a secret."

"And you will also," Hattie declared.

"What? Us? So you really think we're worthy of being the Circle's third generation?"

"Oh, yes sirree," Hattie said. "We've been keeping an eye on you ever since you and Gary rented Olive and Hazel's cabin. We tried to meet for lunch every couple of months so Betty could give me updates on your progress. You were our only hope of keeping the Circle alive. Then we started keeping an eye on Lola and Bridget and really thought we were onto something. Our plans were nearly foiled when Olive and Hazel died in the 1980s, so it was left up to Betty and me. Gaia seemed to be a good prospect too but she'd always disappear. Then Betty died unexpectedly and tragically. My best friend and I couldn't even make it to her memorial because I was so sick with pneumonia...but I was there in spirit. Good golly, I miss her."

"We all do," Lola said.

Hattie smiled at that, then nodded. "Then once again Na'mow and Eru'tan combined forces to bring you three to me...no coincidence, you know...so that you would know the story of the Circle and keep it alive."

"You miss them, don't you?" Bridget said. "The women of the Circle."

"I miss them so much, especially my dear Phoebe." Hattie's voice softened.

Lola spoke up. "Really? After reading those journals, I thought it would be Chimalis. She seemed to be everyone's guiding force. Why Phoebe?"

"Why, because Phoebe was my mother," stated Hattie. "That's how I knew about the Circle. It started with White Sun as you probably read, but then Chimalis expanded on her mother's love of the mountain by starting the Circle of Na'mow with my mother and Martha. The three of them were best friends."

"Did Martha have any daughters?" Ella asked.

"Only Olive," Hattie replied to a round of surprised sighs.

"Olive! It makes so much sense," Bridget said.

"Olive married and moved to Michigan. That's where she befriended Hazel and introduced her to the Circle. I got married and moved to town, glad to know that my brother and his wife were still on the old homestead. Then Betty found her way to the cottage in 1956 during that freak August blizzard that you read about. Betty and I were the same age and became the best of friends. As we grew older, getting together proved more difficult, but we tried. Sorry to say that sometimes life got in the way."

Hattie jumped to her feet, rubbing her hands together with great anticipation. "I have something for each of you. Just stay put. I'll be back in a jiffy."

Hattie came back clutching a beautiful satin bag. She sat, and the girls gathered around. The pendants she withdrew from the bag were circular pieces etched with a spiral surrounded by stars, the very configuration that adorned the door of Ella's cottage.

"Oh, my," Ella said. "Is that…?"

"Yes. Our special design. Our special circle," Hattie said. "The members of the first and second generations of the Circle all decided that we would either die with our pendants on or pass them on to the next generation. That's you three." She smiled broadly and held up three pendants. "So…well, as you can see, I have most of them. All except Olive's. No one seems to know where that one went."

"This first one belonged to Betty, and she wanted you to have it, Ella." Hattie put the pendant around Ella's neck. "Betty always thought of you as the daughter she never had. So sweet."

"Oh, my." Ella was near tears. "Thank you so much."

Hattie took a second pendant and eased it over Bridget's tangled hair. "You get Hazel's since you both hail from Michigan. And besides, she sort of had a wild streak once you got her going. That girl was such a hoot! And I see a lot of her in you."

"Thank you. I'm so honored," Bridget said, caressing the pendant with her hand.

"Lola, you get Chimalis's since the Ancient Ones are near and dear to you, just like they were to her."

"For me? Are you sure? She was so…"

"Special? Yes, she was. As are you, young lady."

"I second that," Ella said, squeezing Lola's arm.

"What happened to Phoebe's and Martha's pendants?" Bridget wondered.

"They were buried with theirs," Hattie said. Then she pulled her own pendant from inside her blouse. "And I have mine safe and sound next to my heart. We never wore them outside our clothing… it was our secret…and we should keep it that way."

"Our secret," Lola said. She reached out and took Ella's and Bridget's hands. "Is that a deal?"

"Deal," they both said.

"Good then," Hattie said. "So…before life snatches you away from me… Hold on, it's been a while. Let me get in 'the Circle mode.' I proclaim that you are officially and forever members of the Circle of Na'mow. Love and cherish that majestic mountain and each other now and forever. Let our Circle spin with your electrifying energy, spiraling and exploding upward and outward into the All of Time!"

Bridget hugged her. "Thank you, Hattie."

"That's it?" Lola asked. "No potions, no smudging, no chanting?"

Hattie laughed heartily. "Always looking for drama, are you? Believe me, you're going to need all your strength just to get through this day. Today, for all of you, simple is what's needed."

The front door opened, and Sam came back in. "It is getting cold out there," he said as he stomped his feet. "But thank God for the weather. How we need it."

The phone rang just then, and everyone jumped except Sam. He answered, said hello, and then just listened. They all saw his shoulders sag. Then he said, "No. I'm on my way…wait…dammit!" Sam hung up.

"Sam, what is it?" Hattie asked.

"Their phone started crackling and then disconnected. Gary and Dan wanted to talk to you two." He pointed to Ella and Bridget. "Guess that'll have to wait. The good news is that the rain, sleet and snow helped dampen the fire, but houses burned…they still don't know which ones. Gary and Dan are okay." He turned his gaze to Ella. "I'm sorry, Ella, but Brice is still missing. Herb too. Gary was hoping we might have heard from them, but I told him no."

"Rain! Sweet, sweet Jesus." Hattie clapped her hands. Then she took Ella's hands in hers and squeezed. "The fire's tamed down now, searching will be easier, Ella. They'll find them. I know they will."

"Thank you. I know they will too," Ella said, trying her best to stay strong and positive. Then she cracked. "I'm trying to be strong, but honestly, my heart is breaking…being torn up to pieces. I can't think of anything else. Where the hell are they? God, I pray they're safe. I'm so scared. I'm slowly dying of heartache." Ella stopped and looked at Lola. "Sorry."

"Yeah, me too. I know, it's the not knowing that gets you. And all of us have that feeling right now, some more intensely than others. It just sucks! I'd love to stay here in the safety of Hattie's little nest and I hate to do it, but I have to leave you three," Lola said, coming to her feet. "I have to go to the hospital."

"We'll come," Bridget said quickly.

"Thanks, Bridge, but I need some time alone with John, and you've got your kids to deal with. I'll call you from the hospital."

"Come on, Lola. I'll walk you to your car." Sam helped her on with her coat and led her to the door. The rest of the women walked out onto the porch and watched as Sam and Lola climbed behind the wheels of their cars and drove away. They shivered from the chill of the early morning and listened to the pitter-patter of the steady drizzle on the roof. All eyes turned westward as a moisture-laden mist settled over the mountain, obscuring it from view.

Hattie took hold of Bridget's and Ella's hands and led them back inside. "Come on, girls, we've got time for more coffee and a few more mountain stories before your girls get up and have to go to school. I have to admit that I'm a bit envious of your youthful exuberance. And since I'm growing darn fond of you and your families, take a minute and indulge an old lady with a few more stories about how you all ended up back on that there mountain."

Hattie poured coffee. "And let me tell you, if past behavior is any indication of future behavior, I bet Eru'tan used all of her *'natural'* powers to rattle and roll your resolve. Oh, and to really make things interesting, I bet she called in her ally, Sla'mina, Ruler of the Wild Ones. Yes, indeed, when she does that, it really gets your attention!"

Late August, 1994

LABOR DAY PARTY

"Freshly fucked," was the phrase that came to Betty's mind watching Gaia skip out of the woods, looking radiant, her face turned upward toward the sun. Gaia twirled around and clapped her hands to a melody only she could hear. Betty blushed, remembering her own naughty woodland interludes as a wild, much younger temptress. *Much younger indeed! It seemed so long ago. Seventy-seven years have passed in the blink of an eye.*

"What're you smiling at, my beautiful bride? Am I missing something?" Herb asked as he came up behind her, patted her butt, and took in the scent of her bare neck. Betty turned toward him as she reached up to her hair, taking out the bobby pins that held her bun in place. Long gray tresses flowed over her shoulders and down her back.

"Smell this air. Look at the turquoise sky…and the shimmering leaves of the aspens. I swear, Herb, it's like a youth elixir! I'm feeling feisty and wild." Betty shook her head, running her hands through her waist length hair. "And it appears that I'm not the only one feeling it!"

"What? Uh oh…what's captured your interest now? This was supposed to be a leisurely walk around the neighborhood and now it's gotten a might mysterious."

Betty shushed him, holding a finger on his mouth and pointing to Gaia just before she disappeared inside her cottage. "Freshly fucked."

"Well, why not," Herb said. "She's young and pretty and, if I'm not mistaken, available. The question is, freshly fucked by who?"

"I doubt seriously if that's any of our business," Betty lied. She would have loved a little gossip to spice up her summer.

"Which brings me to my question," Herb said as if being jolted back to reality. "Where is that son of ours? He comes home for summer break and we never see him."

"You saw him an hour ago," Betty reminded him. "He was talking with Lola."

"And she said she thought he was going out for a beer. A beer? His dad makes the best beer in the entire county. If he wants a beer…"

"Oh, Herb, relax. Henry is a grown man. He's just mingling."

"Well, that's what has me worried. He seems so taken with Lola and…"

"Of course he's taken with her. They're two peas in a pod. She's an intriguing human being and so is he…not the average run of the mill male and female. He's always interested in what makes someone like her tick. He's an epistemologist, for Christ's sake."

"Well, that's the point, Betty. He'll pick Lola's mind without her knowing it and she'll entrance him into her web of mystery. The whole encounter will end up as research for his classes or for his next book or he'll end up in her bed!"

"Herb, you can't monitor your grown son's behavior. So what if he has a little fun on the mountain for the next several weeks. He's visiting us to get away from academia. And, of course, he'll go back to California with a new wealth of information that he can share with his students. That's why the kids at Stanford love his classes. He'll take a conversation he had with Lola or Gaia or whomever and make it applicable to his lecture on feminine epistemology. Reality on this mountain is a lot different than a college kid's reality. Besides, who says Henry's not Lola's type."

"You're kidding me, right?" Herb replied. "Since when did Lola start hanging out with intellectuals?"

"Well, she was married to a lawyer, if I recall, and our Henry kind of reminds me of her ex."

"John? You can't be serious."

"Don't tell me you wouldn't just love to know what Lola and Henry talked about. I bet they're just fascinated with each other. Kind of reminds me of us." Betty batted her eyelashes at Herb.

"God help us. I need more homebrew." Herb sighed and shook his head.

"You do that," Betty said. "Because I have a party to plan."

The party Betty was referring to was set for Labor Day, and it was totally and completely her brainchild.

Being the matriarch of the mountain, she had witnessed decades of family dramas, including her own.

Lately, memories of her past trials and tribulations had been surfacing in a big way. She noticed that she and Herb were laughing less and complaining more, especially about the onslaught of aches and pains that seemed a constant in the lives of two people in their seventies. Short-term memory eluded them. Curiosity ebbed. Driving to Boulder seemed too laborious and dangerous as reflexes slowed.

Visits from friends and neighbors diminished to a trickle. The twilight years of life caught them unaware…days slipped by as the comfort of their beautiful mountain surroundings enveloped them in an isolating cocoon.

Betty didn't like what they had become and was determined for the two of them to metamorphose once again. The couple had promised each other that they would always look at the world with the wonderment of a child, and they needed to get back to that. Breaking free from the routine of just being "old" was long overdue. Betty believed that she needed to be an example for all the women on the mountain, that life still emanated out of her soul, vibrant, joyful, and adventurous. She encouraged Herb to take the men of the mountain under his wing and teach them, among other things, about home brewing.

"It's high time these youngsters feel the love this community has to offer," she proclaimed. "And we need a Labor Day party to end all parties."

Betty sent out a hundred invitations, both to mountain folks and flatlanders alike. She had only one stipulation: No Dogs Allowed. Betty wanted this to be a people party, a reunion of sorts, allowing everyone to reconnect.

When the day arrived, there was a hint of fall's crisp chill in the air and just enough of summer's lingering warmth. Beautiful. Somewhere between sweater weather and long sleeves.

The flatlanders arrived with their coolers filled overflowing with food and drink. Herb and Dan set up a badminton net. A horseshoe pit sparked lively competition. Weekend warriors – at least those with good knees – took to the volleyball area. Screams and shouts were heard over the music coming from a boombox someone had set up on the porch.

September 5, 1994, Labor Day

LOLA

After quenching the parched mountain with a hard rain, Eru'tan had graced its inhabitants with a beautiful morning rainbow, and that was the first thing Lola saw when she woke up that fine Labor Day morning. She loved waking up in her own home after two years of living with Bridget in what they now called the "portal of hell."

Moving back to the mountain was one of a number of exciting changes since then that had given her a new outlook on life. It began after her Christmas party confrontation with John. Soon thereafter, he agreed to pay her tuition at a highly respected massage school in Boulder, the end result being a more respectable job as a therapeutic massage therapist. In John eyes, it wasn't all that respectable – a step or two above a belly dancer – but he also knew Lola would pour herself into it. After all, she loved the human body and was highly intuitive and personable. He guided her through the business end of starting her own business. She would have normal hours at school and at work. It was a win-win for Lola. It was also a win for Nick and John. Nick had his mom back, and John didn't have to worry about Nick fending for himself while his mom worked the belly dancing circuit until all hours of the morning.

The rigid schedule of classes forced Lola into a routine, which made her embrace responsibility. She learned to network, and the networking led her to a position with a psychotherapist massaging abused women. The goal was to get them used to "safe" touch again, and Lola flourished in the position. She was a natural healer and actually had to turn business away.

Lola craved more. She wanted to make her massages as meaningful as possible, so she took neuromuscular classes and energy bodywork seminars. Her job had given her independence and self-confidence, and graduating at the top of her class had reminded her that she was exceptionally bright. With each passing day, her reputation grew.

Lola went to Betty's Labor Day party feeling relaxed and confident. She was surrounded by her closest friends. Listening to the music and feeling the sun warm her skin, happiness oozed out her every pore. She didn't have a boyfriend for the first time in a long time, and that didn't bother her. In fact, her new life was too full to be troubled with a relationship. On the other hand, watching Gary and Ella sneak a quick kiss turned Lola's mind to sex. Big surprise. *Well, she thought, maybe I should do something about that.*

That's when it happened. She spotted the tall, dark, and very handsome man moving effortlessly through the crowd. *Oh my, what a surprise! John's here.*

John was thrilled when Betty called to invite him to the party. He left Boulder early enough to arrive at the party on time, but forgot that the road out of town was a huge pain in the ass on major holidays.

It had already taken him twice as long as he thought it would, and he liked to be punctual. He wondered how elevated his blood pressure was as he continued to climb higher on the mountain road and encountered one obstacle after another. Tourists stopped at every straightaway for photo ops, bicyclists riding side by side stupidly refused to let cars pass, and hikers and wildlife unexpectedly bolted across the road, startling even the calmest of drivers. Besides all of these headaches, he found it particularly difficult to drive by the place where he had "accidentally" met Lola. *Oh, Lola, Lola, Lola.* She could still captivate him even after all their fights and their divorce, and he still cared about her in the most inexplicable way. His logical mind could make no sense out of it. Lola said that they were soul mates and had a lot to learn from each other even though they couldn't be together. Her "woo-woo" was what he loved and hated about her. He found dating boring. Yes, it fulfilled his physical urges, but it was Lola's face he saw no matter who it was he was screwing. Lovemaking had nothing to do with it. He compared everyone to Lola. *Damn her!* How many times in the past had he futilely willed his mind to erase her face from his thoughts? These days he reluctantly accepted it as inevitable.

Emotions amplified the closer he got to his old neighborhood. Halfway up the mountain, he pulled the car over to the side of the road so he could cry...and cry he did. His eyes were red and his stomach upset. *What the hell is wrong with me? Get a grip, John. Whatever the hell your problem is, it's nothing a cold beer won't fix.*

John wiped his eyes and pressed on. He felt like he had been given a hit of acid when he parked his car in front of the Bombers place. Music drifted down from the house. He sucked in the smell of newly wet grass, juniper, and clean fresh air. Every cell in his body came alive. The colors were more vibrant here; the sounds were more intoxicating; the sky seemed close enough to grab. Just like that, the heaviness in his heart and soul lifted. He swallowed hard, put his hand to his chest, and let the realization hit him hard. *God, just say it.* "I love Lola."

John smiled down at the white rose bouquet he had brought for the hosts, and inhaled the sweet fragrance.

September 5, 1994, Labor Day

BRIDGET

Bridget took her time driving up the mountain to Betty's Labor Day party. She was relieved to have a three-day weekend after months of busting her butt at work and traveling abroad more than she could have imagined. She was climbing the corporate ladder faster than any man or woman in the company, which only added to the stress of explosive corporate politics.

For the past year and a half, the firm's executives had held her under an increasingly harsh magnifying glass. They had watched her every move, hoping she would be a marketing director capable of providing a new business strategy that would guarantee funding for her innovative programs, and thus secure them a competitive position in the market.

The budget was meager but the results had exceeded expectations. A vice president job was dangled in front of her like a carrot to a rabbit. She desperately wanted a seat at the executive table to help strengthen out the company's strategic position and propel them past the competition. But this, Bridget freely admitted, wasn't just about the company. She wanted to propel herself to the very top as well…and soon.

Bridget realized that in the early stages of her marriage to Dan, she had taken out her frustrations of "not being good enough" on her family. Her personal life seemed to self-destruct even though she poured all her energy into keeping it stable and moving forward. She had paid a hefty price, but over the last year or so she had made a conscious decision to correct things, starting with Dan. She'd broken it off with Steve, and she and Dan began attending biweekly marriage counseling sessions, which were, they both admitted, difficult. Following each of these knockdown, drag-out sessions, they made it a habit of going out for drinks to laugh at their mutual stubbornness.

Bridget's introspection was interrupted when her son looked over at her and said, "Why are you driving like someone's grandma? Don't we have a party to get to?"

"Yeah, Mom, could you go any slower?" Shauna added from the backseat. The road was quickly drying off. The mountain's perfumed fragrance filled the car, and Bridget pulled over at the next scenic overlook. The kids couldn't believe it.

"Oh great! And now you have to stop and play tourist," Michael said. "You used to live here, remember?"

Bridget ignored the whining and walked out onto a rock outcropping that overlooked the neighboring canyon. Steam vaporized off the rocks and disappeared. Chickadees and juncos chirped excitedly. A small herd of mule deer chewed on the last of the season's fading green grass. It was like a scene from *Heidi*, one of Bridget's favorite books.

"You know what?" she said to her kids. "I feel just like Heidi did when she had to leave her beloved grandfather and mountain and live in a town. I've been feeling like the walking dead for the last year and a half, but, here I am…back where I belong."

"Look at that, Mom." Shauna pointed to a rainbow that arced in all its glory over the valley. She took her mother's hand as she leaned against her. "Hey, Mom, why is everything so much better up here? Even the stars are brighter and the colors…like the rocks…look at the oranges and reds in these boulders."

"I know what you mean, Shauna. It sometimes seems that people down in town are so busy watching where they're going that they don't see anything except for the three feet right in front of their faces. Up here, it's magic. Miles and miles of lofty vistas and the melody of the natural world."

"Jeez, Mom, you sound just like Lola," Michael said as he and Shauna engaged a pair of people-friendly squirrels in a game of pinecone dodge ball. The squirrels bolted, and the kids set out after them.

The moment of solitude gave Bridget a chance to reflect back two weeks to her unexpected and extraordinarily sexy encounter with Dan. She had just delivered the kids to his place, and he wanted to show her the hummingbird nest he'd found in the woods near the house. One thing led to another, and they were like newlyweds all over again.

Bridget hadn't had an orgasm like that in a very long time, and that's pretty much all she'd thought about since. In fact, she was really

looking forward to seeing him today and taking in his smell and…
*shit Bridget, get a hold on yourself, will you? You're reacting like a wild
beast.* And then she thought: *Oh, fuck it…wild beast it is!*

<hr />

Dan's heart started thumping harder the minute he spotted Bridget
and the kids pulling up in front of Betty and Herb's place.

He had two surprises for her, but he wanted to wait for exactly
the right moment to share them. For now, he watched her move with
ease through the growing mass of people. Her cowboy hat sat atop
her head and her mantle of red curls was thrown backwards as she
laughed and chatted with everyone she met, just like old times. Dan
watched with admiration, her long legs and round, firm ass igniting
his imagination. He watched until some twenty-something kid
started doing a bit too much flirting, and he decided it was time to
break it up. He walked up to them and said to the handsome
stranger, "Sorry, I'm going to have to steal her away from you,
partner. Enjoy the rest of the party."

Dan didn't wait for a reply. He took Bridget's hand and headed
for the woods. The last thing the open-mouthed stranger saw was
the redhead jumping up on Dan's back and wrapping her long legs
around his waist. She yelled, "Yeeee haw!" and proceeded to rock
forward and backward like she was riding a bucking bronco.

Their laughter carried them deeper into the forest, and they were
well out of sight of the party when Dan's boot caught on a rock and
sent them tumbling. They hit the ground, laughing wildly. Dan
started tickling her unmercifully.

"Shit! Oh God, please let my Kegels work, please work, shit…I
don't want to pee my pants. Oh, don't make me laugh…I didn't bring
a change of clothes." Bridget slapped Dan playfully on the shoulder.
That's when she saw the little black jewelry box that had materialized
from his jacket. "What's this?"

She tried to grab it, but Dan was faster. "Not yet." He jumped up, took her hand, and led her deeper into the woods.

"What the hell is going on with you, 'cause whatever it is, I like it! Hey, what are you doing now?" Dan had stopped and dropped onto one knee. "Dan, what the fu…"

Bridget grabbed her nose. "SHIT!" The force of the first sneeze sent her reeling forward. Her knee hit Dan in the forehead, causing him to wobble and sending the box into a stand of tall grasses. All she heard in between her convulsive expulsions was Dan yelling, "NOOOOOOOOOOO!"

Bridget finally stopped sneezing and realized that she had to pee and had to pee right then. She said, "Shit," raced into the trees, and relieved herself.

She came back out, zipping up her jeans as casually as anything, and found Dan in a heap with the jewelry box clutched in his hands.

"Much better," she sighed. "Kind of reminds me of the first time we met. Hey, are you all right?"

Bridget bent over, and Dan held out the box. "This is for you. I had it made for you."

Bridget opened the box with exceeding care. Inside was a beautiful silver necklace with a black pendant carved in the shape of a bear.

"Oh, Dan. It's beautiful. But what's the…"

"Bridget, will you stay married to me?" he said sweetly. She looked at him with her mouth agape, speechless. "I thought I'd propose to you this time under better circumstances. If I recall, the last time you *told* me we were getting married."

"Yeah, not real romantic," Bridget admitted.

"The necklace is a token of my love for you, Bridge. It's symbolic of you and me and our relationship," Dan said sincerely. "I love you. You're my partner. You're my best friend. But most of all, you are my one great love."

"Wow! One great love. I like the sound of that! I mean, that's..."

He didn't let her finish. "Oh, and that's not all. Now that I have a steady income again, I've rented the house next to our property so you and the kids don't have to live in Big Pink. What do you say? Please come home."

She stared at him. "Shit yeah, Dan, I'll stay married to you. But tell me this. What in the world made you think I'd say yes after all we've been through?"

"Oh, let me count the ways...that is, let me count the ways from our last encounter. You attack me in the woods, your juices overflowed, you pump my lights out, and growled like a wild animal when you came. All those things added up to basically one thing, that you wanted me badly," Dan said. Then he thought a moment. "But it was the growl that sealed the deal."

Bridget lay down next to her husband and proceeded to point her chin skyward and yip and howl like a coyote in heat.

"Okay, now you're scaring me," Dan whispered as he kissed her deeply.

September 5, 1994, Labor Day

ELLA

Gary held Ella's hand as they walked in the direction of the Bombers house.

For some reason, the sounds of merriment growing louder with each step put Ella in mind of their confrontation two weeks ago with Gary's former lover, Michelle.

It had happened in a local restaurant down in Boulder. They were already seated, both of them with cappuccinos in hand, when Ella saw Gary stiffen.

"What is it?"

"Nothing," he said, and then shook his head. "It's Michelle. She just walked in."

"Oh!" Ella followed Gary's glance as the hostess seated Michelle and her date well across the room from them. Not a minute later, Michelle's date left the table for the restroom, and her roaming eyes found Gary and locked onto him. Then she was getting up.

"Oh, shit. She's coming over here," he whispered to Ella. "I'm sorry."

"It's okay," Ella assured him, even if it wasn't.

"Hey, babe," Michelle said, barely acknowledging Ella's presence. "I mean, Gary. How are you? This always was *our* favorite restaurant and seems it still is."

Gary stood, annoyed at her barbed comment. "Michelle, you remember *my* wife, Ella." He emphasized the word "wife" and felt good doing so.

Ella came to her feet. She was already tall, but her four-inch heels allowed her to tower over the petite woman who had almost stolen her husband away from her. Ella's feet were killing her, but it was worth the pain knowing how good she looked. Her outfit hugged her curves and a new, shorter hairstyle made her look ten years younger. The bloodshot eyes, sallow skin, and pitiful attitude had vanished months before and had been replaced with an inner confidence and radiance.

Ella's inherent glow forced her husband's former lover to take a step back and sent a chill up the woman's spine.

Michelle glanced at Gary's wedding ring; he was wearing it again after several years of going without. "Looks like a lot has happened in the last couple of months."

"For both of us," Gary said calmly.

"Well, you might be interested to know that I accepted that teaching job back home. I'm in the process of moving as we speak."

"Congratulations," Gary said without emphasis.

"So I guess I *won't* be seeing you around," she said, trying her hardest to be sarcastic. Michelle flash a broad smile at Ella, turned in a flourish, and stormed away.

"I think I need a coat, 'cause it just got pretty darn chilly in here," Ella quipped.

Gary laughed uncomfortably, took her hand, and kissed it. Then he started singing. Right there, in the middle of the restaurant.

Ella was stunned. She whispered, "What're you doing? Gary? Everyone's looking!"

Gary didn't care. His melodic voice echoed off the bare walls, his eyes holding hers, and a hauntingly simple melody filled the room.

I've never stopped loving you.
Never stopped wanting you.
Never wanted anything more than a moment just like this...

The restaurant had gone silent, listened as if a minstrel had just wandered into the restaurant, and clapped enthusiastically when he finished; well, all except the table across the room, which was now empty.

Gary sat down beside Ella and said, "I call it *Ella's Song.* I wrote it for you...for us."

The song came back to Ella now and replaced the memory. Gary squeezed her hand and escorted her into the crowded party. She leaned her head on his shoulder, just for a moment, just for a bit of extra support.

So much had changed, she thought. *So much for the better.*

Gary knew how nervous Ella was, attending her first big neighborhood party since getting sober nine months ago.

Her questions were endless. "Will everyone treat me differently? Will they act weird about their drinking and me not drinking? Will

I be able to have fun, because alcohol was my crutch for so frigging long?"

"No, no, and yes." Gary smiled; Ella had always obsessed over what everyone else must be thinking, mainly about her. "Relax. Have fun. As long as you're happy with who you are, everyone will be happy for you. I'll be right next to you every step of the way. That is, until you feel confident enough to go it alone. Then I'll get lost."

They chuckled, and he squeezed her hand even tighter.

Ella took a deep breath, then smiled broadly when she saw Herb nuzzling Betty's neck and the two of them giggling like schoolchildren. *Wow, look at the love between them, and after all they have endured over the years. It's so hard for me to believe that it has only been nine months since I was in rehab. It seems like a lifetime ago. I'm so different. Wish I didn't feel so damn fragile about the changes I've made. God, I can't believe what a sloppy drunk I was.*

It had happened so gradually. She had gone to AA meetings every day for ninety days; sometimes twice a day. She was still going nearly every day and missed it when she didn't go. Alcoholics Anonymous was a lifesaver in every way. After nearly six months, the urgency and the panic she felt about her drinking had eased up a bit. She had also taken up something offered by her church called a Course in Miracles, and it had helped so much with the anxiety. She found that AA's 12 Step program aligned perfectly with the course's daily exercises. Along the way, Ella had also rediscovered her own internal Teacher, she who had led her home. *Home...inside me and right here on this mountain.*

Ella took another deep breath, letting her intention of peace flow through her veins. She felt the thread of truth and wisdom that connected all the teachings she was engaged in, even all the woo-woo stuff that Gaia had introduced to her.

Her hardest challenge in her recovery had been Step Three in the program. Turning her will and life over to the care of God went against her very nature. Ella had always felt compelled to control everything. She was the consummate planner. She organized everything and everyone. She created lists and more lists, all in an effort to keep things running smoothly.

The idea of surrendering to a higher power was still a huge struggle, something she wrestled with daily. On the other hand, the joy she felt in rediscovering the world, in reconnecting with her family and friends, and finding herself again was the best thing she'd experienced in years. Rediscovering herself through this new lens of spiritual awareness was beyond anything she had imagined. Miracles seemed to manifest effortlessly, and she embraced them gratefully.

After Ella returned from her rehab stint at Betty Ford, she found a part-time job at a day care center. It was perfectly suited for her as she regained her strength. After all, she had been the anchor of the babysitting co-op for years and felt highly competent dealing with groups of children.

Sam, of all people, had taken notice of her progress. He saw how the day care job had bolstered her confidence and recommended her for an opening in the police department. It was a full-time position training officers in the D.A.R.E. program. The program's primary mission was to provide children with the information and skills needed to live drug and violence free. Being involved with helping children avoid addiction gave Ella a real sense of purpose, and an understanding of herself and her battle with addiction. How many times had she thought back to one of Gaia's Tarot readings, announcing that the Taurus in her was meant, as Gaia put it, "to teach others how to be in community with the group." Back then the words hadn't rung true, but now she was starting to recognize those unique abilities. Very exciting.

It wasn't all smooth sailing. Brice and Alena seemed the hardest to convince of her sobriety since they'd been the most deeply impacted, so the Labor Day party was a perfect excuse for letting go. Ella could see the joy on their faces as they raced into Herb and Betty's back yard to join their friends.

Ella looked skyward and thanked her parents for the wonderful job they'd done helping to raise Alena during her time in New York. Gary and she had spent the last several months rebuilding their relationship with Brice. This was part of the program's eighth step, making amends with those you may have harmed. Ella had expected this step to be painful, but it had proved just the opposite. Weekly family dinners had transformed from dread to joyful anticipation. She and Gary had also taken to having their own private dinners each week, finding once again immense pleasure in each other's presence and conversation. Ella tried not to project too much hopefulness into these meetings, but the recent run-in with Michelle had actually bolstered her confidence.

The best news of all perhaps had occurred after Alena returned from New York and Gary asked if he could move back in. *Thank God.*

Gary stopped her before they joined the festivities. "Can I tell you something?" he said to her.

"Sure," she said hopefully.

"You know, I never stopped loving you. I just didn't like you very much," Gary said, fumbling his words. "You mean everything to me. You are my Super Glue."

"My, my, Gary, how romantic," his wife teased.

"Guess that sounded a bit science teacher-ish. Let me start again," he said clearing his throat. "You are my True Love. I always kept my wedding ring in the hidden compartment of my wallet. It was my secret from the world. Even in the darkest hours of despair, I would remember it was always close to me…believing in hope… for us. I never stopped loving you, Ella. I just put on a brave front. After all, isn't that what men are expected to do? It's hard for us… we think all you women want is the strongest Neanderthal you can find and then at the same time we get yelled at for not being sensitive to your needs. Nobody teaches us that kind of balance…but hopefully, I'm learning. Running into someone else's arms was a mistake."

His wife's tears fell slowly. She looked thoughtfully into Gary's eyes, took his face into her hands, and tenderly kissed him. They looked deep into each other's eyes, and Gary saw her inner radiance in all its glory. Then a huge, impish grin spread across her beautiful face. "Can you believe I didn't help Betty with one thing for this party? Normally, I would have had a list as long as my arm."

Gary laughed out loud. "Does that mean there will be no more honey-do lists?"

"I wouldn't go that far. Honey-do lists exist to keep you in shape. Otherwise, I'd lose you to a beer belly and football games," Ella said. "No, we'll definitely still need our honey-do lists!"

Ella and Gary put on a united front and joined the party, embracing old friends and allowing the wave of love to feed their spirits.

A half-hour into the party, Ella took a moment to survey the growing crowd and spotted the one guest she had personally invited.

"Oh, there he is," she said to Gary. "I'll be right back."

Ella crossed to the stranger and gave him a big hug. Then she took him by the arm and led him deeper into the party. There were enough shocked expressions at Ella's outward display of emotion to this man that she stopped and said, "Excuse me, everyone. I would like to introduce you to my sponsor. He's done so much to help me on my path of sobriety. My dear friend Jared Davies. But you can call him JD. Everyone does."

September 5, 1994, Labor Day

SAM

The new lady in Sam's life was a beautiful palomino called Dolly, and she was his date for Betty's Labor Day extravaganza.

All afternoon, Sam patiently hoisted children onto Dolly's back and led them in a big circle. Proof of the activity's great success were the squeals of delight that could be heard coming from each new rider.

"Weathered" was how people described the cowboy these days. Deep lines were etched around his eyes and mouth from years of working and playing outdoors. His mustache was mostly gray, but still bushy and prominent. His hair was shorter than in years past but slightly tousled and unruly when he removed his cowboy hat. A yoked shirt with pearl snap buttons, jeans, and cowboy boots continued to adorn his rock-hard, muscularly lean physique.

When the horse rides were over, Sam tied Dolly's reins around a low branch of a ponderosa pine and joined the girls; he hadn't seen the three of them all together in a very long time, and the sight of them laughing like school girls made him smile. "Ladies," he said.

"Sam, how long do you intend to be a bachelor?" Bridget teased. She handed him a cold beer and squeezed his arm.

"Bridget, darlin', I was waiting for you all these years, and then you have to go ruin it and stay married to that husband of yours." Sam laughed, picked her up and swung her around. Her cowboy hat flew off. She giggled with genuine delight. "It just wasn't the same up here with most of the estrogen gone and in town. Although, it was a lot quieter...and duller. Dolly sure is glad she's not the only female around anymore. Hey, now, I usually don't go blabbing about something I witnessed as a PI but..." Sam cleared his throat and met her eyes squarely. "...I have to tell you that I saw Dan flirting with my Dolly more than once. I thought I saw some real chemistry as they gazed into each other's eyes. I'd almost say he was beyond desperate!" Sam stepped back and guzzled half his beer, wiping his mouth with his forearm sleeve. "Ahhh, now that sure does hit the spot."

"You bastard! You had me going for a split second, Sam. Not to worry, Dan doesn't go for blondes." Bridget hit Sam on the arm.

Ella joined them. "I guess I'm going to have to pass this knight in shining armor on to someone else since Gary's back. I was getting used to being the only damsel in distress up here. Sam, you're such a catch. What gives? No date today? You know people are beginning to talk that you might actually like guys just a bit more than you do girls. So…this would be a good opportunity to 'come out,' if you're looking to unburden. You'd only have to say it once because everyone is here…right here in this one place."

"Girls, girls, you look like you're hoggin' this fine specimen of a man," Lola said, stepping up and placing herself squarely at Sam's side. "Sam, we have really missed your manly…well, let's just say… we have missed your cute ass in those tight cowboy jeans." She slapped his butt. "Hmm hmm hmm."

Sam blushed and took a big swallow of beer.

"Lola, don't get too excited. Sam was just about ready to make his 'coming out' announcement," Ella continued to tease.

"Really…oh my…I so love a gay cowboy! Is your boyfriend here? Do we get to meet him? Sam really, I should've put two and two together. You never bring a woman to anything and even my charms don't seem to be enough to entice you!" Lola pretended to look around for his date. "Don't be shy. Point him out to us."

"Whoa, whoa, you fillies. I should have known the minute I saw the three of you together in one place that the drama would begin." He huddled them together as if a quarterback on a football field. "Now I just want to say this once. I am a gentleman, and a gentleman does not kiss and tell like some gracing our presence right now. I have more than my share of female acquaintances. It's just that I have the common sense not to expose them to this here mountain debauchery." All heads turned to look at Lola.

"But what about ending your lonesome bachelor days?" Ella asked.

"And nights?" Lola added.

"Ladies, as my daddy used to say, 'Timing has a lot to do with the outcome of the rain dance.'"

September 23, 1994, Autumnal Equinox

GATHERING

Snow flurries driven down from the North made Gaia's cabin shudder with each chilly blast. The weather was schizophrenic, clearing one moment to reveal radiant blue skies, only to be crowded over the next with precipitating dark clouds. *The arrival of the Cailleach,* Gaia thought. She peered out the window, certain she was seeing the dark, hunched shape of winter taking form in the inky shadows of the trees and through the unpredictable gusts of snow and dirt. Gaia couldn't hold back her smile. *Perfect timing for the autumnal equinox.*

Planning this celebration took up most of Gaia's time following the Labor Day party, and the three women on her invitation list were not privy to her real motivation.

Well, they soon will be, Gaia thought. She pulled herself away from the window and got back to work. A colorful Navajo runner covered a small table strategically arranged with vials, berries, rocks, and crystals. Gaia veiled the items with a beautiful silk scarf to hide them from curious eyes and roaming hands. Atop the wood stove, a dragon-shaped container spewed forth steam as it heated to boiling, reminiscent of the damp heat within a sweat lodge. The smell of juniper melded with the smoky smell of the fire. Condensation dripped from the windows as a mysterious mist lingered within the cabin. What some would have seen as stifling, Gaia saw as comforting and cozy.

Gaia didn't hear the knock on her door, thanks to the howling wind, but she did hear the porch wind chimes as the door flew open, Bridget, Lola, and Ella tumbling in one after another, a fierce gust pushing them in.

"Welcome, welcome, welcome. Happy autumnal equinox." Gaia ushered the women and their crocks of food into her tiny kitchen.

"Holy Christ, Gaia, it's like a friggin' sauna in here! And what's that smell? Or smells, I should say?" Bridget wrinkled her nose and sniffed the air. When she didn't get an answer, she ripped off her down coat and hung it on the coat rack.

"Yummy!" Lola was already test-tasting the eclectic array of food. She hadn't worn a coat. Her body always generated more heat than she could stand, and a thin sweater was all she required, even on a day like this. "Gaia, does this all look good."

"We're in for a real feast, girls." Gaia set Ella's crock pot full of butternut squash soup on the counter and then helped her off with her parka. Elk stew, soup, cornbread, apple cider, and mulled wine teased their noses with pungent odors. "Everyone sit."

Gaia pointed to the pillows scattered on the carpet, and all three women groaned as they lowered themselves to the floor.

"I don't know if my back can take this," Bridget said.

"No complaining," Gaia ordered. "This night is for the three of you, my dear friends. I'll be serving, and I'll be cleaning up. No objections."

"You won't get any from me," Lola insisted.

"I don't think she meant you," Ella teased.

The food came one dish after another, each more delicious than the last. They ate and drank and laughed like they hadn't done in what seemed like ages. They prodded Gaia about her plans for the night, but she didn't relent, saying, "Patience, patience, my little ones. All will be revealed."

Dessert was served: homemade apple crisp and pumpkin pie. "Oh, my God, I'm stuffed," Ella said. "But I will have some coffee."

"Let's take a potty break and stretch. I'll put more wood on the fire," Gaia said over Bridget's objection.

Bridget poured a cocktail. Lola stripped down to her camisole and bent over to touch her toes. Ella entered the small bathroom and marveled at how simply Gaia lived. Gaia stepped outside into the snow and wind, raised her arms, and invoked the divine female energy to guide her. Movement in her peripheral vision caught her attention suddenly. *So you're here, aren't you, my friend.*

Gaia shivered and ran inside.

Her timing was perfect. She caught Lola on the verge of peeking under the veil. "Ah-ha!" she shouted. "Put that scarf down, you sneaky thing!"

"You caught me," Lola admitted.

"Redhanded."

"But Ella and Bridget egged me on, so they're just as guilty as me."

"No one is as guilty as you, Lola," Gaia teased. "Shall we get started?"

"We're all ears," Bridget said.

"Good. Well, I invited you here as honored guests on this very special day, the fall equinox. Today represents balance and harmony... an equaling, if you will...for there are twelve hours of daylight and twelve hours of darkness. This is the night that mysteries are revealed as the veil of the spirit world is stripped away."

"Uh oh," Ella said.

"You mean more woo-woo shit? Sheesh!" Bridget put her head in her hands, rubbed her eyes, and touched her necklace.

"How absolutely divine. Tell us more, oh Great Gaia of our neighborhood." Lola patted their hostess's arm.

"Come on, Gaia. Get to it. I want to know why you requested we bring all this weird-ass shit." Bridget meant their special necklace, a lock of hair, and a sack of dirt. "I'm trying to go with the flow, but my flow is getting kinda dammed up."

"All right then, Miss Impatience," Gaia said. "Get your stuff. Let's get this show on the road."

They sat on the floor, and Gaia talked to them about the deep meaning and importance of the equinox. "This is the time of balance between day and night, just before night takes over and brings the coming winter. I want you to know that this duality between light and dark exists in all of us. It is also part of spiritual transformation. All things must die before they can be born, just like the spiritual must descend before it ascends. If you long for light, you must first face your own inner darkness and overcome it."

Gaia paused. Once again, she sensed movement outside, and her ears picked up a soft moaning.

Ella noticed. "Don't tell me you are seeing ghosts?"

"It's just the Cailleach. The northern wind awaking the winter hag from her slumber to bring forth winter upon the land. It's happening right now, right here." Bridget rolled her eyes. Ella and Lola leaned closer, and Gaia continued. "Remember the waterfall story I told the kids years ago. In the North, the Cailleach's white blanket of snow covered the land. Then, come spring, the snow melted, and the water found its way over the waterfall, reinvigorating the greenness and aliveness of the rebirth of spring."

"Oh, so that's what that was all about?" Lola pondered aloud.

"What? So now you're seeing a hag hanging around outside?" Ella asked, pointing to the window.

"That's exactly what I'm seeing," Gaia said gleefully.

Bridget stood up and headed for the coat rack. She pulled a silver flask out of her coat pocket and took a long draw. Then she said, "While I admit to being a skeptic when it comes to all this la de da woo-woo foo-foo crap, I'll also admit that shit tends to happen when the four of us are all together."

"So you're telling us that you need something a little stronger than mulled wine to get you through the rest of this night, is that it?" Lola said with a grin.

"Exactly," Bridget replied and took another swallow.

"Did you guys remember to bring your special necklaces?" Gaia said. The pendants she was talking about were personal. The emerald heirloom Ella's grandmother had passed down to her and the bear pendant Dan had given Bridget at the Labor Day party. This, of course, elicited any number of comments.

"Your Dan actually gave you a piece of jewelry?" Ella nearly shouted. "I didn't know he knew what a jeweler was?"

"I almost wet my pants," Bridget admitted. "I guess some people can actually change for the better."

"What's the bear made of?"

"Something called jet. An ancient rock, kinda like coal."

"The Indians used it all the time," Gaia said. They all studied it. There was a zigzag lifeline running from the bear's mouth down its body. "That's red coral and symbolizes the bear's life force."

"Dan said the bear reminds him of me."

"You mean crabby, bitchy, and overbearing?" Lola teased.

"No. Strong, courageous, and very protective of family and home," Bridget gently corrected. "The arrow underneath the bear apparently protects her on her journey, and the feather hanging from the arrow is to remind me of the feather he gave me the first day we met."

"Past, present, and future all in one pendant," Gaia said.

"I just love it!" Bridget smiled widely.

And then there was Lola's silver and turquoise necklace, which naturally called for a story that began when Ella said, "Lola, I thought that necklace went missing a long time ago?"

"Well, it's kind of embarrassing to admit. I thought JD had taken it and sold it for drug money."

"That's not what happened?" Bridget wanted to know.

"Turns out John also thought something like that might happen, so he had Nick give it to him for safekeeping. Swiped it right out from under my nose."

"So how did you get it back?" Ella asked.

"Well, after I saw John at the Labor Day party, he invited me out to dinner. It was pretty romantic. Anyway, he told me the whole story and pulled out this beautiful black velvet box, opened it up, and there was my necklace. I literally sobbed over my crème brûlée. I was so touched that, well, you know, he's been very kind to me."

"Oh, my good God, you slept with him, didn't you?" Ella interrupted.

"Uh huh. Several glorious times. You know, he's ambidextrous and…"

"Christ, no more!" Bridget exclaimed.

"Oh my, Bridge, you're getting psychic, cause that's exactly what I yelled after the third time," Lola beamed.

"Please save us, Gaia," Bridget said. "Tell us about your necklace."

Gaia was wearing two necklaces, and her hand unconsciously touched the one she wasn't yet ready to share, the one from her Nana. She caught herself at the last second, and withdrew instead a green tourmaline crystal with an opal set on it in gold.

"Oh, my God. How beautiful, Gaia," Ella said.

"Just like all of yours, it was a gift from someone very important to me, my favorite metaphysical healer. She wanted me to be in the delivery room when she gave birth to her daughter. The pendant was a thank you gift," Gaia said. "Green tourmaline is a conduit for healing. The stone also lets the wearer appreciate life to the fullest, peering into the seen and unseen worlds. The opal awakens the mystical powers of the wearer and lets its owner speak and walk the truth. Gold symbolizes the sun and God. The sun's yellow rays touch everything in its path with fiery warmth."

"That is so cool," Ella said. "What about mine?"

"The same is true for your gold emerald necklace. The green color of the emerald is meant to remind you of the earthly realms, especially those of the elementals such as fairies and sprites. It is also the sacred stone of the goddess Venus. It is a very powerful love stone. It helps remind you just how loved you really are, even though you may not always feel it. And it fights off depression."

"Me next," Lola said.

Gaia reached out and brushed the silver and turquoise of Lola's necklace. She said, "Yours is meant to impart wisdom and help you to find unconditional love. Silver symbolizes the Moon and all of its power. Silver represents the Greek Goddess Artemis, goddess of the hunt, and reminds us to cherish our inner Goddess."

"I like the goddess thing," Lola admitted.

"Bridget, you too have the silver as a reminder of the goddess within. The jet will protect you just like the bear will empower you. It will remind you to stay grounded," Gaia said. "The feather and the arrow, on the other hand, will champion your spontaneity and allow you to take flight were the need ever to arise."

"That's so cool."

"The important point to remember is that all of these necklaces are powerful because they were gifts given to us from someone special in our lives. We now have the important task of infusing them with our intention. Think about what you want to give and receive from your necklace. Take a moment. And then when you're ready, breathe your life-giving warm breath over it…feeling your intention enter into its soul."

"That sounds good, but I have to pee first." Lola ran into the bathroom, disrupting the silence.

"Figures," Bridget said. She looked at Gaia. "I'm having a hard time getting into this infused stuff, but I'll try."

Bridget looked in Ella's direction and watched as she closed her eyes and let out a slow exhalation onto her necklace. Tears appeared when her eyes opened and spilled down her cheek, but she was smiling.

"What?" she asked when she saw Bridget staring at her.

"Nothing. I just thought that was pretty cool, seeing you…you know. Do that." Bridget smiled.

Lola hurried out a moment later, plopped down, and excitedly announced, "I hope it isn't bad karma or anything, but when I was peeing I got some great insight into what I should infuse into my necklace and I did it right there and then…on the john."

Ella, Bridget, and Gaia doubled over in an explosion of laughter.

"Well? Bad karma or what?" Lola asked, looking at Gaia.

"No. For you, Lola, it was perfectly timed."

Gaia served the women coffee. She asked each one of them to say a few words of gratitude about what the last year had given her. When they were done, Bridget toasted their long-standing friendship, and each of the girls followed with a toast of her own. And like the equinox, the balance between laughter and tears brought them ever closer.

The hostess then handed out four small squares of white cloth. To Lola's delight and over Bridget's protests, she asked each of them to prick their fingers and place a drop of blood on each of the four squares. When this was done, Gaia presented them with velvety smooth leather pouches. Finally, she withdrew the veil from the table. She lit the white candle. They formed a circle and held hands, all eyes on the flame.

Then she began, saying, "We begin the initiation into the sisterhood of women…past, present, and future. A gathering of those most worthy ones who have passed the trials and tribulations of the past and will armor themselves with strength, courage and wisdom to persevere into the future."

Naturally, Bridget interrupted the proceedings. "Wait just a minute! Initiation! I don't want to be a metaphysical party pooper, but I didn't sign up for this! I'm just trying to live my life like everyone else in the world, day after day, week after week, and year after year. Taking every shitty obstacle that stands in my way and dealing with it the best I can. It's like cleaning up one shitty mess after another and hoping for a brief respite of joy or peace or quiet before it all starts up again. I mean, damnation. When does it get any easier, or any better? I feel like I'm living my grandparents' and parents' lives all over again, and I wanted something better for my family!" With every word, she got angrier. With every word, she grew closer to tears. "I'm pissed off! Really pissed off."

"But that's the point, Bridge," Ella responded forcefully. "That is life. The good, the bad, and the even worse. And just look at you. You've survived. You've sludged your way through and managed to do it living life passionately. You've taken everything life can throw at you, and you're still alive to talk about it. You are alive! This is it! You've learned how to cope with the ups and downs. The 'wanting something better for your family' part is that you chose your dream and bravely risked getting out of your rut to have it. You've made it, girl. You're financially successful. You've never let that legendary Irish oppression get you down, and you sure as hell don't have the poverty mentality that ran rampant in your ancestors. You wanted adventure and you got it.

"So what if it was hard. So what if it's still hard. Life is hard; achieving your dreams is damn hard work," Ella proclaimed. "Just look at you. You've grown as a human being. You've expanded your soul life. You fought for yourself and this community. No, you didn't do it all by your little lonesome. You were there for us, and WE, WE were also there for you. We were there for each other.

"WE were all drawn here to live our dream, right? And look at us. Look how far we've come. WE ARE ALL BACK and ready to face it all head on, our jobs, our families, and even this mountain."

Now she was really worked up, and the girls looked at her in awe. "WE ARE THE GLUE, HOLDING EVERYONE AND EVERY-THING TOGETHER WHEN THE GOING GETS DOWNRIGHT

SCREWED UP! WE'RE THE WD-40 THAT MAKES IT ALL RUN SMOOTHLY."

"Jeez, Ella, tell us how you really feel. And what's with the WD-40 shit?" Lola piped up.

"Damn all of you," Bridget said. "I told you shit happens when we get together. Damn."

"You okay?" Gaia asked her. "You sounded pretty upset there."

"Yeah, I'm fine," Bridget replied. "That came out of nowhere… just boiled up out of me. I'm all riled up now. I have absolutely no idea where all that came from but…it's out now. God, I was really puking out some anger and resentment. Okay, okay, let me take a breath. Breathe, Bridge, breathe."

"Yes, please. Breathe, Bridget. Breathe," Lola said with a fine mixture of sarcasm and love.

"I'm all right now. I'm just going to say it. Thanks, guys. Thanks for listening to my pity party. How pathetic was that," Bridget said. "I just don't want to carry around the martyr card. I have a hard time admitting how lost I would be without you guys loving me and me you."

Bridget gave Ella's shoulders a firm, loving shake. "Ella, glad you let loose and got in my face."

"I guess I needed to vent too!" Ella laughed.

Lola stared at Bridget, then, out of nowhere, started to sing a made-up tune. "You're getting woo-woo. You're getting woo-woo. Breathe, Bridget, breathe. Breathe, Bridge, breathe. You're learning woo-woo…you're learning woo…"

Ella gently placed her hand over Lola's mouth, then quickly released it when the brunette started nibbling on it.

"Sorry I got us off track, Gaia," Bridget said, though what she was really thinking was that maybe Lola was right. Maybe she was getting into this woo-woo stuff after all these years. *Shit!* "Can we start over?"

"Let's do." Gaia took a deep breath, relit the candle, and looked around the table. "The three of you with me?"

Ella nodded and took hold of Bridget's and Lola's hands, who linked theirs with Gaia's. In the stillness that followed, Gaia said, "The stirrings of the ancient ones awakened us to this mountain. We are now bound by our blood just like those who came before us and those that will come after us." She gave each woman a square of bloodsoaked cloth. "Blood upon blood we join the circle of women who are the nurturers of this land, now and forever bound. Repeat after me."

Bridget, Ella, and Lola mouthed the words along with Gaia, saying, "Blood upon blood we join the circle of women who are the nurturers of this land, now and forever bound."

"And again…"

That's as far as they got when a scream of pure delight and mischief emanated from Gaia's front porch as a loud thud knocked the door wide open. A heap of winter clothes, blonde hair, and peals of laughter rose out of two wriggling bodies and signaled the unexpected arrival of Alena and Shauna. "Surprise!"

"What in the world are you two doing here?" Ella demanded.

"We got bored and decided to play spy," Alena said.

"Your dad let you come out in weather like this?" Bridget couldn't believe it.

"Come on, Mom, it's not that cold."

"There's two feet of snow out there."

The phone rang just then, and Gaia answered it. They heard her saying, "Yes, indeed. They just arrived, two bundles of serious energy… No, it's okay, Gary, they can stay… If they get too rowdy, we'll send them packing… Promise. My pleasure. Bye, Gary."

Gaia hung up the phone. "That was Gary." She gave the girls a wink. "Our adventurers have been traipsing around in the snow for the last two hours, and he decided to try and track them down."

"You've been out in that cold for two hours? Aren't you freezing?" Ella realized how much like an overprotective mother she sounded.

"Well, you girls are just in time," Lola informed them.

"For what?" they both said, as if they'd been handed a script.

"For our initiation into a secret society," Lola said with increasing drama.

"What secret society?" Shauna asked.

"The gathering of a circle," Gaia replied with great reverence. "A circle of women."

"Really? What's so special about that?" Alena asked, shrugging her shoulders. "I just thought it was normal up here on the mountain. Don't other mothers get together, stare into candles, chant weird words, dance around, drink potions and do spells and stuff like you guys?"

Gaia laughed. "Honey, it's a helluva lot more than that! Now if you two want to go get some dessert and watch quietly, you can, but we have more 'spells' to cast, so hold onto your hats."

"Cool," both girls uttered as they went to fill their bellies.

"Here we go again," Lola said. "I think the universe is testing us again. Seeing if we can carry on with this initiation despite all the interruptions."

Gaia giggled. "You women started the initiation process long before this night, but this gathering is so it would be a defining moment in your lives. One you will absolutely remember." *If they only knew there was so much more to come.* A chill ran up her spine.

They circled the table once again, and Gaia added the blood-stained cloths to their leather pouches. "Now do you remember the power animals we designated for each of you at the waterfall?" she asked.

The women nodded, and Gaia held up a fetish meant to represent each of them. "For Ella's pouch, a coyote. A bear for Bridget's. A deer for mine. And a horse for Lola." As the women placed them carefully in their pouches, Gaia said, "Never forget the power of your animal side. Rely on it. Believe in it."

She then took the vials containing the dirt each of the women had gathered from around their individual properties.

"May the power of the earth be always in you," Gaia incanted over the vials, and the women added them to their pouches.

Gaia took a rosehip from the collection on her table and handed it to Bridget. "To remind you of your beautiful nature...that is, once people get past the thorns."

"Naturally," Bridget said with a grin.

Gaia laid a heart-shaped rock in Ella's hand. "To remind you that sometimes tough love is the only way to break through."

"And this is for you, Lola." Gaia placed a rustically hewed arrowhead in her hand. "To remind you not to get so heavenly that you forget your connection to the earth and her earthly tribe."

"Thank you," Lola said, admiring the point.

Granite scrapings from Womb Rock and smooth small rocks that had tumbled into the waterfall's pool found their way into the pouches. Gaia collected locks of hair from each of the women and cut a small amount from both girls. Each lock was adorned with the smallest of strings tied in a teeny bow.

"These bundles of hair represent women of the present and the future," Gaia said. Then she held up strands of obviously gray hair. "These are from Betty, who, by the way I did invite today. Unfortunately, she's home with the flu. She wondered what I was up to and when I told her I was having 'the girls' over for some female bonding she got all excited. 'Just like the old days,' she kept repeating. So I asked for some of her hair. Do you know how long that woman's hair is? Down to her waist! She was more than happy to share...said her hair represents what soon will be your past...and future...the gray hair of the matriarchs that went before and that we are all destined to become. So please add her lovely gray locks to your leather bags."

Gaia noticed the women fighting back tears as Betty's contribution touched their hands. Then she said, "And that's not all Betty wanted us to have."

Gaia carefully filled four small cordial glasses, made from the most beautiful leaded crystal, with an amber fluid – though Ella's was more golden than amber – and handed one to each woman. "This is also courtesy of Betty. It's her homemade dandelion wine. Ella's is her non-alcoholic elixir. Betty's German ancestors handed down the recipe to her. We're to toast to the changing of the seasons. Betty said dandelion wine is liquid summer. Hold your glasses high as we thank her for providing us with this special treat and repeat this toast with me: 'When the north wind blows and the white blanket of winter holds us in her icy dread, may this elixir of summer bring hope of the glorious, warm sunny days ahead.'"

Lola, Bridget, and Gaia sipped the amber potion as Ella reverently sipped her water sweetened with honey. The smells of summer wafted up from the empty glasses, mingling with the savory scents of the hearty stew Gaia had served for dinner and the cinnamon from her desserts.

"Wow, it's sweet and yummy, and it DOES taste like everything bright and sunny!" Lola gushed.

"Sure does." A hint of the honey's sweetness drifted into Ella's nose, making her smile.

"All right you three. Grab your pouches and feel your intimate connection with them. Cherish these pouches; they are part of your history. Every item in them has special meaning. Respect them. Revere them."

Gaia held up her own pouch and said, "I have a name for MINE."

"Well, what is it?" Bridget insisted.

"MINE. My Insight Now Exists."

"What? What the hell does that mean?"

"When I look at the bag, the memories of these items flood my mind, and I remember the insight I had, have, and will need for the future. It's a reminder to use your intuition or your insight or whatever you call it. There's no going back to 'sleepwalking' through your life. You will forever be aware…awake! It's my MINE bag, only for me."

"Very clever," Ella said. Then she clutched her pouch dramatically. "Don't touch that, it's MINE." They all laughed.

"I have one more addition," Gaia announced. "I hope you don't mind."

"What is it?" Lola said excitedly.

From the table, Gaia produced four tiny stones. "These are small amethyst crystal points. The amethyst crystal is specific to our circle. Amethyst calms and balances. It's good for overcoming addictions and the stress of daily life. It protects us from negative energy and helps us transform into our full expression of being."

Gaia handed out the amethysts. "For strength, abundance, illumination, wonderment, and service…so it shall now and forever be given to us by the divine creative source of all that is and will be. Know that you are well loved."

Alena and Shauna were sound asleep in the center of the circle, breathing softly and contentedly. A wave of nausea caught Gaia by surprise. She filled a goblet with water and took a sip. Then she handed out water to the others. "Will you join me once more in our circle."

The four women joined hands once again, and Gaia chanted an ancient melody. Round and round they danced, careful not to step on the sleeping future. The smell of roses overwhelmed the cabin.

The snow drifted against the door. They stoked the fire, gathered their blankets together, and huddled on the floor. Sleep came to each of them. No one stirred until sunrise.

It was only after everyone was awake and well fed that Gaia made her announcement: She would be headed for Oregon before the next full moon. For now, her work here on this mountain was done.

June 21, 1995, Summer Solstice

NATURE'S WAY

Betty had one thing on her mind when she awoke that fine June morning, a good hour earlier than usual. She felt compelled to write in the Circle of Na'mow Handbook. She rummaged through the back of the hall closet and found the old leather-bound journals. She had not written an entry in quite some time. Guilt consumed her as she inhaled the smell of the weathered papers, pages that traveled back many decades, pages that conjured up memories of life's many trials and tribulations and of friendships as powerful as they were treasured.

"Today is the day we catch up, old friend," she said, giving the book a shake for emphasis. Several loose papers fell to the floor.

"Good God," Betty moaned as she bent over to retrieve them. "Time sure flies as you're growing older, and the aches and pains tag along with you no matter how you try to ignore them."

Slowly she made her way to her living room desk where she unceremoniously plopped down in the chair. The chair squeaked loudly and Betty cringed, afraid the noise would wake up Herb. She held her breath for a moment, and then heard his loud, incessant snoring coming from their bedroom. "Fat chance," she said, rolling her eyes.

As she grabbed her pen, a sharp pain shot through her thumb.

"Damn it to hell, come on you, work," she chastised her arthritic thumb. "You only hurt like this when there's a storm a-brewing."

Then she settled in with the journals, thumbing pages and reading bits and pieces. "Good golly…my, my…look at this. I can almost feel you, my sisters, opening up that secret garden in my heart." She let her fingers run over the pages as she recognized her friends' varied and distinctive pen strokes.

"As unique as their personalities. Look at all these stories we shared. Ah…and looky here…the recipe for dandelion wine. Makes my mouth water just thinking about it. Damn straight if it isn't that time of year again!"

Betty jumped in her chair when the little door at the top of the German clock opened and the cuckoo tweeted six times. 6:00 a.m. It had been her grandmother's, ornately carved from trees in the Black Forest. She stared at its numbered face, feeling soothed by its round shape and rhythmic beating.

Good Lord, time is just ticking away! Your hands moving around that face of yours…past, present, and future staring back at me! Yes, I know…your circle of time has value…lets people know where they have been, where they are presently, and where they are headed. But will kids today know…with their digital watches…exact time for that very instant? My God, I hope so. I surely hope so.

Memories swept through her like a fast-paced movie, and the memories brought a flood of tears. Letting herself cry, she felt both the joy and the pain of a life well lived.

Fog rolled off the lake, enveloping the house in its moist whiteness, and within minutes was replaced with the warmth of the morning light. Sun flooded through the window onto Betty's face and spilled over the journals as if a searchlight had found them. She squinted through the brightness, and the window framed a perfect landscape of mountains, crystalline water, groves of trees, and the cloudless turquoise sky. All filled her heart with gratitude, and the words flowed effortlessly onto the paper.

June 21, 1995

The Summer Solstice

"Past, Present and Future provide the momentum of the spiral, the open ended circle of ALL that is, was, and will be."

My Dear Na'mow,

As I look out my window, I feel so blessed and overwhelmed by your majesty, to once again bask in the glow of your glorious day-break. It feels as if the earthly and ethereal realms are lifting the veil between worlds to reveal secrets kept hidden for decades. And you, Na'mow, seem to know the exact moment to expose what lies beyond the veil...beyond your beloved landscape...allowing anyone with the desire to see...to peek at Life's treasures. It's like a huge "Ta-dah...surprise...look at what's been here all this time... wake up, wake up!" It must make you chuckle.

Okay, my friend, I get it! I feel a restlessness rattling in my bone's marrow. I hear a whispering in my unconscious mind, driving my emotions to be expressed. "Something" is pushing, persisting like a virus, giving me signs and symptoms that I can't ignore. Today, like so many other mornings, my lungs crave your mountain air. Each breath nourishes my soul like a well-tended garden, allowing me to grow stronger every day. You are my Home, a place that enlivens my joy and enlightens my very essence. Na'mow, you are the Heart of my evolving history, and I love you for that. Ah! Oh! Goosebumps. "Something" is afoot. I knew it! Change is in the making.

I must admit that Hattie and I worried greatly about the dwindling numbers of the Circle and feared losing all memories of you. But now I feel happy and hopeful, seeing the comforting glimpses of eternity as I watch this next generation of the Circle fall in love with your beauty and magic. And my heart soars with joy right now for I believe that this new generation of the sisterhood has done just that...found you, found Home.

I look forward to sharing this with Hattie...for under your lofty peaks...the Circle of Na'mow will live on forever...never to be forgotten.

Bless you for allowing me the privilege of knowing your mountain majesty.

Betty

Betty tenderly closed the journal, satisfied with her entry. Finding a big manila envelope, she placed the journals in it and licked the top shut. Using a magic marker she wrote "HATTIE" on the outside of the envelope. The sun had invigorated her. She breathed in Na'mow.

"Summer's awakened," she said, marveling at the beauty awaiting her outside.

Summer was Betty's favorite season of the year, and the sight of the sun-disked flowers of the dandelions in full bloom was cause for jubilation.

Over lunch on the back deck, she and Herb watched the clouds roll in and felt the cooling relief from the heat of the day. "It's perfect for dandelion collecting," she disclosed to Herb. "It's always better to collect under a bit of cloud cover so the petals don't wilt too quickly."

"Then you'd better get at it," Herb said, clearing their plates.

"Dandelion wine, here we come." Placing a worn straw hat on her head and leather gloves on her hands, Betty grabbed her dandelion-collecting basket, the very one her grandmother had used in Germany. The yellow and green stains of decades of flower gathering were its only decoration.

Betty stepped off the porch, and the shrill sound of the acrobatic flying of the "hummers" caused her to look at the nectar feeders hanging from the eaves.

"Oh, Herb, come and look," she called. Eight hummingbirds fought for their turn at the feeders, while one very territorial male splayed his tail feathers to proclaim ownership of the one nearest the house.

"Well, my goodness," Herb said, quietly staring at the feeding frenzy. His red hat attracted the attention of several female "hummers," and they darted his way. When they got a little too close for comfort and Herb could feel their wings tickling the back of his neck, he stepped away, kissed his bride on the cheek, and wished her a successful harvest of "the weed," as he called her precious dandelion.

Betty didn't turn away just yet. She was mesmerized by the iridescence of the hummers' ruby throats and the vocal orchestrations emanating from them. The arrival of the hummingbirds was cause for celebration and forecasted warmer weather ahead. The neighborhood would come alive and the bright red feeders would suddenly appear, hanging off the eaves of every cabin and strategically placed in tree branches. Betty and Herb would carry their morning coffee out onto the deck and watch the hummers feed for hours.

"Drink, drink, little ones. Drink in all the sweetness life has to offer," she instructed each bird, as if they were children preparing for the day. The more feeders they had, the more vigilant they had to be, sometimes filling them twice a day. Hummers were not the only creatures who craved the sugary fluid. So did ants, bees, raccoons, and black bears. Many nights they had awakened to the loud crashes of the feeders being raided after they'd forgotten to bring them in for safekeeping. And as they had gotten older and more forgetful, the nighttime crashes became more frequent.

Clouds darkened over Betty's head as she headed for her favorite dandelion patch. It was located near the road among the knapweed and thistles, as many patches were, and substantiated Betty's theory that the tourists' tires carried the seeds up from Boulder.

Betty was a good half-mile from home and her basket was half full when she realized her hands ached with arthritis and were quickly stiffening up. She removed her gloves and tried to massage movement into them. Her back and knees hurt too, and memories of her grandmother's own gnarled joints surfaced. Those days, Grandmother would hand Betty the basket and find a stump to sit on in the shade. From there, she would instruct Betty in the ways of harvesting the yellow flowers and exalt over the dandelion wine they would soon produce.

It was a good memory, except for the fact that Betty wished at this moment that she had someone to pick up her slack.

A deafening crash of thunder startled her back to reality. Lightning flashed nearby, illuminating the mountainside like floodlights on a starless night. Betty glanced up. *Where had the storm clouds come from. Had she been that preoccupied? My goodness, Betty.*

A moment later, thunder and lightning exploded simultaneously, and the sky opened up. The thunderstorm was suddenly on top of her. Hailstones pelted her thin, tender skin as she held her hat over her precious cargo. The wind chilled her to the bone. The shelter offered by needle-laden boughs of the ponderosa pines tempted her, but she knew better; the trees attracted the lightning, and the wood was like a huge conductor of energy.

Then a violent gust knocked her backwards, and she had no choice. She hurried into a small grove of pines and used the trunk of one for support.

Betty's ears nearly exploded from the thunder's deafening clamor. Bright white light flashed all around her. She closed her eyes and then quickly opened them, thinking that someone had called her name. *Could that be?*

In that brief moment, Betty scolded herself for going too far, because she knew Herb would be worried about her, worried sick.

Then it happened. Lightning hit the tree and a searing pain ignited every cell in her body. The basket exploded in her hand, and yellow petals scattered. Betty's ears strained to hear the music of a senescent melody drifting toward her from far away. The volume increased as she focused on the figure approaching her. It was her grandmother, and she was suddenly standing beside her. She took hold of Betty's hand and presented her with a brand new woven container. The basket was adorned with the most beautiful flowers Betty had ever seen. When Betty peered inside, the face of a newborn baby cooed up at her, melding with the flowers, and overwhelming her with joy.

Herb's anxiety reached a fervent level as the hail and lightning forced him back toward his house. A car slowed, and the window lowered. It was Sam.

"Get in, Herb," he called.

Herb held on to his hat as he climbed in the front seat. "Thank you for coming, Sam. Betty...Betty...she's out in this...went to collect dandelions...to make wine. I don't know where she went...can't find her." He put his face in his hands and then used his handkerchief to wipe the wetness off his glasses.

Sam grabbed Herb's shoulder and looked him straight in the eye. "We'll find her," he said with as much reassurance as he could muster.

They set out. Sam turned on the heater and rolled down the windows. Rain and hail entered through the windows as they bellowed her name over and over again. Lightning lit up the road and thunder deafened their calls.

Sam eased the car down the road as water flooded the gullies on either side. Sam cranked up the defroster and turned the windshield wipers on high, straining to see through the deluge. Lightning crashed again, this time directly ahead and to the left of the car. They watched it hit a tree and saw bark arcing overhead.

Herb screamed. The scream echoed within the car like a bullet ricocheting in a dark canyon as he watched Betty's blackened basket arch into the air, spilling fiery yellow petals, and saw her crumpled body. He reached for the door handle, but Sam was already out of the car and running. Lightning and thunder crashed all around him, but all he could think about was Betty.

He got to her first, saw the damage the lightning had done, and knew she was dead. He was taking her in his arms when he heard Herb's footsteps pounding through the rain.

He turned and shouted, "No, Herb, no! Wait! She's..."

Sam didn't have time to finish the warning. Herb had stopped dead, frozen in his tracks not five feet away, his brain trying to make sense of his burned and brutalized wife, her life force fleeing. Then his legs gave way, and he collapsed. On his hands and knees crawling toward her, his strength failing, robotically repeating Betty's name, over and over, sobbing into his wet red hat.

November 23, 1995, Thanksgiving

MEMORIES

Homemade desserts crowded Ella's dining room table. A picture-perfect pumpkin pie, apple pie with an elegant lattice crust sprinkled with sugar, cranberry-orange bread sliced and spread with cream cheese, pumpkin cheesecake topped with shaved dark chocolate, cinnamon-laced apple crisp, oatmeal raisin and chocolate chip cookies, and magic bars were but a few of the delicious treats.

The scent of cinnamon melded with the smoky smell of the wood fire. Neighbors and friends mingled in every room, and conversation moved like a wave throughout the house.

The party marked the first Thanksgiving Dessert Party, as Ella called it, neighbors and friends gathering to share their bounty of food just like they had that first Thanksgiving dinner eighteen years ago. Ella was effusive, wanting more than anything to create a tradition that the people of this mountain could count on, especially after the hard year so many of them had experienced.

She was so glad Herb had come, even though he looked years older and dangerously frail since Betty's tragic death. Their love story was like that of a fairy tale, and a shocked community was still reeling from her absence. Her memorial service had been held at the mountain's outside amphitheater, and Ella remembered Henry giving his mom's eulogy, remembered him saying that his parents had never spent the night away from each other in over fifty years of marriage. Tonight Herb seemed defeated and lost, even though friends hugged him genuinely and his cheeks blushed red from lipstick kisses.

"I need to use the bathroom," he said suddenly, though Ella knew it was an excuse to release the tears that seemed so hard to control even after all these months. He still used "we" instead of "I" in every conversation, because as far as he was concerned, it would always be the two of them.

Herb sat in the bathroom and chastised himself for wishing he could join Betty in death. He missed her more than anyone realized. Watching commercials on TV, hearing certain songs, observing people holding hands, or just seeing them feel joy could open the floodgates of emotion. He splashed cold water on his face, embarrassed that he could not talk himself into happiness.

A knock on the door startled him.

"Herb. Are you okay?" It was Ella.

He opened the door. Ella saw the sadness etched on his face and took him in her arms. She embraced him until no more tears flowed. Minutes later, arm in arm, they reentered the dining room unnoticed.

"You sit," Ella said. "I'm going to bring you a plate of food. I think Gary is about to make a toast."

"The man loves a good toast," Herb said.

As if on cue, they heard Gary tapping his glass with a spoon and calling, "Can I get everyone's attention please."

The noise abated, and Gary asked everyone if they wouldn't mind rising and holding hands.

When the room was quiet, he said, "Eighteen years have passed since fate brought all of us together to share our first Thanksgiving dinner. In those passing years, we've seen a lot of people settle here, only to be brought to their knees by forces beyond their control. The mountain has a way of running off those who can't handle it up here."

Some snickered, some sighed, some just nodded in agreement. "But for those of us who are either too blind or too stupid to get the message, for those of us who are here right now, it has been downright shitty!"

Everyone laughed heartily. Now Gary was rolling. "No really, we came here flatlander greenhorns, and two seasoned veterans took us under their wings to guide us in the ways of living in the high country. We didn't always take heed of your instruction and some of us had to leave in order to realize what a great place this is. There's one man who did more for me than anyone, and I'd like to acknowledge him."

Gary turned his eyes in Herb's direction. "Herb, can I ask you to stand for a moment please?" Herb did so reluctantly, and Gary continued. "We all know that Betty is here too; her presence is everywhere. So if I may say to you both, Herb and Betty, thank you for the kindness you extended to us when we were smart-ass punks. Thank you for welcoming us into this community and helping us to appreciate life here on this mountain. Hell, thanks for showing us what life's all about. Hear, hear."

The spontaneous burst of applause caused Herb to blush.

"Okay, listen, now that you've thoroughly embarrassed me," Herb said as his eyes glistened with moisture. "I want to say something to all you smart-ass punks," he joked. "I brought the last bottles of Betty's dandelion wine and her recipe. 'Liquid summer,' as she called it. Gary, if you wouldn't mind getting some glasses so we can all have a sip and remember my beautiful bride. We, I, would love it if you girls…" His gaze traveled around the room, from woman to woman, and came to rest on Ella. "… would take the recipe and continue the tradition. Just don't collect that damn weed during a thunderstorm." Herb laughed, then choked up. He finally managed to clear his throat and continue. "I will speak for Betty and myself when I say that we had many a discussion about you rascals. Really, we didn't think any of you would stay or amount to anything." The room exploded into laughter. "Come on, think about it. None of you had a chance in hell of staying up here. None of you seemed all that courageous. Then, by some miracle, you all had your own Jeremiah Johnson moment."

Gary handed out the liquid summer, and Herb went on. "I won't take up much more of your time but I never ever realized just how important this community is, to each of you and to me, until Betty's memorial. I remember waking up that morning to the night's gray drizzle. I must admit my mood was understandably gloomy. I really dreaded getting up and stayed in bed longer than I realized. I walked into the kitchen for coffee and saw Henry standing there with a devilish smile on his face. Then he pointed outside. I looked through the big picture window and there you all were, including the kids, in your robes and pajamas with your coffee mugs. Our kitchen was overflowing with food and neighbors. And then...you remember what happened, I'm sure..." People nodded, smiled, and choked back tears. "The most beautiful rainbow appeared...and then another... and another...three at once. And if that wasn't enough, an eagle swooped over us just to make sure we got *it*. Right then and there I knew Betty was orchestrating nature's display. But...and this probably doesn't surprise any of you...Betty wasn't finished."

Lola interrupted, "Herb, before you go on...let's wet our whistles again with a little taste of Betty. Everyone? To Betty and her amber elixir!"

They toasted again, and then someone yelled for Herb to continue.

"So, the memorial was at the amphitheater overlooking the city. I recall feeling a little weak hearted when I began to speak, but as I looked over this entire community sitting before me, I realized that though many of my friends had already passed, the future was staring back at me. You, all of you, filled me up with your strength. Your courage and bravery filled me up, made me stand tall, gave me hope, filled me with gratitude. I'm so proud to be a part of the love we carry for each other and for this rock we call home."

Herb took a short sip of wine and glanced at his son. "Then when Henry took the podium and spoke of Betty's love of nature, especially her little feathered friends, and when he reminded us all to stop to 'taste the sweetness life has to offer,' two hummers just appeared out of nowhere, like they'd been sent just for us. Two hummers, by God…and I knew right then that Betty would live on in our hearts and memories as long as we call this mountain our home."

Herb looked out over his mountain community. He saw them hugging one another, saw tears flowing, felt genuine love. He hadn't expected to feel what he was feeling. The first hints of healing, deep in his soul. A glimpse of hope. Seeing for the first time that the memories of his beloved bride would from here on bring joyfulness instead of sadness. Forever.

January 1996

GROWING PAINS

Fall seemed to last forever. It lingered well into mid-December when, like a hammer on a drum, the winter weather abruptly clutched the mountain in its frigid grip.

The temperatures were schizophrenic the first week of the new year. They would warm up for a day, then drop drastically the next. A deceptively warm rain would suddenly turn into freezing pellets, which would produce sleet and snow that made for hazardous driving conditions, down in town and particularly on the mountain.

On the first weekend of January, the mountain residents went to bed thinking a day of charming warmth had melted the icy pavement, only to find a fast-moving upslope storm had created a layer of dangerous, nicely concealed ice under an ever-growing white blanket of snow.

Sam hated spending the extra money on studs for the tires on his truck, but tonight he was glad he had. He barely made it up the steepest sections of the road, then felt the tires lose their grip, causing him to skid to a stop on the gravel shoulder two miles from home. He usually thought of driving the road as a dance, the tempo slowing or accelerating as he led his car around one obstacle after another, but tonight he was not the one leading. He scolded himself for letting the road get the best of him, but he couldn't take his mind off his date and how well it had turned out.

Time flew by during dinner: the conversation, the laughing, the flirting. The long-haired blonde had invited him back to her place for a nightcap, and they had ended up having a most pleasurable make-out session. She had gone so far as to comment on the bad weather, which led to the overt suggestion that he spend the night. After all, it was after midnight. Sam graciously declined, reviewing in detail all the chores he had to do the next morning. He now regretted it.

Damn, I must have been breathing hard thinking about her soft ruby lips 'cause this here windshield needs some heavy duty defrosting. Hell, I can't even remember watching the road. I gotta get a grip… the road almost got me. Should've taken her up on her offer. Could've been in a nice cozy bed. And now…it's a damn whiteout, and I'm the only idiot out here.

Sam took a deep breath, centered the car back on the pavement and drove on, his pace as slow as molasses, entertaining himself with the low whistling of a romantic melody.

Then he noticed tire tracks swerving off the pavement and tapped his brakes.

"What in the Sam Hill?" he wondered, a thought that usually gave him cause to chuckle. Not this time. He followed the tracks to the edge of the road and came upon a car sitting in a ditch with the lights on and the engine running. Sam recognized Lola's Subaru, but knew for certain that the brunette was skiing in Aspen for the weekend. The Western Slope town was her favorite place to ski because she loved rubbing elbows with the rich and famous, and always found a way to get someone to pay for most of her skiing expenses. He smoothed his mustache, his PI instincts kicking in, and climbed out from behind the wheel. He stepped out of his truck and nearly fell on his ass.

"Goddamnit!" he swore and none too quietly.

His cowboy boots were as good as ice skates as he slid awkwardly toward the car, his flashlight illuminating the movement inside. *Thank God, at least someone is conscious in there.* His hand was reaching for the handle on the driver's door when he saw Nick and Michael staring back at him, wide eyed and half panicked.

"Holy hell, guys, are you all right?" Sam leaned in for a closer look. Nick's legs straddled the gearshift. He was holding his crotch. Michael was scrunched against the passenger side door, looking very uncomfortable.

"Yeah, we're okay. Juth help uth out of here, pleathe, Sam," Nick pleaded.

"Okay, but first you need to turn the engine off. It smells like exhaust fumes in here." Sam didn't wait for a reply. He reached in and turned the key. Then he saw the blood. "Sweet Jesus, where's all the blood coming from?"

Sam's flashlight illuminated the gash on Michael's head, and he said, "Michael, you're bleeding. And it looks bad."

"Are you kidding?" Michael let out a groan. "I thought I was just wet from the goddamn snow. I knew something like this was going to happen."

Then Sam's light came to rest on Nick's lip, which was huge and black. "God, Nick! Look at you...your lip..."

"Hurtth like hell." Nick talked with a lisp, and Michael talked incessantly. Sam used every bit of his strength to haul the boys up and out. Ice crystallized on the surface of the car, making everything slippery. Once the boys were standing, Sam inspected them for more injuries and made a couple of snowballs that he placed over Michael's forehead and Nick's lip. "We're going to have to call the police," Sam advised them.

Michael eyes widened, and he literally shouted, "You can't do that!"

Nick had persuaded Lola to let him spend the weekend alone, and Bridget agreed that Michael could stay with him. The boys were going to have a video game marathon. Both mothers believed it would be good for their self-esteem to give them some semi-supervised freedom, and they took the added precaution of alerting the neighbors. "Really, Sam, you can't do that."

Sam ignored him. He eyes fell on Nick, and he said, "Aren't you due for a birthday this Saturday? I seem to remember your mom inviting me. Sixteen, right? Which leads to the most obvious question. Do you have a license?"

Nick hung his head. Obviously not. Michael explained, "He's got a permit, Sam, and a week from Tuesday he takes the test."

"Well son, I wouldn't plan on that," Sam said between gritted teeth. "Nick, didn't your mom go skiing this weekend?"

"Yeah," the teenager muttered.

"So, this looks like a case of car theft, don't you think? And reckless driving? And Michael, you're an accessory to the crime. Did you think about that?" Sam asked, arching his bushy eyebrows.

"Damn it! Shit!" Michael said, mounting his defense. "We just planned on driving down the mountain and then back up. No one would know. Cops never patrol this road, you know that, Sam. It was supposed to be a secret adventure. But after we got to town, we ran into a group of buds and a girl Nick has the hots for, you know? They wanted to go to a party and no one else could drive out so...so Nick was the only one with a car so he had to do it or look like a jerk. It was super important for him to look cool in front of..." Nick shoved his friend to get him to shut up, but Michael wasn't so easy to shut up. He continued, saying, "We just borrowed the car, Sam. Now that doesn't sound like stealing, to me, does it? Say something, Sam?"

"Cahr thefth? It'th ma mom'th cahr not thome random perthon. It'th not like I thtole it, I bowowed ith. Mom wantth me to dathe," Nick tried to explain through an ever-expanding swollen mouth.

Sam laughed out loud. "Holy hell, son, your big fat lip is going to save your little skinny butt. You sure as hell won't get yourself in trouble by talking too much like your friend here. You sound like you've been in the dentist's chair for one too many Novocain shots. You give a whole new meaning to the term numb nuts. No really, are your balls okay?"

Nick glared at the cowboy. Sam glared back. "So? Was the party worth it?"

"Hell, yeah!" Michael said a little too quickly. "And I'm not an accessory. I just went along for the ride. I had nothing to do with it. Nick was the one who made all the decisions. I was just there to support him."

"Huh?" Nick managed to utter.

Sam decided to take the kids to Bridget's house and to call Lola from there. He would leave it up to the mothers to decide how to handle the boys' freedom ride. As he drove past Lola's house, he noticed Dan's truck sitting where Lola's car should have been. He pulled into the drive, and Dan jogged over.

"Well, son of a...Where in the hell have...?" Dan clearly wanted to throttle someone, but he was also relieved. "Your mom has been beside herself for the last three hours. Do you...?"

Dan stopped himself. "We'll talk about this when we get home."

He ran back to his truck and followed Sam home.

Dan's lecture about trust and responsibility was in full force even before the boys had their coats off. The lecture, however, was civil compared to the fury that his wife unleashed on them. Her red hair swayed crazily with every gesture she made, and there were many. She was so furious even Sam was scared. After thirty minutes of her tirade, she laid down such a rough sentence on Michael that he looked up at the adults and said, "Next time just take me to the cops. I'd rather sit in jail."

"Next time!" his mother emphasized. "Haven't you learned anything from living up here? You two are lucky to be alive. This mountain can eat you up and spit you out if you aren't careful! I thought even if you decided to disrespect us, at least you'd be smart enough to respect it! You don't get another chance, there'll be no next time!" And then she spewed out her disciplinary penalties.

"You're grounded for six weeks, young man," she shouted at Michael. "No phone and no video games for three weeks. Hard labor at the house every Saturday and Sunday for the next month. And you're going to write me a paper on peer pressure...a very long paper."

Then Bridget turned her fury on Nick and let him know he risked ever hanging out with Michael again. She told him that if she felt that he was risking her son's life in any way, she would shut down their friendship in a heartbeat, and then snapped her fingers for emphasis. "And...since both of you are already knee deep in shit, Sam here will gladly let you shovel it out of Dolly's stall for the next two months!"

Sam tipped his hat and grinned.

The phone call to Lola was much less intense since she was slightly groggy from being awakened. She was relieved that the boys weren't hurt and had no idea what to do about the car. Sam told her she couldn't get it towed without a police report. In her most persuasive fashion she begged Sam to use one of his numerous contacts to get the car towed...without police involvement. And she knew Bridget had scared her son far worse than any law enforcement officer could, because she heard trembling in her son's voice.

Michael handed the phone back to the ex-cop.

"I'll make it worth your while. In fact, I'll think up something real special for you, Sam," Lola said, flirting just enough. The PI caved in again, of course, realizing for the hundredth time that she just had a way with him. Sam volunteered to help Dan winch the car out of the ditch, knowing it would be a long, cold night, but also knowing he was saving his friends' sons from a lengthy police interrogation. The whole affair proved a good lesson for young Shauna; she could see that both Michael and Nick were visibly shaken, and followed her mother's orders to find bandages, gauze, butterfly closures, antibiotic ointment and ice to start tending to the boys' cuts and bruises. No one thought they needed to go to the hospital.

Bridget softened some as she played nurse and realized how lucky she was to have Michael and Nick alive and in one piece. She swore to herself that she would not let them see her cry, and she excused herself to the bathroom to wipe away her tears of relief.

Sam had parting words for the boys and he made sure they listening. "Guys, every time one of your friends wants you to do something that you know your parents wouldn't allow and you KNOW is against the law, ask yourself one question. 'If this goes wrong, who pays?' I guarantee the answer will always be YOU and no one else. Just like tonight. Your buddies got off Scot-free."

He then wrapped an arm around each boy and recited, "Boys, good judgment comes from experience, and a lotta that comes from bad judgment. So I'd say at the rate you two are going, well, by the time you're my age, your judgment should be excellent."

Both boys grunted as Sam slapped them hard on their shoulders, and then he and Dan set out for what was bound to be a long night.

Sam's thoughts turned once again to his date earlier that evening. *Damn, she was fine.* The thought got him to whistling again, which caused Dan to question why he was in such a good mood. The cowboy knew he had all night to tell Dan of the great night he was having up until the time he wasn't.

Dammit all to hell. The road really did win this time.

Spring 1996

MUD

Colorado was known for its sunshine, all 300-plus days of it every year. Not this spring. This spring would be different. Eru'tan would make sure of it. Oh, indeed she would.

The mountain residents took to calling it "Mud Season." This morning, like so many others before it, was gloomy and gray and reminiscent of weather you'd see in the Midwest or Northeast. In a word: crappy. It rained at 35 degrees and then turned to snow as the temperature plummeted.

The thick ooze caked every possible surface: boots, pets' paws, stairs, porches, decks. No matter how careful you were, dirty tracks found their way into every room of the house.

For Ella, the weather conjured up bad memories of her hometown and the flood that ruined her high school graduation. For Bridget, it felt like living in a bog. For Lola, well, she was actually having some fun with it by making homemade spa concoctions and catching up on best-selling paperbacks. But even that got old. When she saw that her mountain neighbors were feeling as gray as the sky itself, she decided to plan a potluck brunch.

"Only we're having it at your place," she told Bridget.

Bridget laughed at her friend's brazenness, but the truth was, she was all for it. "Hell yes. I mean, the only good thing about a dreary Saturday is having sex, a pot of chili on the stove, and plenty of cold beer and whiskey. Since the kids are around, sex is out. But I don't know why we shouldn't go for the chili, beer, and whiskey."

Word of the brunch spread like wildfire, and families who were sick to death of being held hostage by the weather headed for Bridget and Dan's place with food and drink in hand.

By 11:00 a.m., trucks and cars lined the front of their garage and house. Mucky boots of various sizes and styles stood guard on the porch since the mudroom was too small to accommodate all the footwear. Most of the guests slipped into their favorite house shoes once inside. Dan grabbed an old clothes tree from the garage and placed it by the front door so rain gear could drip dry. Inside the house, the wood smoke, chili, and stews smelled more like autumn than spring. Conversation was lively, and the neighbors were genuinely glad to be gathered together in one place.

Suddenly, the sound of hail pinging off the roof brought the chatter to a halt. Almost instantly, the battering grew so loud that people had to yell to be heard.

Minutes later, the clouds broke open with a deluge of rain.

"Great! Here we go again," Ella muttered.

"Yikes, that's a lot of negative ions all at once," Lola exclaimed. She stared out the window and wrinkled her nose, taking a big whiff of the wet odor.

"Dammit all to hell!" Bridget swore. She opened the front door and stared out at just one more example of Eru'tan's unpredictability. Three inches of hail covered every inch of open space. Sheets of rain raced through the canyon. Gutters overflowed. A river of water fifteen feet wide and filled with mud, rocks, tree branches, and debris raced down the road and slammed into the cars parked out front. The wall of sludge followed a rut on the low side of the driveway, blasting more cars and slamming into the garage door.

When the rain slowed, Dan turned from host to cleaning brigade drill sergeant, handing out shovels as fast as he gave out orders. The men set to work, shoveling debris out from around their cars and the host's garage door. A far bigger problem was the newly forged channel driving the gathering water straight for the house.

"We have to dig a diversion ditch away from the top of the driveway," one of the men said. "And we better do it pretty darn quick."

They set to work, digging furiously. They worked a good hour. As they heaved the last debris-laden spadeful, the clouds opened up again and soaked them with a bone-chilling rain. The good news was that the newly dug channel diverted the water away from the house and the cars. The bad news was that the front yard and driveway looked like a scene from a disaster movie. Mud was everywhere. It looked like the biggest pile of shit Bridget had ever seen, and smelled just as bad.

Back in the house, the men poured shots of Jameson and ate like there was no tomorrow. They huddled around Sam as he consulted his police scanner. Things had gone from bad to worse. Two hundred feet of road had literally been washed away. "They're not letting anyone up or down the mountain," Sam said.

"And you can bet the rebuilding will take months," Gary said.

"Did the scanner say anything about not partying?" Bridget asked, holding up two new bottles of Jameson.

"Not that I heard," Sam said.

"Well then, we have no excuses. Party on, everyone."

The huge mud and rockslide that had collapsed the 200 feet of road on the front side of the mountain would take six months to repair. Two alternatives existed for the trek into town: the narrow, rocky four-wheel-drive road that ran west of the subdivision, or down a dirt road that led to the adjoining canyon and eventually backtracked north into the city. Both routes took an extra forty-five minutes that most people didn't have.

Lola decided that the second alternative was their best choice and the way she and Nick would drive down on this morning.

They pulled their hoods over their already bad hair, closed the door behind them, and sludged down the muddy path to a car that looked like it hadn't been washed in decades. A steady drizzle wasn't enough to wash away the hardened grime, and things got worse as they settled in behind five other cars who drove like it was Sunday and sightseeing was all they had on their minds. Lola's fuse was already short, and this just made it shorter. When it was clear the five drivers ahead of her couldn't hear her swearing, she turned her attention to Nick and said, "Nick, did you fill up the windshield wiper fluid like I asked you to do yesterday?"

Lola sighed as he gave her a blank stare. As if on cue, a last, pathetic spurt tried to wet the windshield and failed. She leaned forward to see through the muddied streaks. It was hopeless. Worse, it was dangerous. She eased the car onto the narrow gravel shoulder.

"You're going to have to get out and pour some water from your water bottle on the windshield and try and wipe it clean with some tissue."

"Are you kidding?" Incredulous.

"Get your butt moving or you'll be late for school," Lola snarled. "And if we don't get going, I'm going to miss my first client!"

Nick did what teenagers had been doing for centuries: he did a half-assed job, and the tissue he was using disintegrated into a million lint fibers.

Lola was furious. "What's your fucking problem?"

Swearing was not something Lola did often or very well, so when "fuck" came out her mouth, Nick knew how close she was to the edge and clamored back into the car. He put on his headphones and ignored her.

Lola jumped out, slipped on some loose gravel, and landed squarely on her butt. She cried out in pain and frustration.

Who knew what might have happened to Nick if Bridget didn't pull up next to her at that exact moment.

"Hey! Everything okay?"

Lola's expletives startled even Bridget as she harangued about everything from Nick's irresponsibility and the weather to the state of her hair and the disarray of her clothes.

Bridget cut her off. "Listen, Lola, I'd love to have a bitch session with you right about now, but I have a plane to catch and I can't be late. Gary's right behind me. Flag him down. Good luck!"

Seconds later, Gary did, in fact, pull up and was greeted by a sight he had rarely, if ever seen: Lola looking like shit. Her hair hung in damp strings. Her eyes were smudged with black mascara. Snot ran out her nose and coated her upper lip. Her hands and clothes were covered in grit and grime. *A damsel in distress if ever there was one,* Gary thought. He parked and walked over. He knew she probably needed a hug, but, owing an extra change of clothes, Gary stood an arm's length away. He could see that she was in no condition to drive, so he opened the door and looked at Nick. "Out," he said.

Then he guided Lola into the passenger seat, went to the trunk of his car, and handed Nick a gallon of washer fluid.

"Man up, son! Get that reservoir full and then drive your mom down this canyon so she has a chance to pull herself together." Gary turned to go, then stopped long enough to add, "And drive safely. Your mother's enough of a wreck as it is."

"Jerk," Nick muttered under his breath.

Ella left home in plenty of time – she used the small road Lola and Bridget did – but a freight train blocking the intersection hadn't gone into her calculations. She looked in her rearview mirror and recognized half the cars stacking up behind her: Sam the loner, Herb, Mr. Cranky, the JJs, Bridget, Gary, and finally Lola. Thirty painfully slow minutes later, the train inched forward and revealed a long line of cars on the opposite side of the tracks. No one was smiling.

Drivers tried to make up for lost time by taking turns too fast and passing the slowpokes on the few straight sections that the road provided. They tailgated. They swore. They tooted their horns. Bridget was among them. *Why don't these fucking grandma drivers just pull over? It's just plain common mountain courtesy.*

She cursed and fumed her way past three or four cars, but no further. She finally reached the paved part of the canyon road, only to find it was overflowing with commuters. A drizzle had turned to a downpour. She had waited an exasperating ten minutes at the stop sign and finally peeled out in front of a languidly moving Subaru. The guy hit his horn, and Bridget gave him the finger. She had to get to the damn airport, and it wasn't looking good.

Another holdup. Police lights reflecting off the wet pavement and canyon wall a quarter of a mile ahead. Bridget couldn't see around the bend in the road to ascertain the reason for the holdup, but her heart raced as she thought of the school bus, Ella, Sam, and who knew what other neighbor. They were all just ahead of her. *Please tell me they're not involved in an accident,* she thought. A siren split the silence and made her jump in terror; the terror gripped her and wouldn't let go. She prayed out loud. Gary and Lola were just behind her and would be wondering too. Forget her flight; she had friends and neighbors to worry about. She caught sight of a deputy wearing a lime-green vest. He was holding a flashlight and talking to the drivers of the cars ahead of her, one by one. He got to her and motioned for her to roll down the window. Then she recognized him.

"Sam, is that you? You aren't a deputy? What..."

"I'm just helping out until..."

"What about Ella? She was..."

"Ella's fine. She was right in front of me. But there's a long line of cars in front of us. It's not a pretty scene up there. A huge boulder fell off the side of the canyon and caused a serious rockslide. Buried a car."

"Oh, my God."

"Won't know if anyone survived until the backhoe arrives. Witnesses said it happened about an hour ago, just about the time that train moved off the tracks," Sam said. Then he caught her eye. "You must have been driving like a bat out of hell to get down here so fast. I know how far back you were. You ever hear the saying, 'Patience is a virtue?'" Sam teased.

"You're kidding me, right? Patience is not a virtue; it's a fucking waste of time!" Bridget replied.

"Well, darlin', today that waste of time may have saved your sweet ass!"

Bridget looked at him. She bit down on her lower lip and took a deep breath. "Yeah, you're right. I should try being a little more grateful. Thanks for the reminder, Sam."

July 1996

TROUBLE

Ella's kids were more or less just regular kids. In other words, they complained constantly. When Ella picked them up in town that evening, they complained about how hungry they were. When they stopped at the grocery store, they complained about how long it took, especially when Ella stopped to talk with Sam and to invite him up for dinner. When they headed for home, they complained about how long the drive took. Regular kids.

The problem began when Ella realized halfway up the hill how badly she had to go to the bathroom. It was late and pitch dark as the car made its way into the driveway, and Ella was wiggling around in the driver seat, her discomfort obvious to everyone. *Note to self... always pee in town before the climb up the mountain.* She reprimanded herself for not going at the grocery store, but admitted just how much she hated going there. The bathroom was dirty and her germ phobia always got the better of her.

She jumped out of the car yelling, "I gotta pee. You guys start unloading the groceries."

With no chance of making it to the bathroom inside the house, Ella veered behind a couple of trees as her kegels gave way. Thank God she had a skirt on as she fumbled to get her already soaked panties down.

No sooner had she squatted down and felt the first wave of wondrous relief when she heard a grunting noise directly in front of her. The bear that popped out of the trees was as surprised to see her as she was to see him. In Ella's eyes, he was probably the biggest black bear on the face of the earth.

She jumped up, dropped her house keys and screamed, "Kids, get back in the car. Lock the doors."

She turned and ran, her panties stuck just above her knees and defining in no uncertain terms the word "knock-kneed." She got to the car, fumbled for the door handle, and found it locked.

"Open the damn door!" she screamed.

The bear was lumbering her way, holding his nose high in the air, and obviously sniffing Ella's newly purchased provisions.

It seemed to take forever for Brice to unlock the door. When he did, Ella clamored inside and threw the door closed behind her.

"Damn! You reek, Mom," he stated. He stared at the panties poking out from under her skirt. "Gross."

"Oh, my God!" Alena shrieked. She pointed at the huge animal poised at the back of the car. Suddenly, the car was shaking violently, and the bear was working himself into a frenzy, snorting and grunting angrily. His frustration mounted as Ella turned on the lights and laid on the horn.

Alena moved closer to the front seat. She said, "Dad's in the house. I hope he doesn't come out here, or he'll be bear bait."

"My God! I didn't think about that. But where the hell is he? Wouldn't you think with all this commotion he'd at least look out the window?"

"He's probably got his headphones on and listening to some tunes," Brice said, his eyes as wide as saucers.

"Oh...what the hell!" Ella laid on the horn with one hand and handed Alena a flashlight with the other. Alena shined the light right in the bear's eyes, which only served to piss him off even more. Every time he slapped at the window, Alena shrieked even louder. Ella started the car. She was inching in toward the house when two bear cubs suddenly scampered out of the woods and ran straight for them.

"I think we're in big trouble," Brice announced. "I think our bear is a she."

The cubs called out for their momma, and momma bear responded by snarling at the car's occupants and showing her huge incisors. She stood her ground between the car and the cubs like any protective mother would. Ella laid on the horn again, but the blaring noise only caused the cubs to scatter and momma bear to attack the car with increasing vigor.

She looked as if she was about the mount the hood when another car screeched to a stop behind them. It was Sam. Thank God. He fired off a couple of rounds through the driver side window, and the bears bolted for the woods. He got out of his car with the spotlight in one hand and his 9 mm pistol in the other, and tracked the bears until he was sure they had no intention of returning.

Ella rolled down her muddy, bear-pawed window, and said, "Oh, Sam. Thank goodness you came when you did. Are they gone?"

"They're gone. It's safe," he said. The kids scrambled out of the car and headed toward the house.

Sam opened Ella's door and looked down on her. "You're a sight for the sorest of eyes. I remember waking up to a date that had that same look you have right now. She just couldn't believe she had witnessed the fiery intensity of a wild animal: me! Ha ha ha. Now me and her sure did have some fun, but…" Sam stopped and sniffed the air. "What smells?"

By now, Ella's undies had fallen to her ankles. She guided them over her feet and flung them up into the air. The hope was that they would find their way far into the woods, but instead they arched up over her head and onto the roof of the car.

Sam watched her huff away, laughing uproariously at the big wet spot plastered firmly to her ass.

August 1996

ANIMAL SIEGE

The scene in Bridget's office would have looked pretty hilarious even if you didn't know the back story.

The walls were plastered with hundreds of wildlife photos, most of them snipped from magazines and most of them of squirrels. A brightly painted broom decorated with bows and streamers stood upright in front of her desk. A 40-pound bag of premium sunflower seeds was propped up against a galvanized steel garbage can, and the can was secured with a huge chain and a massive lock. There was a trap-cage sitting in the middle of the floor, and it held a stuffed skunk captive. Twenty straw brooms of every size and shape stood like sentries around the perimeter of the office, and all Bridget could do was stare at them in amazement. Her office mates had pranked her good this time. She started laughing, that raucous belly laugh that everyone was so familiar with. Then she turned to see someone in a bear costume roaring toward her and growling. She screamed. Everyone else laughed uproariously.

"You people are all crazy," she shouted. "Thank God."

It was going to be another long day at work, but at least it was going to be a fun one. And God knew Bridget needed some amusement.

She sat down at her desk, and the "decorations" took her back several weeks when a bunch of squirrels, a skunk, a bag of birdseed, and a broom ruined what was supposed to be a peaceful, rejuvenating weekend.

The plan was for Bridget to have the weekend all to herself, and she was wholeheartedly looking forward to it. The kids were at sleepovers and Dan had gone motorcycle camping with his buddies. Bridget's plan was to spend Saturday putting out her birdfeeders, hanging flowering baskets, and setting up the deck furniture. Once done, she would be ready to grill a marinating flank steak and have a few premium beers. The perfect day.

After breakfast, Bridget set to work. She opened a 40-pound bag of birdseed and set it in the middle of the mudroom floor, surrounded by birdfeeders. Bridget filled her favorite wooden feeder and went outside with the small stepladder to hang it in a nearby pine tree. When she got back inside, a squirrel had found his way into the mudroom and was busily filling his cheeks with seed. Exploding with expletives, the mad redhead grabbed a broom and chased him outside and up a tree. *Damn door always sticks. It's just easier to keep it open.*

She stared at the squirrel and snarled, "You little fucker, you stay right up there in that tree. I've got a whole day of chores to do. Do you hear me?"

The squirrel sassed her back with plenty of chatter.

Bridget hosed off the deck furniture and washed off the cushions. She repotted some flowers into her antique baskets and raked up the dead debris from around the house. She went back inside for a glass of water and came face-to-face with a scene from a horror movie about demented animals. Dozens of squirrels and chipmunks were flying off shelves and counters in the kitchen, running over the back of the living room couch and chairs, and scooping up as much food as they could into their overstuffed cheeks.

Bridget pumped her fists and stomped her feet. She spotted her nemesis from her morning encounter and shouted, "This is war, you little bastard. You just couldn't keep from blabbing about the cache you'd found in my house, could you? I'm going to give you a broom whipping you'll never forget. Now, all of ya, get the hell out of my house!"

Managing to sound exactly like a screaming banshee, Bridget took up her broom and swatted every last squirrel out of the house. Then she slammed the door shut. The chatter coming from the pine trees outside was deafening. It sounded as if the mountain's entire rodent population had banded together against the crazy human staring back at them with wild eyes and wilder hair, and then they added insult to injury by pelting her deck with pinecones.

Bridget had to spend a few hours at the office the next day, and she made the mistake of telling the story to a couple of her co-workers. They found it all pretty amusing, of course, and teased her in particular about her weapon of choice.

"I thought about shooting them, but that would have made too big of a mess," she retorted. "On the other hand, my shoulders sure as hell wouldn't be as sore as they are right now."

Bridget figured she may have lost the battle but won the war, and as she was driving home that day her thoughts turned to a relaxing evening alone, luxuriating on the deck with a margarita and a good book.

It was not to be. She knew something was wrong the moment she pulled into the drive. She jumped out and walked around the house shaking her head; every window and door screen had been shredded. *You little assholes! Look at what you've done! You just couldn't leave well enough alone!*

All evidence pointed to the fact that her furry forest loudmouths had tried to get back into the house for another gluttonous meal. She imagined them mocking her from their safe haven in the trees. Too tired to fight, she grabbed a handful of seed and trickled a path to the middle of a clearing just beyond their property line. Then she dragged the bag of birdseed to the clearing and dumped every last seed into an enticing pile.

Have at it, you little bastards. You won...I'm too tired to clean up any more shit.

Bridget didn't even bother changing out of her work clothes. She made herself a huge margarita and sank deeply into her favorite Adirondack chair, watching the screens on the sliding glass doors blow gently in the breeze.

The animal siege resumed two weeks later when the skunks moved in.

Dan had just finished pouring coffee for Bridget and himself when it hit him. "What is that smell? Is it the trash? Ugh!"

"Can't be the trash," Bridget said. "I just took it out."

She walked around the room with a coffee mug in her hand, sniffing the air. She opened the newly fixed screen on the sliding glass door – yes, Dan had finally gotten around to fixing it – and found the source.

"It's right here," she called. "In the crawlspace under the living room. Icky! Ugh!"

"Skunk," Dan said definitively. "Thought I smelled something last night."

"That's all we need," Bridget declared, disgusted. "First squirrels, now this."

"Oh, my God!" Michael said. He and Shauna were holding their noses as they ate their cereal. "Get rid of it, Dad."

"Well, we're going to have to wait until it leaves tonight and I'll see what's going on down there. I should've closed up that hole under the deck when we first moved in," Dan said. "If it is a skunk, we're going to have to kill it once we trap it 'cause in Colorado we aren't supposed to relocate them. They can carry rabies or distemper and they usually find their way back anyway."

"I just want it gone, not particularly dead," Bridget said. "What else can we do? Well, we can see if it moves on its own and then seal up the hole. I read that if you put bright flashing lights and loud music near the hole, the skunk will look for somewhere else to live."

"Oh, that's just great," Shauna said. "Sounds like a skunk disco."

Dan laughed. "Yeah, it does, doesn't it. And it might take all summer to rid ourselves of it."

That night, Dan turned on a strobe light and a radio near the hole leading under the house, and placed some peanut butter in a live trap a couple of feet away.

It was two in the morning when they had heard the gut-wrenching scream coming from outside. Michael and Shauna nearly collided with one another racing down the hall. They found their parents outside on the deck with a flashlight illuminating the baby skunk inside the trap.

"It's a baby!" Shauna shouted. "Dad, what are we going to do?"

The mother skunk bolted onto the scene and started clawing at the trap, desperately pulling at the ends and sides trying to free her baby. Somehow or other, the trap popped open. But instead of bolting toward the safety of the forest, they raced back under the house and their aroma wafted through the air like two-day-old garbage.

"Well, that worked well," Bridget said as they traipsed back inside.

"I've got a feeling it's going to be a long hot smelly summer if we don't get that hole sealed up," Dan said.

The next morning Bridget called Lola, because she had to tell someone her story. "Can you believe it? First squirrels, now skunks. I mean, really! What the hell is going on? It's some kind of animal power shit or something."

"Well, let's find out," Lola said. "Hang on while I get my animal totem book."

Lola was back ten seconds later, saying, "Now, if it were me, Bridge, I would want to know what all of this native woodland activity means."

"Of course you would. You just love this woo-woo shit. The question is, do I believe it or not?"

"Just pretend I'm reading it out loud and you just happen to be eavesdropping on what I'm saying," Lola suggested. "That way you don't have to commit to wanting to know anything."

"Good idea," Bridget said, a little sorry now that she had called Lola instead of Ella.

"Okay, so first off: Squirrel. Squirrel is always preparing for the future. You know, gathering food in times of need."

"You need a book for that?" Bridget said.

"Shush," Lola said. "Oh my! Look at this. Squirrels can evidently get extremely frazzled because of their tendency to do too many things at once. Hmmm. Sounds like a case of ADD to me."

Lola giggled at her own joke and then got serious. "I'd say you need to slow down and figure out what is really important to you. Are you trying to take on too much at work and not making time for the things that are close to your heart? Are you accumulating the wrong things in your life? Is it time to get rid of people or things that aren't serving you and only causing worry and stress? Bridget...Bridget? You listening?"

"Go on," Bridget said. "I'm just sitting here eavesdropping."

"Oh...the skunk. My, my, I never even thought of these quali-ties," Lola said. "My...interesting..."

"Lola!"

"Oh, sorry. So here's what it says about skunks. Skunks demand respect. If their backs are up against a wall, well, you know what happens."

"They let loose," Bridget said.

"Yes, but they only let loose on those who want to do them harm," Lola said. "So here's our lesson. Know who you can trust and who is out to get you. In the skunks' case, their silence gives them an invisibility to accomplish what they need to do under the radar, which means they know when to be humble, and when to toot their own horn, so to speak."

"So to speak," Bridget said facetiously.

"Smell, obviously, is an important part of a skunk's awareness…"

"Stop! STOP!" Bridget shouted. "All in all, it still seems like airy fairy shit. Well, except for the smell thing. That kind of hits home like right now. God, it reeks in here."

~

Bridget may have thought that the skunks were the last of the siege, but she was wrong. A few weeks later, Dan forgot to close the sliding glass door before he went to bed. In the mountains, especially in the summer, this is not a good idea. It was three in the morning when Bridget heard the crashing sound echoing from the first floor. The scene was becoming all too familiar. Michael and Shauna huddled together at the top of the stairs while their parents crept down the stairs.

Dan flipped on the light. A mother raccoon and her five babies stared innocently up at them. Trash was scattered from the kitchen out into the dining room and living room. The pantry door was ajar, and the raccoons were munching on a box of cereal. The overwhelming scent of urine mingled with the stale smell of trash.

Instinctively, Bridget grabbed the broom, her overused weapon of choice. She tried to shoo them out the screen door, but mother raccoon was having none of it, using her little hands to deflect the broom away from her babies. "For Christ's sake, look at this mother, giving me a bunch of raccoon attitude. Move your butt…OUT! OUT!"

Finally, one perfectly placed swipe lifted the raccoon off the floor and out the door, like someone had shot her out of a cannon. Her babies followed. Dan locked the door and turned out the light, but this didn't save him from a string of not-so-kind words, care of his wife. The next morning, Dan and the kids left the house early, while Bridget set about cleaning up the previous night's mess. She was tying up a last trash bag when the screen door opened behind her. She turned and saw the mother raccoon waltz in like she owned the joint.

"What the hell!" Bridget gasped as the raccoon pushed aside the trash bag and headed for the kitchen. "Oh, no you don't, missy!"

Bridget grabbed her broom. By now, she'd had lots of practice perfecting the broom barrage technique and, by the time she was done, felt pretty sure this brazen raccoon would not be back anytime soon.

They say that three times is the charm, but not when it came to Bridget and her ongoing animal siege. It was the third week in August. The skunks had vacated their crawlspace abode, and Dan had patched the hole. That morning, the entire family ate breakfast on the deck for the first time all summer. They were still in their pajamas and basking in the morning sun.

"I need my sunglasses," Shauna said. "It's bright out here."

She jumped up and headed down the drive towards the cars. She got halfway there when she froze mid-stride, her scream reaching an incredible level of ear-shattering decibels. Bridget, Dan, and Michael came running. The doors to both of their cars were wide open and mud covered the windows, doors, and upholstery. A lonely fast food wrapper blew around and under the cars, while Shauna's new sunglasses remained untouched on the dashboard of Bridget's car.

"A bear," the deputy who came to investigate told them. He cited the smeared bear prints staining the windows and marking the dirt.

"You guys are lucky your cars were parked slightly downhill."

"Why's that?" Dan asked.

"The people over the ridge had their car pointed uphill. The bear got inside and the doors closed, locking him inside. He was pissed. Urinated and defecated all over the place and shredded the upholstery. Finally smashed the rear window and escaped. It was a huge stinky mess. Looks like your bear just took a look-see and kept moving. You're really lucky."

"Lucky? You smell that smell?" Bridget said.

"I call that scent à la bear."

"Very funny. But we've had enough smells around here this summer to last us a lifetime," Bridget joked, holding Shauna close.

Of course, Lola was always ready to add her two-cents worth to the ongoing siege, and she showed up later that day with Ella in tow and a mischievous grin on her face.

"Ready to eavesdrop?" she said when Bridget answered the door. She hooked arms with Ella and held up her animal totem book. "I've got my book ready, and I brought along a highly trained social worker to make sense of it all."

"Bridget looks scared all to hell, but I'm ready." Ella laughed. "Wouldn't miss this for the world."

"Do I really want to know this? I mean, what the hell is going on? Did I piss Mother Nature off or something?" Bridget complained. She stepped out on the deck and led them to a well-worn patio table. There were three glasses of lemonade waiting for them. "I just can't catch a break. I'm getting pretty close to trying some serious hocus pocus just to get my life back to normal. Will knowing this stuff really change anything?"

"Well, you're the one who called us, so I would say on some level: YES! Okay..." Lola opened the book to a pre-marked page and immediately began to chuckle. "Oh, this one is cracking me up...but you might not find it all that funny. Oh, yeah, and I have to remember I'm just reading to Ella and myself. You are nowhere around...just Ella, me, and our lemonade...two friends..."

"LOLA!"

"Ha! This is good. The raccoon is the wearer of many masks. You too may be wearing many masks depending on who you are with and what you want to accomplish. The mask lets you feel safe in shifting to and from altered states. Transformation is the key word... wearing the mask lets you explore the world around you without having to give up who you think you are. But, on the other hand, you don't want to hide behind the mask too often or you will lose spontaneity and curiosity for new adventures outside the safety of your box."

"Wow, that is so deep," Ella teased. "This book could put a whole bunch of psychotherapists out of business!"

"Raccoons show fearlessness in most situations, especially in defending their family. And besides, they are so cute." Lola paused. "Well, maybe you didn't think that in your particular situation."

"I can guarantee you that I didn't think they were all that damn cute at the time. Not one bit. And that mother! Damn, she was as belligerent as they come," Bridget emphatically stated.

"Continue eavesdropping," Lola said, "because I can't wait to read about the bear, knowing the bear is just so you. I mean, you and bears...there's something otherworldly about your connection with them. Uh oh! I just got goosebumps all over. You know what that means. It means the Truth is being spoken."

Bridget was unfazed and grunted loudly.

"In...tro...spec...tion...whew ewe...that's so bear! Deep within you are the answers to all of your questions...you can truly meet all your needs," Lola began. "The bear always finds a way out even if others believe he, or she, will not. You are fearless in defending your core beliefs and your family. You will lead. Leadership is one of your inherent qualities and is yours to have if you become silent, listen, and receive the Truth from your Higher Self and use it to transform your everyday life and that of others for their highest good. Listen to your intuition. Use all your senses to full awareness so that you can reach your full potential. Bears have to go deep within Mother Earth for renewal and healing. Mother Earth is your ally. She embraces the way of the bear and always welcomes bear into her nurturing womb. Bear links us to the Ancient Ones who guide us on our path of life. Bear will always make you aware of your existence if you choose to see with the eyes of your soul."

Lola and Ella simultaneously sighed.

"Shit! Shit! Shit!" Goosebumps consumed Bridget's physical body, and a calm understanding filled her spirit.

AFTER THE FIRE

"The universe is wise in the ways of metamorphosis but no matter how the change happens, the timing is always perfectly orchestrated by the celestial composer. Oftentimes, it comes quickly and shocks the soul to the very core but at other times the stirring flutters the heart, a whisper titillates the mind or muscles twitch and spring to action. The song of evolution carries the enlightened along as they ride the flowing melody but others ignore the music reverberating in their cells. Humans always have the choice to follow or ignore but for those that seize the opportunity to harmonize and intermingle within the galactic chorus, their lives will be enriched with the resonance of the one Love and Truth, the cosmic language of interconnectedness, never to be forgotten."

Na'mow

Spring 1998

LOLA

The fire crews broke for lunch.

A buffet style meal had been set up under a tent in the parking area. An array of sandwiches, salads, chips, and cookies had been provided by a group of volunteers from the neighborhood.

Twenty or thirty others – volunteers all, including Lola, Bridget, and Ella – were traversing the scarred slopes of the mountain, re-seeding under the supervision of the Forest Service.

A light drizzle had stopped and the sun had peeked through the mist, creating the most magnificent rainbow.

"The universe certainly likes what we're doing, unless I'm completely misinterpreting her amazing display," Lola said, admiring the rainbow. She took off a pair of brightly colored gardening gloves and looked over at Ella and Bridget with a wistful smile. "Thanks to John, I don't have to spend my time wishing for that elusive pot of gold at the end of the rainbow like I did for so many years. The life insurance and the money he left, well, I really don't know how to express what it means to me. But, you know, I'd trade every penny of it for another day with him."

"I know how much you miss him," Ella said. "We all do."

"Making the decision to turn off those life support machines was the hardest thing I've ever had to do, but it makes my heart glad to know some of his organs are helping a few other people to have a better life. A big piece of him lives on." Lola smiled.

Bridget almost choked on her sandwich. "A piece of him! Shit, Lola you make it sound like a piece of meat or something."

"It does, doesn't it? Well, now that I think of it, he was one helluva piece of man. No disrespect, but he really truly was. If I think about it too much, I just break down all over again, even after two years." Lola's mind drifted off; so did her gaze. "Even in death he planned to help me out. Now, that takes some foreskin."

"Foreskin?" Ella shook her head. She saw Lola staring at Sam's butt as he bent over to wipe the mud off his pant legs. *Yep,* Ella thought. *That is indeed a sight to behold.*

"Hello! Hey there! Earth to Lola. I think what you meant to say was forethought." Ella waved her hand in front of her friend's face.

"Huh? What? Did I really say foreskin? Ha! See. John still has a hold on me even from the great beyond."

"I don't think John has anything to do with it," Ella remarked, glancing in Sam's direction.

"Oh, that! Well, you know Sam keeps complaining about his sore neck, and I keep encouraging him to come into the Wellness Center for a personal massage."

"Damn then! That right there is the problem," Bridget chimed in. "Poor guy's scared shitless of those sensual hands of yours kneading away all his aches and pains."

"If he doesn't feel comfortable with me, then Laurie can do it," Lola said, referring to her business partner. "Ever since we started the center, we've been working on each other, and that girl has hands as strong as steel. Did I tell you that she did some neuromuscular work on Nick's tennis elbow, and he swears she healed him."

"Speaking of the devil, where is that kid of yours?" Bridget asked.

"He's on house duty and hopefully writing a paper for one of his AP classes. Senior-itis is coursing through his veins. I hardly see him anymore," Lola lamented. "You'd think he was already off at Stanford. Which reminds me, I should probably check in with him."

"You definitely should," Bridget said sarcastically. "After all, he's only eighteen and no doubt sick with worry that you haven't already called."

Lola gave her the evil eye and took out her cell phone. When she couldn't get a signal, she strolled in the direction of the lake and found a boulder to perch on. For a moment, she forgot about the phone in her hand and stared out at the magnificent view. A flood of memories came crashing down on her, and with them came the tears.

Her thoughts turned to John and his last day in the hospital. This was a flashback that seemed to haunt her at the most inopportune times, and it played out in her head once again.

———

"No brain function." Those were the doctor's words. He said them with an extraordinary amount of compassion, but they hit Lola like a ton of bricks. She instinctively looked toward the ceiling of John's hospital room, hoping some answer would magically appear to her. What was she supposed to do? The machines hummed and clacked. Lola knew that John's life force had left him days before, but she felt his presence beside her that day, totally and completely. It was as if a cool breeze grazed the side of her body and the scent of Aramis filled her nose. She looked to her left, certain a wavering, translucent sheen was hovering close by. What was it? An angel from God? A messenger from above?

Lola didn't know for sure. She only knew that the words she had been trying to articulate for so long suddenly materialized. "You made me pregnant," she said to John.

She said them again, hoping to give him some power. "Do you hear me? You made me pregnant." The coolness that had been lingering next to her instantly melted into a warm tingling in her heart, a tingling that she could only identify as happiness. His happiness. "You made me pregnant, and I have absolutely no idea what to do."

After shedding an ocean of tears, a calm strength filled her. She called for the doctor. John would suffer no more. She set him free.

Dazed and shaken, she noticed a slight moistness between her legs as she walked down the hospital corridor. She ducked into a bathroom. Her panties were stained with a pink fluid. "Nooooooooooo... noooooooooo! Not now!" she yelled.

———

494

Lola blinked away the tears, the words ringing in her ears. She looked out at the beauty of the lake and felt a huge hole in her heart, a hole left by John, by Candi and Greg, and by so much that had been lost and taken from her.

She heard Ella and Bridget calling to her, but she ignored them, sobbing uncontrollably and allowing her soul to flush the grief from her system once and for all.

Spring 1998

ELLA

The dark charred soil with its smoky smell caused Ella to stop her raking. She folded her hands over the top of the rake and stared out at the burnt, ash-covered moonscape. *How could anything have survived such fiery malice?*

She had been fighting the memories for two years. She was tired of fighting them. Recalling her son's disappearance when the fire was at its worst made her stomach flip flop. She could feel the bile rising in her throat. The blackened landscape triggered an emotional flashback, but she wouldn't fight its appearance this time. She threw aside her rake and sat down; today she would allow the memory to saturate her entire being and hope it would desensitize her to future flashbacks.

⌒⌒⌒

The panic and helplessness she felt when they told her that Brice and Herb were missing that day were beyond paralyzing. The two of them were caught on the outside northern edge of the back burn, they told her later. The back burn had flared far bigger than anyone had anticipated. Blackness disoriented them. Smoke seared their senses. As quickly as the blast approached, a wind blew it backward and away from their homes. Without wasting a second, Brice restarted the ATV and blasted a path to Herb's house. He skidded to a stop near the front porch, but the momentum caused him to fall off and sprain his ankle. Though he could see almost nothing through the smoke, Brice looked down the road and saw that his own family's house was still standing even though flames continued to flare up all around it.

"This way," Herb said. Coughing and hacking, he wrapped an arm around Brice's waist and helped his young neighbor to the safety of his basement.

A small rectangular window was their only view to the outside world. Herb grabbed each of them a flashlight from the stairs. Jars of homemade canned goods and packaged food lined shelves at one end of the room. Two sets of bunk beds sat in a corner with bed linens folded at the end of each bed. A toilet seat resting atop a five-gallon bucket served as a makeshift toilet. Five-gallon jugs labeled "water" were lined up in the center of the room along with a card table and chairs. A table with a crank radio, medical kit, gas masks, matches, paper plates, cups, utensils, can opener, extra batteries and a Coleman stove occupied the space under the window. Brice was fascinated with the self-sufficiency of their temporary home. He stared in awe at Herb.

"Shit, Herb, you're one prepared guy," Brice laughed.

"Damn straight." Herb had already opened the med kit and had found an ace bandage to wrap Brice's ankle. "This here is a bomb shelter built in the sixties. We added the window after the Russkies calmed down a bit. The whole damn country thought the Commie bastards were about to drop an atomic bomb on us, so scared-shitless people were building bomb shelters just like this one in houses all over the country. Like they couldn't find a better use for their basements," Herb explained.

"Never heard of such a thing," Brice admitted.

496

"Son, seems to me you need a little history lesson," Herb said, fiddling with the dial of his radio. "What do you think I was doing when the Forest Service told everyone to evacuate? I was planning on staying right here for the long haul. That was until your mother yanked my ass out of my own house. What do you say we open up a jar of Betty's homemade peaches and have us a couple of home-brews? It's going to take me a while to educate your ass in the ways of the world. Education is key, young man. Yes, indeedy."

The fire had bonded the two, one the aspiring musician and the other a maker of homebrew and homespun philosophy, and Ella often found Brice seeking refuge in Herb's company.

Brice had come away from the fire more determined than ever to take his musical aspirations to California, and Gary and Ella had promised their son he could make the move as soon as his therapist deemed him fully recovered from the dual traumas of John's death and the fire. That proclamation had been made toward the end of March, and Brice had left only last month to room with a high school friend in L.A. He was now playing guitar in the friend's band and getting his feet wet in the music industry.

Because of Herb's influence, however, Brice had also made plans to get his California residency and apply to a community college in pursuit of a degree in musical technology. The whole family missed him badly. The house felt so static with that "boy" energy gone, and Ella even missed their verbal sparring.

"You going to do some work or just sit there in the dirt stewing?" Bridget called to her with a grin.

"I'm mad at you too," Ella yelled at an unsuspecting Bridget. Ella picked up a stone and tossed it aggressively down the slope.

"What the hell did I do?" Bridget fired back.

"This fire still stirs me up. I can't help it," Ella said. "I was just sitting here thinking how worried sick I was over Brice and Herb. And where were they? Getting drunk on beer and sharing stories in the old man's basement, feasting on homemade canned fruit and Twinkies. My heart was torn into a million pieces thinking our home was gone and so were they. Then that got me thinking about you."

"Me?" Bridget replied defensively. "What the hell did I do?"

"Yes, you! Shoving those empty liquor bottles across Hattie's table, accusing me of drinking. That just pisses me off," Ella said, her face red with emotion. "You and everyone else jumping to the wrong conclusion."

"Oh, come on, Ella. The bottles were empty. You were in the damn bathroom, for Christ's sake. How were we to know you poured the alcohol down the sink? And that you had called JD to keep you on the straight and narrow when the stress and anxiety were just about killing you. I said I was sorry, but I'll say it again. I'm so so sorry and I'm so proud and thankful you made the right choice." Bridget grabbed Ella and held her close.

"And Bridge, I'm so glad you made the right choice too," Ella whispered in her friend's ear.

Spring 1998

BRIDGET

"I'm so glad too," Bridget replied.

She hugged Ella for a moment longer, and then let her thoughts drag her back to the aftermath of the fire.

Her boss, Tom, was chomping at the bit to get her to make a decision about his offer. Did she want the job in London or not? It was a helluva promotion, and he needed an answer. "These kinds of offers don't come your way that often, Bridget," he told her.

"Yeah, I know, Tom. And I appreciate it."

From Bridget's point of view, however, the timing sucked. For Christ's sake, she hadn't even told her family about the offer. When would she ever find the right time? The neighborhood was in chaos. People had lost their homes, Sam among them. His was one of the first to go, and he'd been forced to move in with Hattie for a time; not that she was unhappy about having him as a roommate for a while.

Following the fire, both of Bridget's kids attended therapy sessions provided by the county; it was a good way to deal with the trauma, and there was plenty of that going around once they were allowed back in their house.

Dan and Bridget suffered from survivor's guilt, but stubbornly refused any kind of treatment. Five days after the fire, they finally sat across from each other on Dan's deck. Bridget sipped a whiskey.

"This must be serious if you're having a whiskey at 3:30 in the afternoon," Dan joked.

His wife didn't even crack a smile. "You're probably going to need a drink too," she said.

Dan looked worried. He poured a shot. "Okay. Let's hear it."

"Tom offered me the top job in London. Huge salary. Prestige. My big fucking dream job."

Dan swallowed his whiskey in one gulp and quickly refilled the glass. He stared at the amber liquid swirling around and around. "And?"

"It's everything I've ever dreamed of," Bridget said. "No, let me rephrase that. It's more than I imagined. Huge. But...we'd have to move there."

Dan grunted and said nothing.

Bridget decided to rephrase this last thought and said, "Or at least I'd have to move there, anyway."

Bridget's head tilted back against the high back of the Adirondack chair. She pulled her legs up under her and stared into the yard. Birds were busy retrieving sunflower seeds from the bird feeder and chirping happily. Chipmunks scurried underneath the feeder and greedily filled their cheeks with fallen food. Stellar jays, being too big for the feeder, cackled in frustration. The Colorado turquoise sky provided the backdrop for the ravens that were riding high on the thermals. She stared toward the neighborhood where a distinct line separated the burned areas from the untouched, vegetation-rich area.

"Look!" Dan pointed to a doe with two yearlings grazing on the currant bushes in the meadow below them. "It's so great to see all the wildlife coming back home, isn't it?"

Bridget slowly stood up to get a better view. The deer hesitated, heads coming up to watch her. Then, sensing no threat, continued to browse. Bridget watched them for another minute, loving the sight of these beautiful creatures so close to their house, loving the magic of their presence, loving the gift of their presence, and then once again turned her attention to the subdivision. The thought finally coalesced. As she took in the sooty, colorless, and burnt landscape, it reminded her of the house fire years back that had temporarily destroyed their family unit and separated them from the mountain. She remembered her determination to bring back life from the ashes of the fateful blaze. She remembered thinking that she and Dan would work hard to sow the seeds for their family to be healthy, harmonious, and whole again. *And we did it,* she thought. *We did it.*

Bridget turned away from the view and gave her attention to Dan, her eyes steady, her whole being calm. "I've made my decision."

"Well, hold on. We didn't even get to discuss it," he said defensively.

"We don't need to discuss it. It just became perfectly clear to me. Nothing is going to keep me away from you, our kids, this mountain, my friends, and this great neighborhood. Not even the fucking greatest job in the world!"

She marched over to give Dan a big kiss. Out of nowhere, a hummingbird suddenly appeared and buzzed all around them.

"No way!" Dan said in amazement. "Must be one of the last stragglers to fly south."

"That's no straggler," Bridget said. "Shit, that's Betty reminding me of what's important in life. Just like her and that damn hummer, I intend to drink in the sweet nectar of life. So pour me another whiskey. I'm going to need it before I tell Tom my decision."

They both laughed, then tenderly embraced.

"Tom's going to have to wait. And so is that whiskey," Dan said, grabbing her butt with both hands and drawing her close.

Bridget shook her mind free of the memory, a wide grin saying it all about what had happened after that. *Damn, I'm married to a sexy man!*

"Ella, can you believe that once you make a 'right' decision everything else seems to fall into place?" Bridget slapped Ella on the ass, and Ella swatted her hand away. They both laughed.

"Easier said than done sometimes, but so true," Ella agreed. She leaned against her rake.

"I think this damn mountain just wanted a commitment from us that we were here to stay."

"I'm just so glad you guys decided to buy your rental house," Ella said. "What a smart decision."

"It'll do fine until we can plan our dream home on the old pink trailer property," Bridget said.

"Don't worry. It'll happen and probably sooner than you think," Ella said encouragingly. "Which reminds me. How's Dan's new gig?"

Dan had gotten a job helping to build Sam's new "green" home, something he'd always wanted to do since working for the solar energy company down in town. "He's loving it. And Shauna's loving soccer and track and Michael's going to Mesa State next year to study criminal justice."

"Where'd he come up with that, I wonder?" Ella said.

"Well, I know Sam had something to do with planting the seed. Can you picture my son as a policeman or FBI agent?"

"Hell yeah I can," Ella said. "And what about you? You got a promotion anyway and didn't have to move anywhere to get it."

"Yeah, I know." Bridget shook her head. "My life is just fucking fabulous!"

"I know, I know," Ella agreed. "I haven't said that in a very long time but the difference between then and now is that it truly, truly is."

June 21, 1998, Summer Solstice

COMMUNITY

Lola squealed with delight as she sipped her new favorite cocktail. "I found the new Potion drink," she announced to her friends. She held her clear plastic cup up toward the sun. "It usually looks classier than this…'cause it's poured into a martini glass. They call it a Cosmopolitan. Cosmo for short."

Bridget squinted at Lola's outstretched hand. "My God, it's pink! Pink is too 'foo-foo' for me. I think I'll stick to my whiskey. And the occasional shot of tequila."

"Too 'foo-foo'?" Lola teased. "Bridge, when are you going to embrace your sexy feminine nature and quit acting so tough? You need to nurture all your womanly qualities."

Lola casually placed her floral scarf around Bridget's neck and nodded her approval.

"I'll start doing that when you start embracing more of your masculine side." Bridget placed her cowboy hat on her friend's head.

Ella laughed. "You both look ridiculous," she said, restoring the scarf and hat to their rightful owners.

"Okay, okay, you have a point. We're perfect the way we are. But come on. Give this Cosmo a try. I made a virgin one for Ella." Lola handed out the cups. "A toast to the warm green days of summer and its renewal...leaving our past behind...including the old Potion... and welcoming the new. New beginnings and the new Pink Potion! And, thank you Ella, for hosting this Summer Solstice Party for the whole neighborhood."

They touched cups, then took a big swallow.

"Jeez, it's a little sweet for my taste, but not bad, not bad at all." Bridget licked the stickiness from her lips.

"What a delicious surprise. Yum. Cranberry with a splash of lime." Ella smiled, eyeing her drink.

"Speaking of surprises, you said you had one and...does it have to do with woo-woo?" Lola wondered. "Because asking me to bring three urns, I mean, even for me that's weird, Ella."

"You too?" Bridget exclaimed. "She asked me to bring the vials of ashes from our house fire back in '91. What's that about?"

"You'll find out soon enough," Ella said. "I've put everything in a wooden box out on the deck. Follow me."

Ella set down her drink and led them outside. Bridget nearly dropped her vials when she saw the size of Ella's wooden box. "What the...?"

Ella cut her off. "Bridget, get over it. It's part of the surprise."

"God, I can only imagine what you would have us doing if you were still drinking," Bridget joked.

Ella caught Lola trying to peek in the box – great surprise – and slapped her hand away. "Stop it! You just have to wait!"

"I'm not good at waiting," Lola admitted.

"You're telling us something we don't already know?" Ella teased. She took their hands and led them outside.

The neighborhood band tuned up their instruments in Ella and Gary's garage. A white tent lined with tables had been set up in case the weather turned bad or the heat got too intense. Potluck dishes filled the tables. A keg of beer and coolers filled with sodas, water, wine and more beer were lined up against the house. The temperature was pleasant, but the afternoon sun was heating things up, including lively conversations and innocent flirtations.

Sam helped Hattie up the steps to the deck and sat her in a rocking chair next to Herb. She placed a big tote bag down on the deck. Introductions were made, and Herb said he was grateful for the company.

"We met years ago, if you recall," Herb said. He meant back when Betty was alive.

"I'm not that old, young man," Hattie said. "But I sure do miss Betty. Bet you do too."

"Every day," Herb said. "Guess Sam's been living with you for a while."

"Yep. But his new house is ready. He got his certificate of occupancy, so he's now officially living back up on the mountain."

They watched a group of teenagers playing volleyball in the front yard, and Hattie shook her head.

"Ahh, to have my joints working like those young 'uns. Look at all that energy!"

"My knees creak so much you can hear me coming a mile away," Herb said. "I used up my share of energy years ago. It's kind of nice

504

to just relax and take it all in. At that age, you just keep so busy that by the time you stop to enjoy yourself, half your life has gone by in the blink of an eye."

"That's the damned truth," Hattie said.

A comfortable silence followed as they watched the action in the yard.

"You ever been married?" Herb asked Sam's elderly aunt out of nowhere.

Hattie gave him a startled look.

"Oh, I didn't mean to pry," the old man apologized. "Just making conversation."

"That's okay. Land sakes alive, it just took me by surprise. I haven't been asked that question in a very long time." Her eyes focused on the horizon. "Yes, a lifetime ago. He's been gone a good long while. Never had the urge to try it again."

"Betty's been gone three years. In fact, three years ago today. Some days it feels like forever and other days like it just happened. Does it ever get any easier?"

Hattie turned and looked at Herb, and he returned her gaze. "Not really. It just changes. The memories fade, but the tug on your heart remains. I figure once that tugging goes away is when I know I'm not long in this world. It reassures me that love is all that matters, whether in the past, right now, or in the future. And…looking out at all these people up here on this mountain…right here…right now…we surely are surrounded by it. Can't say that about a lot of places."

"No, you can't." Herb bowed his head down to his chest and smiled.

"Oh, good lord, I almost forgot. You and I have something in common besides our youth and vitality." Hattie grabbed the tote bag and placed it in her lap. "Whatcha say we have a little taste of some…liquid summer, Herb?"

Herb's head snapped to attention when he heard this, and Hattie laughed. "I knew that would get you going. I know all about Betty's wine. You know, she's not the only one that made a fine batch of dandelion wine. We flatlanders know a thing or two about making some tasty moonshine." Hattie's belly laugh made Herb chuckle out loud too, and he realized how much he was enjoying himself.

"Now, who's got the better joints, 'cause that person's going to get up and get us an opener and some glasses." Hattie announced.

"I'm your man, Hattie. Don't move a muscle." Herb wasted no time finding what he needed and hurried back to enjoy the companionship with his new friend.

———

Gary turned the grilling over to one of the neighbors and went to find Ella. Finally, he spotted her organizing the food under the tent. He snuck up behind her, put his arm around her waist, and pulled her close. "What's up, hostess with the mostess? I can see the wheels turning in that head of yours."

"You know me too well. Look at this. Our dearest friends and neighbors surrounding us on this beautiful day. Pretty cool, don't you think?" Ella said. "We transformed from kids to adults up on this mountain. All these kids have grown up together and soon they'll be scattered to the four corners. I wish Brice were here to see it. It'll never be the same after this summer, and everyone goes off in search of their destinies. Michael and Nick are off to college and in another year or two the girls will be off too. I'm already missing everyone."

"Me too," Gary admitted.

"Ouch!" Ella screamed when someone pinched her ass.

"Why the long face?" It was Lola, of course, and she hopped in front of the couple.

"Just reminiscing," Ella said. "Wishing I could slow down time for a bit, that's all."

A child's scream pierced through the air at that very moment, and heads turned in the direction of a little girl holding onto Sam's leg. Shauna and Alena, the girl's babysitters for the day, were kneeling down trying to comfort the child.

"Amity!" Lola set out at a run. "Jeez, Sam, she's only a year old, and it looks like you're trying to get a humping dog off your leg."

Lola slapped him on his shoulder and then bent down to pick up her daughter.

"There, there, your momma's here. Shhhhhh, it's okay." Lola wiped the crocodile tears from her chubby cheeks. When the little girl was settled again, she held her arms out to Sam and cried, "Baa, baa, bam."

"I guess she wasn't as upset with you as we thought," Lola said, kissing the top of Amity's head and allowing her to scramble into Sam's reluctant arms. Shauna, Alena, and Lola laughed at Sam's uneasiness.

"Look at that. She loves you, Sam. You're her favorite father figure." Lola tenderly stroked her daughter's back, the gentle scent of honeysuckle rising from her tiny body. Within seconds, Amity had fallen sound asleep against Sam's chest.

"You have to stop saying that or she'll start calling me daddy. And that I'm not! Now what do I do? I feel like I'm caught in barbed wire," Sam complained.

"You're already doing it," Lola told him.

Sam looked a little helpless. But the moment he stopped struggling with his emotion, the look became one of contentment.

"Why don't you see if Aunt Hattie will hold her?" Lola suggested. "Amity didn't have a nap today, so I think she's down for the count. And besides, Hattie is like a grandmother to her."

"Holy hell!" Sam replied as Lola brushed her lips across his, kissed her sleeping angel on the head, and playfully twirled her scarf around Sam's neck. Then, when Sam was thoroughly flustered and blushing a fine shade of red, she slowly circled the scarf around his waist several times before flitting off to join her friends.

"Damn," Sam muttered, trying to walk as normally as he could with the bulge in his pants. "That scarf does it every time!"

⁘

"Uh oh! Would you look at that. Lola's doin' that thing with her scarf and batting her eyes at my nephew." Hattie pointed in Sam's direction. "And he's walking kinda funny, don't you think, Herb?"

Herb chuckled. "This whole mountain has been watching those two tease each other for years. Lola plays with him just like a cat with a mouse. He's been thrown up in the air one too many times to know what direction he's headed. Looks like she got him good this time." The wine was working its magic, and Herb was making conversation and joking with ease.

Sam stepped onto the deck, gently cradling his precious cargo.

"Aunt Hattie, would you mind babysitting Miss Amity for a spell? That Lola just waltzes off like this baby of hers is some kind of a community project." Sam handed the sleeping girl over to Hattie.

"She is the community baby, Sam. Everybody loves this little one. Lola's a good mother but she just needs to spread her wings today." Hattie snuggled the girl close to her chest and inhaled her sweet aroma.

"Looks to me like that girl's scarf and her bewitching eyes are working their magic on someone hereabouts," Herb said, giggling at his own cleverness. "Whoa! Watch out there, young man. You might just get caught in someone's web of seduction."

Sam didn't find it all that funny, but he did take off his cowboy hat and wiped the sweat from his brow.

"Why don't you just admit it, Sam," Hattie said. "You're smitten with her."

"I'll be damned. You two have been having a gay ole time watching me squirm. Christ!" Sam's face reddened as he smoothed out his mustache and replaced his hat. "One thing I know for sure, Lola's scarf twirling around a man's neck is like hearing the rattle of a rattlesnake. You're within striking distance, so you best turn on your heels and run the other direction. And that is exactly what I plan on doin'."

The two elderly cohorts cackled as Sam stomped off the deck looking for a safe haven, most likely in the company of other males.

Dusk lingered longer than usual as an orangish-purple haze hovered over the horizon.

As the sun set, parents gathered their children close to ensure they were safe from the prowlings of nocturnal wildlife. The band was in full swing, energized by the movement of the animated dancers and an unperceivable conductor. Some howled at the darkness of the new moon as their unabated wild natures surfaced. Primal energies manifested as men and women alike inhaled the pine smell of the forest, the sweat of their bodies, and the trepidation of something lurking in the shadows of the night. Magic and reverie entwined.

As the calmness of the night descended, so did the energy at the party. Gary and a couple of the guys built a fire meant to represent the Summer Solstice bonfires of old. Given what everyone had been through recently, they used a decorative fire cauldron with a steel mesh dome to trap flying embers. Not quite as spectacular as a bonfire, but a lot safer. Young and old roasted marshmallows for s'mores and licked the stickiness from their fingers. The music of the band was replaced with the simpler instruments of handheld drums, rattles, and cymbals.

Chairs were gathered around the fire, and one and all started to relax into its warmth. Wool clothing and blankets covered exposed skin. Memories of the past captivated conversations.

"This camaraderie reminds me so much of coming to Colorado for the first time," Lola said. "My friends took me to a blues festival in the San Juan Mountains. It was my first real outdoor experience. I was such a greenhorn. I brought the most worthless crap you can imagine. Don't laugh, but I actually brought high-heeled sandals. Not that I got a chance to wear them for very long, mind you, because of the snow."

Despite her plea, everyone did indeed laugh, and Lola laughed with them. "I'd no idea that the weather in the mountains could change from eighty degrees to wind, sleet, and snow in a matter of hours. There were hundreds of people camped in this one little area, but what I remember most was everyone dancing around this amazing fire. If it weren't for the fire and a blanket and borrowing clothes from my friends, I would have died from hypothermia for sure."

Lola shook the cymbals in rhythm to the drums, her eyes unfocused and dreamy. Dan, Bridget, Ella, and Gary just stared at her.

"What?" she said eventually. "What did I say?"

"What year was that?" Gary wanted to know.

"1975," Lola replied without hesitation.

"No fucking way," Bridget exploded. "I went with my girlfriends to the very same festival. That's where I first met Dan. He was there with a group of his guy friends. I went to pee in the woods and caught him spying on me."

"He what?" Gary said.

"I know, I know, weird. It's a good story for another time," Bridget said, waving him off. "I so remember that fire too, Lola. I can see it so vividly. I remember some chick with flowing dark hair tranced out and dancing with a blanket like she was flying. It was snowing and we were freezing our butts off and that fire was the only real warm place there was. It was so eerie, yet so damn enchanting."

Lola cleared her throat. "The tranced-out girl with the flowing dark hair and the blanket was me," she said meekly.

"It was you! It was so friggin' you!" Bridget stared at Lola and shook her head in amazement. "I swear, it looked like you were floating above the ground, and you got everyone else dancing and circling that fire too. This is too weird!"

"Not to freak you guys out, but Ella and I were there too. We were on our honeymoon," Gary said proudly.

"No friggin' way!" Bridget said it before anyone else, but they were all thinking the same three words.

"Ella was one of the ones who helped get the bonfire started in the first place. There was this guy there named Buck. Buck because he wasn't wearing a stitch of clothes. I'll never forget the guy. He was selling firewood that no one could afford, so Ella talked him into using his wood to build a fire so people wouldn't freeze to death. I'll never forget that night."

"Wish I could," Ella said.

"What?" Lola put down the cymbals to listen to her friend's story. "What do you mean?"

"Well, to put it mildly, I was drugged out of my mind. Just not by choice. Someone put a horse tranquilizer in the hash we smoked. It was terrible. I remember the fire and the circle dance, but it was like I was split in two, experiencing it all on two different planes. It was kind of like the past, present, and future were happening all at once. It sounds cool now, but the feeling of being completely out of control was terrifying. Not a great ending to our honeymoon."

"What I want to know is, how did we not know about this after all these years? The five of us being there at the same festival that same year!" Dan exclaimed. "Especially you women. You talk about everything. How'd this slip by you?"

"Like I always say, the universe is full of surprises," Lola said. Her eyes traveled beyond the fire and widened like saucers. "Oh my! Speaking of surprises! Is that Gaia?"

"Surprise, surprise!" Ella shouted gleefully.

"You knew about this?" Bridget said.

"She swore me to secrecy," Ella replied. "And it was not an easy secret to keep, believe me."

For a moment, the five of them watched their good friend strolling among the partygoers. Gaia seemed to shimmer in the glow of the fire. Time had not aged her. She was holding a little girl's hand, and the girl looked exactly like her.

"Who's that?" Bridget asked, staring at the little girl.

"I don't know," Ella said. "Gaia didn't say anything about a little one."

"Well, let's go find the hell out." They jumped out of their chairs and raced in Gaia's direction, swooping her up in their arms and holding her tight.

"Holy shit!" Bridget said to her. "I mean, holy crap. You just materialize out of nowhere and scare the bejesus out of us? God, it's great to see you."

"We missed you so much," Lola said.

"I've missed you guys," Gaia said. "It seems like forever."

"Who is this little one?" Ella said excitedly, bending down and taking the girl's hands.

"This is my daughter, Celeste Rose," Gaia said proudly. "And today is her third birthday."

"Well, happy birthday, Celeste Rose," Lola said, touching her cheek.

"Thank you," the little girl replied with a shy smile.

"Aren't you beautiful," Bridget said. "You look just like your mommy."

"I have someone else I want to introduce you to, baby," Gaia said to her daughter.

"Who, mommy?"

"Someone special." Gaia took Celeste's hand and guided her toward the porch. They climbed the steps and stopped in front of Hattie and Herb.

"Well, hello there! I'm Hattie," Hattie said, stretching out her hand to Gaia and ruffling Celeste's hair.

"And who is this?" Gaia said, gesturing to the baby Hattie was holding.

"This little one belongs to Lola," Hattie replied. "Well, she belongs to all of us, but she's Lola's daughter."

Lola took Amity in her arms, kissed her head, and smiled an amazingly radiant smile. She said, "This little beauty is Amity Johnna. Amity stands for love and Johnna, well, you know, after her daddy..." Lola choked back a wave of emotion, just managing to say, "Later...we'll talk."

Gaia instantly saw the pain that Lola was still harboring in her heart after all these years, and she said. "Look at me, Lola. I just feel the need to say this to you." She reached out and put a hand on Lola's shoulder. "John loved you very much. He gave you this precious love child. What a gift."

The words lifted Lola's spirit, and she smiled. "I knew you'd know just what to say."

⌒‿⌒

"Okay, now I can't stop myself," Gaia said. "You may already know this, but Amity's etheric smell is honeysuckle, bringing sweetness into your life. Her smell bonds your love for each other with the love John had for you, urging you to move forward in life, balancing discernment with your neverending passion. Amity represents devotion and love incarnate."

Gaia paused. Then she said, "And now maybe we should introduce your daughter to my daughter. I think they probably have a lot in common."

Lola bent down to introduce Amity to Celeste Rose, but Celeste was already making a beeline for Herb. She jumped right into his lap, as if she'd done so every day of her short life.

"Well, my, my," Herb said uncomfortably, hoping someone would come to his rescue. Celeste looked directly into his eyes, and Herb was helpless to look away, for he could see the twinkling of galaxies in her eyes.

He swallowed hard. "Does she always do this? Climb up into a stranger's lap, stare into his eyes, and then without warning, fall sound asleep?" He patted the top of Celeste's head.

"Very rarely," Gaia said. "She's pretty intuitive and chooses wisely. Obviously, to her you're no stranger. Do you mind holding her for a while?"

"Can't say that I mind at all," Herb finally said. "Celeste Rose, you say. That's one beautiful name."

"I was so sorry to hear about Betty's death, Herb," Gaia said to him. "She was like a grandmother to all of us. And I know that today is the anniversary of her death and it's also Celeste's birthday. That Celeste and Betty share the same date is very special. You know what that means, don't you, Herb? It means they are forever linked together by the circle of death and life."

Herb didn't know what to say. He just snuggled up a little closer to Celeste Rose and kissed the top of her head.

"Herb's just an old softy," Hattie said, patting his hand. Then she stood up and took hold of Gaia's hands. "Don't be running off too fast, young lady. I've heard so many stories about you from the girls. And now I'm ready to hear your side of things."

Then Hattie did a strange thing. She placed her hands on both sides of Gaia's face, leaned close, and whispered, "The color of your eyes. So beautiful. I've only seen that amber color on one other person. It was a very long time ago. Her name was Olive."

"My Nana," Gaia whispered back.

"Oh, my. Olive was your grandmother!"

"Yes. And she told me all about you before she died, Hattie... and..." She reached under her sweater and pulled out her grandmother's necklace. "The girls don't know anything about this, but they will. It's a surprise."

Hattie patted Gaia's cheek. "I'm all about keeping secrets," she said.

<hr/>

Hours passed. Dozens of stories were exchanged. What they all discovered was that so much had changed and yet so much had stayed the same.

Herb contributed a story here and there, but mostly he just listened and watched and held as much of it as he could close to the heart.

He was dozing off with Celeste Rose in his arms when he felt a pair of hands grasp his shoulders and a familiar voice say, "Hey, Dad, don't be falling sleep yet. The party's just beginning."

"Henry! Damn, boy, is it you?" Herb turned, and his eyes filled with the sight of his only child, now a full-grown, prosperous man.

"It's me all right. Better late than never, right?"

"Well, I'll be." Herb was beside himself with joy.

"I thought I'd surprise you on Mom's anniversary," Henry said. "But my plane was late and the rental car got screwed up and, well, I'll say it again...better late than never, right?"

"You're here. That's all that matters," Herb said, his emotions rising to the surface. "Let's get you something to eat. Maybe some of dad's homebrew."

"No maybes about it." Henry's eyes went from the little girl in his dad's lap, to the elderly woman smiling up at him from the chair next to him, to the baby in her arms. "I should have known you'd be surrounded by a bevy of younger women."

"Hell, yeah, son. You know me," Herb said. He gestured at Hattie. "This lovely lady is Hattie. A dear friend of your mom's. Hattie, this here is my son Henry."

"Oh, we've met," Hattie said, holding her hand out. "You probably don't remember, but we've sure as heck met. Good to see you, Henry."

"And the little one in her arms is Amity. Amity is Lola's daughter. And this one," Herb said, indicating Celeste Rose, "well, she belongs to Gaia, though she found her way into my heart in about ten seconds. Meet Celeste Rose. Today is her third birthday. Same date as your mother's anniversary. Quite a coincidence."

Herb shook his head. "Gaia sure surprised us with this little one."

"I bet she did," was Henry's only comment as he peered through the darkness, scanning for familiar faces. "What a party!"

"Everyone! Everyone! Can I get you all to gather around?" Ella called. "I have a surprise."

"I think we're being summoned," Hattie said.

A parade of people finally mobilized and followed Ella to the east side of the house where, two years before, the fire had done the most damage to the landscape. Now there were three newly planted aspens, and next to the aspens lay the wooden box from Ella's porch.

Ella waited patiently for everyone to gather round.

"I think we're all here," Gary said to her.

"Well, thank you all for coming," Ella said, raising her voice slightly. "Gaia gracing us with her presence was our first surprise for the day. Her daughter Celeste was our second. And this is our third." Ella opened her hand to the aspen trees and then gestured at the wooden box. "Since the summer solstice is usually celebrated with the burning of a bonfire, I thought I'd put a different spin on it this year. Instead of a fire, I thought we'd celebrate with ashes. And that's why I asked anyone who might have some to bring them along today. Let's face it, we as a community have been through a lot over the years, especially during and after the fire. And I think we need to let go of the past and look towards a bright new future."

A number of people clapped. She heard someone say, "Hear, hear," and another say, "Couldn't agree more, Ella."

"So, we're each going to share that sentiment with our departed loved ones as we spread their ashes around these three aspens," Ella said. "Aspens symbolize community. An aspen grove is a single living organism with all its individual runners. Aspens, as we all know, thrive in the wake of a fire. So, in honor of our community, I would ask everyone to stand in a circle around these trees. Kids too. Herb and Henry. You too, Hattie."

When their circle was complete, Ella looked in Lola's direction. "Lola, would you and Nick do us the honor of beginning?"

"Oh, yes. Thank you, Ella, my dear friend." Lola and Nick broke the circle and stepped up to the newly planted aspens. Lola held two urns in the crook of each arm. She struggled to open them, then struggled to expel the contents and ended up covered in ash.

"Oh my, what a mess!" Lola tried to wipe off the excess soot from her clothes. Then she gave up and looked at the ashes and the trees and said, "Mom, Dad. I know you've been hanging out on that shelf in my closet for a long time, but the timing wasn't right to set you free until now. It's a much better view than you've had the last twenty-plus years, so enjoy the mountain air and the view of our Lake. May this resting place bring you peace. And be glad to know that I'm happy, really really happy and..."

Nick elbowed his mother...hard. Then, in a low voice, whispered, "Mom."

"Oh. I'm sorry." Lola smiled. She took a step back. "Nick, your turn."

For the longest time, Lola's son seemed frozen in place and speechless as he held his father's ashes. His silence made some in the group uncomfortable, but not Michael. In a show of genuine support, he left his place next to his parents, came up behind his friend, and put his hands on Nick's shoulders. "You can do it, buddy," he whispered.

Nick nodded. He walked to the center of the circle. Then he made his way slowly from one person to the next, making eye contact with each as he spoke. He even crouched down in front of Celeste and Amity, and the girls giggled and squirmed.

"I never realized how much every single one of you meant in my life until I left this mountain," Nick said, his mom bawling louder with each word. "I…and my Dad too…tried to fill that void with keeping busy…too busy with sports, school, work, you name it, just so we didn't have to feel the emptiness. My best friends were here, my parents' best friends, all of you…anybody that mattered in our lives…called this mountain Home. We were loved here. And still are. To my Dad, who taught me that even if things didn't work out the way I wanted them to, that there was always one constant. That I am still loved."

Nick stopped in front of his mom. He said, "Mom, Dad never stopped loving you…or me…or any of you. I miss you, Dad."

Nick continued around the circle, scooping out his father's ashes and letting them touch each and every person as he passed.

It took a long time for people to regain their composure after Nick's touching tribute. But then Ella surprised everyone again by holding out a small urn and announcing, "These are the ashes of my dear and sweet friend Hazel. Her daughter gave these ashes to me. It was in her will to have half of her ashes let loose here on this mountain. So…" Ella poured the ashes around the aspen trees. "… may you rest in peace, dear friend."

It was Gary's turn next, and he asked Alena to join him next to the trees. He opened a pewter container. Together, the two of them let the ashes swoosh to the ground, covering their shoes with gray soot. "In honor of our family's loyal friend, Bear."

"We'll never forget you, my big Bear buddy," Alena said as she stifled her sobs.

"Herb and Henry," Ella said when Gary and her kids had rejoined the circle. "Would you two like to come forward?"

"Sure," Herb said. Henry wrapped an arm around his dad's shoulders, and they stepped forward. Tears were rolling down the old man's cheeks as they stopped in front of the trees and opened their urn. Herb called out: "My beloved bride, Betty." Henry added: "And adored mother."

Herb let Betty's ashes fly. He said, "She'd be happy to know she was invited to this party," and his humor broke through some of the sadness. Herb winked at Shauna and Michael, and the pair tried without success to suppress wide smiles.

Dan, Bridget, and their kids were next to move into the circle. They each held little vials of ashes, and Bridget was first to release the contents of hers onto the ground. She said, "Ashes from the 'House that Dan Built.' A great place to live, even if it was cold as hell."

Then Dan emptied his and said, "And to the best damn mountain pooch ever. Laska."

"Our hero!" Michael exclaimed, turning his vial over.

"And the best friend ever," Shauna added.

When her vial was empty, they returned to their places and Ella said, "Sam?"

"Thanks, Ella. I'm honored," Sam said. Then he offered his arm to Hattie. "Will you join me?"

"Oh, indeed I will," Hattie said, taking her place at Sam's side.

Sam placed his cowboy hat over his heart as he opened a mason jar filled with the ashes of his family's original homestead. He poured them out very deliberately and said, "My grandparents and parents found everything they needed up here. It was their slice of heaven tucked right up against this mountain's ridges and hidden within its groves of trees. Protected from the rest of this crazy world."

Hattie patted his hand when he was finished. Then he reached into his coat's deep pocket and pulled out another container. He emptied it. "For Candi and Greg...ashes from their mountain haven and...of them, symbolically speaking."

Sam hit his hat on his thigh, looked skyward, and shook his head, choking back tears. After a few seconds, he cleared his throat, took Hattie's hand, and turned away from the aspen trees and the ashes melding with their soil.

"Gaia?" Hattie called. "Will you share with us?"

"Thank you, Hattie. Yes," Gaia said. She raised the urn sitting at her feet, took Celeste Rose's hand, and stepped forward.

Just then, a twirling wind let loose in the middle of the circle. It swirled around the three aspen trees, picking up the ashes of the dearly departed and lifting them skyward. The timing was perfect as Gaia released the contents of her urn and watched them spiral towards the heavens. Once the ashes reached beyond the trees' height, the wind abruptly stopped, and everyone stood statue-still and awestruck.

Gaia broke the silence, saying, "To my grandmother, who loved me unconditionally, just like she did all of you. To Olive, my Nana and Celeste's great-nana."

It didn't go unnoticed by Gaia at that moment that Lola, Bridget, and Ella unconsciously touched the pendants hidden under their clothes. For it was at that very moment that all knew they shared in the same sisterhood.

Lola fell to her knees, repeating, "Oh, my! Oh, my!"

Bridget let out a bloodcurdling howl like only Bridget could, then shook her head, saying, "Holy shit!"

Ella crossed the circle to Hattie and embraced her warmly.

"And you thought you had a corner on all the surprises this fine day!" Hattie said, with a wide, mischievous smile. If everyone else looked at the spectacle with a trace of confusion, there was also a sense of amusement and comfort.

Once the girls took their places again in the circle, everyone held hands. Old arthritic fingers tightened around the plump fingers of blossoming youth. Hard, callused hands grasped the perfectly manicured. It was then that Gaia stepped forward once again. She gathered two handfuls of ash and dirt, threw her head back, and stared at the sky with amber eyes. She reached out with her arms and released the earth into the air. Then she chanted:

"This Mountain is the Hearthstone of this neighborhood,
transforming all that dwell upon it.
May the sun and moon caress the seasons,
May the earth provide sustenance,
May the snow and rain nourish,
May the wind and fire cleanse and renew,
And may all of us, like these three saplings, join together,
enduring both the harshness and gentleness, to create
one thriving organism, a community.
As above, so below.
So be it!"

"Thank you, Gaia. That was beautiful," Ella said when the chant was complete. "And thank you one and all for sharing in this summer solstice ritual."

Everyone reluctantly turned away from the newly christened trees and gravitated back toward the house. Most of the women and kids made a beeline for the fire. Ella added wood to the small blaze and stoked it. Gaia invited the women to take off their shoes, and all did so without question. Then they formed a circle around the fire. Gaia grabbed a handful of dried earth and gently poured the coolness over the women's feet, anointing them with the Mountain. Little girls danced innocently. Women danced for the sheer joy of it. For those members of the sacred circle – Lola, Bridget, Ella, Gaia, and Hattie – it fed their very souls.

Lola's scarf dance called out to the Ancient Ones, guiding her body to the rhythm of life.

Ella felt that same melody carry her into the deep woods of her beloved Oma, savoring the freedom of her spirit.

Bridget took the feather from her hat, held it gingerly in her hand, and lost herself in the sacred mists of her ancestors' land.

Gaia's aura expanded outward, embracing her mountain family with the shimmering green glow of her heart chakra.

Hattie felt a tear escape from her left eye, sensing her friends from long ago dancing alongside this new generation...celebrating the continuation of Na'mow's special sisterhood.

Round and round they danced, bonded together. Time seemed to stand still as they recognized this moment, a moment of profound kinship; comfortable and easy, yet profuse in its familiarity. Time dissolved into the Infinite.

Gaia opened her eyes suddenly, feeling the heat of an intense gaze, a gaze that penetrated the core of her being. She turned slowly, cautiously. And there was Henry; he was holding Celeste Rose tenderly in his arms, his smile wide and warm with love. He kissed the top of the young girl's head, nodding to Gaia as if the world was suddenly clear to him, the look in his eyes filled with the knowledge that Celeste was his child.

Gaia returned his smile and nodded slowly, binding them as a family. Then she closed her eyes and allowed the circle to consume her.

Round and round the women danced and sang to the cadence of the cosmos. Without doubt, the women on this beloved mountain all knew that their friendships would endure...endure until the end of time.

Their chanting melody rose toward the heavens, climbing the staircase of all life and searching for its origin. The universal language revealed itself and filled the air with an ancient anthem. Supernatural forces guided this sacred incantation to this gathering of women.

Thump, thump, thump! The drums sounded. Their reverberations penetrated the roots of Na'mow's forest trees and traveled downward, reaching the depths of the earth's mantled soul: a celebration of life; a celebration of true friendship and balance.

Eru'tan's earthly sounds, those of the rain, the wind, and the dance of the leaves, intermingled with the divine harmony, creating a cosmic song that resonated into the Forever. Sla'mina, Ruler of the Wild, found voice in the grunting of the bear, the howling of the coyote, the hooting of an owl, and the distant neighing of a horse.

Smoke swirled around each individual, purifying them and honoring their private prayers, hopes, and dreams as it rode skyward on Toh'ria's thermals. Ra'nul, Empress of the Night Sky, hid her face in the infinite blackness, revealing the galaxy's star power. Na'mow, at the center of it all, worked her magic, imbuing all that breathed to remember, to love, to be.

Without a doubt, Lola, Ella, Bridget, and Gaia knew that each had been called to the Circle, the Circle of Na'mow.

EPILOGUE

October 5, 1998, Full supermoon

The luminescence of the orb demanded attention.

Humans and animals alike stopped to take notice. Shadows loomed large over the landscape as the huge round circle illuminated the hidden lairs, concealed dens, and veiled nests of both predator and prey. Not only was the obscuration between darkness and lightness lifted, but also the bridge between spiritual and physical grew less hazy.

Rising from the flatness of the plains, the sheer, precipitous faces of Boulder's Flatirons magnified the brightness of this huge supermoon. The mirrored water of the lake hidden behind these mountains tricked the eye into believing it was as solid as wet pavement. Fish broke the illusion by surfacing and creating concentric circles that moved in perfect harmony toward shore. Silence dominated. The smells of pine and the organic debris of the forest floor assaulted the nostrils of both man and beast. Smoke from chimneys and campfires spiraled skyward. A herd of elk bedded down in the aspen grove, their elegant profiles silhouetted by the stark white light. Sticks and underbrush crunched under the weight of unseen paws, feet, and hooves. The whooshing sound of an owl's wings seemed muted compared to the huffing and snorting of a foraging black bear. Yipping and howling, coyotes called their progeny home, and the melody of this ancient chorus reverberated within the hearts and souls of All that called the mountain Home.

Suddenly, a cloud eclipsed the supermoon's beacon of light, and the void of blackness was immediate. A moment of silence followed, the respite precious in its forced present-ness, a state of connectedness to Woman, the Mother.

"Look at this," Bridget said from her deck. "The moon and stars lighting up the night. Have to admit it, you got me spellbound. Fucking spellbound."

It was too perfect a night not to write in their journal, so Bridget ran into the house and headed straight for her antique desk. The decorative wooden scrolls on either side of the small hutch were actually small hidden drawers. The left one contained the key to the bottom one, and the bottom one contained their three treasured journals. An unexplained urgency deep within Bridget made her fingers tremble as she unlocked the drawer and pulled out the journals. She set the two oldest ones aside. The third was over 500 handwritten pages, a handful to carry back outside, so she sat at the desk with a full view of the supermoon.

She glanced back at the girls' entries from the past three days. Gaia had written:

Here I was, sitting on the porch of this marvelous cottage, staring at the moon and rocking my beautiful Celeste. I was humming a lullaby without a title and snuggled deeper into the layers of blankets that cocooned us.

"Ra'nul is putting on quite the light show for us, Celeste Rose. In a couple of days she'll be as round as she can be. It's nice to witness such celestial glory, isn't it?" Celeste was half asleep, but her eyes opened at the sound of my voice. Is there anything more wondrous than holding your own child and wanting nothing more?

Celeste's eyes closed again, and I found myself smiling at the very thought of her father. Henry proposed to me the night before he left to return to California. Amazingly, I'm seriously considering saying yes. True, I'd have to move to California, but the timing seems perfect for a change.

"So my darling daughter, what shall we do?" I tenderly kissed the top of my daughter's head and inhaled the sweetness of her scent. "My friends will always be here when we need to visit. They wouldn't dare venture too far off Na'mow...we're all connected to this mountain and the Circle even if we're living somewhere else. That'll never change. Plus, there's Herb, your ever doting grandfather. We'll certainly be back

to visit him. And then there's that dad of yours. I think he's grown as fond of us as we have of him. I do believe the three of us are falling in love."

Celeste opened her eyes right then, and looked up at me as if she knew it was decision time. "So, my little one, it sure feels like 'yes' is the right answer."

———

Oh, my, Bridget thought. Gaia. A married woman. How cool is that?

She flipped back a page to Lola's last entry and read the words slowly.

———

I can't believe it. Nick just called to invite Amity and me for Stanford's homecoming. I think I'll pack her and Herb into the car and drive out there. Now that has all the makings of a fine road trip.

Speaking of my baby girl, I'd no sooner gotten on the phone than I heard her awaking from a dream and crying out to me: "Momma!"

I raced into her room – I do a lot of racing when it comes to my Amity – and swooped her up in my arms.

"There, there. Shhhh. Shhhh. You'll be alright, my little angel," I whispered. I rocked her for a minute and then said, "How about you sleep with your momma tonight?"

As I walked past my bedroom window with Amity gently cradled in my arms, I stopped and stared knowingly at the night's shining orb, transfixed. "Okay, you've got my attention. Yes, yes, I feel your magic... I do believe you've got love floating all around Na'mow...love for this lovely night, love for my friends, love for this mountain, and love for this..." I couldn't help but tighten my arms around my sweet girl. Amity's eyes opened and immediately squinted as they peered out the window and upward through the blinding light. I have to say I tried to shield her eyes from the brightness, but my lovely daughter would *have none of it. She actually pushed the hand away and began giggling uncontrollably. And you know me, I didn't hesitate for a second to join in.*

Now Bridget was on a roll, and she flipped back to Ella's entry. "Let's see if you were enjoying the supermoon as much as the other girls were," she said, and started reading.

We knew it was Brice calling when we saw the caller ID, so I put the phone on speaker so Gary and I could both listen.

Brice's excited voice blared from the receiver. "I know it's kind of late, but you guys aren't going to believe what's been goin' on! There's this band here in town...pretty well known and super hot...and they're practically begging me to play guitar for them and do some vocals. They heard me at this jam session I've been goin' to every Saturday night...I played an original song...said they were impressed. Shit! And just like that, they asked me to join! Even made a CD with them. It's in the mail to you guys. How 'bout that! I'm finally livin' my friggin' dream! Look, I have to run but wanted you to know. Keep an eye out for that CD and let me know what you think. Love you guys, tell Alena 'hey.' Whoa, just walked by a window...shit...catch the moon. It's freakin' gi-normous and it's not even full yet! Bye."

The phone went dead, and Gary shook his head in amazement. "Was that the most one sided conversation you've ever heard?" he said.

I kissed him on the cheek. "Did you ever think he'd be so happy? I'm so grateful."

"Me too," Gary answered. He kissed me hard on the lips right then and said, "Let's go to bed...and I don't mean to sleep. Brice is right about the moon...we won't even have to light candles."

"I'll be up in a bit Don Juan. First I have to pay my respects to this gorgeous lightshow."

I wrapped myself in a fleece throw and walked out on the deck. I stared up at the heavens and laughed out loud remembering my magical moon chant from way back when. I let the sky slowly captivate me and drifted off to another place and another time. Bad move.

Suddenly I felt something crawling on my hand. I must have jumped a foot. And then I heard Alena doubling over with laughter.

"Alena! You scared me half to death. My God!" I said. "What're you doing sneaking up on me like that?"

"Oh, Mom! Sorry. I didn't think you'd practically have a heart attack." Alena continued to laugh, so I reached over and started tickling her. She finally screamed, "ENOUGH!"

"Thought you were asleep," I said. "What happened?"

"I was having this weird dream...like some music was following me...I can't explain it but it was like circling around me. I liked it, but it scared me too. So I woke myself up. But it didn't go away. I realized the music was coming from out here. That's why I came out. It stopped when I touched your hand."

"Oh, no. Sorry."

"Yeah, way to go," she teased. "You broke the spell."

Alena started laughing all over again. What an amazing, beautiful sound. I opened up my blanket and invited her into its warmth. I looked up at the sky and whispered, "Empress of the Night Sky, you sure are working your enchantments tonight."

"She sure is," Alena replied. Then, a moment later, she glanced up at me and said, "Love you, Mom."

Doesn't get much better than that.

No, it doesn't, my dear friend, Bridget thought. She picked up her pen. "My turn," she said.

~~~~~~~~~

Just like Ella getting a call from her son, the best part of my night was Michael calling out of the blue at 10:30. At first, it scared the hell out of me. Him, calling that late: it couldn't be good. Turned out he just wanted to say hello. My son, calling from college just to say hello.

After he left for school, I began to realize how much I missed him. How much I missed things like our early morning conversations. That connection was as ingrained as the sun coming up every morning. But things change. Michael's gone. Shauna's turning into a young lady right before my eyes. I picked up the phone. "Hey, Buddy! What's goin' on?"

"I just wanted to call and say hi to you guys and tell you to go out and look at the moon. It's huge!"

"I'm looking at it right now. So ya miss us, do you?" I wondered for a moment if I'd gone too far, but the macho retort I was expecting didn't happen.

Instead, he said, "Mom, you've no idea how much. I miss it all. I just knew you'd be looking at the moon, you and the whole freakin' mountain. Kinda creepy, but special you know?" He was actually fighting back a quiver of emotion. "I never knew how, how...different and special my life was growing up. Mom, nobody grew up like us, and I mean nobody! God, it wasn't until I moved down here, got away from it all, that it hit me...people don't live the way we do. Just the way we were raised, the mountain and animals, the neighbors, all the crazy parties. The guys down here think it sounds like a movie. They keep after me to tell 'em more stories. And believe me, I've got plenty of stories to tell but...when I try to explain...I just can't put my finger on what made our mountain living...the neighborhood...so damn special. How do I explain it to people? What do I say?"

I thought about Michael's question for a moment. I wasn't searching for an answer. I knew the answer; I was just savoring it. Then I took a deep breath and spoke with conviction. "Michael. Son. It's simple. We just took the ordinary and made it extraordinary."

Bridget looked down at her freshly inked writing. A tear rolled down her cheek and spilled onto the paper, landing squarely on the word "extraordinary." The wetness caused the word to expand. It bled into the words next to it, causing the word "ordinary" to become one with it, rippling outward, expanding again, and forming a perfect circle.

ACKNOWLEDGMENTS

We owe tremendous gratitude to all of you who have helped to shape our lives, no matter how briefly. Without our interactions with you, this book could never have been written.

Thanks to Mary, David, Jonna, June, and Kathy, our early manuscript readers; your critiques gave us new insight and vision into making our book better. Thanks to Rich, Anita, Paula, and Kate for reviewing our final manuscript and providing invaluable perspectives.

We offer a very special thank you to our editor, Mark Graham, who believed in us and shared our enthusiasm, vision and passion, taking 600 pages of our storytelling and transforming them into our first novel. We truly value your friendship.

Most importantly, we thank our friends, family, and mountain community, who tolerated our long periods of writing isolation and secrecy. We are most grateful for your unconditional support.

ABOUT THE AUTHORS

Anna McDermott

Anna's personal belief is: "You CAN have it all in this lifetime, just not all at the same time," and the diversity of her experiences is proof of this. They ranged from owning and operating a home day care center to being the CEO of a large international technology company. She currently runs a consulting business focused on executive advisement and management services. Anna loves spending time in her "church of nature" hiking with her dog. Her family, reading, decorating, and sipping fine tequilas with friends are her greatest joy and inspiration.

Anna grew up in Kettering, Ohio. When she was 13, she had a dream of living in the wilds of the Rocky Mountains, and she fulfilled that dream when she moved to Colorado in 1973. She currently resides in the foothills west of Boulder. *The Circle of Na'mow* is her first novel.

Gretchen Wiegand

Gretchen is a storyteller, bodyworker, artist, Universal Life minister, and seeker of new experiences. She earned a B.A. from the University of Colorado in 1976 with a major in art history and minor in Anthropology. For over 20 years, she owned and operated a successful polarity therapy and neuromuscular massage therapy business in Boulder, Colorado.

Gretchen's personal curiosity in metaphysics has been an ongoing fascination since she was a youngster growing up in Elmira, NY. Early in her adult years she had two near death experiences that profoundly influenced her life choices. The Rocky Mountains west of Boulder has been her home for 40 years. She's been married for 37 years and is the mother of one child. The quote that best sums up her view of the world is, "All things are possible if you believe." *The Circle of Na'mow* is her first book.

CPSIA information can be obtained at www.ICGtesting.com
Printed in the USA
LVOW11s1319080914

403026LV00002B/55/P